devious LIES

USA TODAY BESTSELLING AUTHOR
parker s. huntington

DEVIOUS LIES

Copyright © 2019 by Parker S. Huntington

Published by PSH Publishing.

All rights reserved.

No part of this book may be reproduced in any form or by any electronic or mechanical means, including information storage and retrieval systems, without written permission from the author, except for the use of brief quotations in a book review.

This book is a work of fiction. Names, characters, places, and incidents are products of the author's imagination or are used fictitiously. Any resemblance to actual persons, living or dead; events; or locations is entirely coincidental.

The author acknowledges the trademark status and trademark owners of various products, brands, and/or restaurants referenced in the work of fiction. The publication/use of these trademarks is not authorized, associated with, or sponsored by the trademark owners.

Beta, Editing, & Proofing: Heidi, Heather, Janice, Gemma, Ava, Leigh, Brittany, Luis

Cover, Photo, & Model: Parker, Jose, Ryan

A NOTE

This book may contain triggers.

devious
LIES

From *USA Today* bestselling author Parker S. Huntington comes an enemies-to-lovers, slow-burn romance full of revenge and a dash of fate.

"She could enjoy her pretty, perfect world a little longer. Soon enough, everything she owned would be mine."

I had a plan to escape the friend zone.
Step one: sneak into Reed's room.
Step two: sleep with him.

But when the lights turned on, it wasn't familiar blue eyes I saw.
These were dark, angry, and full of demons.

PARKER S. HUNTINGTON

And they belonged to Reed's *much* older brother.

Four years later, Nash Prescott is no longer the help's angry son.
I'm no longer the town's prized princess.

At twenty-two, I'm broke, in need of a job.
At thirty-two, he's a billionaire, in need of revenge.

Who cares if my family ruined his?
Who cares if he looks at me with pure loathing?
Who cares if every task he assigns me is designed to torture?

I need the money.
Simple as that.

I'll suffer his cruelty in silence, knowing there's one thing he wants more than revenge…
Me.

PLAYLIST

Lifeline - We Three
Sober - Demi Lovato
Not About Angels - Birdy
All My Friends - Dermot Kennedy
A Drop in the Ocean - Ron Pope
when the party's over - Billie Eilish
Skinny Love - Birdy
you were good to me - Jeremy Zucker
lovely - Billie Eilish (w/ Khalid)
Somebody to Love - OneRepublic
Outnumbered - Dermot Kennedy
Beside You - 5 Seconds of Summer
All I Want - A Day to Remember
Out of the Woods - Taylor Swift

Darkest Days - MADI
Boston - Dermot Kennedy
I Feel Like I'm Drowning - Two Feet
Somewhere With You - Kenny Chesney
Lover - Taylor Swift
Hot girl bummer - blackbear
Ocean Eyes (Remix) - Billie Eilish & blackbear
THAT BITCH - Bea Miller
Rome - Dermot Kennedy
Before the Storm - Miley Cyrus & Jonas Brothers
Through the Trees - Low Shoulder
Lover (Cover) - Dermot Kennedy

more BOOKS

Asher Black
Niccolaio Andretti
Ranieri Andretti
Bastiano Romano
Renata Vitali
Damiano De Luca
Marco Camerino
Rafaello Rossi
Lucy Black

author's NOTE

HEY, READERS!

This book started as a continuation of the Spring Fling novella... until I scrapped the entire thing and started from scratch. This was, perhaps, one of my crazier decisions of the year.

The deadline loomed ahead. I had no clue how I would start let alone finish this novel... and then it happened. Something clicked. The words didn't flow out of me. They *poured*. I couldn't stop them if I'd tried.

One-hundred and forty-five thousand words. I wrote them faster than I'd ever written anything in my life. At one point, I was funneling them to my arsenal of betas and editors and proofers so fast, none of us could keep up. LOL.

AUTHOR'S NOTE

That's how much Nash and Emery spoke to me.

Usually, I go into a novel knowing exactly the message I want to impart upon my readers. With this one, the idea started vague and spiraled into something else entirely.

Fate.

I have heard the word so often, understand the definition, and recognize it when I see it. Still, what do I really know?

It was daunting to write about two people whose lives come together in so many ways, because I wanted it to be authentic. So, I found myself seeking a different meaning from the word fate—finding it in smaller things than the grand displays people often tout.

And each time I asked myself, "Is this fate?", I would also think, there's a lesson here somewhere. By the time I wrote **The End**, I realized it doesn't matter.

In the words of **Lemony Snicket**:

"Fate is like a strange, unpopular restaurant filled with odd little waiters who bring you things you never asked for and don't always like."

Life throws so much at you, but you still control your decisions.

Nash and Emery taught me to choose what makes me happy. I hope they show you, too.

People will always judge. You can't control that. Move on to the things you *can* control.

At the end of the day, the only people who matter are the ones who care about you and yourself. Fate doesn't determine how you treat them and whether you put them first, too. That's on you.

AUTHOR'S NOTE

Lastly, I hope you enjoy the book. These two hold a special place in my heart for being my first non-mafia characters.

WITH SO, SO, SO MUCH LOVE,

Parker S. Huntington

*For Chlo, Bau, Rose, and L.
My querencia.*

*For wicked princesses who feed themselves with knives
instead of silver spoons.*

For my tribe of dragon-slaying warriors: Ava Harrison, Heidi Jones, Heather Pollock, Leigh Shen, Harloe Rae, Brittany Webber, Desireé Ketchum, and Gemma Woolley.

Thank you for being appalled when I told you my deadline, then getting your asses in gear and helping me succeed. This book wouldn't exist without you.

FATE

(noun) the development of events beyond a person's control, sometimes considered to be determined by a supernatural power

Fate whispers to the warrior, **"You cannot withstand the storm,"** and the warrior whispers back, **"I am the storm."**

— UNKNOWN

part one:
TACENDA

tacenda

/ta-ˈchen-da/

1. Things that are not to be spoken about or made public
2. Things that are best left unsaid

Tacenda originates from the Latin participle taceo for 'I am silent'. Taceo is also the verb for 'I am still or at rest'.
   Taceo reminds us silence isn't a sign of weakness. It is a sign of rest, of certainty, of contentment.

Silence is the best response to people who don't deserve your words.

chapter ONE

EMERY, 15; NASH, 25

nash

I had a habit of touching things that didn't belong to me.

The Stepford wives of Eastridge, North Carolina begged to sample the bad boy from the wrong side of town. If I had a dollar for every time a twenty-something trophy wife ran to me after her sixty-something husband went away "on business," I wouldn't be in this situation.

Sometimes, when I felt irritated with the gluttony of designer this and that, the ten hours a day I worked to repay grad school loans, and the way Ma owned one pair of worn-down, knock-off New Balances yet still spared a few bucks for the church bucket, I would indulge some Stepfords.

(Hate-fuck was the proper term, but no one had ever accused me of being proper.)

Their step-daughters, practically the same ages as them, came to me wet and willing, looking for something to brag about with their friends.

I indulged them, too, though I enjoyed them less. They sought entertainment, whereas their step-mothers sought escape. One was calculated; the other, wild.

And despite how much I loathed this town and the Midas veneer Eastridgers wore like minx on winter coats, I had never crossed the line of keeping something I'd touched. Until tonight with the ledger I just stole from my parents' boss, Gideon Winthrop.

Gideon Winthrop: billionaire entrepreneur, the man who pretty much ran Eastridge, and a piece of shit.

Mounted on the silver-flecked marble of Gideon's mansion, a silver statue of Dionysus rode a tiger sculpted from electrum and gold. The artist had etched the god's cult of followers into the tiger's legs, bearing a remarkable resemblance to Eastridge's cult of wealth.

I had hidden behind the four-legged beast, my hands shoved into my tattered black jeans as I eavesdropped on Gideon Winthrop's conversation with his business partner, Balthazar Van Doren.

Though they lounged in the mansion's office, smoking overpriced cigars, Gideon's voice boomed beyond the open door into the foyer where I leaned against the tiger's ass. Hiding, because secrets were currency in Eastridge.

I hadn't planned on spying during my weekly visit to

my parents, but Gideon's wife had the tendency to threaten Ma and Dad with unemployment. It would be nice to have the upper hand for once.

"Too much money is gone." Gideon sipped his drink. "Winthrop Textiles will collapse. It may not be tomorrow or the next day, but it will happen."

"Gideon."

He interrupted Balthazar. "With the company folded, everyone we employ—the whole damn town—will lose their jobs. The savings they invested with us. Everything."

Translation: my parents will be jobless, homeless, and broke.

"As long as there's no evidence of embezzling," Balthazar began, but I didn't stick around to hear the rest.

Scum.

Ma and Dad devoted their entire savings to Winthrop Textiles stock. If the company collapsed, so did their futures.

I withdrew from the foyer as quietly as I had come, dipping past the kitchen and into the Winthrop's laundry room, where Ma had left the old suit Gideon had gifted me for tonight's cotillion.

I slipped into it, stopped by the storage room, and tucked the joint I'd confiscated last week from my brother Reed's selfie-obsessed high school sweetheart into the outer pocket of the suitcase Gideon took on business trips. A little gift for the T.S.A. And people say I'm uncharitable.

After Gideon had finally left for his daughter's cotillion, I didn't think twice as I snuck into his office to search it. Eight years ago, when my family had moved into the cottage on the edge of the Winthrop estate, I had made it a point to possess every key, every password, every secret this mansion held.

Ma managed the household, while Dad maintained the grounds. Making copies of their keys had required no effort. Extracting the password to the office safe, however, meant creating a make-believe game for Reed and his best friend, Gideon's daughter Emery, to play.

I entered the code into the safe and sifted through it. Passports, birth certificates, and social security cards. *Yawn.* The desk drawers held nothing interesting outside of employee files. I yanked the top one completely off of its track and felt around the hole it left.

Just as I had finished up my search, my fingers brushed against buttery leather.

After pulling off the tape, I latched onto the leather and plucked it from the cavern. Held up to the light, the journal boasted dust on its cover and nothing else. No name. No brand. No logo.

I flipped it open, taking in the rows of letters and numbers. Someone had kept meticulous records.

A ledger.

Leverage.

Proof.

Destruction.

I felt no guilt as I stole what wasn't mine. Not when its owner wielded the power of destruction, and my parents stood in his line of fire. Dressed in Gideon's suit, I looked like an Eastridger as I strolled out of his mansion with his ledger tucked into the inner pocket.

When Ma called, I told her nothing as she begged, "Please, Nash. Please, don't cause a scene tonight. You're there to drive Reed home if things get out of hand. You know how those Eastridge Prep kids are. You don't want your brother catchin' no trouble."

Translation: Rich kids get wasted, find trouble, and the kid with the secondhand uniforms and academic scholarship takes the blame. Tale as old as time.

I could have admitted it then, told Ma about Gideon's misdeeds.

I didn't.

I was Sisyphus.

Crafty.

Deceitful.

A thief.

Instead of cheating death, I'd stolen from a Winthrop. The latter proved more dangerous than the former. Unlike Sisyphus, I had no intention of suffering eternal punishment for my sins.

The ledger couldn't be heavier than a skinny mass-market paperback, but it weighed down the hidden pocket of my suit as I weaved a path through the tables in the Eastridge Junior Society's ballroom, considering what to do with what I'd learned.

I could turn it over to the proper authorities and bring down the Winthrops, warn my parents to find new jobs and sell their Winthrop Textiles stocks, or keep the knowledge to myself.

For now, I would keep it to myself until I formed a plan.

A sea of suit-clad businessmen and manicured women—born, bred, and raised in Eastridge, North Carolina to be nothing more than trophy wives—blurred together in front of me. Not one of them piqued my interest.

Still, I ran a palm across a Stepford wife's exposed back to distract myself from the fact that I'd taken something from the most powerful man in North Carolina—one of the most powerful men in America.

Katrina's lips parted at my touch, and she let out a shaky exhale that had Virginia Winthrop cutting her frosty glare in my direction. From a table over, Katrina's step-daughter Basil took a vicious stab at her white-truffle Kobe strip steak, her eyes trained on where my fingertips rubbed at Katrina's bare back.

The steak reminded me of my little brother—glistening on the outside, full of blood, and ready to burst at the slightest cut. His on-again-off-again girlfriend, however, wouldn't be the girl to cut him.

As soon as Reed got his head out of his ass and realized she was in love with him, Emery Winthrop would own his heart.

Girls like Basil Berkshire were pit stops. They fueled your tank and helped you along the road, but they weren't the destination.

Girls like Emery Winthrop were the finish line, the goal you worked for, the place you strived to reach, the smile you saw when you closed your eyes and wondered why you even bothered.

Reed was fifteen. He had time to learn.

"There's a seat at the kids' table," Virginia offered, a chute of Krug Brut Vintage cradled between two fingers.

She resembled the Hera statue she'd had Dad place at the center of the Winthrop's backyard tree maze. Pale beauty frozen in a towering, too-slender frame. Virginia wore her blonde hair straightened until it mirrored frayed bamboo skewers kissing the tops of her shoulders.

The glossy strands swung as she nodded at the table her daughter sat at. The daughter she'd molded into the spitting image of her. But Emery possessed quirks that slipped past the cracks, like sunlight filtering into a prison cell through a single pinhole.

An expressive face.

Too big eyes.

A singular gray iris only noticeable up close, but I'd once overheard Virginia demand her daughter to cover it with a colored contact that matched her blue eye.

Sitting eye-level with Katrina, Virginia managed to look down her nose at her as she threw at me, "You may sit at the children's table."

My finger twitched, tempted to finger fuck Katrina at the "adults' table" to provoke her because I had no doubt Virginia took part in her husband's embezzlement. If Gideon Winthrop was the head of Winthrop Textiles, Virginia Winthrop was the neck, moving the head whichever direction she pleased.

I kept my fingers to myself as Mom's pleas bounced around in my skull.

Don't cause a scene.

Easier said than done.

Without another word, I pivoted and nabbed the seat between Reed and Emery's date, Able Cartwright. Able appeared as slimy as his lawyer dad. Black, beady eyes and blond hair slicked back like he'd come from an audition for the part of the vulture in that D-grade Laurence Huntington flick.

"Little brother. Emery." I nodded at Reed and Emery, then quirked a brow at the rest of the table, some prepubescent teens desperate to hide beneath five pounds of makeup. "Teenyboppers."

Basil's flushed cheeks clashed with the almost-white shade of blonde on her head. She wore enough perfume to fumigate a gymnasium. It killed my olfactory receptors as she leaned toward me and tittered into her palm.

"Oh, Nash, you're so funny."

I gave her my back, effectively finishing the conversation. I studied Emery, one seat over. She sat with her brows furrowed and hands on her lap, trying to unravel a Snicker's mini without drawing attention to the contraband candy.

I wondered if she had any idea what her parents were up to.

Probably not.

Ma once told me that people are wired to do the right thing.

It's human instinct, she'd say, *for people to want to do right by others, to please others, to spread joy.*

Sweet, naïve Betty Prescott.

The daughter of a pastor, she grew up spending her free time in bible study and married the altar boy. I lived in the real world, where rich assholes fucked the little guy —in the ass, without lube—and expected to be thanked after.

And Emery's dad? He put up a good front. Charities, volunteer work, a sunny smile. I had thought Gideon was different. Look how wrong I'd been.

But Emery Winthrop... I considered what to do with the ledger in my pocket. She complicated things.

Not that I was particularly attached to her. I'd had maybe a handful of conversations with her over the past eight years, but I loved Reed, and Emery knew how to love Reed better than anyone else.

She'd spent her childhood sharing her lunch money with him and sitting through tutoring lessons she didn't need. The shit school we'd transferred from had left Reed practically two grades behind. Even at seven, Emery understood the only way my brother could hire a tutor was if she pretended she was the one who needed it so her parents would pay for it.

Hurting Emery would hurt Reed. Simple math. And as jaded as I had become, as much as I hated

Eastridge and the people inside this ballroom, I didn't hate the girl who was fiercely loyal to the point of reckless, the girl with a thousand years' worth of wisdom gained in only fifteen, the girl who loved my kid brother.

"Emery," Basil began after I'd ignored whatever she had said. "I heard about your fail in Schnauzer's class. Bummer."

Schnauzer. Why did that name sound familiar?

Reed dipped close to Basil, his voice a low whisper everyone could hear. "That's not nice, sweetheart." His North Carolina accent was strong, and he'd somehow managed to make the situation worse.

"Do you hear that noise?" Emery tilted her head to the side. Her brows tipped together in mock concentration.

Able invaded Emery's space. "What noise?"

"That annoying buzzing."

"Sounds like a gnat," I offered as I leaned over Cartwright, plucked the Snickers mini from Emery's fingers, and popped it into my mouth.

"Nope, that's not it." She thanked me with a glimmer in her eyes. A fleeting salute to solidarity before they shifted to Basil. She went in for the kill. "Just Basil."

Basil jerked forward as I realized who Schnauzer was and cut off whatever stupidity she'd intended on spewing. "Isn't Dick Schnauzer that AP Chem teacher? The fucker who leverages blow jobs for As? And those who don't, well..." I cocked a brow at Basil. "Hey, you got an A, right?"

Basil's eyes turned to Reed. She waited for him to defend her. He looked between me, Basil, and Emery, a type of helpless that had me questioning if we were even related. But maybe he had a higher power looking out for him because Virginia chose that moment to intrude on our table.

Her eyes skimmed the uneaten cold fennel soups across the table like they were an affront to her skills as the chairwoman of the Eastridge Junior Society. Perhaps they were, because no sane person would look at a menu and say, "I'd love the chilled fennel soup, please."

"Emery, honey." She turned to her daughter and tucked a loose strand of hair behind Emery's ear. Like a real-life sequel to *Invasion of the Body Snatchers*, Virginia had a team of stylists create Emery in her vision.

Before I left Eastridge for grad school, I had lived in my family's cottage for years, from my year at Eastridge Prep to the four years I had spent commuting to a state college to save money. Enough time for me to witness the sheer amount of hours devoted to plucking, prodding, and dyeing Emery into a body Virginia could inhabit… or whatever she had planned for her daughter. Death by Eastridge's high society, probably.

"Yes, Mother?" Emery didn't look at her mom with love. She looked at her with resignation. The stare you gave a cop when he pulled you over for driving five miles above the speed limit. Disdain cloaked in civility.

I swore, the only spine Reed possessed grew from years of proximity to Emery.

"Be a dear and run into the office for me?" Virginia licked her thumb and swiped at a stray hair on Emery's forehead. "I need the tiara to crown the debutante of the year."

Debutante of the year. As if that was a title someone wanted.

Emery's eyes darted from Reed to Basil, so transparent I didn't bother holding my laughter back. She leveled a scowl at me, then turned to Virginia. "Can't you ask somebody on the wait staff to grab it?"

"Oh." Virginia clutched at the pearls choking her neck. "Don't be silly. As if I'd entrust a *server* with the code to the office's safe."

"But—"

"Emery, do I need to send you to Miss Chutney's etiquette classes?"

Miss Chutney was the borderline abusive lady who'd trained Eastridge's female population into the La-Perla-panties-up-their-asses women they were today. She didn't leave bruises, but rumor had it, she walked around with a ruler she used to slap wrists, necks, and whatever sensitive flesh it could reach.

Able pulled out his chair. "I can grab it, Mrs. Winthrop."

"That's a wonderful idea!" Virginia cooed. "Able will escort you, Emery. Run along now." Virginia's face remained frozen, like someone had slipped plaster into her Botox.

Irritation dilated Emery's eyes. The gray one darkened, and the blue one brightened. She muttered a few words I couldn't make out, but they seemed angry. For a split second, I thought she would surprise me.

In fact, something in me needed her to surprise me to restore my faith in a world where people like Gideon could take advantage of the Hank and Betty Prescotts of the world.

Instead, Emery pushed her chair back and allowed Able to take her arm, as if we lived in the eighteen-hundreds and she required a damn escort to go places. The defiance in her eyes had fled.

In this moment, she looked nothing like the eight-year-old girl who punched Able in the face for stealing Reed's lunch.

I watched with detached interest as Emery submitted to Virginia's will.

She was just like the rest of fucking Eastridge.

chapter TWO

Emery

Sometimes, I wondered if Eastridge wasn't a small, affluent town in North Carolina, but a circle of Dante's Inferno. Problem with that theory—Eastridgers didn't limit themselves to one sin. We were voracious with our sinning.

Lust.
Gluttony.
Greed.
Anger.
Violence.

Fraud.

Treachery.

Even heresy, because let's face it. Most Eastridgers might have called themselves Christians, but they sure didn't act like it when they turned up their noses at helping the other half of Eastridge—the half that slept in houses still damaged by the hurricane two years ago as they used the salary from Dad's textiles factory to pay for food.

Take tonight for example. Cotillions presented debutantes to society, but we'd all lived in this town since birth. A cotillion was no more useful to us than a stack of sequential hundreds.

A bottle of bourbon nearly toppled off Dad's alcohol cabinet, but Able caught it and held it up like he'd meant to knock it over. "Can I drink this?"

"Do whatever you want," I muttered, bending over to access the wall safe behind the desk.

I still wasn't sure if it was Dad's office or Mother's, but they had sunk their claws everywhere in Eastridge. Even The Eastridge Junior Society, an offshoot of The Eastridge Country Club.

Able gulped down a generous swig of the bourbon behind me. I pressed the lock combination Mother had whispered to me minutes ago. His footsteps beat against the hardwood before his hand rested on my back.

I pushed it off with a small smack. "Excuse you, I'm entering the combo. Look away."

Cursing, I pressed the wrong combination and had to try again.

The sound of Able chugging the bottle like a frat house initiate filled the little room. "C'mon, Em, don't be like that."

With a voice like Adam Sandler circa *Little Nicky*, I

could give a million and one reasons why Able couldn't land a girlfriend to save his life. He was my date because his dad was my dad's lawyer and fighting every ridiculous request Mother sent my way exhausted me into submission some days.

"*Dye your hair to match mine.*"

"*Maybe another liquid fast will get rid of that extra five pounds of baby fat.*"

"*You'll take Able Cartwright to the cotillion, won't you?*"

"*Be a dear and grab the tiara.*"

Perhaps the only reasonable demand I'd gotten lately.

I bit my tongue and did as she pleased, because my plans for college and a career in design required money. As a grantor on my trust fund, Mother possessed the power to bleed me dry.

Silent rebellions, however, were my bread and butter. Wearing a stained dress. Using the pastry fork rather than the fish fork. Tossing out odd words at inopportune times. Anything to make that curly vein on Mother's temple bulge.

"My name is Emery," I corrected, cursing Mother's choice in my friends. "Turn the other way."

"Fine." He rolled his eyes. Already, I could smell the liquor wafting from his mouth. "This fucking blows."

Must. Not. Stab.

I swiped hair out of my face and tried another code.

The code is your birthday, sweetie, my ass.

I should have known Mother had no clue when my birthday was.

"It's a cotillion, Able." I typed in Dad's birthday, but the screen flashed red twice, taunting me. "It's not supposed to be fun."

Dad had called it "vital networking," sympathy in his

eyes as he watched the hairstylist tame my hair with what could only be described as the technique you'd use on a wild animal.

Mother hadn't bothered with half-hearted apologies as she reminded the stylist to touch up my "truly awful" black roots and add more lowlights, so my shade would match her blonde exactly.

"Emery," Able groaned. I finally entered the correct code—Mother's birthday—and pulled out the tiara, leaving it in its velvet case. "Let's ditch this place. My parents will be here, occupied by the rest of Eastridge's heavy hitters." He leaned closer, his bourbon breath caressing my cheek and neck. "We'll have my mansion all to ourselves..."

"You mean your *dad's* mansion?" I straightened and took a step back when I realized how close Able stood. "You can go home. I have to stay."

The image of Basil's fingers clenched around Reed's thigh burned my mind. We'd been eating soup. Who mauled someone's thigh while eating chilled fennel soup? Not the kind of psychopath I should leave alone with my best friend.

"Babe..."

"Emery." I shook my head. "It's just Emery. Not Em. Not babe. Not Emery in a whiny voice. Not Emery groaned out. Just. Emery."

I dodged to the left to brush past him, but his palms slammed against the wall on either side of me, caging me in. "Fine. C'mon, Just Emery."

A brief burst of fear seized my limbs. I thrust it aside as quickly as it came. "Move."

He didn't.

"Move," I tried again. Firmer this time.

Still nothing.

I rolled my eyes and pushed at his chest, trying to keep calm when two-hundred pounds of Southern linebacker didn't budge. "I'm sure you think this is hot, but FYI, it's not. Your breath smells like a brewery, your armpits aren't too pleasant either, and I would rather be out there at the fucking cotillion than in here."

When he narrowed his eyes, I rethought my approach and the millions of times my big mouth had gotten me into trouble in the past. I'd known Able my whole life... He wouldn't hurt me. Right?

"Look," I began, my eyes darting around the room for anything to help me. Nothing. "I have to get this tiara out there or my mom will flip and send everyone in here for me."

Lie.

Mom wanted nothing more than for me to marry Able and pop out two-point-five blue-eyed, blond-haired children. Even if that meant her fifteen-year-old daughter fornicating in the Junior Society office.

I scoffed like I wasn't freaking out as Able closed the distance with another step and forced his entire front against me. The alcohol on his breath could put an elephant to sleep. It was all I smelled as he leaned forward and squeezed a sloppy, wet kiss to the tip of my nose. His saliva slid into my nostrils, and I had never felt anything more disgusting.

My eyes flicked to the bottle of bourbon on the table behind him. The contents sat low behind the glass, nearly gone. I prayed to whatever higher power existed that Able had found it that way. That he was not plastered out of his mind.

"This isn't funny, Able."

I shoved again, but it was hopeless. I weighed barely a hundred pounds, and he doubled my weight. I parted my lips to shout, but his meaty fist covered it as he ground his hardness against my stomach.

Fight, Emery. You've got this.

I tried.

I kicked.

I clawed.

I screamed, even when his hand swallowed my cries.

Desperate, I sunk my teeth as deep as I could into the fleshy part of his palm. He cursed and released me long enough for me to run two steps before his arm wrapped around my midsection and hauled me against him.

Granite muscles met my exposed back. He carried me to the desk and bent me over it. My palms hit the mahogany with a hard *Smack!* I used the backs of them to cushion my head as it banged against the table. It was useless.

My vision blurred. I still saw stars by the time Able had torn the back of my dress and started peppering sickening kisses all over my flesh. His kisses formed a scattered constellation of saliva across my skin.

I gasped when I finally found my voice again. I could scream, but I was too far for anyone to hear and he would just covered my mouth again.

Switching tactics, I begged, "My lips."

"Hmm?"

His tongue swiped a trail along my spine.

"My lips. Kiss my lips."

Able spun me around and dug his erection into my stomach. "Emery Winthrop. So eager to please. Who knew?"

He let me run a hand through his hair as I stretched up to meet his kiss, standing on the tips of my toes to reach his lips despite my height. He groaned into my mouth, a palm splayed on my lower back and the other trying desperately to unzip his pants.

I covered his fumbling fingers with mine, moved them to the side, and pulled the zipper of his dress slacks down. When they pooled around his feet and his boxers dropped with them, I kneed him as hard as I could in the balls.

Shock coated his face. I grasped the opportunity to knee him again. I refused to be the girl in the horror movie who died because she didn't go in for the kill. I didn't watch as Able collapsed to the floor.

Toppling the desk chair over him and lifting the hem of my tattered dress as high as I could, I took off into a sprint toward the hallway, barely making it a foot out the door before I crashed into something rock solid.

Emery, only you, I chided, *would escape a near-rape and run into a wall.*

I grabbed whatever I could to steady myself. Guanashina fabric slipped through my palms before my fingers latched onto it, digging slightly into the owner of the suit.

"Easy, Tiger."

Relief flooded my limbs at the sound of Nash's voice. I blinked away the tears that built behind my eyes while Nash came into gradual focus. Time played tricks on my mind as I took my time stitching the image of him together like patchwork on a quilt.

Nash Prescott was thrift-shop beauty, threadbare and jaded, the memory of something once beautiful lingering as he looked on the world with war-torn eyes. His contempt for Eastridge reflected on his face, hard edges and endless rage that, on normal days, forced me to look away.

The women of Eastridge fawned over him, the dead

eyes and the self-assured sneer. The sheer masculinity that clung to him like an expensive cologne. But when *I* stared at him, I saw something sad. A priceless shirt with a stain on the front.

I meant it as a compliment. There was something arresting about someone who regarded the world for what it was. Even if he couldn't see the beauty, he saw the truth. And because that truth was layered with ugly and flaws, I struggled to look at him most times.

And yet, at my most vulnerable, I'd suddenly caught tunnel vision for him.

Blatant wrath shifted Nash's hazel eyes from golden brown to green, like aragonite and emerald gems had battled inside a kaleidoscope and neither had won. With his aquiline nose and too-full lips, he looked too pretty to touch. Still, I couldn't pry my fingers from his forearms if I'd tried.

Tufts of jet-black hair stuck up in several directions on his head, like he couldn't be bothered to tame it. Cropped closely at the sides, he kept it long on top in silky, uncultivated waves.

Cafuné, I thought, disconcerted when I realized I'd whispered it.

Cafuné—the act of running your fingers through the hair of someone you love.

The word came to me at the speed of an earthquake, sudden and unpredictable, shaking my already cracked foundations.

It didn't make sense.

I was staring at the wrong Prescott.

"Your mom sent us to grab the tiara," Reed explained from beside his brother.

Reed. My best friend. The school's golden quarterback. A blond-haired, blue-eyed, All-American Southern boy with a charming drawl and a reliable smile. And those dimples. One on each side, gracing us each time he smiled.

Reed was here, and I was safe.

Time slammed into me until I teetered backward. It felt like an hour had passed since I'd bumped into Nash, but it was probably more like ten seconds. Nash steadied me as I registered Reed's words.

Mom had sent them.

For the tiara.

Not me.

I said nothing.

I *couldn't*.

Was this the type of truth—the type of ugly—Nash saw that had his lips permanently down-turned? For a second, I imagined my escape. No Eastridge Prep. No future at Duke. No designer threads laced with expectations.

Nash stayed silent. His eyes traversed a clinical path along my body—the disheveled hair, the mascara-stained cheeks, the ripped Atelier gown in Dusty Rose, a color that had looked cute when I'd left the house but just looked depressing now.

Tacenda.

Arcane.

Dern.

I mouthed words I loved to calm myself, letting them form on my lips without releasing them into a universe that destroyed.

My fingers clasped Nash's button-down, one I recognized as my dad's, but I couldn't let go. Even as my torn dress made a slow descent down my torso.

"Whoa, Em." Reed reached out and adjusted my corset.

Whatever he had done fixed it enough that it stopped slipping, and still, I couldn't let go of Nash's arm.

"Emery," I corrected Reed. My tone spoke of a calmness I didn't feel. A detachedness I desperately sought.

Some distant recess of my mind remembered Reed had always called me Em.

That this was normal.

That I was safe.

You are Em.

You are Emery.

You are okay.

"Emery?" The concern in Nash's voice sounded real.

I clung to it like my hands clung to his suit. My dad's suit. It still smelled like Dad, a mix of Cedarwood and Pine that settled in my chest. A balm to my nerves. I pressed my face against the shirt and inhaled until I sucked it dry of Dad's scent, and the only thing that remained was the distinct smell of Nash Prescott.

Citrus. Musk. A heady vanilla that should have been feminine but wasn't. Anarchy displaced rationale and rendered me speechless. I couldn't speak. So, I focused on Nash's scent, even when all I wanted to do was hide under my covers from mortification and never leave.

"Emery," Reed started again, but the office door slamming open cut him off.

Wincing, I curled my head down, bracing for a hit.

Stop, I ordered myself. *Able didn't hit you. He tore your dress, touched your flesh, and pitched you onto the desk, but he didn't hit you.*

I snapped out of it when Able groaned. Swiveling in time to see him stumble past the doorframe, I scowled at the sight of him zipping his pants up and yanked myself away from Nash.

Anger fueled me, thrumming along to the beat of

my pulse until my palm twitched with the need to hurt Able back. I needed to slap him. Punish him. Rob him of his dignity. Embarrass him like he'd embarrassed me. I considered how I'd look in an orange jumpsuit, doing twenty to life, but I lunged for Able anyway.

I parted from Nash, bridged the space between me and Able, and slapped him across the face. Twice. Nash stepped in front of me when I went in for a third slap. He captured my hand and released it.

Without a word, he pulled something from the jacket and shoved it into his pants pocket so fast, I only caught a glint of brown. He slipped off my dad's suit jacket and slid it over my shoulders. I'd never felt more like a child than I did now.

"Take her home, Reed."

Nash pressed the car keys to his 90s Honda into Reed's palm and curled his fingers around it when he wouldn't grab it. Reed had once said Nash's car was quite possibly the only thing he'd ever formed an attachment to. It didn't seem like it as he gave the keys to Reed without so much as a flinch.

Behind Nash, Able dragged a foot back, trying to slip away, but Nash gripped his shirt and tugged him back to us.

"Nash," Reed tried to argue, his eyes blistering angry and streaking a flash of violence I'd never seen in him before.

The ferocity excited me, though a part of me feared it made him look too similar to his brother. The boy who used to stumble into my kitchen to steal ice for his bruised fists and black eyes.

"You should see the other guy," Nash always said with a half-assed smirk before he vanished out the back door, and I'd have to pinch myself to make sure I wasn't hallucinating.

I'd been too scared to narc. Even the temptation of eating a bowl of ice cream without fielding Mother's judgment couldn't lure me back to the kitchen. I'd stopped the midnight munchies trips until one night, Nash had been arrested and Reed told me Betty Prescott had made him swear to never get into trouble again.

And he hadn't. I'd been safe to eat my ice cream in peace, and our ice had been safe from Nash Prescott's blood. I'd also never talked to Nash Prescott again until tonight, not that today nor back then constituted as talking.

"Take. Her. Home." Nash gave Reed a long stare-down, and one, two, three seconds passed before Reed finally nodded his head.

I let out a pent-up breath, realizing I didn't know what Nash would do if Reed disobeyed him, and I didn't feel like sticking around to find out. I liked Reed's face arranged exactly as it was, thank you very much.

"Fine." He spared Able one more glare. "Yeah, okay. Fine."

I felt like I was coming up for air as Reed interlaced his fingers with mine. That choking feeling evaporated, and another feeling took its place. Like something had grabbed my chest and dug its claws inside.

"I'm okay," I promised Reed.

But I wasn't.

I'd realized what this feeling was.

chapter THREE

Emery

L ove.
It always felt wrong that people chased something so fickle. Something that could be there one day and gone the next.

Love reminded me of Nash's car—scattered with bruises from a past owner; well-cared for by its current tenant; and still ticking as it awaited its fate, abandoned in some North Carolina junkyard.

The shrink Mother had sent me to when I was eleven and caught Mother a little too close to Uncle Balthazar would tell me I was examining life too carefully again. Mother also paid her to keep my mouth shut by all means. I had overheard that particular conversation on my way back from the restroom.

The whole thing was pointless. It didn't matter if I told Dad. The maids gossiped about my parents' fights, saying he'd leave her as soon as I graduated high school. I believed them. Dad and Mother rarely talked, and when they did, their conversations revolved around business.

During my sessions, my shrink told me Uncle Balthazar was my mind's representation of my demons. My mother was supposedly an analogy for strength, if you could believe that. *Strength.*

And the proximity between Uncle Balthazar and Mother? According to North Carolina-certified psychologist Doctor Dakota Mitchum: strength slaying my demons.

Dad was a planner. He anticipated moves like a Chess grandmaster and countered them with a ruthlessness I envied. I figured if I rebelled too hard against Mother before she and Dad divorced, I'd set off a butterfly effect. So, I kept my mouth shut, attended the shrink sessions, and spent the full hour wondering how Doctor Mitchum would rank in the Hunger Games.

I *had* learned something from Doctor Mitchum, though. She'd told me I needed an outlet for my creative mind. One for my emotions, too. She'd suggested drawing. I had taken up putting people on blast instead.

The t-shirt printer Dad had given me on my sixth birthday had laid dormant in the back of my closet. I'd pulled it out, brushed off the thick coating of dust, and printed a Winthrop Textiles shirt that read, "Horizontal Sundays." When Mother asked what that meant, I had insisted it was an indie band she'd never heard of.

Shirts became my way of dealing with life, and eventually, they became Reed's way of helping me deal with life. Fitting for the Textiles Princess of North Carolina. Mother had no clue. All she knew was she hated the tees, and she forbade me from leaving the house in anything but designer threads.

But Dad? My brilliant, attentive Dad... He always noticed the T-shirts of the Day—TSOTD, as Reed called them—meant I was dealing with something.

"Ready?" Reed waved his white shirt like a flag, hiding the front of it. It was my favorite cut that Dad's factory manufactured, something snug and soft that made me want to curl up against Reed and turn on a scary flick.

I'd already slipped out of my ruined dress and into a freshly-printed tee. My knees pressed against my chest. I sat on my bed, covering the words I had placed on the shirt ten minutes ago.

The adrenaline had fled during the drive home, and I'd spent the rest of the time since pretending I was okay when all I wanted to do was turn back time and make Able Cartwright pay.

I was not a forgiving person. I latched onto grudges and raised them like a favorite pet, never forgetting to feed them, entertain them, and keep them company. I needed revenge, or I would spend every second obsessing over every detail of Able's touch.

Reed flicked off the t-shirt printer and unbuttoned his button-down. I pretended to look away from the sinewy muscles no boy his age should have and waited with actual closed eyes as he slipped the fabric over his head and down his torso.

"I'm ready." I ran my fingers through my knotted hair before covering my chest with both palms and scrambling off the covers.

The desire to roll my eyes at this childish game we often played gripped me, but I didn't because the idea that a day would come when we wouldn't do this scared me. I wanted to be old and gray, making ridiculous shirts with Reed.

Reed stepped closer to the bed. "1... 2..."

On three, he flipped his shirt over and I dropped my hands with practiced synchrony. We fell onto the sheets, snow-angel style, laughter filling our veins and happiness staining our cheeks as we realized we had printed the same sentence on our tees.

ABLE CARTWRIGHT HAS A SMALL DICK.

It was funny, but not *that* funny. I knew what he was doing, though. Getting my mind off of what had happened in the only way he knew how. I appreciated it, but nothing short of Able suffering would ease my shaky fingers.

"You're my best friend, Reed." It escaped as a breathy sigh I should have chained inside me.

I waited for myself to regret it, but the feeling didn't come.

Instead, the one from earlier fogged the room. I didn't dare give it a name as it possessed me, nudging my hand closer to Reed's. Our fingers brushed, but I pulled mine back and played it off like an accident, flicking fake lint nearby.

Subtle.

Reed flipped onto his stomach and studied my face. Those golden locks matched mine, though his were natural, and he had two blue eyes, unlike my single one. I wanted to brush my fingertips against his eyelids until he closed them and press a kiss to each one.

Holding back had never been my strong suit, but I did with Reed because I had too much to lose. Even when I craved to grip, claim, kiss, I held back.

His fingers toyed with the ends of my hair, bringing them up to my cheek and using them to tickle me. "Are you okay, Em?"

I tugged at his ear until he stopped and considered ignoring the question but didn't. He would ask and ask until I spilled. The Prescotts were a relentless bunch.

Betty could interrogate a terrorist armed with nothing but a gap-toothed grin and homemade apple pie.

Hank's kind eyes doubled as weapons of mass confessions.

Reed had never heard the word "no" in his life.

And Nash... Well, Nash was Nash. All he had to do was breathe, and people tripped over their feet to please him. He possessed a presence money couldn't buy.

"Sheep gravitate to likable people. Likability is not a quality you can learn, but one you are born with," Mother once informed me after Basil had invited everyone in our grade to her tenth birthday party except me. She looked down her nose at me, disappointment staining her voice. "I am likable; you are not. I lead the Junior Society; you are an outcast. Perhaps you should learn to be like sheep."

Nash's existence poked holes in Mother's theory. He was simultaneously unlikeable and magnetic. Fuck the sheep. When I grew up, I wanted to be like him.

"Are you okay?" Reed repeated.

No.

Yes.

I didn't know. Physically, fine. Mentally? A little shaken and a whole lot of bloodthirsty. But Reed was a pacifist at heart, and I had no clue what he would say if he knew what I would do if I ever got my hands on Able.

The adrenaline had pacified me in front of the office, but now that I was home, my body demanded I fight or I would shake and never stop.

"Yes," I finally spit out. When Reed continued to study me, I shoved my hair out of my face and sat up. "I promise. I'm okay. I wouldn't lie to you."

But a lie of omission...

It occurred to me that my lies had piled up like an intersection crash. One after the other after the other. I needed to stop, but the alternative—a.k.a. the truth—appealed to me less.

"Are you sure?"

"Yes. Stop asking, Reed." I shot him an exaggerated eye roll, glanced at the clock, and slipped under the covers, hoping he would drop the subject.

After a minute of staring at me pretend-sleeping, he did. Truthfully, Able Cartwright didn't bother me. I had fought him off. I had stopped him. I had won.

Able Cartwright was a cockroach. It might take a ridiculous amount of attempts to crush him, but make no mistake—life will crush him.

Cockroaches die eventually.

This crush, on the other hand?

I'd tried everything from dating other boys to kissing Stella Copeland in her closet during seven minutes in heaven.

And still, it had a heartbeat.

Vibrant. Loud. Pulsing with life.

And I didn't want to kill it.

chapter FOUR

Emery

"I don't understand!"
"What is happening?"
"Stop, please! I'm begging y'all."

An argument pervaded my dreams. I reached out, my hands finding empty sheets in the starless dark. Reed had left. I crossed my fingers and hoped Dad hadn't found him sneaking out of my room. I would sooner lunge on a blade than let Reed take the fall for making me happy.

Slipping into drawstring shorts under my oversized shirt, I forced myself out of bed and into the hallway. My arms found their way across my chest, and I shivered in the cold, cursing my mom and her need to keep the AC at sixty-five degrees.

"Only poor people suffer in the heat, darling."

I followed the voices into the living room. A yawn in my mouth died down the second I caught sight of both my parents, Hank and Betty Prescott, Reed, and Nash. They stood wrapped around the walls of the room like an exhibition at Madame Tussauds, frozen in varying degrees of rage and anxiety.

The Winthrop mansion comprised of cold marble with a farmhouse twist. Reed joked Dad was the farmhouse, and Mother was like the cold marble.

Tonight, the marble had taken over, and we stood inside a tomb of statuario, gold, and silver—mummified, waiting for life to move on and forget about us.

I rubbed my bleary eyes and took in the scene as quick as I could. Mother wore that frozen stare of hers. Dad stood like a Hummer, imposing, arms crossed as if daring someone to talk to him.

Tremors rocked Betty's round frame. Hank stared between Betty and Nash, whose relaxed shoulders spoke of boredom, but instinct demanded I not be fooled. He was more alert than the rest of us.

It made the baby hairs on my arms stand up as I brought my focus onto Reed. Handcuffed beside his brother, his fury left no feature of his unscathed. I barely recognized him through his scowl.

In front of the fireplace with hands on their hips, two detectives took turns speaking, police badges proudly displayed. I'd been transported into a *Dirty Harry* flick, except instead of Clint Eastwood, I got cheap suits and a frantic Southern mother. (Betty, not Virginia. My mother couldn't give two shits.)

"Reed?" My voice halted the yelling.

The two detectives scrutinized me in unison. I didn't want to think of how I looked with the mascara-stained cheeks and bed head, my arms clenched around my chest to fight the chill and feet shoved into the hot pink bunny slippers Reed had gotten me as a gag gift last year.

Instead, I turned to Reed. "What's going on?" My eyes dipped to the cuffs interlinking his wrists. "Why are you handcuffed?"

"Able is in the hospital." The voice belonged to Reed, but it didn't sound like Reed. It sounded like rage, thinly veiled, looking for a target. "He woke up long enough to tell the police I beat him up."

One detective approached Reed. "Is that a confession?" His eyes lingered on Reed's Able-Cartwright-has-a-small-dick t-shirt, and I realized we'd never taken them off. Great.

Nash stepped in front of his brother, blocking him from view. "It's not a confession, because *I* did it."

The other detective shook his head. His man bun bobbed with the movement. "Mr. Prescott, you expect me to believe you assaulted a boy ten years younger than you with whom you don't spend time, do not go to the same school as, and no longer live in the same town as? Allow me to remind you hindering an investigation is illegal, and the victim has already identified his assailant."

"Nash!" Betty glanced between her sons, desperation turning her brows into a mountain peak that met at the middle. "You will not take responsibility for something you didn't do."

"Ma—"

"*Nash.*"

Their stare-down lasted a full minute. Tension swarmed the air, and no one dared to breathe loud.

Meanwhile, I kept my head down, confused as I tried and failed to make sense of this. Reed wasn't violent. That sounded more like Nash, who Basil used to gossip would punch a man out for breathing at him the wrong way.

Reed was a pacifist. He took out his aggression on the football field. Even then, he was a quarterback, and I'd never seen him tackle anyone. Ever. And I'd gone to all of his games since his mom had become our housekeeper and his dad had taken up the mantel as our groundsman.

One time, a fight had broken out on the football field, and Reed had been the first to walk to the sidelines and wait for it to subside. Yet, he'd fought for *me*. That pleasure in my chest, like a balloon filling the space around my heart with air, returned.

"Detectives..."

Dad stepped forward, pulled a cigar from his front pocket and a lighter from his back pocket, then lit it. We waited as he tilted the cigar above the flame, taking his time to turn it until the foot ignited.

When Dad spoke, everyone listened. It happened without fail. All he'd said was one word, and we'd stopped. Even as he brought the cigar to his lips, inhaled, held, and exhaled, we waited.

The people at the cotillion today? They were rich because Dad had made them rich. Everyone in town—with or without money—invested in the Winthrop name. The richer we became, the richer they became.

The detectives knew of Dad. They shared a glance, not a complaint on their lips as he took his damn time. He lowered his cigar. The smoke clouded the living room, bringing the warmth it lacked.

The pitter-patter of rain against the roof filled the silence. At one point, I'd loved the noise until Mother caught me and Reed dancing in the rain, and I'd come down with a cold that lasted three weeks because she had refused to get me medicine until I promised I had learned my lesson.

My dad had returned from a business trip a week into my cold. By then, my tenth birthday had been a week away, and I'd feared he'd make me stay home from our Disneyland trip if I told him I'd gotten sick.

Dad had rented out the park, and I'd spent the entire night on Space Mountain with Reed, pretending I didn't need to throw up every time the ride lurched to a stop.

Mother knew, but she'd pulled me aside and said, "Punishment is the backbone of this country. Being sick is not your punishment; it's suffering in silence."

"I'm sure we can figure this out." Dad stepped closer, looking at ease despite the tension in the room.

He still possessed a head full of dark hair, graying at the temples in a way that made him look distinguished rather than old. He'd once joked that I'd gotten my gray eye from him and my blue eye from Mama.

As soon as he'd said it, my gray eye had become my favorite, because that was Gideon Winthrop. He had the ability to make everything better, including this.

"Mr. Winthrop." The detective with the man bun swiped at his baby hairs, transferring sweat from his forehead to his fingertips. "With all due respect..." He trailed off when Dad interrupted him.

"With all due respect, you are in my house at midnight without a warrant." Dad held the cigar in front of his lips as he finished, "I am telling you we can figure this out, and you will listen." He drew the cigar to his lips and pulled.

"Mr. Winthrop, someone is getting arrested tonight." The detective glanced at Reed's shirt, coughing a bit when Dad exhaled the cigar smoke in his direction. "A fifteen-year-old boy is in the hospital with a broken nose, rib, and leg; a separated collar bone; and a dislocated shoulder."

Mother gasped, and it took everything in me not to.

Holy crap.

Reed had done that?

For me?

Thump.

Thump.

Thump.

My cheeks flushed when I realized how fast the knowledge had my heart beating. I pulled my arms tighter across my chest as if they could protect me from my feelings. They couldn't. Nothing could.

This would be our fate—childhood naivety repaved by darkness.

"His father, Eric Cartwright, is my attorney—" Dad stopped as soon as he'd caught my wince at the mention of Able's dad. "Emery…" Wrathful eyes dipped to where my arms met my shirt. He lowered the cigar and stepped toward me. "What does your shirt say?"

I backed up a step and considered the cost of moving to Eritrea and opening up a seawater farm. Somewhere no one in this room but Reed could find me. We'd live on white-leg shrimp and milkfish and would probably die of mercury poisoning before twenty, but it would be a better way to go than death by mortification.

"Dad." I almost shrugged but dug my crisscrossed arms tighter to my chest. At this rate, I'd never grow boobs because I'd suffocated the cells before they could grow. "It's no big deal."

"Emery."

"Please."

"Emery."

Another step back, and my heel hit a wall because, apparently, I didn't know how to walk a straight line out of here. Truth was, I didn't even need to show him.

He knew.

No way did the fury in his eyes escape anyone's notice. My arms shook. I succumbed to inevitability and lowered them. Not that I was ashamed of what had happened to me. I didn't want it to follow me.

Once one person knew, the whole town knew. That was how Eastridge worked. And people always, *always* blamed the girl. Since everyone from Eastridge would undoubtedly go to Duke with me and Reed, they would forever remember me as the girl who'd fucked up Reed's and maybe Able's future.

My burden and mine alone.

Dad was a good person. Most times judicious, and sometimes even rational in a way most blue bloods weren't. He wouldn't blame me. Reed wouldn't blame me. Neither would Hank nor Betty. Hell, I even knew Nash wouldn't stoop so low. But Mother? The two detectives I'd just met?

I felt vulnerable as I laid my secrets on the table without speaking a word. I should have said something or explained that nothing had happened; instead, I appreciated the silence, because I knew it'd be the last time I heard it before my dad blew his lid and destroyed the Cartwrights and possibly Eastridge with them.

The two detectives glanced down at my shirt, piecing things together before Reed and Nash stepped in front of me in tandem. I peeked around the brothers but let them cover most of me.

Dad pulled out his phone and dialed. "Eric. My home office. Now."

Classic Dad.

Always standing up for me.

I wanted to grab his hands, drag him to the Harry Potter World theme park, and drink ginger beer with him. Or dance in the rain with no music as I replaced my memories of Able with his ridiculous eighties moves.

Dad turned to Hank and Betty, tossed the cigar on the floor, smashed it with his heel, and ignored Mother's irritated gasp. "Eric Cartwright is on his way. As far as I am concerned, your son did nothing wrong, and Eric will agree with me. No charges will be pressed." He said it with such certainty, I believed him. That, and he was Gideon Winthrop, and that meant everything in Eastridge.

The detectives didn't even argue as he asked them to un-cuff Reed and wait in his office. Satisfaction unfurled in my belly. I had no plans on telling Dad what had happened because I had no plans on giving it more attention than Able deserved, but revenge felt good at my fingertips. They burned with the urge to raze, dismantle, devastate.

I wondered if this was how Nash felt as he blazed his own path, doing as he pleased with no concern over consequences. When he'd played football for Eastridge Prep, he'd start fights with the players, the mascots, the refs without considering the consequences. Or perhaps he had considered them and simply didn't care.

He'd ditch school, to be found behind the gym with his hands up a senior's shirt. And I'd never forget those nights in the kitchen, a spoonful of ice cream in my mouth, watching blood drip from his fists onto the floor as he tried and failed to ebb the flow with ice and towels.

"Honey…" Mother placed a palm on Dad's shoulder, hard enough that his shirt bunched at her touch. "Gideon, don't be silly. Think about this." She ran her palms across his shoulders and down the length of his arms. All six carats of her engagement ring winked at me, sandwiched between two diamond-encrusted wedding bands. "The Cartwrights are great people. What about Winthrop Textiles? Eric Cartwright knows all our company secrets."

Rage expanded in my chest, lacing itself with the oxygen I inhaled, momentarily blinding me. I struggled to focus my vision. I stared into the backs of the Prescott brothers and counted down from ten, allowing myself a moment to hide behind them as I processed in silence.

Calm down, Em. Don't say a thing. Let her think she's winning. Dad has this handled.

People assume strength is loud. In reality, strength is silent. It is resilience, the will to never surrender your dignity. And sometimes, the only person who knows strength exists inside you is you.

Nash's muscles tensed. He seemed coiled, ready to burst. I didn't know what to do, but I felt like I owed him. Touching him felt weird. Forbidden. Like I had broken a boundary no one had warned me existed. Still, I placed a palm on his back, hoping it brought him some comfort, like he and Reed had gifted me today.

If anything, he became tenser until I drew invisible lines on his back with my finger and began playing Tic-Tac-Toe with myself. Nash twisted his head and arched a brow at me, but his muscles had loosened. A lopsided grin tilted my lips up. I slashed a finger across the imaginary grid, pretending it was Reed's back I was touching.

"Winthrop Textiles?" Dad raised his voice and pivoted to face Mother. His heel crushed the cigar against the marble, scattering dusky ashes like a shattered urn. "Able Cartwright hurt our daughter, and you're worried about Winthrop Textiles?"

"Yes, I am. You should be, too." I could picture her waving her arms around, gesturing to the cold marble of the living room. "How do you think we afford all this?"

I peeked around Reed and Nash a bit, in time to see Dad spear Mother with a glower that suggested he might hate her. I wasn't my mom's biggest fan, but Dad seemed pained, betrayed, some mixture of feelings that hurt me to witness.

"What if we did nothing?" I rested my forehead against one of the brothers. "What if…"

I considered Reed in juvie, all golden-haired and bronze-skinned beauty. He wouldn't last. He'd come out jaded and acting like… well, like Nash.

"What if we could find a way to make this all disappear?" I finished, louder this time, peeping out from behind my wall of brothers to do so.

Betty Prescott shot me a grateful glance, hope in her eyes along with guilt. I understood it—the need to protect her sons at all costs. Her hope was mine, too.

"Wonderful idea, sweetie." Mother stepped forward, the pep back in her step, and clapped twice. "Let me talk to Eric. We'll get this settled. No one presses charges on either side. It'll be like nothing ever happened."

Except something had happened.

To me.

Did she even care?

Laughing and making dumb t-shirts with Reed pushed tonight away, but standing in front of an audience, vulnerable… what had almost happened hit me hard. I dipped behind the Prescotts and fell forward into Reed.

A broad hand reached back to steady me, and I realized I'd actually fallen onto Nash's back.

He looked over his shoulder and whispered, "Easy, Tiger."

I stared into his eyes, trying to figure out what he was trying to tell me with them. In front of him, my parents fought, but I focused on the Prescott brothers, my fingers finding purchase on Reed's arm and Nash's words.

"Why a tiger?" I asked.

We had one in the foyer, but I'd never thought much about it. It had a gaudy silver-skinned version of Dionysus riding it and Dionysus' cult tattooed on its hind legs, none of which I identified with.

"It's a saying," Reed offered, still refusing to stare at either of us. He trained his eyes on Betty and Hank. His rage hadn't lessened, but at the very least, I knew it wasn't directed at me.

Nash shook his head. "You're the tiger."

I waited for him to explain. He didn't.

"When you say it to me, I can't figure out if you're being nice or making fun of me."

He shook his head, laughter on his breath. The amusement in his eyes carried levity I clung to. "Why can't it be both?"

"Gideon!" Mother shouted. Her shrill voice broke the Prescott spell. "We are not jeopardizing our relationship with the Cartwrights over this!"

"And you're okay with jeopardizing your relationship with your daughter?!" he called out to her retreating back, but she'd already left the room toward the office.

Finally, Dad turned to me, Reed, and Nash. "Are you okay? Did Able..." he started, then stopped as if realizing the company.

I bit my lip to stop it from quivering. Winthrops were strong.

"Nothing happened, Dad. He tried, but..." I trailed

off, feeling silly because I was still hiding behind the Prescott brothers when I'd done nothing wrong. I stepped to the side and stared Dad in the eyes, my chin tilted up and voice steady. "I'm fine. I swear. And if Able is in the hospital, he got what he deserved, though I think I did a pretty good job kneeing him in the balls if I do say so myself. *Twice.*" I leaned against Reed, who wrapped an arm around my shoulder. "For the record, Dad, these shirts are accurate. Able Cartwright has a small dick, and now he has a gazillion broken body parts to go with it." I squeezed Reed's hand on my shoulder, a silent thank you.

Dad scanned me, examining my face for any signs of lying. "That's my girl, but it ain't enough for me." He shook his head. Someone cared. Warmth blossomed across my chest. "He deserves jail."

"No."

"Em?"

"If I press charges, he'll press charges against Reed. You know this."

Dad and Nash cursed at the same time. Dad swiped a palm down his face and shifted his weight onto his back foot.

"Please, Dad, do this for me," I added.

Silence trickled between us. He finally relented and shifted his eyes to Nash, like he was the leader of our little trio. "I want the three of you in Emery's room. I don't want Cartwright to catch sight of y'all when he shows up. Okay? It'll only make it worse. I'll do my best to fix this."

"Yes, Dad."

"Hank. Betty. Join me in my office, please?"

As soon as the room emptied, Reed had his forearm pressed against Nash's throat. "What the fuck, man?!"

I caught the flash of remorse in Nash's eyes before it

fled, and he couldn't have looked calmer even if he had a cigarette dangling from the corner of his lips. "I'm sorry."

Two softly spoken words.

An apology I didn't understand.

Still, I bore witness to the scene, an interloper they didn't bother acknowledging.

Reed pressed harder against his brother's throat before letting go. "Fuck you." He shook his head. "Fuck Mom. Fuck Dad." He strode off and out of the back door, ignoring my dad's demands to hide.

Ignoring me.

"Reed!" I stumbled after him, but a hand tugged my shirt back. I jerked away, and Nash released me, even when I fell into the wall.

"Let him go."

For a fleeting second, I wished to be Nash Prescott. I wished to have whatever chemicals in his brain allowed him to see the people he cared about and let them go.

But I wasn't Nash.

I was Emery Winthrop.

And Emery Winthrop?

She'd realized her crush on Reed Prescott wasn't as small as she'd thought.

It was an itch inside my heart.

I wanted to rip my flesh and tear him from my system.

part two: BOLT

bolt

/bōlt/

1. To hold together
2. To separate by fleeing

Bolt is a contronym—a word that is opposite itself. If you bolt something, you hold it together. If you bolt, you separate by fleeing.

Bolt is a reminder that words were made by humans, and sometimes humans make mistakes.

Mistakes are powerful, not because they have the power to ruin your life, but because they possess the power to make you stronger.

The worst mistakes make the greatest lessons, and those who learn them... **bolt**.

It's your journey to figure out which bolt.

chapter FIVE

EMERY, 18; NASH, 28

Emery

Starless nights rarely descended upon Eastridge. They reminded me of golden tigers—one-in-a-million, striking, intoxicating. Like golden tigers, they seemed bigger, as if the emptiness of the sky meant I could fill more space.

Reed had once informed me that starless nights were a sign secrets needed to be shared. The abyssal darkness provided protection, and he'd said, if I was going to tell a secret, it had to be under an empty sky.

We were nine, and Timothy Grieger had given me a

secret Valentine's day card Reed begged me to show him. I did, sneaking into the tree maze in the backyard and handing it to him with my cheeks flushed red.

Until we'd realized it was too dark to read it under a half-hidden moon without stars.

We ended up leaning against the Hera statue in the center of the maze as I told him what the card said from memory. It was one of those fill-in-the-blank, store-bought cards, where the first five lines had been typed out and all Timothy fucking Grieger had to do was figure out the last word, and he'd written "poop" in brown crayon beside a picture he had drawn of, of all things, a briefcase.

Dear **Emery,**

I love you more than pretty birds
and all the words.
I love you more than clear blue skies
and fresh apple pies.
I love you more than **poop.**

Love, **Timmy.**

Poetic.

He'd even spelled my name right.

It seemed fitting that, all these years later, a starless night numbed my fingers as I decided to spill my biggest secret to Reed.

If you want to date a boy Dad doesn't own, you'd have to leave the state, I reminded myself as I snuck my way from Dad's mansion to the servants' quarters.

The chill of the North Carolina winter taunted me,

nipping at my bare arms. Like it was trying to tell me something. Maybe even stop me.

I lifted my phone and reread Reed's text again, twice to be sure.

I broke up with Basil. For real this time.

Hope spun threads of excitement and anticipation through my body, and I ignored the rest—the part of my brain that told me to turn around, to preserve us because once I professed my love for him, I couldn't take it back.

We would never just be friends anymore. Either he felt the same way and we became a couple, or he didn't and something ugly and awkward would cloud whatever remained of our friendship.

Don't worry, Emery. You know what you're doing. It'll be worth it.

Plus, I'd never possessed an aversion to risk. I jumped first and dealt with the consequences later. Only this time, I had too much to lose. Anxiety tied a chain around my legs, weighing them down with each step I took.

Toska.

Lacuna.

Kalon.

I muttered unique words that made me happy, keeping my voice low. I shut my phone off in case it rang inside Reed's house. Because I had no pockets, I slid it into the Prescott's wooden mailbox, the same mailbox Reed and I had once watched Hank Prescott make.

Reed's dad had let us paint it. It ended up a royal blue with the Duke logo on Reed's half and black with wilted, gunmetal roses on mine. Betty had pretended to love it, while Hank laughed, patted my head, and said I was something else.

Tucked beside a purple heart pergola, the Prescott's tiny three-bedroom cottage seemed ant-like compared to my parents' mansion. I slipped my key into the back-door lock and turned it as quietly as possible. The door creaked and so did my steps as I slithered through the kitchen and crept into Reed's room, ingrained memory of the cottage allowing me to navigate it without light.

Are you sure about this?

I could almost hear Reed asking me that, his smooth accent dipping its way past my ears and into my heart. He was ever so cautious, the one to watch my back as I leapt. And he always caught me.

Always.

Countless scraped knees and a constellation of faded scars told tales of childhood adventures on my body, but they didn't speak of the golden-haired boy who stood beside me for them all, even when Mother sneered at him and made jabs about his secondhand clothing as if she couldn't pay the Prescotts what they deserved to make in the first place.

(If Dad ran the house rather than Mother, I bet Reed would never wear used clothes again and I could eat more dinners at the Prescott's without feeling like I was taking something I shouldn't.)

Bottom line—Reed had my back. The scar across Able Cartwright's face proved that. It sent a secret thrill down my spine each time I passed Able in the halls of Eastridge Prep and saw it.

Being near Reed made my stomach quake like it'd been hit by an avalanche, and tonight, I was going to sleep with my best friend.

"Are you awake?" I winced. My voice had come out tentative, but the Southern drawl still filled the room louder than I'd intended.

I inched deeper into the small space and shut the door behind me, not bothering to turn on the lights. No sense in waking Mr. and Mrs. Prescott. Not a hint of moonlight filtered in past the black-out curtains, but I'd been in Reed's room enough to reach his full-size bed in the center without missing a step.

"Wake up," I urged, not quite knowing what I'd tell him when he did, indeed, wake up.

I'd planned a speech on the flight back from winter break in Aspen, but standing in front of Reed's bed, it felt stupid. Like something one of Nash's groupies would say to him after spending the night.

"You're so sexy, Nash."

"The things you do to me, Nash."

"I think I love you, Nash."

Reed and I would press our ears to his bedroom door, our cheeks tinged pink when we heard things we were too young to hear. After he sent them away (and he always did), they left in tears, and we would pretend we didn't see them.

The sheets rustled as I sat on the edge of the bed and shook Reed's shoulders a bit. He stirred, groaning before settling again.

"It's me." I exhaled all my uncertainty, closed the distance, and made my move, straddling his bare chest before he could speak. Pressing a finger to his lips, I spoke before he could, "Don't say anything." *Don't stop me.* "Please. I just... I've been waiting too long. I want this. I want *you*. Now."

He didn't answer, so I shook his shoulders again and whispered, "Wake up."

Slipping my silk robe off my body, I tossed it to the floor. My lace bralette and matching panties might as well have been nothing with how naked I felt right now. Reed's hands found the narrow curve of my waist, lazily, as if he was still half asleep. The sheer size of his palms made me feel small.

I rubbed myself against his broad chest. His body cut sharply, all marble and bold strokes. Everything about how he felt was unexpected. The toned abs and rough ridges that met my palms. The energy he radiated that vibrated around us like an earthquake.

I lowered my lips to his, and then he was on me, flipping me onto my back as he took over with an eagerness I'd hoped for but couldn't anticipate.

"Took you long enough."

His words sent anticipation spreading through my body like embers igniting a fire. His voice sounded deeper with lust, his groan like a man's as I reached between us and stroked him.

Oh, god.

He wasn't even wearing underwear.

Reed was bigger than my ex. I wasn't quite sure he'd fit inside me, but my determination wouldn't allow that to stop me. I stroked him again. My lips sought his, catching his cheek in the dark instead.

His day-old stubble scratched my chin, longer than I was used to seeing, but I hadn't seen him since I'd left for winter vacation two weeks ago. I tried to kiss his lips. He didn't let me. He grabbed both my wrists in one hand, held them hostage above my head with a single palm, and sucked on my nipples through my bralette.

"These feel bigger." He licked the underside of my breast and whispered against the skin "Boob job?" His voice was so low, I almost convinced myself I hadn't heard him right.

"Um... No?" I kept my voice even lower than his was, half mortified, hoping he wouldn't be able to make out my words and would drop this line of questioning.

"Hmm..." he hummed against the curve of my neck, and I felt him speak against my skin, "I'm not doing period sex. Too messy."

What the hell, Reed?

"I'm not on my period..."

"Not doing pregnant sex either."

I was sure I hadn't heard him right this time, but I wasn't about to ask him to repeat that louder.

I stroked him again, hoping he'd shut up and stop ruining the moment. He thrust himself into my palm and bit down on my neck, sucking so hard it would leave a bruise. His movements were confident. Experienced. Like he knew precisely how to make my body come to life.

In all the years I'd pictured this moment, I'd never thought it'd be this feral, this instinctive, this *good*. I didn't know if I'd done such a great job of convincing myself we were meant to be or if we really were fate, but it felt like destiny, like gratification, like three thousand jigsaw pieces finally coming together.

Reed's other hand explored my body as if he knew exactly what to do with it. I whimpered when he tore my panties off, ripping them without a care. Pain lashed at the top of my ass where the panties had snapped off and bit my skin, but he didn't give me a chance to dwell on it.

This.

This was better than all my fantasies of Reed put together. It was passion. It was lust. It was all the reassurance I needed to make taking the first step worth it. I felt his need for me, and it drove confidence into my body like nothing else could.

Reed's fingers glided up my inner thigh and found me soaking, sliding inside with embarrassing ease. The adrenaline rushed to my head.

"I've wanted you for so long. You make me so wet. So, so wet. I've touched myself to you in the shower. In bed. In..."—I hesitated before admitting—"... my ex-boyfriend's bed."

He let out something like a laugh, a possessive half snarl that sent shock waves straight to my core. "Fuck your boyfriend."

"Ex," I corrected.

"Don't care," he said, his voice still groggy and different from sleep and lust.

He slid his finger out and pushed himself inside me. I bit my lower lip to hold back my moans, pressed my forehead against his shoulder, and closed my eyes, meeting each of his thrusts. One of his palms gripped my ass and squeezed while the other held my waist.

He flipped us, so I sat on top of him. I'd never done it this way, but I moved on instinct, grinding myself against his skin.

"Atta girl." He leaned back against his pillow as I placed each of my palms on his chest and took over. "Ride my cock."

His gruff voice was almost indistinguishable past the hoarse lust, so deep and different, his desire something I wanted to explore until I knew it just as well as I knew him.

"I'm close," I gasped.

It felt deeper this way, like he reached a part of me I never knew existed and my body hinged on the brink of explosion. My fingers dug into the skin of his shoulders. Each of his hands met my waist.

I needed to mark him, to claim him as mine as I left bruises and scratches all over his chest, hoping I'd leave evidence that this happened, that this was real. That tomorrow, when we both woke up, I could look at him and call him mine.

Reed took over from below, meeting me with so much force, it rattled the bed, and I feared his parents would discover us.

"Oh, God." I leaned forward, buried my head into his neck, and whispered against his sweat-stained skin, "I'm coming. I'm coming, Reed."

He stumbled a moment, halting his thrusts, but I was too far gone to stop. I pushed myself down harder on him and came, clamping around his length, biting down on his shoulder to quiet my moans. He came with me, his tongue brushing the shell of my ear as he let out a harsh curse.

I'd been with other guys in the past, and they'd never made me come. Inexperienced teenagers, fumbling to clumsy completion compared to the sheer masculinity Reed fucked me with.

Maybe having feelings changed sex. A part of me considered that he felt better because I was in love with him and I'd never been in love with any other boys, but I dismissed the notion. The way Reed slid inside me, the way his hands explored my body, the way he knew exactly what angle to push into me...

It couldn't be my head making it up.

We fit perfectly.

We settled into silence as I came down from bliss. Reed's hand rested on my thigh, his fingers brushing the crease where my thigh and lips met until goosebumps lined my arms. I didn't dare move, refusing to be the one that interrupted this.

Chaos ran laps around my body. I needed to figure out what this meant. Still a little hard, Reed pressed deeper inside me as he reached for the lamp on the nightstand, his breathing a ragged exertion I felt against my skin.

I blinked away the post-orgasm haze as the light flickered on. When my sight cleared and I finally got a look at him, I froze. Shock bulldozed into my body, nearly pushing me back had I not been gripping his flesh.

Black spots scattered across my vision, and for a second, I thought I'd faint—and it would still be less mortifying than this.

Anything would be less mortifying than this.

It was almost too much to process.

To make it worse, he was still inside me.

This wasn't Reed Prescott.

This was a six-foot-two, hazel-eyed Adonis with short black hair and bedroom eyes that made you picture him naked if you looked long enough. Only he was actually naked and, I repeat, still. Inside. Me.

Nash Prescott.

Reed's older brother.

His *nearly thirty-year-old* brother.

chapter SIX

Emery

"You're soaking my brother's bed," Nash remarked as he leaned back against his pillow and took in the sight of me. He looked annoyed, liked I was a pest who had royally fucked up his weekend plans.

"You—I—What—" I floundered, my mouth opening and closing like a fish.

You slept with Nash Prescott.

Nash Fucking Prescott.

And it felt amazing.

Don't freak out.
Don't freak out.
Don't freak out.

I was totally freaking out.

Nash raked his fingers through his hair, leaned over to snatch my robe, and tossed it to me. "Just fucking relax, would you? You'd think the goddamn orgasm would loosen you up."

For a split second, all I could think was, *you weren't always like this.*

Perhaps to other girls, but never to me.

Nash was a fierce protector, the guy who would stop by my table with his brown paper lunch bag when my mom 'forgot' to give me lunch money. And while we'd rarely talked, even when he would share his lunch, I always took comfort in knowing I had two protectors—Reed and Nash.

Something flipped the night of the cotillion. And after cops almost arrested Reed, the rift between him and Nash became unnavigable. They barely spoke. If they did, it was with a cordiality that reminded me of my relationship with Mother.

My heart wept for Betty, who tried desperately to mend things. Surprise parties. Homemade dinners. Family outings they couldn't afford with a son going off to college and one fresh out of grad school.

Reed placed all his focus on Basil, football, and school. And Nash? He became a different Nash around us. One who lived up to his reputation. Gorgeous. Arrogant. Insufferable. Whenever he visited, he'd spend the weekend fucking every bored twenty-something housewife in Eastridge.

I don't recognize you anymore.

The words sat at the tip of my tongue. I would never

release them. That was Reed's hill to die on. I cared because I hated the way Nash stared at me sometimes, accusations stabbing me from his eyes.

Snide comments I would never ask him about because I was loyal to Reed, and even talking to Nash felt like picking the wrong side.

"Such a Winthrop, Emery," Nash once said when I stole capers from Reed's plate after Betty made Chicken Piccata.

"So good at hiding things." He caught me sliding extra money into Reed's stocking. I lied about it being from Dad. *"Gideon has you sneaking around for him often?"*

"Betrayal. Taste it often?" I'd spit out a rotten peach from the garden. It landed by his foot, a few inches past my target.

I wanted to take a few seconds to study Nash, to process my mortification, to enjoy the aftershocks of my first orgasm, yet all I could feel was Nash's overwhelming gravitational pull, one more dangerous than that of any other boy I'd ever met.

But Nash Prescott wasn't a boy.

He was a *man*.

One who made me feel like the little girl I'd convinced myself I wasn't.

My arms slipped through the robe. The second the tie wrapped around my waist, my body solidified. My underwear remained lost somewhere, but at least I was covered.

I ignored the sting of his derision, shook my head, and pushed aside the embarrassment. "Did you know?"

The sharp accusation unfazed him. He stretched his arms, drawing my attention to the deep V of his body. I clenched around him. A reflex. My mortified eyes flicked up in time to catch his cocked brow.

"I figured it out when you moaned my brother's name while coming around my cock." His eyes dipped down as if to remind me I was still on him.

I scrambled off the bed, pushing the blanket over with the rushed movement. Horrified didn't even begin to describe how I felt, but it was the plain irritation on his face that almost undid me.

Couldn't he at least pretend he enjoyed it?

Because I did.

I'd come.

I *never* came.

I'd spent the past two years filling out my body, my full chest the one thing about me that didn't scream runway model. Riding Nash made me feel like a goddess. As if my body possessed magic, I controlled my pleasure, and something that had always worried me didn't need to be anything but bliss.

Yet, I obviously did nothing for Nash. He stared at me like he wanted nothing more than to forget this had ever happened. Like he disgusted himself for screwing somebody so young.

It wasn't as if either of us intended this to happen, and I didn't have the guts to ask him why he looked slightly sickened and a hundred percent scornful.

Pulling the sheets had left him bare, but Nash didn't bother covering himself as he ran a hand through his hair again. Maybe if I were a guy and I was as big as Nash, I wouldn't cover up either. Still, you'd think he'd at least have the decency.

Then, I remembered there was nothing decent inside this man.

Reed had warned me.

"Careful, Em." Reed glowered at his brother's retreating Honda the weekend after the cotillion. "Nash does unforgivable things without bothering to ask for forgiveness."

I dug my nails into my thigh, hating this cycle of hurt. "Can't you two talk it out?"

"What would be the point in that? He's a devious liar. I can't trust anything he says."

I'd never been able to reconcile Reed's version of Nash with the one who saved me too many times to count. Even if three years passed since he flipped a switch, I'd still hoped Nash hadn't become as bad as Reed accused him of being.

Until tonight.

That hope died a painful death.

Rocking back on my heels, I faltered for something to say before settling on, "Who did you think I was?"

"Katrina." The words were blunt, like it wasn't a big deal that he'd been waiting for a married woman to have sex with him.

Worse—he'd mentioned a boyfriend, which meant she was cheating on Basil's dad and another man with Nash.

What happened to you, Nash?

He had gone from Knight in Shining Armor to a version of Maleficent that was so indifferent toward me, he didn't even bother extending a poisoned apple.

Until now.

Only the apple was a rock-hard penis, and I imagined it felt much better than a poisoned apple tasted.

I whisper-shouted, conscious of Betty and Hank one door down, "You fucked me thinking I was someone else?!"

My hypocrisy wasn't lost on me. So what if I thought

he was his brother? It was different. I was in love. He thought I was a married woman. Okay, we both mistook one another for other people, but for my sanity's sake, I needed to believe we were different.

You are not as bad as Nash Prescott, Emery. This is his fault.

Nope.

Even I didn't believe my bullshit.

I'd been the one to climb onto him, not bothering to confirm his identity.

Stupid. Stupid. Stupid.

"Fuck," he toyed with the word, looking genuinely surprised. "Dirty word for a goodie two shoes..."

Good.

Like being nice and biting my tongue every time Mother spoke somehow made me less than him.

It pissed me off. I raised my arm stupidly. I wouldn't hit him. I didn't know what I would do, but it was a reflex, and it amused him.

"Easy, Tiger."

He didn't waver as he desecrated two words he'd said to me years ago when I'd run into his and Reed's arms at the cotillion. I pushed the past away, not wanting to humanize Nash while I felt so furious at him.

He continued, either oblivious or uncaring, "I figured it out a second before you came. I wouldn't have fucked you if I'd known it was you. I don't fuck teenyboppers."

A wave of awkwardness and embarrassment descended upon me.

I fought it.

Hard.

Lifting my chin, I glared at him. "I'm eighteen."

Barely.

The ten-year age gap between us felt unbridgeable.

But at least it gave me something to focus on besides the fact that I had sex with the wrong Prescott.

Fuck.

Reed.

I continued, "Reed—"

"—won't know," he seethed. "You tell him and you fuck up your friendship."

His tone didn't match his eyes.

One screamed, *you'll fuck yourself over.*

The other screamed, *you'll fuck me over.*

It wasn't only me who didn't want Reed to know. It would damage their relationship beyond repair.

I knew you still care about Reed.

The realization returned a sliver of my confidence. He still had a heart, and needs, and feelings. Blood ran through his veins, just like mine. He wasn't invincible.

I folded my arms across my chest, pulling the material tighter around me. "Aren't you supposed to be in New York, opening some destined-to-fail business venture?"

At least that's what Reed had told me a few weeks ago. Not the destined-to-fail part, but a wound named Ego bloomed beneath my skin, and I didn't like it. Cruelty was a knee-jerk reaction, one bred into me through years of catty prep school drama, and I almost apologized but couldn't quite bring myself to.

Two hazel eyes hardened, and he leaned back against the headboard, studying me with a scrutiny I wasn't used to. Even with Virginia Winthrop as a mom.

"Not that it's any of your business, Winthrop, I'm in town for a business meeting. Reed is spending the night at Basil's, so I figured I'd crash in his room since Ma turned my room into a fucking craft room. I didn't think I'd be accosted by an eighteen-year-old child."

Fury exploded from my chest to my fingers at his coldness, and I wanted to punch him back—because that was exactly what his words were.

A punch I felt in my gut, worse than anything a physical hit could land.

He'd transformed from the older brother Reed had once idolized to this monster neither of us could recognize.

It hurt more than I'd thought it would.

I buried his jab beside my pride.

Nash grabbed a spare pillow and wiped our cum off his cock with the case, uncaring of the audience or the fact that I laid on that pillow every time I lounged in Reed's room. "Do you often come into my brother's room, looking for a quick lay?"

Never, I almost defended, half transfixed and half horrified as I watched him express his nudity so comfortably.

But I didn't say it, because it made me feel vulnerable. The one night I professed my love for Reed had backfired in spectacular fashion, and Nash Prescott had the misfortune of witnessing it.

"All the time," I lied to save face. "He's a better lay than you."

Another lie.

I couldn't imagine anyone being better at sex than Nash Prescott. He made my toes curl and my lungs burn from exhaustive pleasure. He had pushed my body past its limits, and part of me wanted him to try again, just to see if the first time had been a fluke or if sex was supposed to be like this every time.

I still craved him, felt an obsessive thrill at the angry, rose-colored marks my nails had left across his chest. The thought terrified me. I wanted to run, but I also wanted to take a picture of the way I'd bruised him like he'd bruised me.

Deranged would be the perfect word to describe me. I had several teachers younger than Nash, and the idea of having sex with them sickened me.

Nash's eyes narrowed as he studied me, lingering on my collarbone, where he'd sucked so hard, I knew his mark would last for weeks. "If he can make you come harder than you did around my cock, he deserves a medal." His knowing eyes took in my flushed skin and the way my lips parted at the word *cock*. "My brother has a girlfriend. You know this, right?" he spoke as slow as he implied I was.

"For the record, Reed texted me, saying that he and Basil broke up." I clung to the robe's fabric.

"So your idea of being there for him is being his rebound fuck? Classy." He ran a hand through his hair, messing it up more than I already had. He snorted a laugh. "That break up lasted all of thirty minutes before he apologized to her, practically begging on his hands and knees."

I flinched.

The worst part was, I knew it'd be like all the other times they'd "broken up" and gotten back together ten seconds later. I'd succumbed to the magic of a starless night, convincing myself it would be different because that was what I wanted to believe.

For a startling moment, Nash's arrogance fled, and he took me in.

Really took me in.

My whitened fingers clenched the robe. My chest rose and fell to a staccato rhythm as I reminded myself I needed to breathe to live. The alarm gleamed within my eyes. They darted from Nash to the framed picture of me and Reed laughing on the wall, and I realized that I'd ruined my chances of ever being with Reed after having sex with his brother.

It was pity mixed with that damned disgust I saw in Nash Prescott's eyes.

He glanced at the alarm clock on the nightstand and said, "Either sleep or leave. I have a meeting in a few hours."

His words were harsh, but I recognized them for what they were.

Sympathy.

He was giving me an out, a way to flee without addressing any of the mortifying details that brought me here tonight. I latched onto it like he'd thrown me a life raft.

"You're unbelievable," I retorted, but they were half-hearted words, because if he treated me any differently, I'd probably cry.

And I was *not* a crier.

"Here's what we're going to do." He nodded to the mess of cum we made on the sheets. "We're going to forget this ever happened. You didn't fuck the wrong brother. I didn't fuck an eighteen-year-old." His lips curled into a sneer as he said my age. "Neither of us will tell Reed. Understood?"

Finally, something I agreed with.

"Crystal clear." I grazed my lip with my front teeth. "Promise you won't tell Reed?"

Nash watched me for a moment, something like disappointment flickering in his eyes, before he reached over and switched off the light. "Get out of the room, Winthrop."

"Gladly, Prescott."

I dashed back to my house, fumbling with the lock to

my back door and rushing my way into my room. Flipping the lock behind me, I turned the knob twice to be sure and dove onto my bed. Pulling the sheets completely over my head, I panted into the silky fabric.

I'd left my ripped underwear on Reed's floor. I prayed Nash had the decency to throw them in a ditch somewhere or burn them in a fifty-foot bonfire. My breath fogged under the covers, but I couldn't bring myself to lower them or do something sane like take a shower.

Five-thousand threads of bliss stained with sweat and our cum.

I'd learned two things tonight.

First—I could orgasm during sex, and I would never be the same.

Second—I hated Nash Prescott.

chapter SEVEN

EMERY, 20; NASH, 30

EASTRIDGE DAILY

GUEST COLUMN

On the Anniversary of The Winthrop Scandal, We Remember Victims
by Aaron Bishop

We remember the sirens, the surprise F.B.I.-S.E.C. joint raid, the rumors spreading like wildfire across Eastridge: Gideon

Winthrop allegedly embezzled from Winthrop Textiles. None of us could believe it. Not even after acting Mayor Cartwright announced the formal FBI investigation launched into Gideon Winthrop and Winthrop Textiles.

Two years later, a company that once employed over eighty percent of the Eastridge workforce has shut down, the life savings of Winthrop Textiles employees who had the misfortune of investing in Winthrop Textiles have been obliterated, and two people have lost their lives. Yet, no concrete evidence has been found, and no charges have been pressed against Gideon Winthrop.

On the anniversary of The Winthrop Scandal, we remember the victims.

We remember those who fell homeless after losing their jobs.

We remember the elderly who have continued to work past retirement age to recuperate what they can of their savings.

We remember the children who went hungry.

We remember Hank Prescott, who died of a heart attack working three jobs to provide for his family after losing not only his job but also the life savings he invested in Winthrop Textiles.

We remember Angus Bedford, who committed suicide after losing his job at the Winthrop factory and his son's college fund.

Gideon Winthrop may have fled Eastridge, North Carolina and no charges may have been pressed, but we remember.

Note: If you or anyone you know has suffered from The Winthrop Scandal, The Eastridge

Fund, set up by Eastridge's very own Nash Prescott, provides 24/7 support, including over-the-phone counseling, a 100% anonymous pen pal system, and a suicide prevention hotline.

COMMENTS:

Mary Sue: I invested all my savings in Winthrop Textiles! I lost my home. That wicked family deserves to burn in Hell. God will not be kind to the Winthrop family.

Derek Klein: The Winthrop family should have died! Not Hank! Not our Angus!

Beth Anne: Bless Nash Prescott. To lose a father then make The Eastridge Fund after the fact. Kind of makes you wonder what would have happened if he had struck rich sooner. Would Hank Prescott still be alive?

Joshua Smith: If I see Gideon Winthrop, he's dead. No two cents about it, no hesitation. That man deserves to meet the Devil.

Ashley Johnson: @Beth Anne, that's an awful thing to say. Delete your comment!!!!

Hallie Clarke: Does anyone know what happened to Emery Winthrop? Her social media is silent. My daughter goes to Duke and says she's not there.

Demi Wilson: @Hallie Clarke, no clue.

Bruce Davey: @Hallie Clarke, don't know either, but as far as I'm concerned, she's just as guilty as the rest of 'em.

part three: MOIRA

moira

\\'mȯirə\\

(noun) a person's fate or destiny

In Greek mythology, the three Moirai spin the threads of Fate. Men, women, and gods submit to them, forced to accept Fate as Destiny.

    Moira is the idea that each person possesses a predetermined course of events that shapes his or her life. It is the *idea that some events are inevitable—a person's fate (every decision leading to the present) and their destiny (the future) is not always in his or her control.*

Moira reminds us some things happen no matter how hard we fight them.

chapter EIGHT

EMERY, 22; NASH, 32

Emery

Burn. It crept up my fingers, down the side of my wrist, and across my palm.

My fingers flexed. Straight. Curled knuckles. Straight. Fist. I did this eight times until I could pick up the needle and thread again without wanting to chop off my hands.

I would withstand this torture every hour of the day if it meant I'd created something tangible. Something that couldn't be taken from me. Something I could latch onto and call mine.

Five yards of curtain laid in front of me. The fabric pen sat uncapped beside my thigh. I dropped the needle and thread, picked up the pen, and dragged it across the fabric in a sweeping motion.

Empty.

I shook the pen and tried again.

Still empty.

"Motherfucker."

I didn't have money for a new one, and my next paycheck didn't come for a week.

"What happened?"

I took Reed off speaker and pressed the phone to my ear. "Pen's out of ink. No big deal. It's a recreational project."

All my projects were recreational, including this curtain-turned-peplum-dress. I had zero design gigs lined up and a stack of unpaid bills I hid in my freezer so I didn't have to see them. Every time I thought of the bills, I was tempted to dip into my trust fund. I never caved. That, and Mother dangled stipulations over my head like poisoned mistletoe.

The tension in my neck was another sign I needed to get my shit together, or I'd die of a heart attack before I turned twenty-three. Thanks to shitty construction and my inability to afford AC bills, the heat sweltered in here despite the cool fifty degrees outside.

It was always either too cold or too hot in my two-hundred-square-feet studio, but at a hundred bucks a month for rent, I had no reason to complain. And no super around to complain to.

My phone dinged with a message from the Eastridge United app.

Benkinersophobia: I finally looked up Durga. A goddess of war? Please, tell me you have a *sari* you roleplay in.

The snort slipped out before I could stop it. The Eastridge Fund had assigned Ben as my anonymous pen pal three years ago. I shouldn't have signed up for the app. I wasn't a victim. I was the daughter of the victimizer.

But I'd been lonely and a little drunk, two dollars short of my utility bill, and clinging to a torn quilt for warmth.

Desperate for comfort, to put it bluntly.

I'd meant to stop. Truly. But Ben turned out to be something I was in low supply of—a friend. Sometimes, we felt like one mind in two bodies. Then, one night when the flirtation transformed into something more dangerous, we'd made each other come with nothing more than dirty messages. And, well, that was a rabbit neither of us could put back in the hat.

I shot a reply to Ben through the app.

Durga: You waited three years to look up my username? I Google'd Benkinersophobia day one.

Benkinersophobia: And?

Durga: You don't know what your username means?

Benkinersophobia: I used the random username generator. I don't have time for frivolous things.

But he had time to look up "durga." I rolled my eyes, but a smile tipped my lips up.

Durga: Benkinersophobia is the fear of not receiving a letter from the Hogwarts School of Witchcraft and Wizardry on one's eleventh birthday. I was sure I'd hit the jackpot with a Potterhead. I would have enjoyed that more.

Benkinersophobia: A Potterhead?

Durga: God, your lack of knowledge of pop culture references is horrifying. You could always change your username. Perhaps 'Underwhelming' would be more accurate.

Benkinersophobia: Underwhelming. I've never heard that complaint before, but don't trust the Yelp reviews. You're welcome to try for yourself.

My lips parted and my cheeks flushed before I reminded myself I didn't even know what he looked like. I typed out a response, deleted it, typed out another, deleted, then settled on one word.

Durga: Rules.

Sweat lined my palms as I remembered the gift he'd sent me—a vibrator I kept tucked under the corner of my mattress. He'd found a way around the Eastridge Fund's anonymity rules by sending it to me through a gift list service that made recipient addresses anonymous. As if we needed a middleman to broker my nightly pleasure.

Benkinersophobia: Fuck the rules. And no, I've never considered changing the name.
Change implies regret, and I do not regret.

Durga: Ever?

Benkinersophobia: No.

Durga: I call bullshit.

Reed groaned out. "Emery, are you even listening to me?"

Oops. How long had I been ignoring Reed?

Remorse had my fingers twitching. Reed didn't know about Ben. No one did. That was the point. Hell, it was the single rule the Eastridge Fund swore by. Anonymity. That meant no meetings and no discussing identifying details.

I placed Reed on speaker again, tossed my old smartphone on my raggedy mattress, and massaged the back of my neck. "Yes. Sorry. I spaced out."

"You've been doing that a lot."

His evident frustration settled in my chest, the guilt nothing new to me. Reed and I had made a pact to attend Duke together. Instead, I'd left for Clifton University in Alabama without telling him.

The people of Eastridge hated my family—and me by default. The same people that had followed Reed to Duke. I'd needed to get out of North Carolina. As far away from the Prescott brothers, The Winthrop Scandal, and Eastridge as my wallet would take me.

Four years ago, that would have been far.

Then Dad became the subject of a very public F.B.I.-S.E.C. joint investigation for embezzlement and stock tampering, and the textiles business he owned—the same one that provided jobs for almost everyone in town—went out of business.

Dad still had money—a lot of it—and so did Mother, but I wanted nothing to do with the dirty money that, as far as I was concerned, had become blood money as soon as Reed's dad and Angus Bedford had died.

"Who calls someone to read their emails? I'm not your assistant," Reed complained.

It was almost odd how we pretended everything was normal, that my dad's actions hadn't led to his dad's death, even if indirectly. I knew Dad hadn't forced Hank's heart to give out... just like I knew it never would have happened if he hadn't been so stressed about losing his life's savings and had to work three jobs to make it—and Reed's college tuition—back.

"I know. I'm sorry." I bit my lip and let my apology linger, because as always, I meant it as more than what I was supposed to be apologizing for. *I'm sorry I'm too chicken shit to read my own emails. I'm sorry I screwed your brother. I'm sorry about your dad.* "But I literally can't bring myself to read the email."

Tap.

Tap.

Tap.

Each click-clack of his keyboard sent my anxiety skyrocketing.

"Okay." He let out a heavy breath. "Headline: Emery, prepare for your successful repayment."

Next door, my neighbor's chihuahua barked as if he could sense my anxiety. I heard my neighbor yelling at the puppy through the thin walls, but he barked louder. My spirit animal was a three-month-old chihuahua who weighed one pound and three ounces and responded to the name Muchacha.

(Muchacha was not, in fact, a young woman but a male dog with a very real penis I'd witnessed him licking on occasion.)

I switched my phone off speaker and drew it to my ears.

"I know what the headline says," I snapped after Muchacha finally stopped barking. "Fuck. I'm sorry."

Here's something people often say about being poor but you never fully understand until it happens to you: being poor is stressful.

Unpaid bills always found a way into your mind, and when you stood in front of a grocery store cashier, holding up the line as she read out a number you were a few bucks short of, the desire for the ground to open up and swallow you whole became a permanent fixture of your life.

In reality, I knew what the email would say. I'd graduated a semester early, and my six-month student loan grace period would end soon. I needed a job. Preferably one away from home, not that anyone in the state would give me one.

The Winthrop name was radioactive in North Carolina. For good reason. Too many lives had been lost, including—I reminded myself for the millionth time—Reed's dad.

"You good, Em?"

I could never thank Reed enough for his patience, especially when I got Hulk-like, which was often lately.

"Yeah. Continue, please?" I toyed with my hair, which I'd let grow back to its natural roots. For starters, I had no money for highlights and hair dye. Also, I'd never thought I looked good as a blonde carbon copy of Mother.

"Once your loans leave the grace status, your Monthly Payment begins. Blah. Blah. Blah." I waited for him to finish reading. "Basically, your loan payments start in about two weeks."

"Shit."

I cursed myself for getting a degree in design when the present market for clothing designers in the South was practically non-existent and for not accepting the minimum-wage job I'd been offered last week. In my defense, at those rates, I might as well work for Daffy Dee's Diner as a waitress on rollerblades, which was my current hustle.

"You could work for Nash," Reed suggested, but I could gather how much he hated the idea.

I didn't understand what had happened between them. I didn't feel like it was my place to ask either. No matter how curious I was. A part of me always wondered if it had to do with me, but no way.

I shook my head, even though he couldn't see me. "Nope."

"Why not?"

Because four years later, I'm still mortified.

I hadn't talked to Nash Prescott since that night in Reed's bedroom. Not that we'd talked much before that. He was always Reed Prescott's older brother to me. Unattainable. Forbidden. Something I'd never even considered.

Until he had given me the best sex I'd ever had, and I still revisited that night in my head when the Alabama nights got too cold and I had nothing but fantasies to keep me warm. One night, when Ben had sent a slew of dirty messages my way, I'd come to the image of Nash over me.

I shook my head and picked at the cheap threads of my swap meet sheets. "Because he's your brother, and that's weird. Plus, you hate him."

I hate him, too.

"I don't hate him," Reed lied. "As for the rest, that's a horrible reason to deny an opportunity most would kill for."

I loathed that check-your-privilege tone of his, something he'd picked up from being my best friend during my high society days. The worst part was, he was right.

I'd left my parents and their money as soon as I'd turned eighteen, but that unshakeable guilt nagged me. It reminded me I was still more privileged than I deserved. I had a roof over my head, a bachelor's degree, and a few Hamburger Helpers in my cabinet.

Truthfully, there were signs I'd ignored, conversations I'd overheard, and pieces I should have put together but didn't. The way Mother never wanted me to visit the factory. The way Dad forced me out of the room every time his business partner Balthazar visited. The secret argument I'd heard between Mother, Dad, and Balthazar just weeks before the F.B.I. and S.E.C. raided our home.

When Mother had sat me down and told me Dad had defrauded everyone, that she was leaving him, and that she and Balthazar had tried to stop him, I hadn't believed her. The fucking F.B.I. had been looking into Dad, and still, I loved him with a loyalty he didn't deserve.

He'd screwed his business partner over. He'd screwed the town over. He'd screwed my mother over. And he'd screwed *me* over.

The worst part? My ignorance made me as

complicit in The Winthrop Scandal as my dad. Sophomore year, on the heels of a bomb threat at Eastridge Prep that had turned out to be Teddy Grieger's bail-out plan for the A.P. Physics test, the school's administration had held an assembly with the Eastridge Police Department.

Officer Durham gave a cheesy speech about being young adults, having responsibility, and looking out for one another. He'd made one point that, years later, always echoed in my mind when I laid alone in bed and felt particularly masochistic.

If you see something, say something. This isn't just a slogan. It's a creed. There is no such thing as an innocent bystander.

I was not an innocent bystander.

My sigh transformed into a long exhale as I bundled my design materials into a ball at the base of my mattress.

"If by horrible reason you mean horribly valid, yes, I agree." I couldn't be more petulant if I had jutted my bottom lip out.

"Mature." I could almost hear Reed shaking his head. "What's your beef with him? You know what? Don't answer that. Nash won't know you work there. The company is huge, and you're going by Emery Rhodes. Plus, you haven't seen him in four years, and you look nothing like you used to."

"You mean, I look like a mess."

Mother reminded me of this in her monthly emails.

Speak of the Devil...

My phone beeped with another call. I pulled it away from my ear and checked the caller ID. Mother flashed on the screen, a picture of her portrait-style in front of The Eastridge Junior Society displayed in full HD.

She was probably calling to pry info out of me, to see

if I'd finally visited Dad or if I wanted to do brunch with her and her boyfriend Balthazar.

As in, Uncle Balthazar.

As in, my dad's business partner Uncle Balthazar.

As in, the man who had been so close to my family that Mother had instructed me to call him "uncle" since birth.

I hadn't talked to my mother in months and didn't plan on starting now. I would sooner talk to Dad.

Anagapesis.

Aesthete.

Yūgen.

Gumusservi.

Muttering pretty words that made me happy, I declined the call and pressed my phone back to my ear in time to hear Reed laughing. "I didn't say that."

A woman's voice drifted over the line in the background.

I winced, absently rubbing at my chest, right above the spot that housed my jealous heart. I wasn't jealous because I wanted Reed. I knew that ship had sailed as soon as I'd slipped into bed with the wrong Prescott.

Loneliness fueled the jealousy. Mother had Uncle Balthazar. Reed had Basil. And I had a broken heater and endless Netflix binges of *F.R.I.E.N.D.S.* on my ex from freshman year's account. I dreaded the day he realized I was using it and changed his password.

"Is that Basil?" I bit a strand of hair, a nasty habit Mother would disown me for. "Tell her I said, 'hi.'"

We both knew I didn't mean it. He thought I disliked her for the way she treated me in high school, and I let him believe that rather than tell him the truth, which was that I thought he deserved better.

My neighbor's chihuahua, perhaps.

Whereas I'd ditched Reed for Clifton University, Basil and just about every other filthy rich Eastridger had followed him to Duke.

They'd been together since and were two seconds away from getting married and having perfectly behaved, blonde-haired, blue-eyed babies. Not the chaotic, wild, black-haired, heterochromia-eyed demon children I'd probably give birth to.

"She says you'd be a fool not to take a job with Nash."

Another lie from Reed.

When had we started lying to each other so much?

"No, she didn't."

If there was anyone Basil Berkshire wanted more than Reed, it was Nash. Though he wasn't as wealthy as us—as blue-blooded, as pedigreed, as groomed for nine-figure trust funds—he was always above us in some intangible way no one could explain but everyone gravitated toward.

And now, Nash Prescott was filthy rich. No one had an explanation for how it had happened, but it didn't surprise anyone either.

"Okay, she didn't," Reed admitted, "but I think you should work for Prescott Hotels. At the very least, maybe take one of their design internships for new graduates. You'd be designing a hotel, not clothes, but at least it's kind of close? Maybe? I don't know. Either way, it's a good, paying job. Nash doesn't even need to know if you think it's awkward. I can get Delilah to set it up for you. She owes me one."

Beggars can't be choosers.
Beggars can't be choosers.
Beggars can't be choosers.

I repeated the mantra in my head. Let's be real, I was

a fucking beggar. Probably would be for the rest of my life.

"Delilah?" The largest hole in the blanket widened as I toyed with the loose threads.

"The head of his legal department and his best friend, though he'd deny it, the cranky asshole. They're opening a new hotel in Haling Cove. It's in North Carolina, but it's far enough away from Eastridge that..." Reed's voice trailed off, but I got his point.

"I'll think about it," I relented before ending the call about the same time another email pinged on my phone. This time reminding me of a two-thousand-dollar payment I had to make.

Fuck.

I hit redial immediately.

"Yes?"

I ignored Reed's amused tone and Basil's whispers. "Set it up, please."

I swear, I could be naked and on display in the Metropolitan Museum, and my heart would beat slower than it was beating now.

"Just do it, please," I added when I sensed he'd give me shit for changing my mind so quickly.

"Under Emery Rhodes?"

Rhodes was my grandmama's maiden name. I'd been using it since I had left Eastridge. Winthrops weren't exactly popular in this neck of the woods, even as far as Alabama, but at least with my hair back to its natural black, I survived most of my undergrad with no one recognizing me.

That last month, though... I wouldn't wish it on anyone. Not even Basil fucking Berkshire.

I chewed on another strand of hair, wondering how to

ask this without sounding ridiculous. I spit it out, "Please, don't tell Nash."

"Keep a secret from my brother? Easily."

No hesitation.

Nothing.

Reed liked people. Whereas I had gone full-on hermit in college, Reed joined a frat, went to parties, and made more friends than Facebook allowed. But for the past seven years, he liked everyone except his brother.

"What's with you two? You used to be close."

I'd broken the unspoken rule. Asked the question I'd known I instinctively shouldn't have asked.

"Nothing."

Flat.

Emotionless.

Not Reed, yet somehow Reed.

Some rustling on his end filled my ears, and instinct told me he was done with this phone call.

"Look, I have to go. I'll talk to Delilah. This is the right decision," Reed assured me before he hung up.

I knew he was right. There wasn't a market for inexperienced twenty-two-year-olds with degrees in design in Clifton, Alabama, and there was nothing for me back in Eastridge, North Carolina. An internship at Prescott Hotels would afford me a head start I would be stupid to give up.

But the idea of seeing Nash again, of working for him...

I buried my face in my pillow and screamed before glaring at myself in the mirror. Desperation clashed with my pitch-black hair.

My phone pinged. *Ben.* The one person I could talk to about the Nash Prescott fiasco, but it felt weird to use Nash's app to discuss accidentally having sex with Nash.

Benkinersophobia: I didn't change it, because it reminds me of a girl I used to know.

My fingers twitched with the urge to ask him more, but I held back. I was better off not knowing.

Durga: If you had to change your username, what would you change it to?

I waited an hour for him to respond, and as soon as he did, the green active dot beside his name turned red.

Benkinersophobia: Sisyphus.

Sisyphus.
A fallen king.
A liar.
A cheat.
I could relate.

chapter NINE

nash

The one-word name should have been the first indicator I couldn't trust Fika.

His name reminded me of Emery Winthrop and her penchant for obscure words, which should have been the second indicator.

Fika is Swedish for a moment to slow down and appreciate the good things in life, and that should have been the third sign.

For starters, there were no good things in life.

And Fika wasn't even Swedish.

He was a Wonder Bread white, North Carolinian,

Keith Mars wannabe, a disgraced Eastridge sheriff ousted almost two decades ago, around the time I'd touched my first boob.

"I think you should stop this crusade of yours." A curtain of bangs swept hair over one eye until he brushed them to the side. He resembled the Jonas Brothers before they'd realized straightening hair was for pussies. The leather chair squished under his weight as he leaned forward and placed two elbows on my office desk, close enough I could see my reflection in his eyes. "It's destroying you. There's no light in your eyes. I didn't think it's possible, but each time I see you, it's worse, Nash."

Fika patted his pockets as if searching for the cancer sticks that had fucked up his lungs in the first place. When he didn't find them, he snapped at the litany of rubber bands that formed a colony up and down the length of his forearms.

"I didn't invite you inside my home at four in the morning for your opinion of me. I hired you for a job." Tracing my fingers along the stack of hundreds in front of me, I watched Fika's eyes follow their path across Benjamin Franklin's pasty, sunken-eyed face. "I tell you what to do. You get paid. That's how this works."

Thumbing the currency strap, I lifted the bills and fanned them, my fingers brushing against each hundred (and there were many). I should have shown mercy, but all I could feel at the mention of a Winthrop was rage.

The medical examiner had ruled my dad's death a heart attack, but he'd left out the three jobs he'd taken that led to it. If he and Ma hadn't lost their home, jobs, and savings, Dad would be alive and I wouldn't catch Ma staring at an empty dinner setting with misty eyes every time I visited.

As far as I was concerned, the Winthrops killed Hank Prescott.

Case closed.

Vengeance pending.

Fika's jaw ticked when I pulled out my desk's drawer, dropped the bills inside, and slammed it shut with an audible thud.

I believed in power over mercy. People possessed needs, and when you determined someone's needs, you ruled him.

Fika's need was money. His second cancer diagnosis arrived eighteen months ago. It sucked away the fat on his cheeks until he resembled something more like a ghoul than a man. Since his remission, he'd gained back some of his weight, along with medical debt that could fund a third-world coup d'état.

To be fair, I'd never had to pull the money card in the past. I'd done some less-than-legal things to become the C.E.O. and founder of a company Forbes valued at over a billion dollars last year, and Fika had done a stellar job of covering my tracks for me.

I'd stayed out of jail this long, a phenomenon in itself.

I asked him to do something. He did it. That was how transactions worked.

Until now.

"Did you swallow a bad batch of chemo?" I lifted a second stack of hundreds and tore at the edges of one bill because I could—and it left Fika on edge, a near miracle with the hippy bullshit he'd turned to after he'd beaten cancer the first time. "Have you forgotten the English dictionary? Transactions require an exchange, and for you to get this"—I rattled the stack of bills—"you have to give me what I asked for."

"Look, man..." He eyed the money before shaking his

head. "I get it. You've got a thing against the Winthrops, for good reason, but nothin' good will come out of finding Gideon Winthrop. Trust me."

I trusted no one, another reason Gideon needed to go. I didn't mean die. Death was an easy route; long, drawn-out suffering pleased me more.

Movies like *Taken* and *John Wick* skewed the general public's conceptions of revenge. It didn't happen in a day. Like all things worth doing, revenge—true revenge, the type meant to annihilate its target—took time.

The Space Race, for instance, began in 1955. The Apollo 11 didn't reach the moon until 1969. It took over fourteen years to land on the moon. Fourteen years. More than the average lifespan of a dog.

My revenge, on the other hand, had been in the making for a mere four years.

"I'm not looking for an ethics lecture, Fika." His hands shook as I spoke, but I spared him no mercy. "You found Gideon."

"I did." He worried his bottom lip and swiped at the Jonas Brothers wig again until it sat slightly crooked on his head. "Sometimes people do bad things for good reasons."

The argument of someone who'd taken bribes during his tenure as sheriff to pay for his cancer treatments.

How much evidence had he stolen? How many wealthy Eastridgers had he given a free pass? If Gideon had approached him, would he have brushed those crimes under a rug, too?

Unbuttoning my cuff plackets, I rolled up my sleeves on both sides until the tattoo on my left forearm peeked out.

Penance.

My bold, unapologetic truth.

Fika had misconstrued its meaning in the past, and I allowed him to do so again as his eyes dipped to the word then back to my face.

"I won't bullshit you," he began, his hands clasped together in the shape of a church steeple.

"Then don't."

"I found Gideon Winthrop." Fika dropped a hand to his distressed jeans—a fucking fifty-something-year-old in distressed jeans—and toyed with the frayed strands at the knees. "He seems happy and thriving. He sends his daughter postcards through email often. He has new friends, new neighbors, and even a new Golden Retriever. They know of his past, yet they still befriended him. In return, he treats them well. I've never seen a man smile more. He's discovered his own paradise, Nash."

I wanted to raze it all to the ground.

Destroy his daughter.

Steal his money.

Break his friends.

Tear down his neighbors.

Kidnap the damned Golden Retriever.

If he owned it, I wanted to watch him suffer as I took it from him.

"That's all good and dandy, but I didn't pay you to give me the Hallmark summary of Gideon's life." I poured each of us a glass of Bowmore 1957 and slid one Fika's way, knowing he craved it but couldn't accept it thanks to the diet his doctor had him on. "I asked you to find him for me. Where. Is. He?"

He eyed the liquor, his hand twitching before he dug it into his Slim-Jim-thin thigh. "I can't tell you that, kid."

I'd turn thirty-three years old this year, and he still saw me as the twenty-five-year-old who had come to him sprouting wild accusations about the Winthrops.

Unbelievable.

"Why."

A demand, not a question.

It slid past clenched teeth into stale air. I tapped the table, drawing his attention to a pack of cigarettes I'd left there for the sole purpose of keeping Fika off balance. I'd never smoked a day in my life, but they tempted me as I pictured the way they'd rile him up.

Seething didn't begin to describe me. If I were a volcano, I'd be spewing lava, an ash cloud the size of the moon hovering above us as I burnt Fika to a crisp. I settled for pulling the ten-thousand dollars from my desk and tossing the money into my fireplace with the precision of someone who'd spent his teenage years throwing shit out of windows and running for it when husbands came home too early.

I had a hotel being built in Haling Cove, a contract to negotiate in Singapore, and four suppliers to fire by sunrise. Stopping by my house in Eastridge for a meeting with Fika sat low on my to-do list, and my time was too damned valuable to be jerked around by a corrupt ex-cop in a Jonas Brothers wig who had forgotten his place.

Fika leapt for the money, but the flames swallowed it, bright sparks shooting past the mantel at us. He whimpered as it burned, withering away to nothing but smoke and ashes.

Meaningless.

"I feel sad for you, kid." When the last bill metamorphosed to dust, Fika turned to me and sat on the leather ottoman beside the fire, shaking his head like I was his son and my existence disappointed him. "Do you know what Fika means? It means to have a coffee, but it's more than that. It's a way of life. Stop. Have coffee. Enjoy your own company. Enjoy the company of others. You can't appreciate what you have now if you're fixated on what was taken from you in the past."

I stood, pushing my chair with the backs of my thighs as I remembered the fourth sign I shouldn't have trusted Fika. He answered to a moral compass skewed by his idiotic perspectives. He was, after all, the type of madman who played Christmas music year-round and, worse, sang out loud with the songs.

"Before you quote another CBD-laced fortune cookie, Hank Prescott isn't the kind of man who can be forgotten." I opened my office door and stared Fika down until he got the hint and left, sans the fifty-thousand dollars he would have received had he delivered Gideon Winthrop's location as promised. "Learn your place."

Slamming the door just as he exited so he felt the bite of the wood, I gathered documents into a briefcase for my trip to Haling Cove and considered the obvious. Emery knew where Gideon lived. Gideon and Virginia had separated soon after news of the scandal broke, but Gideon still sent messages to his daughter.

Stripping a man of his wealth, dignity, and happiness was an art form, and like all art forms, it required a great deal of patience and suffering. I had the patience, but I refused to suffer any more.

Emery Winthrop, on the other hand, made perfect collateral damage.

I could break her spirit in half and not feel a lick of guilt.

Sin number one.

She'd known about her dad's extracurricular activities. I'd overheard her parents discussing it the night Reed almost went to jail.

Reed had run to the cottage, and Emery had hidden in her room, but I'd found myself against the tiger sculpture's ass again, leaning behind Dionysus, listening in on Virginia, Gideon, and Able Small Dick Cartwright's dad argue.

"If Emery finds out, I will cut you off, Virginia, and I will sue you for everything you own, Cartwright," Gideon had warned, his voice steady and threat real.

"Please," Virginia scoffed, unladylike without an audience, "she already knows. Why do you think I sent her to that shrink to set her straight?"

The ledger had only left my suit's breast pocket once since I'd stolen it, and I felt the heat of it burn my chest. Emery Winthrop knew about her parents' scam, and I... I'd made two mistakes tonight that I couldn't take back.

Sin number two.

The day the F.B.I. and S.E.C. had raided Emery's McMansion, she'd led an agent to my parents' cottage, covering for her dad as she listed our names—Betty. Hank. Reed. Nash. They stood in front of the mailbox, staring at the door, but I'd heard enough.

I dipped into the maze and retrieved the ledger I'd hidden before some government smuck found it.

I had a plan to atone for my sins.

I had a plan to fix my parents, Eastridge, everything.

I had a plan.

Then, Dad died.

And I was just as guilty as the Winthrops.

chapter TEN

Emery

Weessalth.

I never realized it had a scent, but I'd been away from Eastridge for so long, I almost couldn't recognize the familiar stench as it assaulted my nostrils. Prior to last week, I'd never been inside a Prescott Hotel before. I had no intention of stepping foot in another after I finished my internship.

It reeked of wealth I'd worked so hard to distance myself from.

So pretty. So fragile. So breakable.

It reminded me of a snow globe. A picture-perfect world trapped within delicate glass that would shatter if handled too roughly. Just like my world had shattered four years ago.

The features spoke of wealth. Marble lobby. High ceilings. Over-the-top chandeliers. A floating pool built one hundred feet into the Atlantic Ocean. The fact that I could picture my mother here had me looking over my shoulder as I dipped back into the ballroom from the restroom.

"Adagio for Strings" and the hushed sound of the country's top point-one-percenters living their best lives accosted my ears.

Most of the hotel remained in a partial construction stage, waiting for finishes, flooring, and paint. You wouldn't know it if you stood inside the ballroom.

Over the past week, I'd helped furnish half of the suites on the sixteenth floor, the main part of the lobby, and the ballroom for a masquerade party my boss had dropped on us last minute.

We were designers, not event planners. But Chantilly viewed the masquerade as an opportunity to cement her name as America's foremost designer. I saw a thinly veiled attempt at assuring the who's who of North Carolina were on board with the fast-tracked creation of this hotel.

Worse, Reed had promised I wouldn't be in the same room with Nash, yet I felt him here tonight with intimate, uncanny precision I had no business possessing. Dipping past a group of men discussing Chinese tariffs, my skin tingled from the sensation of being stared at.

I'd felt it all night, two eyes tracking each step I took. I needed to run. I also needed money for food, loans, and penance.

Pivoting abruptly, I gave the source no time to turn away as I tracked him down. Two brown orbs watched me from three tables over. Their owner lifted a glass to me. I struggled to place him beneath the distance and his distinct, emerald-colored masquerade mask, but I knew it wasn't Nash.

The eyes were wrong.

The lashes too short.

The hair too orderly.

The goosebumps on my arms too absent.

Neither of us broke eye contact, even when my vision blurred and I spelled *cryptoscopophilia* in my head. The urge to secretly peer in windows of homes as one passes by. Except it was a mask my eyes itched to stare past.

The stranger unsettled me, like my brain knew something the rest of me didn't. Reckless. Gutsy. Stupid. I wouldn't argue against any of these descriptions of me as I planted my feet and tilted my chin up—daring him to approach me.

Reed always hated this side of me, but I could never fight it. I was made to go down swinging, which explained why I wouldn't be the first to lose the staredown, except an arm latched onto my hand and jerked me toward the wall.

Countless politicians canvassed the room with their Aubercy shoes and artificially whitened smiles, extracting votes from rich men who expected favors in exchange for money. Businessmen dressed in Dormeuil flipped from conversation to conversation, sealing investment deals and assuring business contacts of past opportunities.

Near the open bar, socialites gossiped about illicit affairs and unsuspecting victims wearing last-season gowns. Over a hundred people shared the room with me, yet Chantilly managed to isolate me in the corner. She harrowed me with problems I had no intention of solving.

My skin continued to prickle, and I fought the temptation to turn and see if the masked man still stared at me. Worse—I dared him to. I'd be the first to admit I'd grown more reckless in the past four years. (And I'd already been reckless to begin with.)

"Where the fuck is the caviar?" Chantilly waved her arms until the strap of her gown slid down her bony shoulders. Shifting with me as I tried to dodge her, she backed me into the wall. "Fuck me! We need the caviar." Her wild hands gestured to the throngs of guests behind her. "Which one of us is fucked if someone complains that there's no caviar? Me! I need the fucking caviar, Rhodes."

She'd managed to use *fuck* as a noun, verb, and adjective. Her Vancouver accent sharpened with each shrieked syllable. She reminded me of Moaning Myrtle, and I couldn't escape her on account of her being my boss.

I pictured myself as the storm outside, whipping around the room until dresses flowed with water and conversations halted. Until silence met my ears, and I found peace for the night. Until I wiped the ballroom of its occupants, except for myself and the food.

I spelled the word *procellous* on the roof of my mouth with the tip of my tongue and focused on my red-faced boss. Hunger pains pinched my sides. I fought them and lost, clenching onto Chantilly's shoulders a little tighter than necessary. I turned her toward a waitress the modeling agency had sent to us.

Blonde hair rested in a severe bun on the top of her head, paired with dramatic black eye shadow and a suit dress she wore absent of a shirt or bra beneath. She held the tray out to guests, but she walked so slowly in her six-inch heels, she must have been new—to heels *and* to catering.

"Maybe one of the male models can take her place so she can rest her legs," I suggested.

We both watched her skinny legs wobble.

They weren't skinny in the way mine were. Hers spoke of intention, sculpted with lean muscles and a tan that looked natural but I knew from experience wasn't. My legs resembled two sallow, vegetative twigs that told tales of poverty and malnourishment.

In the past four years, I'd lost weight off my already slender frame. My hip bones jutted out, taunting me with the food I craved but couldn't afford. That was my mission tonight—binge eat free food. I had no doubt Chantilly would be an obstacle.

"We don't pay for servers to take breaks." Her head shook in furious waves. She lifted her hand to scrub at her face but stopped the instant her palms brushed her mascara-coated lashes. "No breaks," she repeated. "That's what the complimentary Red Bull and caffeine pills we provide are for."

For a second, she abandoned her hatred of me and took off after the poor waitress, and I couldn't bring myself to feel anything but relief. Chantilly had done everything except take out an advertisement announcing her disdain for me.

My first day of employment had begun with a speech on nepotism as the eighth deadly sin and spiraled downward since. I didn't dare mention that I'd never actually met or talked to Delilah, because knowing Delilah was infinitely better than knowing Reed or Nash. Chantilly's head would probably explode if she learned I knew the Prescott brothers.

I popped out my phone, rereading my messages from Ben. My lifeline. My single thread of sanity this past week.

Durga: Tell me not to quit. I need this job, but my boss is borderline abusive. It's driving me insane.

Benkinersophobia: You—the woman who told me to guzzle a gallon of TheraFlu and suck it up when I thought I was dying from the fucking bird flu—want to quit? There's a word for this. Irony? No... Oh, wait. Hypocrisy. That's the word I'm looking for.

Durga: Ha. Ha. You're so funny. Laugh it up. I'm miserable.

One text, and he'd cured me. I swore, he could bottle himself up, sell it, and become as rich as Nash.

Benkinersophobia: You aren't miserable. You are the person who sees beauty in every situation. The one I turn to when I'm stressed and need someone to lift me up. Someone so strong, I marvel at your existence. You know what you're not? You. Are. Not. A. Quitter. You are a warrior, but it's okay not to feel like one all the time. Even warriors take breaks.

Durga: I almost don't want to ever meet you. You're too good to be true.

Benkinersophobia: I'm not. I'm a full-time dick. Just not to you.

Durga: No one else gets the Nice Ben treatment?

Benkinersophobia: My mom.

Durga: Ah. A mama's boy. There's the thread that pulls apart the hot man fantasy.

Durga: Thank you.

Benkinersophobia: If it's any consolation, my night is shit. I'm spending it with uptight dicks whose favorite games include Whose Net Worth is Bigger? and How Punchable Can I Sound Without Actually Getting Punched?

Durga: Misery likes company. Have fun suffering.

Benkinersophobia: Ass.

I pocketed my phone, a smile on my face that Ben never failed to stamp there. With Chantilly gone, I pivoted in the other direction, narrowly avoiding this month's Forbes 30 under 30 cover model.

What had I said to Nash Prescott all those years ago?

Aren't you supposed to be in New York, opening some destined-to-fail business venture?

Well, that business venture had turned into the first Prescott Hotel, which soon morphed into a second. Then a third. Then a fourth. Until the Prescott Hotels brand cemented itself as one of the most well-known and coveted luxury hotel companies in the world. A powerhouse hotel chain that put names like Hilton and Kensington to shame.

The boy who borrowed suits from my dad and spent his nights getting in fights had become the king of Monopoly, collecting property even when it wasn't his turn. I wanted to hate him for it. I couldn't. Not after what had happened to Hank.

A hand caressed the fabric of my dress, followed by a compliment intended to stroke my ego. I smiled politely at the girl, told her I absolutely died over her Carolina Herrera gown I'd seen on two other women tonight, and snagged a gruyere sandwich from a waiter before she could sentence me to mundane conversation.

When I finally made my way back to the table, the emerald-masked stranger had left. I gave myself two-and-a-half seconds to indulge my fantasies of stealing all the food in the ballroom and slipping upstairs to the sixteenth floor. All my worldly possessions sat in a closet there.

A crate of plain Winthrop Textiles t-shirts.

My t-shirt printer.

A cardboard box of random knick-knacks and jeans.

Pricey tourist traps like Haling Cove were a real estate investor's dream. An excess of small units crammed into sky-high buildings, then up-charged by five-hundred percent. Rather than choose between food and shelter, I slept in the closet.

It felt duplicitous, but so was getting a job at Nash's company without him knowing.

Beggars can't be choosers, Emery.

Shuffling through the crowd and into a small opening, I came face-to-face with one of Dad's old friends. He stood in a corner, his gray hair glistening as he spoke to an older couple.

"Have you considered investing through a new firm? The stock market is ever changing, but at Mercer and Mercer, we are always ahead of the curve."

Yeah, through insider trading.

I pretended I had something in my nose when a guest stared at me.

Dad once told me the Mercers had spies inside every large American corporation and had made a science out of insider trading. I'd balked at the idea back then, but now, it seemed like the least significant crime in a room full of people who had done worse than my dad and only hated him for getting caught.

I dodged past Jonathan Mercer, fake smiling at his mistress who clutched onto his arm with her umber coffin nails. The tight corset of my floor-length gown labored my breaths. I plucked a bottle of water from the bar, ignored the persistent feeling of being stared at, and chalked it up to paranoia. The sensation often pricked my skin since my last semester at Clifton, after everyone had figured out who I was.

The dress I'd repurposed from a woven black curtain I'd found at a swap meet had the distinct displeasure of being made from black-out fabric. I stopped for drink breaks every fifteen minutes to fight the heat, alternating between ice water and Amaretto sours because something had to make this night tolerable.

I pressed my back against the standing freezer, exactly where the dip in the dress exposed a stretch of skin. The thigh-high slit had risen from half-assed stitch work, but it did the job. I looked like I belonged here, which pissed Chantilly off.

I'd done nothing to her, yet she'd hated me from the moment I stepped foot into this building a week ago. I slanted my head until my hair covered my face and adjusted my self-made masquerade mask. Too many familiar people here to take chances.

A violent thunderstorm brewed outside, but you wouldn't know it with the way the investors laughed and drank without a care in the world. Meanwhile, Chantilly had sent the other intern off to make sure our back-up plan was ready in the likely event the storm made its way inside. Hannah had been stacking buckets in the utility closet beside the ballroom all night.

Two shoes popped into my line of sight, and I followed them to their owner, a Daniel Henney lookalike. The Roman nose, sharp brown eyes, and gentleman's cut—all eerily familiar echoes from a past I'd rather bury.

Still, my skin itched.

I tried and failed to place him.

Chantilly eyed me from across the room as he offered a hand.

"Brandon. Brandon Vu."

He spoke without the North Carolina accent I loved, his voice stripped of identity and stamped with the General American label. Generic. Boring. Another clue to a puzzle I yearned to unravel.

I swore I knew him from somewhere. Skimming his features once more triggered nothing. I hated puzzles I couldn't solve; I was better off ignoring him and occupying my mind with food. The urge to flee the hotel and chase the petrichor forced my toes to curl inward and dig into the soles of my Converse.

Brandon's hands lingered in the space between us, but he kept his grin easy until I caved and folded my palm into his.

Pretending I didn't feel the heat from Chantilly's glare, I added, "Emery."

Instead of shaking my hand, he pressed a kiss against my knuckles. Warm breath teased my skin until he released my hand.

"I know."

He stared at me like a cat stared at a mouse caught in a trap.

No remorse.

No guilt.

Unsatiated, waiting for his prey to die.

You should have run, I scolded myself.

Still, my feet remained planted on the freshly milled Macassar ebony. I forced my eyes to his and scanned his face.

No recognition.

Nothing.

Just a twinkle in his eyes I didn't like nor understand.

chapter ELEVEN

Emery

"Do I know you?" I eventually asked, cursing my buzz.

He dipped his chin to the name tag pinned at the upper swell of my left breast. "Your name is right there."

I released the breath I'd been holding in, laughed at my paranoia, and finally gave him some semblance of a grin. "How are you enjoying the party?"

A waiter snagged my empty water bottle as I observed Brandon. Shoulders pulled back. Easy smile on his face. Movie-star looks. He seemed at ease here, his well-fitted suit stretching across his broad frame like a knight's armor as he worked the room as if he owned it.

The lack of designer threads was the sole indicator he didn't belong here, which begged the question—why the hell did I recognize him?

Brandon shrugged and made a circular gesture with his pointer finger. "Not my thing."

I should have been offended. After all, I had helped to plan the masquerade—and not in the sense that I'd dished out orders to Dad's staff and an overworked, underpaid event planner.

No, I'd spent the past week running around Haling Cove; double-checking floral arrangements; sitting in on the orchestral practices; and taking the bus to a different mall after I'd spotted my ex-neighbor Matilda Astor at the boutique Chantilly had ordered me to buy eggshell-colored tablecloths from.

She made me return all one-hundred and eight of them, and I had the pleasure of purchasing the original brand after she berated me for my incompetence in front of everyone I worked with.

Then, she'd decided the new ones weren't the right shade of eggshell and demanded me to return them and repurchase the ones I'd bought in the first place.

Whatever grunt work needed to be done had fallen on my bony, underfed shoulders.

And I was proud.

Truly.

If not exhausted and ready for it to end.

"Not my thing either." I snagged a soup spoon of scallop ceviche bathed in coconut foam from a waiter, who shot me a polite smile.

He'd witnessed Chantilly yelling at me earlier for

seating the design team too far from Nash's table. As it was, I'd made it a point to avoid looking at him all night except to make sure I always stood on the opposite side of the room from him, far enough that I couldn't even tell the color of his suit.

Aside from Brandon, Nash was the one man in the room who hadn't bothered with a masquerade mask. Didn't matter. With or without a mask, I would have recognized him.

He had that kind of presence. The type that had you turning around and looking over your shoulder to make sure he wasn't behind you because, from across the room, I could feel him near me.

Even now, it took everything in me to push his presence out of my mind.

"Oh?" Brandon sipped his drink, something clear. Water, whereas everyone else had taken the open bar as an invitation to get plastered. The insight unsettled me. "You look like you fit in with this crowd."

"I've been to more of these things than I'd like to count." I shrugged, uncomfortable with the direction of the conversation. "Doesn't mean I like it."

I did, however, like keeping my job. Forgoing another night at the soup kitchen didn't hurt either. I usually went during off-hours when it wasn't busy, but lately, with how unpredictable the weather could be this time of year, people constantly filled it, seeking shelter from the harsh heat and sudden rains.

"Are you an investor?" He didn't seem particularly interested in the answer.

I inspected his features again. Curiosity rooted my feet to the floor, even as instinct yelled at me to retreat. Assembling the mystery of Brandon reminded me of starting a book and being told not to finish. I'd never possessed the willpower.

"No. They're wearing the gold name tags." I didn't elaborate, snagging a fruit tart off a passing tray. My mission tonight was to eat as much food as I could, so I wouldn't have to stop by the soup kitchen in the morning.

"Not a date, then?" An amused grin lifted his lips. He watched me struggle to remove the wrapping from the tart.

Malaise.
A general feeling of discomfort or unease.

I couldn't grasp where I knew him from, but I'd pinpointed the feeling his presence evoked from me. Despite my bravado, it gave me pause. The last time I'd felt that had been the night Angus Bedford committed suicide.

"I work here." The catering and design teams shared sterling-colored tags, etched with our first names. I thumbed mine, the movement unintentional.

"Why do I get the feeling you're not as invested in this conversation as I am?" He didn't look offended, but I had the decency to pretend that I felt bad.

I shoveled the tart into my mouth as gracefully as I could and sent him an apologetic smile. "Sorry, I haven't eaten all day."

"You have nothing to apologize for." He snagged a chocolate strawberry and offered it to me. I considered returning it to the waiter before giving in to my hunger. "I actually approached you because you look so familiar. Do I know you from somewhere?"

I knew it.

We did know each other.

I resisted the urge to adjust my mask. I'd stitched it myself with the sole intention of making it large enough to hide my identity. I no longer wore my hair blonde, my lashes didn't boast eight-hundred-dollar extensions, and my hair fell down to my waist in a wild mixture of wavy, straight, and curled locks. I looked nothing like the Virginia Winthrop clone I'd once been.

The single identifying feature I still possessed were my eyes. One gray. One blue. But not noticeable enough that he'd realize it unless he searched for it or he'd been around me all of his life. And since he seemed familiar…

Déjà vu eased its way inside me. My stomach took the hit first, nausea replacing some of the hunger pains. It still ached from starvation and exhaustion, but I no longer possessed the self-destructive urge to stick around and find out how Brandon Vu recognized me.

I bit into the strawberry, buying time to consider my words carefully. "I think I have one of those recognizable faces." My shoulders shrugged, and I pretended to wave at Chantilly, who frowned at me in response. She was *still* frowning at me. "My boss just waved me over. I'm so sorry, but it was nice meeting you."

Trotting off before Brandon could say anything, I sidled up next to Chantilly at the open bar and discarded the strawberry stem into the nearby trash can. Chantilly had moved past glaring at me to gawking at Nash.

The woman was as transparent as a hologram. She wore a crimson faux fur-lined mask to cover her face, not sunglasses to cover her eyes. She could at least pretend she wasn't staring.

Metanoia.
Tarantism.
Marcid.

Mouthing the words, I filled my fist with oyster cracker packets from a bowl laid out, shoved them into my clutch for later, and twisted to Chantilly. "Can I leave?"

She finally turned to me and toyed with the ends of her auburn hair. Her olive-colored eyes popped beneath her mask, and I'd classify her as gorgeous if she wasn't such a horrid bitch to me.

A flawlessly threaded brow arched. "After you screwed up with our seating arrangements and the tablecloths, you want to leave early?"

Fuck this.

"You're right. You know what?" I lifted my chin in Nash's direction, defocusing my eyes because if I saw him, I'd stare like Chantilly. Or worse, perhaps, since I knew what he looked like beneath his clothes *and liked it*. "I should introduce myself to our boss," I bluffed. "I've never met Nash Prescott before. He's gorgeous… I've heard he's even more gorgeous up close."

It was like a game of two truths and a lie.

Truth: Nash Prescott was gorgeous.

Truth: He was even more gorgeous up close.

Lie: I had met Nash Prescott. I'd met more nooks and crannies of Nash Prescott's body than I wanted to admit, least of all to Chantilly.

Her brows furrowed, and she looked like she was trying to work out if I was serious or not. I kept my face neutral until she cracked.

"Fine. You can leave. But don't think I'll be paying you overtime for tonight. The design budget is tight enough as it is."

She'd made room in the budget for her Versace gown, but she didn't have room to pay me four hours in overtime. Got it.

Whatever.

It was either stay and relinquish myself to Brandon's

scrutiny or leave and be free of Brandon *and* Nash. I chose the easy choice. The right choice.

Snatching two shots of top-shelf liquor from the bartender, I downed them both in front of Chantilly, arched a brow, then left. I kept close to the walls as I snaked my way out of the ballroom, cursing when someone spilled an entire glass of vodka on my dress.

I dabbed at it with a cocktail napkin before giving up and continuing my path to the elevators. I'd nearly reached the lobby when Ida Marie cut me off.

"Ugh." Matching my stride, she groaned with each step. "My feet are killing me. I need a break."

Precisely why I wore Chucks over heels. That, and I no longer owned heels. Mother would disown me if she knew.

Ida Marie flicked lint off her frilly dress and asked, "You going up?"

Out of the four others on the design team, I liked Ida Marie most. The only one who didn't view our coworkers as competition in the quest for a promotion. Everyone wanted to be the person assigned to the following hotel so much, they lost sight of the fact that we were supposed to be focusing on *this* hotel.

This job.

Not some fancy upcoming Singapore location Nash's company had sent a memo about.

"I'm headed to the fifth floor. I have to grab my work bag from the office," I lied. "But Chantilly said I can leave after that."

The design team had made a makeshift office out of the fifth floor. It consisted of an oversized couch, a TV, some company-owned laptops, and two desks that went to Chantilly and Cayden.

Ida Marie's white-blonde curls bounced as she walked. "You mean she was actually nice to you?"

"I threatened to introduce myself to Nash Prescott." She laugh-snorted.

I stalled near the archway where the ballroom met the lobby, not quite wanting her to follow me to the elevators and realize I wasn't headed to the fifth floor.

"Chantilly has been salivating over Mr. Prescott since she heard he would be here tonight." Ida Marie lowered her voice after a few heads turned our way at the mention of Nash. "Last year, she managed to get someone to take her as a date to the annual company party so she could meet Mr. Prescott. Hannah told me she got so wasted, security had to escort her out. The lone reason she wasn't fired was because the company parties are always masquerades. They didn't know it was her."

The alarm on her phone beeped out before she muted it with a curse. "Shit. I have to be back. I'm on drunk assholes duty. Chantilly has me bringing them water and begging them to return to their rooms before they make her look bad in front of Mr. Prescott."

She paused for a second as the lights flickered, courtesy of the wicked storm gathering force outside the hotel. "You don't think…" Alarm dilated her pupils. She shook her head, dismissing the idea of a power outage, as if rich people and their parties were untouchable. "Nah. You guys don't get, like, power outages down here, right? There are fail-safes and stuff."

Ida Marie had grown up in the SoCal high desert. The storm last week had been her first in decades. First storm. First lightning. Being around her reminded me of witnessing a child experiencing the world for the first time.

"I'm sure it'll be fine," I offered, hoping she'd leave

already because the last thing I wanted was to share an elevator with a guest. The longer we stalled her, the more likely it got.

"Knowing my luck, the power will shut off, and we'll be stuck here all night." She leaned forward for a hug. "Better get out while you can. See you in the morning?"

"Wait..." My fingers latched onto her upper arm before she slipped away. "The morning?"

As far as I knew, we worked Mondays through Fridays.

"Yeah." She nodded her head.

I released her. The wilting flowers on a nearby table caught her attention, and I repeated my question before I lost her to the melaleucas completely.

"Eight in the morning. Sharp," she said. I followed her to the table and watched her fingers flutter around the flower stems. "Some last-minute meeting. Didn't you get the memo?"

"Must have missed it," I lied.

Chantilly also hadn't told me about the dress fittings the company had set up for us, which meant I'd ended up pulling this outfit together with minutes to spare while Chantilly had strutted into the ballroom wearing in-season Versace.

Pushing past servers, partygoers, and a holier-than-thou Chantilly talking up an investment banker who'd once had an affair with a classmate's mother, I made my way to the exit.

I left, my eyes holding Brandon's the entire time.

I backed away slowly before a flash of something green peeking from his pocket snagged my attention.

I recognized it.

The same mask worn by the man I'd caught staring at me all night.

chapter TWELVE

Emery

My singular near-death experience had come on the eve of my ninth birthday. My nanny cried as the storm rattled our private jet. She cried harder when the pilot announced an emergency landing.

Mother sipped the glass of Château Margaux she shouldn't have owned. (Money bought things like famous wine once belonging to a founding father.) I didn't know whether she was a badass that couldn't be fazed or the 'preventative' Botox had smoothed her face to the point of no expression.

The landing flung my head against the leather headrest until the only stars I saw were the ones blurring my vision. Dad held my hand, telling me stories of a war he'd never been to, the analogy being we were warriors fighting a storm or some bullshit I no longer believed but had clung to at the time.

Our private jet shook against the pavement in some podunk Southern town Mother deemed too gross to step foot in. The emergency landing hadn't budged her face, but my nanny wore streaks of mascara on her cheeks as she helped Mother to the back of the jet for a nap until we could leave for Greece again.

I stood to follow, but Dad tugged at my hand and led me to the emergency exit. The slide inflated within seconds of the door opening. I didn't have the opportunity to scream. Dad pushed me, and I flew down.

Wind whipped hair against my cheeks. Rain made my teeth chatter. Sharp lightning lit up the sky. Sparks of thrill sent delicious electricity through my body that reminded me of staying up past my bed-time and not getting caught. And I swore, I'd never experienced magic before that day.

Dad slid down after me, singing the lyrics to "Every Little Thing She Does is Magic," so off-key, I enjoyed his version more than the real one. When he grabbed my hand, we danced to no music, switching from ballroom to 80s moves, feeling reckless, happy, like a two-person family was greater than a three-person one.

I laughed until I collapsed onto thick mud, making lazy angels with my arms and legs as I told Dad I wanted to move here forever. I didn't even know where here was.

Dad tapped my chin and fell to the mud beside me.

"It doesn't matter where we live, Emery. We can balter anywhere."

I scrunched my nose, inhaling salty rainwater that shotgunned to my head and rendered me dizzy. "Balter?"

"To dance—artlessly, with no grace, no skill, but always with enjoyment. All you have to do is ask. I will always be here to balter with you."

The pilots had delayed another day until they could replace the emergency slide, which forced Mother to sleep in a town she thought she was too good for, and Dad and I spent the entire vacation with a cold.

Mother called us stupid on her way to the spa, but I shared secret smiles with Dad and drank hot chocolate with mini marshmallows in the library of the *yposkafo* we rented, scouring English and Greek dictionaries for special words.

On my ninth birthday, I'd learned that my dad loved me fiercely, storms were magic, and unique words were the prayers that fueled them.

The first lesson had been a lie. Dad wouldn't have stolen from his company and taken that risk if he loved me.

The second and third lessons were probably lies, too, but I'd never been able to shake the idea of magical storms and transcendental words.

I whispered five magic words to force Brandon out of my head. I speed-walked my way to the alcove of elevators. My fingers made quick work of my pin, loosening my name tag before a guest noticed an employee headed to the sixteenth floor.

Before the power crew had left for the day, we'd had them turn an extra elevator on for the guests to reach their rooms.

Two elevators.

More than a hundred guests.

I dropped my hands and ran to the last one on the right. Its doors had begun to close. A crowd of businessmen approached behind me. I didn't know how I could explain not having an actual room on the sixteenth floor to nine people, so I took my chances that there were fewer people inside the closing elevator.

I broke into an all-out sprint, which wasn't the best look in Converse and a floor-length dress made of restricting curtain fabric, but I'd been working since eight this morning, and it was two hours past midnight. I needed a whole day of rest if I had to spend it on the damn closet floor. Plus, I'd drunk just enough to make me drowsy, my eyes droopy and begging for a good night's sleep.

"Wait!" I called out to the two occupants, so dizzy from alcohol and hunger, I thought I might faint.

The man had his head tucked downward, focusing on his smartphone, but the woman looked up. We made eye contact as the doors continued their path. Neither of them bothered holding them open. I dove inside the elevator, barely escaping the heavy metal doors.

I bumped into the man, who steadied me with a large palm before stepping back. My cheeks burned a horrifying shade of scarlet from exertion, and I averted my eyes from his towering build and bespoke suit, almost certain my mask was a second from slipping off.

Ignoring my irritation with them both, I pressed the button to the sixteenth floor, brushing against the woman's arm.

She scooted as far away as possible at my touch, her silver-coated mask shifting with the movement. Her runway-thin body looked svelte in the sequined dress she wore, the same color as her mask.

Meanwhile, I resembled the aftermath of a category four tornado. Vodka stained the left half of my gown. Slate-black hair swept in dizzying directions. Multi-colored eyes framed by melted mascara and eyeliner, in the shape of a wilting raccoon.

I could kiss my mask for hiding most of the liquified makeup, but I kept my head down in case. I didn't want one of Dad's old business friends to recognize me, and the prospect of anyone seeing me like this unnerved me.

A nagging awareness spread through my chest, something I couldn't pinpoint but knew I had to. The wall tempted me. I wanted to face it, bury myself in the gunmetal velvet lining, and hide until the invisible needles pricking my body ceased their assault.

I lowered my head down and tilted away. Pulling my phone out, I typed out a couple of messages to Ben for something to do.

Durga: You know what would be an awful way to die? In a room full of people you don't know.

Durga: Or worse—a room full of people you hate.

I waited, breath baited. The circle by his name remained red, indicating he either wasn't on his phone or he wasn't on the app. I suppressed my sigh but flipped off its push notifications in case an alert came in during work and someone realized I was from Eastridge.

My fingers continued typing idle messages on the notes, pretending I had a reason for keeping my head down other than a body-seizing fear of being recognized.

The lights flickered. I crossed my toes in the Chucks my dress hid well and sent a mini-prayer to the powers that be that the electricity wouldn't shut off, and I wouldn't be stuck in this elevator with these two.

The elevator shook at the next rumble of thunder. My thin, silver name tag fell to the floor. I'd forgotten I even loosened it. I bent to pick it up the same time the man did. He reached it first, lifting it with delicate care I hadn't expected.

I extended my hand out for it, but he didn't return it. His thumb brushed against my name engraved on the tiny silver rectangle. He stood, his movements abrupt and jerky. It remained clutched between his fist, the grip so tight his knuckles had turned white. He would have crushed it, had it not been metal.

I kept my head down, torn between facing him and demanding he return my name tag and turning to the wall and forgetting it existed.

What the hell was happening?

I straightened after him, confused and too tired to draw conclusions. He pressed the button for the next floor—the seventh.

The doors opened almost immediately. I glanced at his date from the corners of my eyes.

The girl stood frozen, her jaw unhinging. Her furrowed brows dipped into her mask. "What?"

"We're done for the weekend." The clipped tone seemed familiar. I wanted to study him, but it was more reason not to. I refused to be recognized while confined to a small box. "Wait for the elevator to return to the lobby. I'll add a bonus for the taxi."

She clutched onto his arm as the elevator pinged. "But I thought—"

"I don't pay you to think." He took a step back, extracting himself from her grip. I refused to glance at his face. "Your flight is booked for 8 A.M."

In six hours.

I nearly winced for the poor girl, but I was supposed to be minding my business, my head down, my damn name tag still in this stranger's fingers. Plus, if it had been up to her, the elevator doors would have closed on me.

She dipped her head down and left the elevator without another protest.

He was an asshole.

Clearly.

But it was not my problem.

Nope.

I just wanted my name tag.

"Can I have my name tag?" I shifted at the awkwardness in the air.

I'd met men like him before. I didn't need to look at his face to know his type—classically handsome with all the money and power in the world. A man who thought he could toy with people as he pleased. A man like my father.

I loved my dad, but I didn't love who he had turned out to be. Obligatory love, my mom had called it when I'd tried to explain the pain in my soul. It seemed too inadequate of a description.

The man toyed with the metal in his hand and whispered, his voice as deep and rich as his Westmancott suit, "Emery."

My name sounded like it'd touched his lips before. It spoke of a familiarity that alarmed me, and I prayed against all odds he hadn't recognized my name.

It wasn't only my dad people dragged through the mud. My mother and I bore emotional battle scars from the last four years, but I supposed I might have had it easy compared to her. She refused to leave Eastridge.

No one wanted us there.

"Look at me," he demanded, shocking me.

I refused. It felt like the coward's way out, and I'd never been a coward in the past. I criticized my dad, but I'd failed to mention what I thought about myself.

The person I'd become since The Winthrop Scandal would never have earned my respect back then. One moment, fearless to the point of reckless, jumping with little regard for consequences. And the next moment, spineless, both victim and victimizer. A bear ensnared by a simple trap, once mighty, now fallen.

Once a tiger. Now a whelp.

Aside from Dad's victims, that was, perhaps, the biggest tragedy of it all. I'd lost my dad, but I'd also lost myself. Not all the time but enough for my pride to shrivel.

The man placed the name tag in my palm and curled my fingers around it. The gesture was innocent, but it felt too intimate for strangers. Electricity traveled from my fingertips to my heart, spearing me until my chest heaved in a pant.

What the hell was happening?

Witchcraft.

Had to be.

I jerked my hand back, falling off balance when the elevator screeched to a halt with a synchrony that had me wondering if fate had spent my entire life conspiring against me. My body stumbled forward at the same time the lights flickered off.

We were trapped, and I was dizzy.

Falling.

Falling.

Falling.

Black.

chapter THIRTEEN

nash

Storm season in North Carolina always took tourists by surprise.

It attacked suddenly, vibrant sun peeking out after the rain had cleared. I'd grown up with it, and still, I found it odd, like a quirk Mother Nature branded to remind us she held the power.

I glanced to the body on the floor, sprawled out in a right angle. Not dead. Unconscious, drunk, and snoring louder than a broken carburetor. And not just anybody. Emery Winthrop, an interesting but not entirely unwanted turn of events.

A few days ago, Fika had revealed that she knew where her dad was hiding, and as if Fate had decreed it, she'd landed on my lap. Literally. Facedown, her temple pressed against my thigh until she'd lolled off with a loud thud and an annoyed groan that might have made me wince if I cared about murderers and their accomplices.

Thunder growled so loudly outside, it shook the metal box. I planted my feet, cursing when something pricked at my heel. Shining my phone's light on my foot, I pulled the long pin of Emery's name tag out of my shoe, clasped it together, then tossed the tiny metal rectangle at the elevator doors.

The flashlight illuminated her skinny frame, bonier than I'd ever seen her. Her slit had risen and torn, leaving most of her leg bare to me. She'd grown taller in the past four years, and she laid sprawled across the elevator floor, taking up all the space.

My space.

My elevator.

My hotel.

A drunk and unconscious kid, the last thing I needed in a hotel swarming with politicians, a Presidential candidate, and Secret Service agents.

The name tag tugged at my mind, begging me to unravel how she had one—how she worked for my company.

She had Winthrop money, meaning she'd been a member of the Three Commas Club since birth. College degrees doubled as ornaments, jobs were merely a formality, and if she wanted, she could never work a day in her life and still live as luxuriously as a Saudi oil prince.

A loud snore jerked her thin frame until she rolled over, revealing her clutch in the same black fabric of her dress. She reeked of alcohol and poor decisions and looked like a victim of the storm.

Swiping at her hair, I checked her scalp. No blood or bumps, but she smelled like a brewery, and her head would pound when she woke up. My fingers caught in a tangle, taking three tries to pull it out.

The long locks could have doubled as a bird's nest, and I swore, if this was the direction fashion trends were headed, I was hitching a ride on Elon Musk's newest rocket to Mars.

Bye, bye, human race.

Adios to your pumpkin spice lattes, cookie butter ice cream, and charcoal toothpaste.

Good fucking riddance.

I shook Emery's shoulders and snapped my fingers next to her ear. She sat up with a whine on her lips, shoved my hands aside with surprising strength, and muttered, "fuck off." The scent of vodka swarmed my senses before she curled onto her side and fell back asleep.

Unbelievable.

I snatched up her clutch, unclasped it, and sifted through the contents. Several packets of oyster crackers scattered to the floor the second I opened the bag. I shook my head, noting she hadn't changed a bit.

Emery used to walk around with candy and snacks shoved deep inside her pockets, mostly Snickers, a habit she'd picked up after Virginia neglected to give her lunch money too many times. Usually on accident, but sometimes on purpose to encourage her prepubescent daughter to lose a few pounds.

Pieces of work, the Winthrop family.

Flicking Emery's wallet open, I flipped through her cards. An expired driver's license sat on top of her

Clifton University student I.D., reminding me how young she was.

The license read, "Emery Winthrop," whereas the student I.D. read, "Emery Rhodes." Amusing, but not surprising, given she was born and bred from liars.

The photos in her wallet told me nothing of Gideon's location. A Polaroid of a field of stars with the word *balter* written in Sharpie under it. On the back, she'd drawn a small animal that resembled a tiger, but it had no stripes, and crayon wasn't the best art medium for precision. She'd scrawled, of all things, "ride me" beneath it, and I swore, if Emery weren't rich, her quirks would land her in an asylum.

The other Polaroid featured a Valentine's Day card that compared love to shit. She had glued another picture to the back. Reed smiled at me, his arm around Emery's shoulders while she held a tattered football.

I remembered when Ma had taken the photo. A row of red maple trees grew near the garden on the Winthrop estate. Reed had gotten his football stuck in one, and Emery climbed up the tree, limbs moving with no grace yet no hesitation, even when she fell to the ground in a bed of sanguine leaves and twisted her ankle.

Reed had screamed for Ma although I stood thirty feet away in the garden, tearing out weeds since Dad had popped his hip and couldn't afford to get fired by Virginia. Ma came running, and Emery refused to see a doctor until Ma took a picture of her with the football. She wore a toothy smile on her face, looking nothing like Virginia despite the matching dyed hair, sharp bob, and single colored contact.

Shoving the photos into the trifold wallet insert, I pocketed the whole thing, keeping it as leverage. She'd want them back, I was sure. Two years ago, I'd wired a cool twelve million dollars (a small fortune for a home in North Carolina) to a shell company. In exchange, a discrete broker had transferred ownership of the Winthrop estate to me.

The purchase had set me back a pretty penny, and I loathed the idea of Gideon profiting from me, but I'd tried to track the payment to his location. That failed, and now I owned a mansion I refused to step foot in.

Point was, the real estate agent informed me I'd be buying the house as is, including everything in it. From the listing images, Emery's room appeared untouched. She had taken nothing with her to college that I could see.

Her pictures of her and Reed still decorated the walls. Her photo albums remained on the shelves. The Polaroid camera she loved peeked out from beneath her bed. I'd pegged her as the sentimental type, and now I owned every memory of hers, including the ones in my pocket.

I shook the purse upside down until another cracker packet fell out. Ripping the seams with deft fingers, I fished around the hole, sliding my finger beneath the fabric until I was sure she had hidden nothing inside before discarding the clutch a foot from her snoring body.

Figuring Emery was passed out for the foreseeable future and the storm didn't seem to let up, I loosened my tie, pulled out my phone, checked a few emails, and began crushing candy. Twenty minutes later, I'd eaten all of her crackers and paid my way through a couple dozen levels of the game.

A groan that could awaken a bear in hibernation was the first indicator she had woken. The second indicator came as she swiveled her head to take in her surroundings and realized the lone light originated from my phone—and I'd set it on the lowest brightness to hide my face.

To her credit, she didn't gasp. She pawed at the back of her head and sat up. I watched as she blinked rapidly, unadjusted to the dark, and swiped at the mess of sweat, tears, and mascara.

She faced my direction, staring at me crush two more rows of candy. The words "cold," "emotionless," and "bastard" left her lips, a rapid mutter—in that order. I ignored her, letting her sweat it out a few more minutes.

"How long have we been in here?" No hesitation seeped into her voice.

I allowed myself to wonder if anything could shake her before remembering the night we'd accidentally slept together. Wide, innocent doe eyes that made me want to fuck her all over again.

Now I was hard as a rock, and despite the darkness, adjusting myself would bring attention to it. Plus, the Winthrops might have abandoned their morals, but I hadn't. Getting hard at the thought of someone who'd been an adult all of two seconds was all sorts of fucked up.

"About two-and-a-half hours," I responded, voice level, though it was closer to thirty minutes.

Amusement lined my lips as she jerked upwards and flung toward me, barely stopping herself from launching completely at me. I was quick to shut my phone off, so she couldn't see me with the light. The darkness blanketed me, concealing my identity. Concealing our past.

Her heavy pants brushed her chest against my abs. I could only hear her. *Feel* her. So close, she had my jaw ticking and my pulse racing. Her energy mobbed me, chaotic like the storm. Unpredictable, despite fifteen years of knowing her.

She didn't back away even though I heard one of her feet slide back like she wanted to but couldn't bring herself to show weakness.

"Two and a half hours?!"

The vodka on her breath assaulted my senses, but she sounded more sober than I had given her credit for. That, or the situation had sobered her up quickly. Beneath the alcohol, a rich scent hit my nostrils.

Citrus.

Mango.

Vanilla.

Musk.

Almost masculine.

Something familiar.

The scent invaded my space.

She tried to get into my face, probably on her tiptoes to reach it. "I was knocked out for two-and-a-half hours, and you didn't think to check for my pulse? To see if I was still breathing?"

"You were snoring, and you smell like you took a bath in vodka," I offered.

"Unbelievable." She muttered a few curses and stepped back, which did nothing.

I could still sense her.

Feel her.

Breathe her.

"For the record," she added, "someone spilled their drink on me."

I caught a quick movement of her hand and *tsked* twice. "I know you're flipping me off."

"It's dark. How—" She stopped herself, but I had an answer.

Because I know you.

I kept it to myself, content in the knowledge that

everything about this situation bothered her. She hadn't looked at me once earlier, even as I was hyperaware of the long legs and generous cleavage—then disgusted with myself when I saw the name on her name tag.

She plummeted to the floor again, the sound of her snapping off her mask filling the air.

It's cute that you think you've hidden your identity from me, sweetheart. I know your secret. Wait until you discover mine...

As if she could hear my thoughts, she pushed herself away from me, sliding across the marble until her head hit something loud. Probably the metal bar that wrapped around the elevator.

"Ugh."

My eyes had long since adjusted to the dark, and I caught the outline of her hands reach behind her head and probe. The wince was obvious, her body curling inward before she took a deep breath and straightened.

I felt sorry for her for a split second before I buried my sympathy in a grave beside Dad.

Emery Winthrop secreted wealth from her pores. A trip to the doctor's and a few bags of fluids to fight the hangover would do nothing to her wallet. Meanwhile, poor people—people who'd grown up like me, like my dad—had spent their lives without the luxury of doctors, refusing to escalate health concerns to situations that required money.

Not until it was too late.

chapter FOURTEEN

nash

Emery dropped her hands to the elevator floor, beating out an uneven rhythm on the same statuario that lined the mansion she'd grown up in. *The mansion full of people who'd ruined my family.*

The beat dragged out, rapid and loud in the confined space.

Tap.

Tap. Tap.

Tap.

"Stop," I demanded, hating her ability to fill the room with her presence.

She didn't. If anything, her fingers fluttered faster, brushing against a cracker wrapper I'd discarded on the floor.

Tap. Tap.

Crinkle.

Tap.

"Stop."

Louder.

As if she had one compliant bone in her body that didn't bend at anyone but Virginia's will.

Her tapping persisted.

Tap. Tap. Tap.

Crinkle.

Tap. Tap.

The elevator felt smaller, like the walls sucked in her direction, pushing me with them. Our breaths fogged the little container—hers heavier than mine. Her chest heaved to the point where her breasts hit her chin after a sharp exhale.

Her lips moved fast, quick mutters I could barely make out.

Tacenda.

Moira.

Koi no yokan.

I'd either heard her wrong, or she'd made up the words. You never knew with Emery. Her palms pawed at the floor, pushing her body further into the corner opposite of me. She stared blindly at me, unable to adjust to the dark as she blinked rapid blinks.

A smile curved my lips. I watched her fall apart, accompanied only by blackness. No mother to tell her what to do. No daddy to run to. No Reed to serve as a conduit of bravery. Meanwhile, I looked like the poster child for Xanax, calm and uncaring as I pulled out my phone and continued to crush candy.

Ding.

Ding.

A game played by children, yet my success brought me pleasure.

"I hope his battery dies, and he suffers with me," she muttered, probably to herself, but I wasn't deaf.

My attention clung to her side of the elevator, enraptured by the little differences becoming clearer with each second. Anxiety, mostly. The same quirky Emery, packaged differently and stamped with extra baggage.

Good. How does it feel to live a fucked-up life, Princess? Welcome to the club.

I paid the ninety-nine cents for five more lives after I used my last one and turned the volume all the way up until the crushed wrappers and pinging drowned out her insanity. The distinct sound of a zipper unzipping halted my fingers above a coconut wheel. I waited to see where she'd take this.

Her hands worked at the corset of her dress until it loosened, and she heaved out another exhale. She bent both knees, rested a forearm on each one, and leaned her head between her legs.

The first dry heave elicited an eye roll from me.

The second one had me pulling up my Spotify app.

The third one pierced my ears until my fingers ran marathons across the keyboard.

The fourth one came, and I pressed play on "Shut Up" by Black Eyed Peas.

One second.

Two.

Three.

"Turn that shit off!" Her voice bounced off the walls,

an unbridled shout. Her anger formed tsunami waves in the elevator, lashing at me. "I swear, I will smash your phone against your head unless you turn that shit off!"

Following orders had never been a strong suit of mine.

I let it play, "shut up" repeating over and over again. She shot up from her crouch and pushed me, putting all her weight into the effort. A kitten who'd mistaken herself for a tiger.

My phone clattered to the floor between us, but I planted my feet, not budging an inch, even when her tiny fingers flexed against the hard ridges of my pecs and her tits delivered her rapid heartbeats onto my abs.

They fluttered like hummingbird wings across my skin, sending goosebumps up and down my arms. Her scent repelled and lured me. I leaned forward when I should have leaned back.

I wanted to fuck with her.

I wanted to fuck her.

I couldn't do one, so I settled for the other.

Stepping into her touch, I reveled in the sound of her breath catching as I whispered against her ear, my lips touching the delicate curve, "Faking a panic attack is not cute attention-seeking behavior."

Pulling back, my body hit the wall and my hip brushed against her pinched waist at the movement, conjuring a breathy gasp.

So fragile.

So delicious.

So *wrong*.

"Word of advice," I drawled. Slow. The speed you'd use on someone just learning English. "If that's how you sound after sex, I suggest cardio."

The words made me as much of a liar as the

Winthrops.

Her hands still sat on my chest, clenched around the shirt fabric, breaths coming out in quick pants.

She sounded like sex.

Reeked of sex.

Moved like sex.

The last thought I needed was of Emery and cardio with the memory of her riding me branded on my brain.

Tiny nails grazed my pecs. Her hips rolled forward, unaware my eyes had adjusted to the dark half an hour ago as she sought something I'd never willingly give her. She had to steal it from me. Rob me.

A little thief.

Like her father.

Like me.

"I hate you," she whispered.

That's okay, little Tiger.

I hate you, too.

And if she ever asked for forgiveness, I'd throw her pleas back in her face and ruin her life for sport.

Her family killed my father. It might as well have been tattooed onto my flesh, because I would never forget it. I would never *forgive* it.

I pressed a pointer finger to her forehead and pushed until she took the hint and stepped back with the attitude of an unfed dog. "You don't know me, sweetheart."

She laughed, lazy, psychotic, maddening. It was the kind of ceaseless laughter that didn't have a beginning or an end. Just noise.

Raucous.

Unhinged.

Worthy of a horror movie soundtrack.

She'd lost it.

Emery Winthrop had finally lost it.

But crazy had always fueled her blood. She sought adrenaline highs like a junky, climbed trees and fell down without blinking an eye, snuck into beds, proudly wore her emotions on t-shirts, and defended herself fiercely.

She reminded me of a cornered predator, ready to lash out, desperate to differentiate herself from the Virginia 2.0 her mother demanded her to be.

It made her wild.

Reckless.

Foolish.

So, so foolish.

"I know your type." She swiped at my finger, swatting it to the side. Her dress bowed forward, unzipped, but she either didn't notice or didn't care. "Not just rich but *wealthy*."

The word spat out like a curse. She edged herself onto me. Not edging herself onto me—edging herself onto my phone. She drove her heel into the screen and twisted until it cracked, a kaleidoscope of reds, greens, and blues that did nothing but light up the Converse she wore beneath her floor-length gown.

"Handsome." Another word she'd turned into a curse. "Over-privileged. You think you're better than everyone else, that you can do whatever you please and get away with it. You disgust me."

It wasn't lost on me that her description suited her dad. I didn't tell her this, though, because doing so would reveal my identity. I unveiled a saccharine smile she couldn't see and laughed. Loud. In her face. Spearmint caressing her skin.

She could enjoy her pretty, perfect world—her emails from Gideon and the fat sum that sat in a trust fund under her name—a little while longer. Soon enough, everything she owned would be mine.

Her hopes.

Her dreams.

Her future in the palm of my hands.

I was hard at the idea of revenge.

Beneath us, my phone sputtered out.

Dead.

Another casualty to the Winthrop name.

Anger stained her voice. I let her revel in it. My pulse thrummed at the realization I might have lost my final photos of Dad on there. Dad's birthday party. Ma had packed a picnic because it was all she could afford, but it was the last time I'd smiled. *Really* smiled.

My fingers itched to snatch my phone and fix it, but I couldn't do anything while stuck here.

"Do you have a last name, Emery?" I enunciated her name, taking pleasure in the way her body stilled.

Her bravado vanished.

She backed away from me. "Who's asking?"

"A concerned guest, who'd like to report an ill-mannered employee," I lied.

She nestled herself in the corner, relieving me of the vodka scent. Of *her*. "Don't bother. I'm with the catering staff, and we're gone after the night."

The puzzle clicked into place. The name tag. The rail-thin frame. Prescott Hotels hired models to serve at every event. Usually, ones who hadn't made a name for themselves and needed money.

Emery needed money like I needed a bigger dick. Any more would be excessive.

Silence spread until her legs twitched, tapping on the floor again.

"Claustrophobic?" I could have hidden the amusement in my voice. I didn't.

"Not really. Just bad in confined spaces."

"That is literally claustrophobia."

She also hadn't had it when I'd known her. I took pleasure in her baggage, tangible evidence justice existed after all. Not in the court systems. Guilt and evidence lived separate lives, rarely meeting one another.

Hence, her baggage delighted me.

An appetizer for the main course to come.

"I know what claustrophobia is," she snapped. "I don't have it." She sat in her corner, legs straight out. They brushed against my shoes until she jerked them back to her chest like she'd been stung.

I allowed silence to settle between us. Sitting, I palmed my broken phone and felt around the edges. Definitely smashed, tiny little pieces of shattered glass digging across my palms.

Hopefully, it only required a new screen.

An hour later, Emery caved, shaking her head, probably to stop herself from falling asleep. "What's your name?"

"We're not doing this." My clipped tone spoke of finality, unyielding to her pathetic probe.

"Doing what? Introducing ourselves?"

"Talking."

"You are such a piece of work." She pulled at her dress, adjusting the top around her, and I imagined she'd at least become somewhat used to the darkness by now, but it was still too dim to capture my face. "No wonder you hired an escort as your date."

"What I do with my money and whom I do with my time are none of your business, Emery." I enunciated each syllable of her name, taunting her.

I know who you are. Do you know who I am?

She edged forward, closer to me, her voice sounding like she was a hundred percent awake now. "You people are all alike." The words came in pants. She seethed at me, and I realized my first assessment had been right—she needed cardio.

"You people?" I humored, because there was nothing better to do while stuck in a box than watching Emery Winthrop lose her shit.

"Rich people." She drew it out, like it disgusted her. "People like Nash Prescott. People like *you*."

I almost snorted at the irony.

Instead, I scoffed, like the idea was laughable. And it was. Had she ever looked in a mirror?

"Tread carefully," I taunted. "You don't know me."

"Or what?"

Or you'll look like a fool.

Too late.

"You're reckless," I observed, ignoring her question.

She'd inched closer since picking this new fight with me. Always picking fights, this one. "Reckless is hiring an escort, then getting an S.T.D."

"Not that it's any of your business, but I don't fuck them. Even when their legs are spread, fingers dipped knuckles-deep inside their soaking wet pussies, begging me to make them come, I don't."

I hired escorts because I worked in a world that required dates for corporate events, and I had neither the time nor inclination to fend off Eastridge housewife wannabes, who saw me as nothing more than a golden ticket to a privileged life.

A sharp inhale met my words, but she recovered quickly, never one to back down. "You leave women unsatisfied. Fits the profile."

"Of?"

"Rich men whose only claim to fame is their net worth. I've met hundreds of men like you. They have no skills to call their own, other than the money in their bank accounts. And when their money is gone, what's left of you? A man who can't satisfy a woman he paid to satisfy."

"For starters, you're objectifying these women. Such solidarity," I mocked. "Secondly, the escorts are simply a means to an end. They're dates, not fucks, and I compensate them well for their time."

Her biting laugh turned into a sharp cry. Her hand met the crown of her head. For a second, I allowed guilt to swallow me, because maybe she hadn't been as drunk as I'd thought she was. Maybe she was actually hurt.

I'd never been nice. Ma said I grew up hating the world because I saw what it was rather than what it could be. But... I'd also never been the asshole to see someone hurt without offering a hand.

Dad would have been pissed if he were here. The knowledge settled inside me, carving ugly marks into my chest, but I didn't rectify it. I looked up at the ceiling, careful to move my eyes and not my head, knowing Emery could probably see me by now but not very well.

What do you expect me to do, Dad?

I could picture him in front of me, the clearest I'd ever seen him since he'd died. His heavy brows pulled together, crow's feet rimming the edges of his eyes. The tan came from all those years working in the sun, forgoing sunblock because there was nothing like warmth on naked skin.

He opened his mouth, I edged forward to latch onto his words, and when they neared fruition, Emery spoke, breaking the spell, "I'm not objectifying those women or even judging them for how they earn their money. That's their situation. Their business."

Of course, you're not judging. How could you when your family earned its money through theft?

I became irrationally angry. She could never have known that was the closest I'd felt to Dad since he had died, but still—I hated her more than I ever had in that moment. Even more than I had when she hadn't shown up for Dad's funeral, for the man who used to call her his third child.

I curled my fist to the point of white knuckles. My fingers dug into my palms, the pain distracting me from the gaping hole in my chest.

From the fact that, sometimes, I could remember Dad so clearly, and other times, I struggled to recall where on his forehead his mole sat.

From the fact that no matter how hard I fucking tried, I couldn't hate Emery.

Not all the way, anyway.

Not with the same careless freedom I possessed when hating the rest of the world.

I bit my tongue.

Emery continued, so oblivious, I could have died from disbelief, "But if you're judging me for being panicked while trapped in this tiny metal box with a jackass, I'm judging you for hiring escorts in the first place and leaving them unsatisfied." She inched closer and taunted, "Performance anxiety?"

"Never been the type," I bit out.

"Prove it."

"What are we? Five? Are you going to dare me next?" I wouldn't put it past her. Dares were currency for thrill-seekers like her.

The elevator shook. She latched on to my shoulder, her hands flying forward so fast, I knew it was instinct. The lights flickered on, a quick blink like a camera flash. Moments later, the light reintroduced her features to me.

She opened her eyes, blinking rapidly, taking a few

seconds to get used to the brightness before she focused two different-colored eyes on me. Realization blossomed across her face until her fingers unlatched from my shoulders.

Déjà vu punched my chest hard.

Emery wore the same deer-in-headlights expression she had four years ago when I'd switched on the lights, and she realized I wasn't Reed. I watched, unmoving. She stumbled backward, her jaw nearly unhinging from its socket.

The spread of wrappers almost tripped her.

"Easy, Tiger."

I could tell that was the right thing to say because she narrowed two hate-filled eyes at me, the gray one stormier than the blue. When the elevator doors opened behind her on a random level, she grabbed the clutch I'd pilfered and stumbled out.

My fingers jabbed the button for the penthouse floor before I realized I'd never asked her why the hell she'd taken a catering gig when she didn't need the money.

chapter FIFTEEN

nash

I'd grown up as an only child.

Sharing seemed like a simple concept, mostly because it was foreign. I'd never been asked to share. Maybe a chip from a nearly empty bag (Dad did this when Ma wasn't looking) or my bed on a rare occasion (Ma did this when Dad worked long hours and snored like a tractor). Insignificant sacrifices since my parents worked hard to make me happy, and everything else in my life felt like mine.

Until Reed came along.

The accidental child they couldn't afford.

When I was eleven and Reed was one, Reed took over my bedroom. He cried so much, he messed up Dad's sleep (and therefore work) schedule. Ma moved Reed from their room to mine, which left me on the living room couch. A dinky, secondhand thing that previously occupied the waiting area of the Chinese restaurant down the block.

When I was thirteen, Reed caught a bad case of croup and spent three days in the hospital for observation. Every spare dollar for the next five years went to that bill. That Christmas, Dad taught me how to play soccer in the snow with a half-flat ball he found somewhere in the apartment complex. All the other kids sat inside playing their new video games.

When I was fifteen, some asshole punk drew a dick on Reed's forehead with Sharpie and stole his lunch bag. For the first time, he ran to me for help, and I accepted that sharing my parents wasn't so bad, because in return, I'd gotten someone who looked at me like I was the solution to life, not a problem.

When I was twenty-five, Reed told me I was dead to him after the cotillion. Ma cried the entire night, then cried again the next morning when she realized he'd meant it.

Dad turned to me, placed his calloused palm on my shoulder, and said, "Life hurts something stupid, kid, but being brothers is a lifetime commitment. He'll realize that."

I listened to Dad and waited it out, convinced it was a phase, because from the moment Reed had been born, I'd done everything for him, given him all I could, and loved him more than I did myself.

Seven years later, I was still waiting.

The email sat on my laptop, the words unlikely to

change in this lifetime, but I wasn't opposed to funding time machine research. I'd go back and reverse a lot of things, starting with the cotillion. I told Durga I didn't feel regret, but I lied, knowing she'd call me out on my bullshit. Someone had to.

Here's what people who sit around smoking ganja and quoting Gandhi won't tell you. There's always that one mistake that changes your life. If you're lucky, it's for the better.

Spoiler alert: I'm not lucky, and regret is life's longest punishment.

I felt it now, reading Ma's email, wondering how someone who shared my blood could turn into a coxswain, Vineyard Vines-wearing, Niçois salad-ordering, country club-attending, nouveau riche douchebag, who surrounded himself with people named Brock, Chett, and Tripp with two Ps.

From: betty@prescotthotels.com
To: nash@prescotthotels.com

Subject: 4th of July Weekend

Hi, sweetheart!

I was hoping to catch you on your phone, but you didn't answer and your voicemail inbox is full. (You should really consider hiring an assistant. It's been like this for months. I've been meaning to tell you.)

Your brother says he'll be spending the weekend in Eastridge with Basil, Chett, Brock, and Tripp for the country club's fourth of July brunch. I think Reed and Basil are ready to take the next step. Seems like he's gonna pop the question. I mean, we always knew this was coming, but I'm happy that he's happy.

You know I love you, and I hate to ask you this, but would you mind not coming that week? We both know he won't come home to see me unless I assure him you're not in town, and I haven't seen him in months.

I ain't happy about this. It hurts to even ask, but it won't always be like this, baby. I promise.

Love,
Ma

I couldn't blame Ma.

Growing up, Reed used to think Ma favored me, so Ma worked extra hard to prove she didn't. What Reed never got was, Ma didn't love me more. She'd just loved me longer. Ma had ten extra years to learn how to love me best. She'd been figuring out how to love him, which he made infinitely harder by having mood swings that would make teenaged girls seem tame.

I typed out my reply.
One word.

Nash: *Sure.*

Then, I wired the allowance I sent Reed each month —apparently, he couldn't take my calls, but he had no problems taking my money—and slammed my laptop shut, discarding it on the pillow next to my head.

Some asshole knocked on my door, but I sunk back into my mattress and closed my eyes. The knocking persisted. I muttered a curse, reached out to the nightstand, blindly fished out the bottle of painkillers, tossed two into my mouth, and swallowed them dry.

Padding barefoot to the door, I yanked it open, knowing I'd throttle whoever it was if they said the wrong thing. I didn't know why I thought it'd be Emery, but it wasn't. Disappointment burned my tongue.

A uniformed staff member stood on the other side. He tossed me a loopy grin, his feet shuffling back and forth like he bought a new bong and couldn't wait to get out of here and try it.

"Mrs. Lowell sent this up for you." Dudebro held up a folded piece of paper with the Prescott Hotels letterhead sticking out from the flap. "She left this letter for you, too."

I snatched the letter and let him in. He pushed a cart past me, a smile on his face, too damn chirpy for a Saturday morning. My nudity didn't faze him. I greeted him in boxer briefs, taking in the food as he unveiled it.

A full breakfast. Eggs, bacon, bagels, coffee, hash browns, and French toast. Beside the silverware, a fruit basket of bananas, strawberries, and Fuji apples had been arranged in a phallic shape, ejaculating into a bowl of Nutella.

The clock in the open-plan kitchen read eight in the morning exactly. This spread hadn't been to feed me. It'd been to wake me up with an extra side of fuck you.

Delilah Lowell thrived on passive-aggressive bullshit.

Breakfasts screamed wake the fuck up.

Lunches doubled as a reminder not to pile any more lawsuits onto her plate.

Dinners cemented the fact that I'd be flat-out broke and most likely dead if she didn't exist to put out my fires and occasionally feed me.

I never bothered with dessert. Learned my lesson the first time when she'd brought her rat and asked me to pet sit the monster. (Rosco and I do not and will never get along.)

The alarm on my spare phone set off two horns. I'd set it up last night after carefully sealing the broken phone in a plastic bag in my nightstand. Swiping the screen up, I shut off the noise and noticed the eight missed calls from Delilah.

Pressing the return button, I spared the guy feelings of inadequacy at the sight of my dick and stepped into the en suite bathroom before stripping out of my black Calvin Kleins. The rainfall shower heads shot out water.

I connected the phone to my shower's Bluetooth speakers.

Delilah answered my call on the second ring with a *tsk*. Her voice came out in pants like she'd been walking. "Do you ever answer your phone?"

So much tact, this one.

"Eventually." I dumped shampoo onto my head, wondering if I had any unread messages from Durga. "Is the breakfast from last night's catering staff?"

The memory of Emery Winthrop against my body drove my line of questioning. Her existence pissed me off. A trust fund princess. A daughter of a thief and (as far as I was concerned) murderer. Someone complicit in his lies. Complicit in Dad's death.

The worst part wasn't seeing her last night. It was

feeling her against me. I could write our first time off as a mistake, but she was still young. So damn young. She'd been an adult for all of two seconds, and I'd already fucked her.

Remembered it.

Liked it.

My dick hardened. I stroked it twice before telling it to fuck off.

"Nope. I bought it." Delilah cooed at the naked rat she called a dog. "Did you pee, Rosco? Did you pee? Such a good boy." Her voice came out louder this time, "From the place down the street. I paid some kid fifty bucks to dress in a uniform and cart breakfast to you. Cute, right?"

And I'd left him alone with a fat wad of cash in my suitcase, designer everything, and my company laptop.

Perfect.

"You are so extra."

"And you are so fucked." In the background, the wind whipped around her until I could barely make out her voice. "Why did building security call me this morning to inform me that a man from the Security and Exchanges Commission came here to see you?"

The S.E.C.—high-and-mighty, Paul Blart rent-a-cops who aspired to be the real thing. Unfortunately, the crimes they investigated included the ones I'd committed.

I bit back a curse and tightened my fingers into fists before returning my hands to my head and lathering the shampoo. "Is he still here?"

"I bought you an hour. He'll be back. Do you need me there?"

"No."

It was probably a good idea to have the head of my legal department with me because, let's face it, I'd broken a shit ton of laws this decade, but I knew Delilah. She would demand that I spill everything to her, and that sounded as appealing to me as a blow job from a piranha.

"Nash..." she trailed off, and I could picture her scrunched up nose and crossed arms. That bulging vein on her forehead she claimed she only got around me. Apparently, I was responsible for aging her ten years, too.

"Delilah, if you can't understand simple words like 'no,' you're in the wrong line of work." I rinsed the shampoo, watching it swirl down the drain in a Rorschach pattern. It looked like Sisyphus shouldering a boulder.

"You are such an ass." The words held no bite.

"I'm also your boss."

"Now that you mention that, I feel incredibly underpaid. You know, I may take the liberty of hiring you an assistant if you're going to be too stubborn to do it yourself." Rosco barked in the background, starting a chain reaction where five dozen dogs barked back. The last thing I wanted to hear with a hangover. "I didn't go to law school to be your twenty-four-seven bitch, Nash."

"What's that? I think someone just called my name."

"You're in the shower," she deadpanned.

"Gotta go, D."

I finished showering, brushed my teeth, dried my hair off with a towel, and tossed on a Stuart Hughes suit, F.P. Journe watch, and a pair of Testonis.

Delilah liked to coat herself in diamonds and designer threads for country club dinners with her husband. She used her looks, her wealth, and her bitchiness to intimidate catty, rich housewives into submission.

For men to intimidate men, you needed to be taller, stronger, smarter. But a show of wealth and a sculpted face didn't hurt, which was why I filled my closet with overpriced clothes I didn't need and thanked Ma for my good genetics.

When I re-entered the bedroom of my suite, Rosco sat on my bed, the long strands of black and white hair sprouting from his gargantuan ears and onto my sheets. His bare ass pressed against my pillow, precisely where I liked to lay my head. The only fur he boasted budded from his head and tail, and he looked like a dog like Shawn Spencer looked like a psychic.

Delilah held a slice of French toast to her mouth, swallowing half in one bite like the damned Neanderthal she pretended she wasn't. Grade-A syrup dropped from her lips to the carpet. Rosco yelped, then dove off the bed and lapped it up.

"The rat better not vomit on my carpet." I grabbed the toast from her fingers and took a bite. Cold, like everything in this room, including me. "If this were 1690s Salem, you'd hang for witchcraft."

She rolled her mint-green eyes and licked at the syrup that had smeared onto her cheek. Her tongue waggled across her cheek like one of those inflatable tube men at car dealerships. "I choppered in earlier this morning." She allowed Rosco to lap at her fingers. I watched on, vowing never to get a pet rat. "Security just let me up."

"Remind me to fire them."

"I repeat, I am not your assistant."

"I repeat, I don't need you here."

She ignored me, her favorite pastime and the sole person on my payroll I allowed the privilege. "I looked into the S.E.C. agent. They have a pending investigation into you, Nash. My source wouldn't say much, which tells me this is serious." Furrowed brows and a half scowl formed her don't-bullshit-me face. "What did you do?"

"Delilah—"

"Are you going to tell me what you'll be investigated for?"

This was what happened when you worked with someone for too long. They got comfortable and thought they could ask questions I didn't want them asking.

"Do you remember the catering company from last night?" I redirected.

Why the hell was Emery Winthrop working a catering gig, anyway? I understood the modeling part. She had the height and face, but catering? Her family's net worth dipped into the ten figures. Her trust fund had to be at least eight if not nine figures. She could finance a war and not want for money.

Maybe Virginia had sent her on the heiress equivalent of an apology tour. A few magazine covers, and I was supposed to fucking forget she'd known about her dad's embezzlement.

"Don't change the subject." Delilah tucked a dirty blonde strand of hair back into her French chignon and folded her hands on her lap. She took a seat on the absolute edge of my bed, like she feared she would catch my germs. "I asked around about the lead investigator. Brandon Vu. He's ambitious. Moved up the ladder fast, looking to be the chair of the S.E.C. If you did something, he'll find it. You have to tell me everything."

Like hell I would.

"No. Fika took care of it." I didn't elaborate, merely pulled out the bundles of bills from my suitcase and shoved them into the built-in safe I'd had installed yesterday. I thumbed through one of the ten-thousand-dollar stacks and pointed at Delilah with it. "You act like I'm a sketchy person. I'm entirely innocent."

Delilah watched me shove half a million dollars into

the safe, my ritual for every penthouse in all my hotels. A fail-safe in case I ever got caught and needed cash quickly and a go-bag to run. "Ugh. Fika. You trust him to take care of it?"

"*Took* care of it," I corrected, cramming a small go-bag into the remaining space. "As in, it's already done. Stop worrying about it. I think I see two new wrinkles on your forehead. You look forty."

"I'm thirty-one, and I look twenty-six," she corrected, fingers dabbing her forehead for the aforementioned wrinkles. "It's Fika. Trusting Fika is like giving Rosco a full bag of treats and trusting him not to finish it."

No love lost between them. Odd, considering they both shared similar views on the law. Fika pretended it didn't exist. Delilah dedicated her life to defending people who bent it. Either way, they both treated it like a nuisance.

I didn't acknowledge this. Keeping them at odds with one another compartmentalized the less-than-legal portion of my life.

"Don't underestimate Fika."

I closed the lock and set an anagram for Emery Winthrop as the password. When I realized what I'd done, I swore and jabbed at the keypad, trying to undo it, but I didn't know how to change the password. *Perfect.*

Pivoting to face Delilah, I leaned against the wall and added, "Beneath the Jonas Brothers wig, the distressed jeans, and the litany of addictions, Fika is an ex-cop whose calling in life is to break the rules without getting caught."

She scowled when I adjusted her fingers to where two non-existent wrinkles sat, just to fuck with her. "He literally got caught. It's why the people of Eastridge fired him as the sheriff."

"Semantics."

"No." Both hands met the air as she tossed them up. "That is not what semantics means. Look, I need to know what you did. How do you expect me to do my job with my hands tied behind my back?"

Readjusting my tie, I pulled off the tag and made a point of feeding it to Rosco in case D got any crazy ideas of asking me to pet sit again. "If you need hand-holding, you're in the wrong building. I'm sure some midlevel firm will be happy to have you."

Delilah snatched the tag away from Rosco's thin lips. "Fuck you, Nash."

"I'd rather eat a bag of dicks, thank you."

She glanced down at her phone when it vibrated. "He's on his way up. Let me do the talking."

"Fine."

"Say as little as possible."

"No shit."

"I mean it. I will do all the talking," she repeated slowly, like I'd given her a reason not to trust me in the past.

She'd stopped trusting me the week we'd met when I fired a supplier without pay and suggested he take his shriveled-up dick and shove it into a pussy that didn't belong to the now-ex-wife of one of my board members.

The lawsuit hadn't been pretty, but that's why I paid Delilah double what she would earn anywhere else. She won cases no one else could. Better—she rarely had to step foot in court because she performed miracles before the cases ever reached the steps of Lady Justice.

I mocked a zipper across my lips and pretended to feed the key to her rat. "Maybe you can get your rat to bite him and give him rabies."

"He's not a rat." She picked Rosco up, held him close

to her chest, and followed me into the living room, where Cayden from the design department had set up a mini-office for me two days ago. A mahogany desk and a high-back leather chair. "Rosco is a hairless Chinese Crested Dog. A four-thousand-dollar dog, for the record."

"I could blow four grand on a flea-infested crack den in North Korea, and it'd be a better investment."

She pressed a kiss to her pet rat's temple and whispered, "Don't listen to the bad man, Rosco."

My knuckles flexed along the handles of my chair. She set Rosco down and swung the front door open.

Delilah didn't understand the accuracy of her words.

I *was* a bad man.

Sisyphus.

With blood on my hands.

Penance in my future.

Tick.

Tock.

chapter SIXTEEN

nash

After acquiring my wealth, I realized half the power of money came from possessing it. I could spend it, sure, but I didn't need to. It was a nuclear weapon. A threat looming over enemy heads.

It said, "I have the power to destroy you. Don't make me use it."

Flexing that power became an art I valued.

A way of life.

As natural as breathing.

By the time Delilah took her stance a step from my shoulder, the elevator dinged in the hallway.

The window behind me spanned the length of the room with panoramic oceanfront views, and Delilah and I had positioned ourselves in front, so Brandon had no choice but to look at what my money could buy.

Delilah wore enough jewelry to sink the Titanic, while I leaned back against my seat, shoulders relaxed and my new phone pulled out like I hadn't a care in the world. I downloaded the Eastridge United app, opened it, and logged in.

Brandon Vu entered. I didn't bother to glance at him as I read Durga's messages, noting she'd been up as late as I was last night.

Durga: You know what would be an awful way to die? In a room full of people you don't know.

Durga: Or worse—a room full of people you hate.

"Delilah Lowell." Beside me, Delilah reached a hand out to Brandon as I shot a reply to Durga.

I ignored the death portion of her messages. It wasn't like I avoided death, but I preferred not to think about it. After Dad had died, Ma invoked an unspoken do-not-go-there rule, and I had no arguments.

If I ever went there, I'd drown in the woulda, coulda, shoulda of my life. Death was a mistress approaching her expiration date. To be held at arms' length, until one day, you forgot about her.

Problem solved.

Not the healthiest solution, but I'd never been the type to eat my vegetables, and even Michelle Obama ate at Shake Shack every now and then.

Benkinersophobia: You've never struck me as the type of person who hates people.

Brandon stepped closer, but I still didn't glance up. "Brandon Vu, S.E.C."

Durga: What type of person hates people?

I considered it for a moment, but the answer was obvious.

Benkinersophobia: Me.

Delilah's elbow dug into my shoulder, and I waited fifteen seconds to piss her off before I slid my phone into the inner pocket of my suit and gifted the S.E.C.'s errand boy my attention. "Why are you here, Brandon?"

The cocky tilt of his lips had me questioning whether I'd left a trail of evidence. I hadn't. Fika pissed me off, but I hadn't lied to Delilah when I'd said years of being a corrupt cop had given him experience in hiding crimes.

Brandon eyed the oceanfront view, his attention lingering on Delilah before he turned to me. "I'd like to ask you a few questions if that's okay."

"Rhetorical questions are a waste of my time." I leaned against my seat and pressed my fingertips together like a church steeple. Probably the closest I'd get to a church, because I was sure I'd burn alive if I ever stepped foot inside one. "Get to the point."

Delilah made a show of checking her hundred-thousand-dollar watch with the hand not buried in my flesh. "We only have a few minutes to spare, Mr. Vu."

Brandon focused on me, his smile something more

fitting for a wax museum. "Do you have your lawyer at every meeting?"

Delilah's elbow dug deeper into my shoulder as I spoke, "I'm sure this is a foreign concept for you, but I'm not in the habit of paying people salaries out of charity."

"Charity. You do a lot of this." Brandon lifted a finger with each charity he listed. "The Eastridge Fund. The Eastridge United app. Healthcare for All. Soup kitchens across the South. I could go on."

Not exactly classified information.

Internet trolls accused me of doing charity work for good P.R. all the time. They were wrong. I couldn't give two shits about P.R., but I did have an ulterior motive and talking about it always put me in a mood.

"I'm impressed. It's almost as if you know how to use the internet." I cocked a brow, daring Brandon to accuse me of something. "Is there a point to this or do you enjoy wasting my time?"

He'd come here expecting to rattle me. Maybe get me to make a mistake. I could see it in his face, the down-turned lips and the pinched eyes. He could continue to be sorely disappointed for all I cared.

D's stiletto heel found my shin, and she kicked. Hard. I didn't wince, but she'd drawn blood. I felt it trickling down my shin and staining my suit.

"Forgive me. I'll get to the point." He eyed the rat before stepping closer. "Mr. Prescott, do you know what insider trading is?"

Rosco approached Brandon and sniffed his leg. I imagined him taking a piss on the fucker's shoes. For a second, I thought he'd finally make his four-thousand-dollar price tag worth it. But the traitor curled up against it and laid down.

The motherfucking rat.

"Toddlers from Old Greenwich know what insider trading is." I powered on my laptop and began sifting through the emails my Singaporean contacts had sent me. "Spare me the dramatics, and actually get to the point when you say you'll get to the point."

When I glanced up, Brandon's face remained frozen for a half-second longer than necessary, his cool slipping like melted FroYo before he collected himself. "Fine. Let me lay it out for you."

He placed two palms on my desk as if the movement would intimidate me. Leaning across the table, he lessened the gap between us until his chest brushed against the back of my laptop.

I responded to an email as he continued, "You came from a poverty-stricken family, yet you've amassed a substantial fortune in the past four years, particularly right after the fall of Winthrop Textiles. Two parties gained a large sum from the collapse of the company. You're one of them."

He gestured around the penthouse suite, which despite being sparsely furnished until the designers had the opportunity to do their jobs in here, boasted an ocean view I'd paid tens of millions of dollars for.

"Before I accuse you of anything and before you deny anything," he bit out, "I saw Emery Winthrop here last night, a name tag pinned to her dress, working for you. Too many threads connect you to Winthrop Textiles for it to be coincidental. I am good at my job, and if there's anything for me to find, I'll find it. You may as well save both of us time and talk to me now. We can work out a deal."

I pressed send on the email and glanced up at him in time to see his self-satisfied grin. Ripping out of his Saks Off 5th outlet suit and eyebrows so neat they had to be waxed, he looked more like a Tod with one D than a Brandon.

He knew too much for me to dismiss him, but I stood knee-deep in this shit I'd helped create for me to shift the blame onto someone else. If anything, this very moment had been in the making for seven years.

It seemed as inevitable as taxes.

I tilted my head to the side, taking the time to look down my nose at him despite the fact that he stood while I sat. "Does that ever work?"

"More often than you'd think."

Delilah stepped forward, the picture of calmness. She reminded me of the principal parents and students secretly feared. Eyes that had seen everything in the book and remained unimpressed. "Agent Vu, I think it's best you leave now. We have a strict schedule to adhere to, and if you'd like to talk any further, you may contact me and only me."

Brandon's eyes flickered between me and Delilah before he straightened and nodded. "Think about my offer, Mr. Prescott." He tossed a business card onto the desk. "A deal doesn't have to be a bad thing."

After Delilah shut the door behind Brandon, she turned back to me, a vein bulging on her temple. I'd once named it Delilah Jr. "What part of 'do not talk' do you not understand?"

"The words 'do', 'not', and 'talk'."

"Nash, this is serious."

Wasn't that the truth?

In my opinion, insider trading fell on the lowest rung on my list of crimes. I always knew I couldn't hide the money I'd made from trading in Winthrop Textiles stock, but insider trading was difficult to prove, and I'd done a good job of cleaning my tracks.

What I hadn't known was someone else had profited from the fall of Winthrop Textiles.

I slid out my drawer and brushed my knuckles over the charred leather I traveled with. "Get me a P.I."

Delilah's nose curled up at the sight of the burnt leather, but she said nothing. Her naked, furless rat pawed at her legs to be held. "What about Fika?"

"Fika is gone." At the horror in her eyes, I rolled mine. "Relax. Gone as in fired. Fucker's still alive and kicking."

"Jesus, Nash."

"Let's not involve him. He's never been my biggest fan."

She ignored me. "You don't tell someone a man with cancer is 'gone.' You also don't pay me to be your assistant. Find your own P.I."

I would have taken her more seriously had she not picked up Rosco and pet the five strands of hair on his body. "This shit again?"

"I deserve a raise."

"Done."

"But I don't need one."

Truth.

Her husband came from old money. The next ten generations of her family could stop working and still fund ten Star Wars franchises.

"What do you need, D?" I quirked a brow, giving her my full attention.

"Why do you assume I need something?"

"No one does anything out of the goodness of their heart."

"You do." So she thought. "You're a cranky asshole, but you spend your nights feeding people at soup kitchens regardless of the town we're in, you take care of your family, you donate a shit ton of your income, and you have never passed someone in need without expensing help."

She made me sound like the saint Eastridge had made me out to be. The reality couldn't be further than that. The word penance tattooed where my forearm and elbow met reminded me of this each time I stripped myself bare and forced myself to look in the mirror.

I ignored her Nash-Prescott-is-a-saint canonization speech and got to the point. "I need someone not connected to the company. Not the investigator with your legal department. An independent private investigator who isn't afraid of getting his hands dirty."

Someone like Fika, I didn't say.

Burning bridges seemed to be a habit of mine. I'd go as far as considering it a hobby if I didn't need those bridges to walk across.

"What's being investigated?" Emerald eyes studied me, waiting for me to give something away.

"Vu mentioned a second party profiting off the Winthrop Textiles scandal. I want to know who."

"Are we going to talk about how you're one of those two parties?"

"No."

She paused a beat, and finally, something other than indifference flickered into her eyes. Guilt, maybe. "About Emery Winthrop..."

I held up a palm to stop her. "I know. Spare me the lecture. She had a catering gig last night. We won't hire them again."

"What?" Her head shook until Rosco nipped at her neck to stop her. "No, that's not it. Why would you think that?"

I pushed aside my laptop, ignoring the last question. "Spill."

She cocked a hip against the wall and rubbed at Rosco's belly, a nervous habit of hers. "Reed called me."

Already, I knew I'd hate the punchline to this story.

Not because I hated Reed. I didn't. The opposite. He was the one who hated me, and I didn't blame him. I deserved the hate, definitely more than I deserved Eastridge's naive adoration.

Didn't mean I accepted it.

"Spit it out, Lowell."

"I owed him a favor. He cashed it in. He wanted me to get Emery Winthrop a job for the company under Emery Rhodes. That was before I knew about the S.E.C. investigation. If I'd known it would cause problems, I wouldn't have done it."

This was the thing I admired about Delilah. She possessed the rare ability to admit when she was wrong. Her confidence was unmistakable. The humility required to pinpoint and admit her mistakes didn't lessen it.

"Where is she working?" I asked, wondering if I could fire an entire department without a settlement.

"The design department as an intern."

Fitting.

She'd always had her head buried in a sketchbook.

I pulled out my phone and shot a message to Durga.

Benkinersophobia: How would you treat someone who fucked your family over? Who hurt your family so badly, it'll never recover?

Durga: Assuming I like my family?

Benkinersophobia: Clearly.

Durga: Like dirt.

Durga: Like less than dirt.

Great minds think alike, Durga.

Delilah continued, "It's for the duration of the Haling Cove project, and the upper half of the floors are mostly designed based off old schematics. The budget is tight because we had to grease too many fingers to get the zoning and plans approved so fast. We took the money from the design budget." When I didn't speak, Delilah asked, "What aren't you telling me?"

I hate Emery Winthrop.

She epitomized everything I stood against. Also, she'd known about her dad's embezzlement and had done nothing about it. To think I ruined my relationship with my brother over her.

I didn't say any of that.

Instead, I pressed the shin Delilah's heel had pierced against the desk's leg until the pressure drew more blood. "I got stuck in the elevator last night."

"Stop changing the subject."

"I got stuck in an elevator last night with Emery," I amended.

"Fuck."

One word, but it summed the entire situation up. I had a Winthrop working for me while a nosy S.E.C. prick was investigating me for insider trading over Winthrop Textiles. Fuck, indeed.

Delilah paced, her heels putting temporary little dents into the carpet.

"For almost two hours." I watched the dents disappear before lifting my head to face D. "Maintenance had left for the weekend, and a twenty-four-seven crew won't get hired until the hotel is done. The electricity didn't come back for about two hours."

"You were stuck in an elevator with Emery Winthrop for two hours?"

"She spent a part of those two hours knocked out."

"Sleeping?"

"You could call it that."

"I'm not even going to ask what that means, except to say I'm not representing you in that lawsuit. Her parents are loaded." She picked a strand of lint off Rosco that I'd mistaken as a fifth hair. "Knowing the Winthrops, they'd probably bribe the judge." Delilah stepped in the kitchen and filled a bowl with water for Rosco. "Is she going to be a problem? I can fire her. I included a thirty-day clause in the employment contract she signed. She's been here about a week. Totally fireable."

I considered it for a moment, but Reed didn't need more reasons to hate me. It would only hurt Ma. "No. I'll take care of it."

By take care of it, I meant I'd put Emery Winthrop in her place. The liar. She'd told me she was a caterer, and I'd believed it because Reed had mentioned to Ma that Emery was figuring out what she wanted to do with her life. I should have expected her to lie. The Winthrops had turned lying into an art.

Reed would blame me if I fired Emery. He couldn't say anything if she quit. Making her job miserable enough would bring me pleasure.

Delilah disappeared into the spare bedroom before exiting with a giant L.V. suitcase she must have brought while I was in the shower. "I know you're here until the hotel is done, so I'm staying in the room next door until we take care of Vu. I had it set up this morning."

Rosco lapped at the bowl while Delilah lugged the suitcase toward the door and called one of the security guards to help her move in next door. I side-stepped him and leaned against the kitchen island, watching her stack her Birkin bag on top of the suitcase.

Delilah had moved to Eastridge years ago to work full-time in the company headquarters, but she basically traveled with me as I jumped from new hotel location to new hotel location in order to oversee their construction.

She referred to me as a walking liability, and I referred to her as my personal Swiffer, cleaning up my messes with a quick spritz and a back-and-forth swipe. Convenient. Effective. Reliable.

"How much does your husband hate me?" I pulled out my phone to check for messages from Durga, not really caring about the answer.

My software designer had encouraged me to try the Eastridge United app and test functionality. I'd never intended on keeping a pen pal, let alone for this long. If you could call Durga a pen pal. Did other people who used the app sext late into the night?

I palmed my dick. Delilah grimaced at me, pulled out her phone, and dialed a number.

She covered the bottom microphone of her phone with her fingers. "Only when it's cold at night, and he wants something to fuck other than his hands."

"Lovely image."

"I thought you'd appreciate it."

I picked at the breakfast spread and popped a fresh strawberry into my mouth. "One more thing."

"Great."

"Pay last night's date a bonus."

"What did you do this time?"

"Booted her without a place to stay until her flight at eight this morning. It might have been storming."

"You're an ass."

"So you keep saying."

One of the security guards showed up and grabbed Delilah's bags. Rosco trotted after her as she left, leaving me alone in the room with the half-empty water bowl still on the floor—and a puddle beside it.

Loneliness sometimes felt crippling. Not in the sense that I needed someone near me at all times, but in the sense that I found no difference between standing in a crowded room and standing in an empty one. I still felt hollow with every breath I took.

Dipping my eyes to my phone, I read Durga's message.

Durga: Would you shoot your best friend in the arm for five million dollars?

As always, I wondered if Durga had a wiretap into my head.

Benkinersophobia: I don't have a best friend.

Durga: Color me as surprised as a cheerleader being chased down by a man with a machete five minutes into a B-grade horror flick.

I snorted before gunning a response I knew would make her laugh.

Benkinersophobia: I'd do it for twenty.

Durga: Twenty better include dismemberment, too.

Unraveling the notes on my table, I prepped for the design meeting. One where I planned on confronting Emery Winthrop, my little liar, and endeavored to make her life as miserable as she'd made mine.

She reminded me of the rat I accused Rosco of being, and though I couldn't extinguish her without pissing my brother off, I'd happily trap her inside a box she couldn't escape with a smile on my face.

And maybe, just maybe, I'd learn where Gideon Winthrop was hiding in the process.

Fitting.

I was the downfall of my family, and she would be the downfall of hers.

chapter
SEVENTEEN

Emery

The morning after seeing Nash again came on the same day as the apocalypse. No floods full of dead marine life. No falling skies. No ground opening up and swallowing me whole. That would be too easy.

Ben leaned forward to kiss me, his nose nuzzled into the nape of my neck.

He whispered words of platitude. "Kiss me, Durga."

When he leaned back, it wasn't a faceless avatar I saw, but pitch-black hair and cruel hazel eyes.

Nash.

"Pathetic," he drawled out, tracing my collarbone with the tips of his fingers.

I panted.

Needy.

Desperate.

Craving him.

Wetter.

He flicked my nose and tutted. "You don't come before I do."

Nash was straddling me, a leg on each side, not bothering to hold up his weight. He pulled himself out of his jeans and jerked off onto my chest. He was as long as I remembered him, thick with two veins I yearned to lick running down the sides of his cock.

Long ropes of cum shot onto my face and breasts, and I came with him, crying out his name as if I owned it.

"Nash!" I screamed it out, like I'd had a nightmare.

When I opened my eyes, I laid alone in the closet. Dark. Empty. Heaving for breaths. No Nash, just me and a brand-new stain on my tattered sheets between my legs.

Hunger whipped a hurricane in my stomach. Dizziness pinched at my vision until I coaxed myself back to sleep.

Two more hours until the meeting. You can do this, Em.

Two more hours to go without food. Maybe there'd be a breakfast spread at the meeting.

My plan had been to eat the crackers I'd stolen from the party, but Nash had taken them all, along with my wallet. Ironic, considering Nash used to be the person to feed me when Mother refused to.

"And so the savior becomes the villain," I whispered to the dark room.

The Polaroid of stars in my wallet was the one thing that reminded me of Dad that didn't immediately make me hate him.

The golden tiger on the back was supposed to be me.

A warrior.

A survivor.

A fighter who never backed down.

But after a slew of death threats post-Winthrop Scandal, I'd written, "ride me" in angry bold letters on the bottom, a reminder that the tiger wasn't a warrior.

The tiger was ridden.

By Dionysus.

By Durga.

Dionysus and Durga were the god and goddess.

They were warriors.

And the tiger? Nothing but a glorified pet.

The pictures of Reed and Teddy Grieger's card served as untainted memories of my childhood. Snapped in Polaroid, a series of smudged ink and blurry pixels. Moments I didn't know were valuable until they'd already become faded memories.

On the days I felt small, I looked at those pictures and reminded myself that I might be one person, but I was also a thousand memories, a million feelings, and infinite love.

I was immeasurable.

Now someone owned the Winthrop Estate, which meant someone owned all my memories.

And Nash had stolen the only ones I had left.

I didn't know who was worse.

The faceless monster or the monster I knew.

On top of the fucked-up wet dream starring some warped hybrid of Nash and Ben, I woke up a second time to a piercing hangover and an email from Mother. One I actually replied to—the second sign of the apocalypse.

I idled around, flicking lint off the blanket, looking up unique words on my dictionary app, refolding some shirts in my worn cardboard box, replaying memories of Nash in the elevator, and sewing up the hole that had formed on the curve of my Converse.

Anything to put off reading it.

I caved after twenty minutes and pulled up my email app, already knowing I'd hate whatever she had to say. I always did.

To: emeryrhodes@cliftonuniversity.edu
Fr: virginia@eastridgejuniorsociety.com

Subject: Exciting News

Emery,

I am writing to request your presence at brunch on the fourth of July weekend. I have happy news to share, and I would like to do it in person. The country club has reserved a table for us. I expect you to be there exactly at noon. Do not be late. I will not have you embarrassing me again.

I realize you possess an aversion to Eastridge, a weakness that has never sat well with me. It's time you get over yourself and think about others. Your Uncle Balthazar has been dying to see you. He asks about you often.

The other women at the club whisper about your absence. It makes me look like a terrible mother. We both know I am not. You have become a stain on my reputation. You can make it up to me by showing up on time, dressed appropriately for brunch—and for goodness sake, do something about your hair.

I can have Darynda ship you a brush if the need arises, or you can simply accept poverty is as disgusting as it sounds and dip into your trust fund. I'll allow it if you follow my conditions. Return home, find a suitable husband, and stop embarrassing me.

In case you decide to be selfish, remember I know all your secrets, Emery *Rhodes*. If you do not show up on the fourth, I have every intention of revealing your new name to the press. I look forward to seeing you soon.

With love,

Virginia, Chairwoman
Eastridge Junior Society

Why did anything regarding Mother make me feel like I'd been dropped off in a jungle to fend for myself, armed with a designer handbag and six-inch heels?
 I scraped my teeth against my bottom lip, pretending it was food. Maybe my stomach would get the message and swallow me whole. My fingers hovered over the keyboard, wondering how to reply to the email.
 The *threat*.
 I didn't think she would dox me, but Virginia Rhodes also wasn't a fan of idle threats. Even if my poverty and unkempt hair embarrassed her, she would rather suffer Eastridge's rumor mill running rampant about my new name and appearance than not have her way.

To: virginia@eastridgejuniorsociety.com
Fr: emeryrhodes@cliftonuniversity.edu

Subject: Please use lube next time you decide to fuck me in the ass...

My dearest, most-beloved Mother;

Excuse the typos. I'm finding it hard to see straight through the pain. Next time you fuck me in the ass, please consider using lube. I've attached a link to my Amazon wish list. On it, you will find my favorite brand of numbing lubricant. Please keep your brush and ship *this* to me if the need arises.

Thank you for inviting me to brunch. I have plans to stay at home and memorize the lyrics to Beyonce's "Lemonade," so the next time it plays, I can impress my new coworkers.

However, because you've been such a great inspiration in my life, I've decided to put my plans aside and spend the Fourth of July at the country club with you and all of Eastridge's finest patriots.

(I heard the Mercer family managed to pay zero taxes on their fifty-million-dollar income last year. They're living the American Dream. I aspire to be them.)

Please assure the women at the country club I will be there. We wouldn't want you to look like a terrible mother. I'll be wearing my black sundress with the wilting roses. Remember that one?

I wore it to Easter mass. You pulled me to the side and told me, in front of all my classmates, that even the Devil wouldn't take me in that dress. What charming memories we share. I love walking down memory lane. Don't you?

Speaking of memory lane, I absolutely adored our family trip to Hollywood, where you returned with two ccs of lip fillers and a new butt you swore came from hours at the gym. I feel it prudent to remind you I know many of your secrets, too… including the tummy tuck scar you've managed to convince the Housewives of Eastridge is from a C-section.

With so many hugs and kisses…

Your favorite daughter,

Emery
Demon Spawn

- Sent from Beyond Virginia's Uterus

Darynda, my mother's assistant, filtered through her emails. Sweet, pearl-clutching, pumpkin-spice-cereal-eating, Prada-obsessed, God-fearing, serial-gossiper Darynda. She had the mouth of a hippo. Always open. Always spilling secrets. Always spreading rumors.

I would love to see my mom explain her way out of that email.

A text from Mother came through my phone a few minutes later. An actual text, which was how I knew I'd entered the apocalypse. Virginia Winthrop didn't text. She sent emails, wrote letters, and spoke on the phone, but she never texted. Texting was for millennials and the Tide Pod generation.

Mother: Emery, I raised you to behave like a lady, not some untamed animal. I expect you to treat me with the respect and dignity I deserve as the woman who raised you. Darynda will reach out with details for brunch. Kisses.

She followed up with:

Mother: Oh, and honey, you're old enough now that calling me Mother just sounds silly. Virginia will do.

See?
Apocalypse.

Reed called before I could fixate on the fact that my mom wanted me to refer to her by her first name; I slept in a six by eight closet; my boss had kept today's meeting from me; and I'd been stuck in an elevator with Nash Prescott, who had torn apart my clutch and stolen my wallet, food, and dignity.

"I need your help." The first words out of Reed's mouth as I answered the call.

I flipped onto my stomach and toyed with my sheets, the ones barely holding it together. An accurate metaphor for my life. My bodyweight on my stomach made it feel more hollow, its growl filling the air.

Again, I thought of my trust fund before reminding myself it was blood money.

"What do you need?" I asked, voice low and raspy, knowing it couldn't be any good after the morning I'd had.

The third sign of the apocalypse, no doubt.

"Why are you whispering?"

Because I don't know if any stragglers remain in the building I am currently squatting in.

I didn't say this, of course.

"My neighbors finally finished having morning sex, and I'm afraid if they hear me, they'll ask me to join again." The lie slipped out so easily, I felt very much like a Winthrop in this moment.

"Again? As in you've joined in the past?"

"Again, as in they've invited me in the past. I said no."

I pictured my imaginary neighbors, a rail-thin rockstar with a two-inch goatee and a redheaded plus-sized model he couldn't get enough of. Harlan Felt and Alva Grace, in case Reed asked.

He didn't.

"I swear, the weirdest shit happens to you."

Probably because I make half of it up, so you don't worry about me.

"That's the life." I fought off the sudden surge of homesickness when Reed laughed. Clearing my throat, I asked, "What did you need?"

"Ideas." His ragged breathing filled the line. "I want to propose to Basil."

I switched the call to a video call, so I could see his face as I asked, "Are you sure?"

What I really wanted to do was scream, "What the fuck!" and check him into an involuntary psych hold.

He scrubbed a hand down his face and tugged at his hair before staring at me. The poor lighting made his hair darker. He laid in bed, the silky strands flying in several directions. For a second, he looked so much like Nash.

My stomach flipped with stupid butterflies, and my fingers hovered over the red button, so close to ending the call before Reed asked, "Am I sure that I want to propose or am I sure that I want my best friend to be supportive and give me ideas?"

Point taken.

"Well, Basil likes big gestures." *Huge, ridiculous, ostentatious gestures.* "Maybe take her to *Hamilton* and have the cast weave your proposal into the play? Like, a local version, because I doubt Broadway would do it."

Perhaps Wicked. *I'm sure Basil will identify with the Wicked Witch of the West.*

"Can't do *Hamilton*. Basil's dad thinks *Hamilton* is a bastardized take on American history with too much diversity."

And that's the family you want to marry into?

I bit my tongue until I tasted copper and flipped the phone off video call, so I could talk without worrying Reed would discover I was living in a closet like a less-glamorous version of Harry Potter. Only, I was a Muggle, and life couldn't get much more fucked-up than that.

"How about a helicopter—"

Reed cut me off, "No helicopters. Basil refuses to ride in one that isn't manufactured by her dad's aerospace company, and you know he hates me."

Forgetting why I'd been whispering in the first place,

I pushed my face into my make-shift pillow of shirts and screamed.

"What was that?" Reed asked.

"I think Alva Grace just screamed into her pillow."

"Is that your neighbor's name?"

"Yep."

"Must be some sex."

"Yep."

"Any other ideas?"

"Not off the top of my head. I'll think about it," I promised and hung up.

Reed and Basil. Married. I no longer loved Reed like that, but I still thought he could do better. Nash's escort perhaps, because at least she was willing to work for money.

I dragged my bottom lip into my mouth, wishing I could get full off lies and unfulfilled dreams.

I'd never starve again.

The fourth sign of the apocalypse came when I snuck down to the fifth floor, our makeshift design office, at exactly eight in the morning on the dot. Chantilly sat on the couch, watching *The Titanic*.

She paused on the scene where Rose pretends there's no space on the debris she's laying on and Jack dies. When Chantilly turned and saw it was me, she pressed play on the remote without a word.

If I'd surprised her, she didn't show it. Maybe she hadn't left me out of the email chain on purpose. And maybe that overweight bird I'd seen flying like a drunkard outside the window was really a pig with wings.

Chantilly ignored my existence and continued watching the movie, a tear trailing down her cheek as Rose's selfishness kills the man she supposedly loves.

"Gets me every time," Chantilly whispered to herself, not a hint of sarcasm in her voice.

Murder?

"Umm... okay," I drew out, wondering where everyone else was. Ida Mae had told me eight sharp. "Where is everyone?"

"The meeting was pushed back an hour. Not my decision." She swiped at the mascara trailing a path down her cheek. "Shit. I need to fix this," she informed me as if I cared.

I whipped my phone out, typed out a message to Ben, and waited for everyone else to show up. I considered telling him I'd had a wet dream about him, but I decided to go for something PG, especially because I'd pictured him as Nash.

Durga: Would you shoot your best friend in the arm for five million dollars?

Fair question.

Rose had sacrificed Jack, and Reed currently sat

pretty high on my shit list. Marriage? To Basil Berkshire? The girl who'd filled my locker with Tampax the day after I'd gotten my first period in the middle of gym class.

Thankfully, the clothes I'd stained were gym clothes. I'd also dipped the tampons in red food coloring-laced water and left them in her locker, because "rise above" was not in my vocabulary, and my pettiness reached acceptable levels, in my opinion.

(Reed once informed me I was made of 99% pettiness and 1% white cheddar mac 'n cheese, but he loved me anyway. I'd kissed his cheek and called him my best friend.)

Benkinersophobia: I don't have a best friend.

Naturally.

Ben had the personality of a porcupine in heat, pricking every surface of your skin with a voraciousness I personally reserved for hating people. He once told me our friendship was nothing short of a miracle. I had taken it as a compliment, but I wasn't sure he had meant it as one.

Durga: Color me as surprised as a cheerleader being chased down by a man with a machete five minutes into a B-grade horror flick.

He didn't answer for a while, so I sat on the couch, shoved my hands into the pockets of my black zip-up hoodie, and lifted my Chucks onto the coffee table. Because I was bored and enjoyed dishing Chantilly's cruelty back to her, I sped the movie and hit pause at the part where Rose dumps the expensive necklace into the ocean instead of donating it to charity.

Benkinersophobia: I'd do it for twenty million.

I gave an unladylike snort that had Chantilly scrunching up her nose as she walked back in, and I swore, if I died before meeting Ben, I will have died having lived an incomplete life. Reed held the title of best friend, but Ben was Macaroni noodles drowned in Vermont White Cheddar cheese. Comfort food for the soul. The person who always knew exactly what I needed to hear to feel better.

I might have lost my family, my belongings, my future.

But he'd helped me find something important.

My smile.

AND FINALLY, THE fifth sign of the apocalypse occurred after Hannah, Ida Mae, and Cayden had arrived—when Nash Prescott walked into the room and pretended he didn't know me.

chapter EIGHTEEN

nash

I never wasted my time explaining myself to anyone. Ten out of ten times, people have already made up their minds about you. Time is too valuable to waste it on people devoted to misunderstanding you.

Delilah Lowell, however, was the exception. We had gotten off to a rocky start. I told her to fuck off, mistaking her for an over-talkative intern. She'd told me my insults didn't faze her, and she owned a dog more threatening than me. (Had I known the dog was Rosco, I probably would have laughed in her face as I slammed my door in it.)

Four years later, she and Ma were the two people who had the privilege of knowing my phone number. Everyone else, including Reed, had my email address.

"Nash." Delilah placed a hand on my forearm after I stepped out of the elevator onto the fifth floor. "That scowl on your face screams impending lawsuit. Whatever you're thinking of doing, don't."

Her hair stuck out in multiple directions. She carried her rat in one hand and dug through her orange Birkin with the other. I was ninety percent sure she'd been having phone sex with her husband before I'd forced her to follow me down here.

Two spruce-colored eyes narrowed, looking for any signs of trouble on my face before she added, "I'm already swamped overseeing the contracts on the Singapore location." Her free hand continued rifling through her bag, stopping to grab my arm again when I turned to leave. "I'd like to be able to spend time with my husband sometime this century."

I turned back to her, removed her hand from my arm, and deepened the scowl. "First, I'm not scowling. Second, I have nothing planned. Third, last I checked, overseeing the contracts on the Singapore location is your job. If you dislike your job so much, perhaps you should find another line of work. I'd be happy to hire someone to write you a letter of rec."

Her attention had fled, returning to her bag. "I never said I dislike my job." She stopped digging when she found what she'd been looking for. "And the you're-not-the-boss-of-me routine? Seriously? We're above that."

"It's a routine because it's true. I *am* the boss of you," I enunciated each word and buttoned up my suit. "Feels nice to have lowly minions."

Finally, she pulled out a stack of papers, wrinkled at

the edges and stained in brown by—I hoped—coffee in the center. Anyone who fell for Delilah's manicured fingers and freshly-steamed power suits possessed stupidity I wanted no part of.

She was as likely to be put together as I was to fuck without a condom. (Re: a once in a lifetime mistake that, thankfully, did not end with a crying newborn I was bound to emotionally destroy.)

I relieved her of the papers and skimmed them. A list. Bullet points, a litany of action verbs, and thumbnail pictures, but my eyes honed on Emery's. She posed like someone taking a mug shot.

"And this is?" When Delilah opened her mouth, I added, "Give me the CliffNotes version."

"A list of everyone on the design team. They're all on the younger side, but we do that for longevity. Chantilly —the redhead—is in charge of the team while Mary-Kate is on maternity leave.

"Cayden is second in command, a senior design associate. He's British and tactless but good at his job. Extremely efficient. He set up the office and furniture in the penthouse while we were at a meeting with the mayor the other day.

"Ida Marie, the lanky blonde, is a junior associate and my favorite of the bunch. Sweet and dull as Marmaduke. Every time I see her, I have to resist the urge to pet her head. You would hate her.

"Hannah and Emery are interns. You know how Emery looks, and Hannah is the one with brown hair and nothing good to say." She pulled a sheet from the bottom of this stack. "This list is the most important. It's full of things you cannot say to your employees without getting a lawsuit slapped onto my workload."

Dragging my eyes from Emery's mug shot, I spoke, "I know how to avoid a lawsuit, Delilah."

She arched a brow. "Do you?"

I swiped the second paper from her and scanned it. "Do not swear at employees. Do not bully employees. Do not make employees cry." Staring up at her, I double-checked to see if she was serious. "This is Soviet Union bullshit. I have no control over their emotions."

"Just follow the list." Rosco barked twice and leaned forward to nip my shoulder. I side-stepped the rat. Delilah pulled him back, plopped him into her thirty-thousand-dollar bag until everything but his head vanished, and continued, "I'll see you tonight for dinner. I hate eating alone, and King doesn't fly in until Wednesday."

"Can't. I'm volunteering at the soup kitchen."

Like melted ice cream, she softened—first her eyes, then her posture. I waited for her to pool onto the floor in a puddle I could step in. At the very least, we'd be done with this conversation.

Her voice dipped lower as if she intended on spilling national secrets. "You're a good person, Nash. When I first met you, I wanted to quit, then I realized you are the best person I know."

"I'm not. Perhaps you should still quit."

"You didn't see the resignation letter on your desk?"

"That's what that was? I shredded it along with your raise."

She turned to leave but pivoted and exhaled, her voice a little too loud for comfort, but telling the one person who could stand me (besides my mom) to shut up seemed like a bad idea.

"I had my resignation letter written. Four years ago." Delilah pulled her coat tighter around her. "Then, I saw you at that Italian place on eighth. You walked in with a homeless woman. They wouldn't serve her, so you walked out. By the time they'd brought me and King dessert, you had taken the woman to get a haircut, new clothes, and makeup, and you returned to the restaurant, bought her a meal, and tipped everyone a thousand bucks except the asshole who wouldn't seat her."

She swiped beneath her lashes even though she hadn't shed a tear and added, "You gave her her dignity back, because you are a good person, whether you want to believe it or not. Sometimes, I wish you'd give yourself a break."

I almost appreciated her speech.

Almost.

Then she had to ruin it with, "You blame yourself for your Dad's—"

"Delilah," I warned. Sharp.

It fell under the do-not-fucking-go-there column of our friendship.

"Fine." She threw her hands up, causing her purse to swing. Rosco yelped. "Never talk about it. Live life an insufferable jerk, and die in bed with only your arsenal of paid dates to keep you company. None of it will change the fact that I know your secret."

In one second, she'd gone from pissing me off to enabling the part of me that sought destruction at all costs. I was on a warpath, ready to annihilate my lone friend just so my secret could die with me.

And then she opened her mouth, and I relaxed as she finished with, "Deep down, you're a good person."

She'd had enough of me, pivoting without another word and poking the elevator button with the same vigor you'd use to stab someone attacking you.

And that was our friendship in a nutshell. She stood

up to me. I let her. At the end of the day, I didn't budge, but at least I had the company of someone who gave a shit without trying to get at my dick.

We never even parted with hugs or handshakes. Delilah knew my boundaries. Skin-to-skin contact was one of them. I could touch someone, but I'd be damned if I let anyone touch me.

I tossed the lists she'd given me into the trashcan next to the elevator and continued my path down the hall, stopping short of the door to the conference room. From my vantage point, I could spy without anyone on the design team seeing me.

My eyes honed in on Emery, Durga's messages on my mind.

Like dirt.
Like less than dirt.

Emery sat on the couch, her eyes trained on the television, on the part where Ariel undergoes the fish version of plastic surgery to please her man and then loses her ability to talk in the process, but hey, it's not like the woman had anything valuable to say.

(Note to self: If Reed ever has a daughter, she cannot watch princess movies unless it involves an essay dismantling them.)

Emery wore a black hoodie, unzipped except at the bottom, where she'd fastened the zipper without bothering to pull it up; a shirt that read *eccedentesiast*, which for all I knew could be an S.T.D. warning; and black Chucks that looked like they'd been bought used from a pigéage facility.

Meanwhile, Cayden dressed in a three-piece suit, outfit completed by a striped pocket square tucked in a double-point fold. The other girls wore dresses and heels, their hair actually brushed and faces congealed by makeup.

"Oh, come on!" Emery's zipper unfastened as she threw both arms in the air, nearly hitting the blonde sitting on the couch beside her. She turned to the woman, eyebrows pointed at the ceiling, "Tell me this pisses you off, too, Ida Marie."

Wide-eyed and bearing remarkable resemblance to an Asian tarsier, Ida Marie stuttered, "Um... what?"

"Ignore her," Hannah remarked from one of the desks, not bothering to glance up from the computer screen. She sounded harsh without the Carolinian drawl to soften her vowels. "She's been doing this for the past thirty minutes."

"Past hour," Chantilly corrected from the other desk. Her tiny scarlet dress inched up her thigh as she leaned forward and squinted at her screen.

An F5 tornado couldn't faze Emery as she gestured to the television, this time almost hitting Cayden on her left. I recognized him from our Redondo Beach project last year. He had a keen eye, sharp wit, and a British accent that landed him more ass than a stripper pole.

Emery stood and turned to Cayden and Ida Marie. "This chick basically changes how she looks for a guy, then she washes up on shore, and dudebro prince sees a hot naked chick and wants to smash? Are y'all for real?" Her Southern accent strengthened the more worked up she got. Wide-eyed and jaw unhinged, she looked manic, a second from being escorted out in cuffs by security. "This is worse than *The Titanic!*"

"What's wrong with *The Titanic*?" Ida Marie crossed her arms and inched away from Emery. "It's romantic."

"It would have been romantic if Rose had shared her raft."

"What about Snow White?"

"She's fourteen, Ida Marie. Fourteen!" Emery shook her head, then swiped the drawstring of her hoodie aside when it swung at her face. "Snow White trusts a twenty-something dude she's alone in a forest with because he sings to her? *Sings*. And the Queen gets jealous of how pretty a fourteen-year-old girl is and decides to poison her. Unbelievable. She didn't need seven dwarves. She needed a knife and two body bags."

"You are disturbingly violent."

Her chin tilted up. "Thank you."

Chantilly lifted her wrist and glanced at her watch. "It's two past nine. He should be here by now."

True, but I wasn't in a rush to end this amusing display. In another life, I might have liked Emery. Unfortunately for her, liars and murderers appealed to me as much as making out with Able Small Dick Cartwright did. As in, I'd rather take my chances with a Guillotine.

"Who should be here right now?"

Chantilly ignored Emery's question and gestured to her shirt. "What are you wearing?"

"I've been here for an hour. If you had a problem with what I'm wearing, you should have told me while I had time to change."

"This is an office of business. I shouldn't have to tell you it's inappropriate to wear jeans and Converse to a meeting. Delilah Lowell may have gotten you this job, but I don't play favorites in *my* department."

"This is a half-finished construction site," she corrected. Her eyes dipped to Chantilly's open-toed Louboutin pumps. "There's still a closed-toed shoes policy."

She reminded me of an active minefield. Volatile.

Dangerous. A liability to herself. Because when a mine exploded, it'd take her down with it.

"So..." Ida Marie began, her voice trailing off as the silence persisted. "What do you think about Mulan?"

Emery scoffed and finally took a seat on the couch again. "She's sixteen, and he's, like, ten years older than her *and* her boss."

Our age gap, I noticed.

She spoke as if the very idea disgusted her.

It didn't matter.

Touching her once was a mistake.

Touching her again would be sinful.

chapter NINETEEN

nash

I stopped the conversation before it escalated into a brawl. Clearly, the quirky girl I remembered had grown into an unhinged nut case.

"If it helps, the original version had Ariel committing suicide and turning into sea foam, Mulan becomes the new ruler's prostitute and commits suicide, and Snow White..." Five sets of eyes turned to me as I entered the room. "Well, that one actually does have a happy ending. Snow White and Prince Florian marry, invite the Queen to the wedding, and force her to wear hot iron shoes and dance until she dies."

"Charming," Emery muttered as if she hadn't been the one to suggest a knife and two body bags.

I walked past the three on the couch, pretending I didn't know Emery, and sat on one of the desks, my back to Chantilly as I addressed the room. "My name is Nash Prescott. I'm here to share the aesthetic Prescott Hotels is looking to achieve with the Haling Cove location. Which one of you five is an intern?" I made a spectacle of scanning their faces before landing on Emery, whose glare dared me to mess with her. I did, raking my eyes down her body as if I disapproved. "You look like an intern. What's your name?"

Fight back, Tiger. Don't be weak. Show me your claws.

She didn't answer for a second.

Three.

Two.

O...

Finally, she bit out, "Em—"

I cut her off, "Actually, don't care. I need a coffee from the cafe down the street."

"I'm not getting you coffee."

"You do work for me, right?"

We were at war with our eyes, neither of us budging.

I'll make your life miserable, mine promised.

You have no clue what you've started, hers dared.

Oh, I do, little Tiger. Game on.

If she were anyone else, I would have admired her fight. The only feeling I had toward her was destruction. By the time I was done with her, I had no doubt she'd quit. If I acquired the location of Gideon Winthrop in the mean-time, even better.

"Emery, get Mr. Prescott his coffee," Chantilly chimed in after the silence lingered too long. Panicked eyes darted between us, confusion with a dash of jealousy.

I cocked a brow, daring Emery to defy me. She stood on reluctant legs, her eyes screaming how much she hated me. I slid my wallet out of my inner pocket. *Her* wallet, actually. A distressed leather square peppered with cigarette burns that looked like it once belonged to a coked-out rock star.

Her breath escaped her pouty lips in a rush. She did that thing she always did, where she mouthed a bunch of words. Two tiny hands clenched into tight fists. Her tits jerked with her breaths.

Emery held destruction in her eyes. She looked like she wanted to wrap her hands around my throat, snatch the wallet from me, and stomp all over my new phone for good measure.

Destroy, destroy, destroy.

But I knew her. If Chantilly hated her for getting the job from Delilah, no way would Emery reveal she knew me. She held a hand out for the twenty-dollar bill I pulled out. *Her* twenty-dollar bill. The lone bill housed in this war-torn wallet. For one of the richest women in the world, she traveled light.

I pulled the twenty away before she latched onto it, holding it above her head like she was a child begging for lunch money, and conjured the most obnoxious drink order I could think of.

"Get me an iced coffee in the largest size." When she reached up again for the bill, I *tutted* and held it back above her head, probably the one person she'd ever met who could make her five-nine frame feel short. "I'm not finished. Three ice cubes. Two pumps of vanilla syrup, pure cane sugar only. One pump of hazelnut and cinnamon. Two mocha drizzles. A layer of whip cream, but I want it in the cup before the coffee is poured in. A splash of oatmeal milk. Two tablespoons of cookie butter stirred in, not shaken or blended. Four shots of dark-roast coffee. Double-blended."

She snatched the bill from me before I could hand it to her, tearing it at the corner in her haste. Before I could add to the order, she pivoted and darted out of the room.

"Hurry or you'll miss the meeting," I called at her back, an actual smile on my face.

As soon as she left, the air thinned. I exhaled easier, taking the time to lean against the table and observe the other four designers. Chantilly's breathing heated my back for a few seconds too long before she walked around me and sat on the couch, taking Emery's place.

She reminded me of someone, but I couldn't quite place it.

I eyed the designers, a circle jerk of (over) paid fresh-out-of-college kids, teenage acne scars still clear on their faces like I ran a casting call for *High School Musical*. When I started the company, Delilah mentioned young employees were more driven, highly productive, easier to manage, versatile, and adaptable.

I hired them because they were more affordable, but also for those reasons. The downside was, people like Chantilly received promotions before they paid their dues. Power corrupts fools, and Chantilly looked one hundred percent foolish in a red mini dress on an active construction site.

"Mr. Prescott, it's wonderful to see you again," Chantilly said after twenty drawn-out minutes of silence I spent ignoring them.

"We've met?"

She paused, her cheeks turning a shade of scarlet that outdid her hair, before she smoothed out the nonexistent wrinkles on her skintight dress and laughed. "You're so funny."

Basil.

Basil Berkshire.

Reed's self-absorbed girlfriend.

The one addicted to Gucci, Balmain, selfies, and sugar-free açaí bowls.

That's who she reminded me of.

"Not particularly," I replied, and though Emery wasn't here, I knew if she had heard me, she would have had one of those ghost smiles on her face—hidden just beneath the blasé expression she wore so well.

Since the idea of Emery smiling nauseated me, I added as Emery walked in, "In fact, I only recognize Cayden."

Emery held out a hot coffee for me. I brought it to my lips, my fingers clenched around the double layer of heat sleeves. Her smile told me she had spit in it. I held eye contact with her as I took a sip anyway, never one to back down from a challenge. We were the same people in that regard.

Her smirk and the fact that she stood in front of me, hovering, should have warned me. The coffee was black and near boiling, about the exact opposite of the frozen monstrosity I'd ordered. It scalded my tongue, but I swallowed it anyway and smiled even when the liquid lashed at my tonsils, burning a path down my throat.

Whatever I ate in the next few weeks, I knew I wouldn't taste it. She'd fried my taste buds with a smile on her face, then lifted a blended drink to her mouth, a litany of add-ons written on the side like hieroglyphics, informing me she held the drink I'd ordered.

The smile on her face taunted me, even as she pressed the straw to her lips and sucked in sugary crap neither of us needed in our bodies. I drew the black coffee—what I would have ordered anyway, for the record—to my lips, even when she mouthed, "I spit in that," her face angled so the room couldn't see.

"Change," I demanded, holding out a hand. "I have a no-tolerance policy on thievery."

Panic took over her eyes, along with pure rage. She dug into her pocket and slammed two fives and some loose change into my open fist. I made a show of sliding the money into her wallet and shoving it into my inner suit pocket before turning to the rest of the group, dismissing her like she meant nothing.

"As I was saying," I began. Emery hovered beside me, no doubt talking herself out of first-degree murder. "I only know Cayden." I shot him a nod of acknowledgment and continued before the rest of them had the opportunity to start introductions. "But Delilah, whom some of you may know as the head of the legal department, gave me the rundown on your names."

Emery finally took a seat on the couch, but Chantilly made a show of stretching and stood, blocking Emery from my view.

I ignored them both and addressed everyone else, "Let's cut to the chase. I'm looking for something dark and white. Muted colors. This is a beach hotel, but we want to stay true to our brand. Some base flooring and materials have already been chosen to match different locations, but each hotel still maintains its own identity."

When Chantilly shifted, Emery finally peeked into view. She gnawed on her bottom lip, her brows furrowed in concentration. The ideas in her eyes brought more life to them than I'd ever seen.

A dash of hope, too.

My depraved sense of justice made me want to extinguish that hope.

After Reed hit high school, Ma gave him two gifts—a door and her permission to redecorate his room. My brother had the aesthetic vision of a prosopagnosiac, so he'd pushed the responsibility onto Emery.

My parents' budget wouldn't put a dent in a single Prescott Hotel bathroom, but it had been enough for a few buckets of paint. Unintentional as it was, I'd listed everything Emery had done to Reed's room.

Dark on white. Minimalistic. But she'd added a mural wall, one that could only shine if the entire room had been dulled. Pictures hidden within pictures. Gray shades that blurred together, and each time you looked at it, you saw a different image.

Magic, she'd declared out loud when she unveiled it to us.

I stared Emery directly in the eyes and said, "No murals. This is a Prescott Hotel, not a decrepit building ripe for some Banksy wannabe to paint on. I expect you all to treat this like the billion-dollar hotel chain it is."

Prescott Hotels had one worthy rival—Black Enterprises' hotel chain, owned by billionaire entrepreneur Asher Black—and the company hadn't stepped foot in North Carolina yet. I'd bought up every ideal property along the North Carolina coast, making this state officially mine.

Truthfully, it didn't matter how the hotel looked. I could rent out a human-sized fishbowl and sell out a year in advance, because these rooms went for two-thousand bucks a night, and people were hardwired to believe money meant value.

Plus, my name was attached to the building in giant letters. Like Asher Black, I'd acquired my seed money through shady means. Unlike Asher Black, the general public regarded me as a saint. I could do no wrong in their eyes, a privilege I hadn't earned but used to my full advantage despite the guilt that nagged at me.

"But," Ida Marie began, stumbling over what words to choose. "If we stick with muted colors without some sort of a focal point, won't the design be..."

"Boring," Emery finished for her.

So much fire burned in her eyes, watching her reminded me of feeling alive again.

Chantilly flinched, waiting for me to explode.

My jaw ticked. I checked my watch and loosened its grip on my pulse, feeling hot every time I looked in Emery's direction. "It's not my job to design this hotel for you. If you can't make it work, I can find someone else."

I realized, as she stared at me like she wanted to kill me, that it wasn't only irritation I felt. Her defiance turned me on. I set the shitty coffee on the table, pulled a chair out, and sat on it backward so they couldn't see I was hard as shit behind it.

She and her family fractured yours. When my dick didn't get the hint, I added, *remember when she basically forced herself onto you and roll the hell out of you?*

It saluted her as if the idea made it want her more.

"No need to find someone else, Mr. Prescott." Chantilly shot a glare Emery's way. It bounced off her like a quarter off Nicki Minaj's ass. "We'll make you proud."

"I'll see you all when the mockups are complete and ready for my approval. Miss Rhodes," I emphasized her new last name, "a word."

"I have somewhere I have to be."

"It wasn't a question."

Chantilly froze first, taking her time to collect her belongings. Cayden left quickly, twisting the car keys to his Civic around his middle finger. Hannah shoved Ida Marie out of the room when she all but shouted to catch Emery's attention.

Emery and I waited in silence until everyone left and the elevator in the hall dinged. I stood and leaned against the table, my hands gripped around its edge.

"Your hair is black." It slipped out, a lapse in control I hated myself for.

"I'm well aware, considering it's my head."

My eyes scraped a path down her body, cataloging all the similarities and differences. The shirt would have hugged her curves if she had them, but she didn't. Two hip bones jutted out.

Outside the elevator's shitty lighting, I could study her better. She looked thinner than I'd ever seen her, borderline fragile and breakable if it weren't for the expression on her face. She looked like the type of girl to brandish her middle finger as a weapon. I knew from personal experience she'd do it while hiding a knife in her other hand. Better to stab you in the back with.

"You're dressed oddly for a catering gig." She didn't even have the decency to look ashamed. I continued, "If you're going to continue working for me, and that's a big if, you'll have to learn I don't tolerate lies," *unless they're my own*, "and respect is demanded. Oh, and do keep your hands out of the proverbial cookie jar. I don't need the prepubescent offspring of a thief caught working for me, let alone stealing from me."

"At least I don't need to pay people to date me."

"It's a choice, not a need. Speaking of dates, at least buy me dinner before you mount me next time."

Her cheeks flushed. "No need to worry. If you recall, the lights were off. Had I known it was you, I would have been looking for a toilet to puke in. I hate you, Nash

Prescott, and every time you step into a room I'm in, I'm unsure if I want to vomit or stab you."

"I know I inspire your gag reflex. It takes time and experience for women to blow someone my size. I wouldn't worry about it until you get your first period."

"I'm twenty-two," she fumed, absently tugging at her shirt until it pulled against her chest and I noticed I made her nipples hard.

"Wow, you've been an adult for two seconds. Congratu-fucking-lations." I tore my eyes away from her nipples. "Nevertheless, I appreciate that—this time—you're able to keep your hands to yourself. It must be difficult, considering the past two times we were alone in a room together, you forced yourself on me."

I stepped forward until her tits brushed against my stomach, just like they had last night when she'd pressed against me in the elevator, angry breaths caressing my skin.

She's Reed's age, I reminded myself when the urge to turn her around, flip her over my lap, and mark her skin gripped me. She needed to learn discipline, yes, but she was too young and too tempting for me to be near.

"I didn't force—" She stopped herself, flicked her eyes down to where our bodies met, stepped back, and delivered a saccharine smile. "Is there a point to all this or did you want to isolate me so my coworkers can hate me more?"

I studied her. The daughter of a thief. The woman whose actions could never be justified. I didn't know who I hated more—her or myself for wanting her.

"The point is, Prescott Hotels is not Winthrop Textiles. I will not allow another Winthrop to ruin the livelihoods of thousands of people. Any stealing, scheming, and general misbehavior will not be tolerated."

"You're the thief," she seethed, ignoring the whole part about the merry band of thieves she called a family. "I want my wallet back."

"Or?"

Her eyes flashed, but she said nothing. What could she say? The one thing she had that I wanted was her dad's location, and I wouldn't let it slip that I wanted it. Not until the perfect moment.

She retreated. Chin up and silent.

I stood alone in the room, staring at her ass as she left.

Victory felt bittersweet on my tongue, and if she was defeat, I wondered what defeat would taste like.

chapter TWENTY

Emery

I'd always had an obsessive fascination with storms. They reminded me to breathe, smelled like fresh starts, and were teachers in a world full of lessons.

Sophomore year of high school, Reed and I shared drinks on a backroad deep into my family's property, the area no one ever went to or even bothered to maintain. Tipsy and reckless as always, I hopped behind one of Dad's Range Rovers, careening down the road at high speeds.

Half a mile later, Reed swearing in the passenger

seat, I crashed the car into a ditch when the rain started slamming against the windshield and visibility went from a hundred to zero fast. By the time Reed and I climbed out, the thunderstorm raged in full force.

Involving Betty or Hank would risk Virginia's wrath (and their jobs), and Nash had moved out by then—long gone and only showing up every other weekend to eat dinner with his parents and screw whatever slice of the month he graced with his presence.

That left Dad.

I almost begged Reed to call Virginia instead, because even though Virginia would be furious, Dad would be disappointed and that was worse.

He came within thirty minutes, dropping his meeting with a fabric supplier to make it back by dark. The rain poured down on the dirt road. I could barely make out his silver Mercedes.

Reed and I leaned against a tree stump off the path.

"How mad do you think he'll be?" Reed whispered, tapping his fingers against the ground as Dad drew nearer.

"Not at all." My words accompanied a groan.

Please, be mad.

Please, be mad.

Please, be mad.

I took in Dad's face. He shut his door and rounded the SUV to us. Nope. Not mad. Let down. *So, so much worse.* Eyebrows pulled together, giving me the look parents gave their kids when their report cards came back all Cs.

"Told you he wouldn't be mad." I ran a palm along my jaw.

Reed wrapped an arm around my shoulder as if he could shield me from Dad's woeful eyes.

Dad took in my face, flicked a glance at Reed, and cataloged our limbs to make sure they were still attached to our bodies. "Anything hurt?"

Reed stood up with me. "No, sir."

"Emery?"

I shook my head. "No, Dad."

"Good. Follow me."

Reed and I trailed behind Dad. He swung open the trunk to his G-Wagon and pulled out two child-size bikes.

"No way." I backed up a step, ignoring the rain. It lashed at my face, punishing me for my mistakes. I could guess where this was going, and I hated it with a capital H. "Dad, that's child torture."

"You two are going to get on these bikes and take yourselves home. When your calves are burning and your lungs are struggling for air, I want you to think about the consequences of your actions. By the time y'all get to your rooms, I expect you to be sober with your heads on straight. Y'all got that?"

"Yes, sir," Reed agreed.

Not me.

I went down swinging.

Always.

I flung my arms out, splashing rainwater in Reed's face. "That's insane! Dad, it's freezing. The rain—"

"You mean the rain you drove drunk in?"

I shut up. I mean, what could I say to that?

He leaned down, placed a hand on my shoulder, and forced me to look him in the eyes. "I can bring you bikes and bail you out of trouble all day, but I won't always be around, sweetheart. Storms will always rage. Don't run from them. Face them. Some things in life can only be learned in a storm."

Dad pressed a kiss to my forehead and sped off before I could complain. The downpour cloaked my sight as we biked back. All I could feel was icy water splattering my face until my vision blurred and my teeth chattered.

I wasn't sure what lesson Dad was trying to teach me on that bike, but I learned that storms could be relentless.

They were supposed to come and go.

But when you needed it to most, the storm never receded.

Working at Prescott Hotels, I felt trapped in the middle of one daily, like every conversation was a battle I had to fight unless I wanted to be drenched.

Shivering.

Defeated.

My throat burned from arguing all day. Chantilly had overspent on flooring we didn't need, which meant our already dwindling budget had been blown on statuario marble with silver and gold veins nearly identical to the Winthrop Estate's.

The Winthrop Estate reminded me of a boomerang. Every time I gained some distance, it always came hurtling back at me. I couldn't escape it. I saw pieces of it in the Greek statues at the park down the street; in the floor-to-ceiling curtains at the soup kitchen; and now, in the floor I was expected to walk over every day of my internship.

Hannah suggested reducing the design to the absolute basics, creating a minimalist effect like Kim Kardashian and Kanye West's sixty-million-dollar home in Hidden Hills, California. The one that possessed the personality of a peanut—all beige and not much to look at.

(For the record, the property tax on that home is over seven-hundred and five grand a year. I Google'd it. A

UNICEF donation in that amount could vaccinate nearly four million toddlers. Google'd that, also. Virginia spent triple that each year on chartered private jets alone. Didn't have to Google that. She bragged about it to anyone who would listen.)

The five of us had all reluctantly agreed to the minimalist aesthetic. What choices did we have? The budget had been nearly wiped out. Anything else wasn't possible. I argued we could cut corners in some design aspects, like using remnant materials and spending the money that saved on a centerpiece that would make the hotel design less boring.

Today, Chantilly took that idea and twisted it, so the extra money went to custom cabinet handles that I swore resembled butt plugs. By the end of the day, I'd checked my project calendar five times, ticking down the days until my internship ended.

After I clocked out around five, I sprinted to the soup kitchen, shoveled as much food into my mouth as I could while listening to two kids—Harlan and Stella—talk about their new friend at the soup kitchen, a volunteer who brought them presents every time he came.

Sounded nice. Wish I knew Santa, too.

I kissed them both on their cheeks, hugged their mom Maggie goodbye, and checked my email from the office of donations at Wilton University, an insanely expensive Ivy League university based in New York City.

To: emery@winthroptextiles.com
From: donations@wiltonuniversity.edu

Subject: Atgaila Scholarship Fund

Dear Ms. Winthrop,

We are emailing you in regards to your anonymous scholarship fund. With our recent tuition hike, the sole recipient, Demi Wilson, will need to pay the difference in a total of $500 per month for her enrolled semesters.

You may choose to continue to pay the $2000 per month scholarship or increase the scholarship coverage to $2,500.

As always, we appreciate your patronage and assure you our discretion.

Lexi Wheelander
Office of Donations

Five hundred extra a month. I could barely make the two grand a month work. Prescott Hotels paid well, but after taxes and the donation, I was left with too little to care for myself. I squeezed my eyes shut and muttered the prettiest words I knew.
When that didn't work, I imagined baltering in the rain with a thousand happy puppies.
Breathe, Emery. It'll be okay. You have no choice. It's the right thing to do.
I shot an email agreeing to the extra five-hundred, then ran as fast as I could to the Mom-and-Pop gym near the hotel. My shower caddy and towel bumped around in a black knock-off Jan Sport backpack held together by

duct tape and amateur stitches (I'd been a novice at the time. Bite me).

I paid twenty bucks a month for a gym pass. Instead of working out, I stopped by every morning for a shower. Ben had kept me up all night with dirty texts messages, which meant I'd overslept this morning and hadn't been able to stop by for a shower.

Careening to a stop in front, I took in the sign on the door.

Dear Valued Customer,

There was a leak from the last storm. We are closing down for the next few days to repair it. The three days will be comped from your next billing cycle. We are so sorry for the inconvenience. Stay happy. Stay fit!

- Haling Cove Fitness Staff

"Ugh." I groaned out, kicking a rock on the sidewalk, which undid the quick patch job on my Converse.

Ripping the shoe off so it didn't get worse as I walked, I made my way back to the hotel, ignoring the people who stared at my single bare foot with upturned noses. On the bright side, I must have looked like a mess because everyone I passed gifted me a wide berth.

Pulling out my phone, I shot a message to Ben.

Durga: I am having an awful day. Make it better.

Benkinersophobia: Roses are Red. Violets are Blue. You give good phone sex, and I guess you're okay, too.

I snorted an obnoxious laugh, the shoe in my hand flinging at the movement. A toddler pointed at me before his mom hurried him away.
At least I was smiling.
Always smiling when it came to Ben.

Durga: You're a poet. I'm filing that under the employment column. Mystery solved.

Benkinersophobia: If you think that's impressive, you should see my side hustle for cash.

Durga: Does it include something soft and small?

Benkinersophobia: And here I thought we were friends...

Benkinersophobia: Hey, Durga?

Durga: Hey, Ben.

Benkinersophobia: Did I make you smile?

Durga: Always.

At the hotel entrance, I swiped my employee card.

Panic bit its way up my throat when it wouldn't work the first time.

No, no, no.

Dipping my head back, I glared at the sky. Angry, dark clouds covered the expanse, no stars in sight.

I have no secrets for you, starless night. I swiped hair out of my eyes, the movement jerky as I glared at the abyss above me, daring it to do its worst. *Actually, here's a secret for you. I'm tired. So fucking tired. Are you happy? Is that what you want?*

Pressing my forehead against the glass door, I suppressed a scream. The first mist hit my hair, cheek, neck. It would downpour soon. If I didn't get inside, I'd be fighting a cold by the morning.

I wiped the magnetic strip of the card against the inside of my hoodie until it was completely dry.

Swipe.

"Oenomel. Phosphenes. Kilig," I muttered magic words, hoped they'd grant me good luck, and waited for the red dot to turn green.

It made me wait a solid two seconds before it did. I exhaled, shakier than I wanted to admit. I was okay for one more night.

When I walked into the lobby shoeless and misted with rain, the night guard drew his phone away from his ear and winced at the sight. "Long day?"

"You have no idea," I managed to mutter.

Joe knew I squatted. He never judged me. Never tattled. Especially since he'd been in this situation himself once before. In another life, I liked to think I would have fallen for someone like him.

The nice guy with the tanned skin, evergreen eyes, and megawatt smile. The hot guy with a rough past who never let it faze him. I'd beg him to kiss me, and he'd give it to me without taunting me for wanting him.

Someone like Reed, I reminded myself, dumbfounded when I realized my childhood crush might have existed because he felt like a safety net.

Four years later, I didn't want safe. I wanted someone who made my heart pound like getting stuck out in the rain, drifting at sea without a home. Someone who gave me the same thrill as being reckless and taking risks.

Dipping my toes past the rules, seeing how far I could fly before I crossed a line.

With Ben.

With Nash.

The unattainables.

"You're the last one left." Joe walked me to the elevator, hand on the taser of his belt. A habit of his that almost made my love for quirks smile. "Mr. Prescott left for dinner with Mrs. Lowell and her husband a few minutes ago. They were dressed nice. The three of them probably won't be back for a while."

He winked at me, and I wanted to want him, but I didn't. Relief hit me fast, two scraggly shoulders sloped forward as I jabbed at the elevator button. Scraping my nails against my palms, I considered hugging Joe for the good news but settled for a wave.

He patted my shoulder and left, lips tilted up as if to say, *it won't always be like this.*

Compassion.

Such a beautiful, foreign sentiment.

I hoped he wasn't lying, because I couldn't take much more before I succumbed to the fact that I wasn't made of fortitude.

Maybe I was a kitten who hid behind a plucky front, mistaking herself for a tiger.

Swallowing the wave of self-pity, I dipped inside the elevator and considered my options. If everyone had left the hotel, I could sneak into the office and rifle through the master keys for a key to one of the rooms we'd finished for the masquerade party guests.

My pointer finger pressed "5" before I could talk myself out of it. At Cayden's desk, I ransacked the drawers, making my way through stacks and stacks of paint and fabric samples until I found a lone key. The word *Penthouse* had been written in cursive with a Bic pen on a sticky note and pressed onto the keycard.

I juggled it between two fingertips, considering.

Could I take it?

Cayden wouldn't notice. After the long week we had, his normally tidy desk resembled an avalanche, mountains of paper that slid outward each time he piled another sheet of paper on top.

If he did notice it, he wouldn't say anything for fear of Nash's wrath. Everyone thought Nash was ruthless for the way he'd treated me. They feared him like hypochondriacs feared Ebola. Paranoid. Irrational. Yet, somehow rational at the same time.

Truthfully, the Nash I used to know only lashed out at people who had wronged others. Virginia for her treatment of his parents; Basil for bullying me; me for, well, I didn't know how it had begun, but he must have had a reason. He didn't do things without a reason.

If I had to venture a guess, it'd be for what happened to Hank or siding with Reed in their feud, which was ridiculous, considering I would always side with Reed.

At the reminder of his cruelty, I pocketed the key. If he was gonna treat me like dirt, the least he could do was offer me a shower to wash it off. I pressed the penthouse button in the elevator, my heart pounding with each floor I passed.

By the time the elevator doors opened, I'd assured myself a million different ways that Nash was out to dinner and wouldn't be back soon. I could sneak in and out in under fifteen minutes. Ten if I didn't bother to hide the evidence that I'd been there.

I swiped the key to Nash's penthouse suite, flicking on the light as soon as I entered. It smelled like him. A new scent mixed with old. Intoxicating in a way I hated him for.

The first week at college, I'd stood in front of rows of body soap at Walmart, overwhelmed by the choices.

Some guy shoved past me, nearly knocking me over, but he'd smelled good. Familiar. Something that reminded me of home. So, when he grabbed the bottle of Tiger's Bane, I'd snatched up the same kind.

Tigers were predators.

Loyal.

Tough.

Resilient.

I wanted to be a tiger.

It wasn't until Reed mentioned that Nash used the same body wash that I realized why I recognized the scent. But it was too late. I was hooked, even drizzling it into my laundry detergent, so my sheets smelled the same way.

I felt like a thief, stealing his scent as if it were my own. Perhaps I was one, since I squatted in his hotel and stood in the threshold of his penthouse without his permission. I took it in, feeling like a voyeur.

An interloper.

A stranger.

A kitchen bare of cabinet doors and countertops sat

at my left. Gray low-pile carpet made up the living room, along with two desks. One sat in front of the floor-to-ceiling, wall-to-wall panoramic windows. The other rested two feet from the perpendicular wall.

The window lured me in. I pressed a palm against it as if I could touch the storm outside. The life of luxury formed most of my life, but I would never get used to this feeling. Being on top of the world, staring a storm in the eye and feeling like I could win.

Think about winning later, lunatic. It's time to haul ass.

Doors lined the left and right sides of the penthouse. I took a guess, venturing left, immediately knowing Nash slept in this room when I entered. An Alaskan King-size bed rested against the wall, the one piece of furniture.

My fingers twitched with the need to toss the room for my wallet. I held back. Barely. I dipped into the en suite bathroom, my nipples instantly puckering after I stripped off my clothes. Something about being naked in the place Nash slept felt dangerous. Exposing. Intimate.

Pulling my shower caddy out of the backpack, I plopped it into the standing shower and slung my towel onto the spare towel hook near the door. The shower was made completely of glass on all sides, sitting in the center of the large bathroom.

I felt like a statue in a museum display as I padded barefoot into the shower and stood directly under the built-in rainfall shower head. Shampoo, conditioner, and body wash from the Prescott Hotels skincare line sat in a row on the built-in shelf. His new scent, I realized, after I popped a cap and sniffed.

I flicked on the water switch, groaning the instant the hot liquid lashed my back, pounding onto my head like I was standing beneath a North Carolina thunderstorm.

It was almost—*almost*—enough to forgive Nash.

I'd managed to avoid him all week, feeling zero-percent guilty about serving him scalding-hot coffee. He'd robbed me of my wallet and the money in it when I needed every dime I owned. Was this how all the Winthrop victims felt? Desperate and penniless, fingers ready to dig under couch cushions for every spare cent?

I twisted another switch, and the water spread across the entire shower ceiling, a torrent of hot rain I could barely breathe through. The onslaught eased my sore muscles, and I relaxed under the spray, my limbs loose and body begging for more.

I stayed longer than I should have. Unlike the studio I'd lived in near Clifton University, the water didn't turn cold after seven minutes and twenty-three seconds, telling me it was time to leave.

It remained blissfully hot. A luxury sauna. I rubbed at my neck, cursing when I felt how pruned my fingers were since I hadn't even begun to wash. My body swayed under the pouring water, eyes closed. I hummed the melody of Jeremy Zucker's "you were good to me."

My eyes popped open. I reached for my shampoo, but my eyes met Nash's.

I froze.

Couldn't think.

Couldn't speak.

Couldn't *move*.

Nash wore a suit that hugged his body, his hair the same mess and his eyes the same shade of irritation. For a fleeting second, I wondered what he looked like out of the suit. I'd seen him naked once, but I'd been too preoccupied by the fact that I'd slept with the wrong brother to pay attention.

The woven fabric of his suit taunted me, hiding something I'd probably never see again.

You don't want to see him naked, Emery.

Lie.

I did, but in the way you'd stare at a car wreck as you drive by—with morbid fascination at witnessing something destructive.

Dangerous.

Deadly.

The dark scowl on Nash's face never left. He pressed his phone to his ear—a new phone, I noted with some satisfaction.

If I could break you, too, I would.

His lips moved at a rapid pace I couldn't keep up with. I heard nothing beyond my heartbeat and the water. My palm darted to the switch. I turned it so only the middle strip of the shower head remained on. I could hear him better that way.

He knew, because he narrowed his eyes on me, never once dipping below my face to my body. If our situations were reversed, I never would have had the willpower. Or maybe I really disgusted him, and he didn't need willpower to resist looking at me. He simply didn't want to.

"Don't call security, Delilah." Whitened fingers gripped the phone, tight enough it should have cracked from the pressure. "No one broke in. False alarm." His clipped tone pierced me. He bit out, "Yeah, I'm fucking sure."

I stood in silence, at a loss at what to say for once in my life. I wanted to wrap my arms around my body and cover myself. Instead, I lifted my chin and stood proudly, daring him to stare at me.

The tight peaks of my nipples pointed directly at

him. I kept myself bare, completely shaved. A mistake, I now realized, as I felt the rainwater trickle down my body, past my folds, caressing my clit.

My breathing grew shallow in the silence, the water feeling suddenly warmer. Too hot. I fumbled with the latch, telling myself I needed to keep my cool if I ever expected to live this down.

My fingers twisted the knob in the wrong direction. I jumped out of the water's trajectory when it scalded my skin, suddenly closer to Nash, like a caged animal on display.

Not a tiger.

A kitten, running from hot water.

He finally ended the call. When he opened his mouth, I braced myself for his words, wishing I could step back into the safety of the water without getting burnt.

"Get the fuck out. You're not worth the orange jumpsuit, Jailbait." Slipping his phone into his pocket, he added, "Don't forget to wash behind your ears."

Anger whipped at my chest. Resentment chewed its way up my throat. I wanted to shout my age for the millionth time, but it would fall on deaf ears. He'd humiliated me time after time.

In Reed's bed.

In the elevator.

In front of my coworkers.

But I knew I affected him, because I refused to believe he affected me this much without at least some reciprocity.

So, *fine*. If he wanted to make my life miserable, I could dish back what he served. I needed this job, but he needed his reputation.

And I was bad for it.

So, so bad for it.

chapter
TWENTY-ONE

nash

Ticked.
      Everything about me was ticked.
      My jaw.
The vein in my neck.
The vein on my temple.
The vein on my fucking cock.
    Emery's hand shot out, reaching blindly for the temperature control. She twisted it and stepped back. Water cascaded down her face, dripping past the curves of her eyelashes, over her lips, and lower.
    I refused to pay attention to her body, even though

she filled the room with her presence. Everything about her was too much.

Too destructive.

Too toxic.

Too reckless.

"Such a simpleton," I lied, burning at the way those discordant eyes speared me.

Hot mist boiled the room, sheathing my clothes and whatever skin it could latch onto. I leaned back against the sink, letting the counter carry my weight as I stripped my suit jacket off, tossed it on the steam-coated tile, and took my time rolling up my silky button-down sleeves.

My neck felt choked, but I kept my collar buttoned, unwilling to strip anymore with a twenty-two-year-old girl naked in front of me. Especially when I noticed the distinct red bottle with the blue label and prowling wolf behind her.

She used my old body wash. Same brand. Same scent. A thief, stealing my essence for reasons that evaded me.

That's why I recognized her scent in the elevator.

She rubbed *me* all over her body.

"I pity you, Miss Rhodes." I emphasized her last name, taking pleasure in the way she reacted to it. Like I'd delivered a lashing onto her back. "Incapable of comprehending basic words. So dull. So desperate. You remind me of your mother."

They were polar opposites, actually.

Virginia Winthrop's societal contributions included encouraging anorexia in the Eastridge youth, slut-shaming housewives who got the dick she wanted but would never receive, and drinking enough champagne daily to render an overweight elephant unconscious.

Meanwhile, Emery made a sport of defying her

mother, fighting against the Virginia 2.0 mold like her sanity depended on it. At the end of the day, however, she'd known about Gideon's embezzlement and did nothing.

Thousands lost their jobs and savings. Angus Bedford died. Dad died. Maybe Emery was like Virginia after all.

"Take that back!" Defiance slammed into Emery's posture as she shouted, sloping her chin upward and body forward. I had no doubt she would have lunged at me if thin glass and four feet of space didn't separate us.

"It's cute that you think you have any control over me."

I stepped up to the shower until we stood nose-to-chest, the fine layer of glass and my diminishing thread of sanity the only things separating us. I dipped my fingers into my pocket and pulled out her wallet. *My* wallet.

The picture of Reed caught my eyes first. Sliding it out of the insert, I licked it exactly where her face sat and slammed the photo onto the shower door. The wetness bound the picture to the glass.

She flinched as it rattled, looking like she'd taken a punch in the gut. I allowed her three seconds to stare at it, memorize it, *savor* it one last time before I tore the Polaroid in half. A yelp traveled up her throat, and she lost the defiant edge to her face.

Good.

I wasn't here to be friends with her.

I wasn't even here to acknowledge her.

How desperate for attention was she that she needed to break into my penthouse and strip in my shower?

Two halves of the photograph fluttered to the floor, Reed on one half and Emery on the other. As far as I was concerned, I'd done her a favor.

Lesson number two, baby. There is no you and Reed. He is wrong for you. Docile. Predictable. Tame. The sooner you get that, the better.

"I hate you." A faint hiss. Soft and oddly feminine. I wanted to bottle it up and listen to it whisper dirty things.

She'd said those words before in the elevator under the guise of darkness. She hadn't meant them then, but maybe she meant them now.

"Strong words," I taunted, kicking one ankle across the other. "Do they make you feel like you have a spine? Because all I see is something breakable."

Fingers swiped at her hair, whipping the thick, black strands out of her face. That fire returned, tenfold, sucking up all the air in the room. If I looked down, I knew I'd see bare tits heaving with panted breaths.

I didn't look down, but my dick wanted me to. It pointed straight at her in my dress slacks. Instead of noticing, she glared at me.

She looked so rebellious, it reminded me of when she'd turned sixteen and asked her mother for a car. I stood at the edge of the pool, cleaning it while Dad met with his doctor. Virginia reclined on a lounger, sunbathing topless as she read the latest *US! Weekly*.

"I know what I want for my birthday," Emery declared before cannonballing into the pool. She popped back up at the shallow end a minute later. "A car. One of Dad's old ones from the garage. He doesn't use half of them."

Virginia set her magazine down and tilted her oversized sunglasses on top of her head. "Sweetheart, the riffraff drive cars. The Winthrops have drivers."

And that was that.

Emery was gifted a Birkin bag made of ostrich skin the shade of vomit, which she sold the next week before begging me to drive her to the used car dealership in good ole Honda Yolanda, my 90s Accord that still ran a gazillion years later.

She bought a used junker, and on the way home, donated the rest of the Birkin money to the animal shelter, passing Virginia and her friends at the country club along the way.

The next day, Virginia had Dad drive the car to the junkyard to be crushed, and Emery had turned to Reed and said, "It was worth it," her face making the same expression she wore now.

Defiant.

Smug.

Unbeaten.

I waited for her to say something, but she was doing that thing she did where she muttered words I couldn't hear and drove me mad in the process. I studied her lips, trying to decipher what they were saying until I realized I was just staring at her lips.

Meanwhile, the shower head worked above her, pounding out enough water to save California from its next drought.

Finally, her eyes locked on mine, and she pressed a palm against the glass door, right beside my cheek. "I like when you call me Jailbait, Prescott. It means you want me."

My nostrils flared, eyes ticking. I had no idea where she intended on taking this, but she was playing a dangerous game. One I had no intention of losing. Part of me considered she had an angle, and I wanted to nip it in the bud.

"Careful, Winthrop, you're looking at me like you want to fuck me, and we both know the only way that will happen is if you pretend to be someone else."

"You haven't changed, Nash." Her belittling scoff dug at my ego—I hated myself for it. "A decade later, and you're still picking fights for the hell of it."

She looked at me like she knew me.

I needed to prove to her she didn't.

"You have no idea what you're talking about." I unbuttoned my collar and loosened it, my words and movements unhurried. Let her sweat at the hands of water. "I didn't get into fights for the hell of it. I went out and bruised my knuckles, spilled my blood, broke my bones for my dad. That is the kind of loyalty a Winthrop would never understand."

You don't know me as well as you think you do. Do you, baby?

The bravado dropped like a curtain closing. "Your dad?" She faltered in an instant, but I didn't fall for her tricks. I'd sooner trust Bin Laden with national security.

"Color me shocked—something the all-knowing Emery Winthrop doesn't know." I unfastened the top three buttons of my shirt, hating the way she caved and stared, hating the way I liked it. Hints of my chest peeked out, coated with torrid mist in an instant. "Dad had a heart condition that required monthly medication. Medication that cost more than my parents could afford. I found out when I overheard Ma and Dad arguing over bills.

"I needed a job, but none paid well enough. We had no healthcare, and the pills cost three grand a month. Wealthy Eastridgers would drive up to Eastridge High School and pick up some poor public-school kids who needed the money." Two more buttons. "I had friends who told me about the fights. Next thing I knew, I was in the ring night after night.

"I won often, made a lot of money for myself—and

even more for the assholes who bet on me. I told Ma I'd taken a job to help out with the bills. I think she always suspected I made my money fighting, but she never pushed it."

"Until you got arrested," Emery finished, recognition dawning in those eyes. "Betty made you promise to stop."

I'd met Fika that night at the station. He stood near the front, flirting with an officer, but he'd stopped when he saw me, a frail palm rubbing at his bald head.

"You're Hank Prescott's kid," he'd said, nodding to me.

I armed myself with a sneer, ignoring the blood when it trickled from my temple down my cheek. "What's it to you?"

"I see him often. At the hospital." Oh. *The fight deflated as he continued, "What are ya in here for?"*

"Fighting."

He nodded and fist-bumped my shoulder because my arms remained cuffed behind my back. I didn't see him again until an hour later when he kicked at my legs, waking me up.

"Come on. Let's go."

I scrambled up from my seat when he pulled a key out of his pocket and dangled it in between us. "Just like that?"

"Just like that." He uncuffed me with the grace of a horse on ice, jabbing my wrists with the key twice in the process. "I got connections here, kid."

"You stopped fighting after that," Emery added. "I remember."

Actually, I'd fought once since, but I would hardly consider that a fight. He was severely outmatched. I didn't tell her any of this as I unbuttoned the final two buttons and let my shirt slide down my arms.

Emery's eyes widened. They took me in. I knew what

she saw. I had to look at them in the mirror every day, knowing they weren't enough.

Constellations of scars and cuts littered my chest and arms. Below my ribcage, a knife wound stretched from my front to my back. It had healed poorly, still raised and angry against my skin.

She cataloged each one in silence, taking in the corded muscles and stains of battle, mismatched eyes lingering on my tattoo before she flicked them up to my face. Something gnawed at my stomach when I realized she liked what she saw.

"Why doesn't Reed know?" she croaked.

"He does. Now."

And the chip on his shoulder hunched his back as soon as he'd found out. He didn't realize how good he had it. Ma, Dad, and I let him be the golden boy. For as long as Dad lived, we never let the problems touch Reed.

He never had to pick up food at the grocery store with Dad, wondering if he had to explain to Ma how Dad dropped dead in the feminine hygiene aisle.

He never had to give up a scholarship from an Ivy League school, knowing it was too far to visit and help Dad if something ever happened.

He never had to give up his body, submitting it to a battering of fists—and knives when some overprivileged asshole bet on the wrong side.

Reed remained pristine as a sacrificial virgin, a purity we all fought to maintain at all costs. So, he could be pissed at all of us, but his anger rested on a cracked foundation.

"He kept it a secret from me?" Oddly, Emery didn't sound hurt. It made me study her closely, lured by the idea of peeking inside her head.

"No." My fingers itched for a joint, something it

hadn't done since high school. "Ma and I didn't tell him anything until after the funeral." Actually, Ma had told him. Reed still hated me for the cotillion. "Dad didn't want him to know. Reed would have quit football and used the gear and registration fee to pay for Dad's meds."

"He should have."

An instant response, absent of hesitation.

It made me hate her a bit less, which transferred my irritation onto myself.

I wondered what she'd say if she knew Gideon had known. He'd offered to use his connections to get Dad into a trial. My parents didn't give two shits about pride. They cared about their kids, staying out of trouble, and spending as much time with each other as they could. Nothing else.

The drug trial helped until the Winthrop Scandal broke, and the lead researcher booted Dad from the trial in retaliation. Like my parents, he'd invested all his savings in Winthrop Textiles. Like my parents, he lost it all. Unlike my parents, he lashed out.

"Dad didn't want him to," I finally said.

"Is that why Reed hates you? Because you three kept that from him?"

It struck me as an odd place to have this conversation, but I kept my face level with hers, even when the idea of water dripping down her bare flesh enticed me. "Part of it, but he was mad before that."

Since the night of the cotillion when he'd almost gotten arrested, to be specific.

"Hank died of a heart attack... because he stopped taking his meds?"

"He couldn't afford them after he and Ma lost their jobs for your parents and their savings."

After he'd been cut off from the trial drugs, Dad was

a ticking time bomb. He didn't have three thousand a month for the other drugs. I had a plan, but I'd been too slow. Reed left for college, and I'd moved back to a shitty one-bedroom apartment in Eastridge and let my parents take the room.

"I'm sorry." A strand of hair dropped over her eye, but she didn't move. Surprise sliced across her face. It didn't set well with me.

Always a great actress. From pretending to be Virginia's bitch to stabbing my family in the back, you deserve an Oscar.

"Emery," I warned.

More than anything, I hated apologies.

The thing about apologies is, they come after the fuck-up.

It's like saying, "I admit it. I fucked you over, and now you have to forgive me for it."

Why would I?

"No." She stepped closer until the tip of her nose touched the glass. If the door was open, she'd be touching me. "Let me get this out. I know people throw the word sorry around like it means nothing, but I don't. I believe in the power of words, and I'd never abuse them. So believe me when I say I am so incredibly sorry about your dad."

Believe her? Never.

Water beat the floor. Flecks of liquid speckled the glass between us, fat teardrops chasing one another toward hell. She didn't deserve a response, so I didn't gift her one.

"That's why you hate me," she whispered.

So, so clueless.

I didn't hate her for the sins of her parents. I hated

her for knowing about them and doing nothing. I hated her because dad didn't have to die.

It was why I hated myself, too.

"No, little Tiger." My eyes finally caved, dipping to her tits. Two full, pear-shaped tits with hard nipples pointing right at me. If I looked lower, I could make out her pussy. I mustered the willpower not to and flicked my eyes back to hers. I promised, "I hate you for so much more."

I'd told her about Dad. Got it over with, so she could wallow and languish in guilt like I did every day. A single lilac struggling to live without sunlight.

Wilted.

Withered.

Empty.

This conversation changed nothing.

There was still blood to be spilled.

Gideon's.

Virginia's.

Emery's.

chapter TWENTY-TWO

Emery

All my life, I'd been accused of being too much.
"Too out there."
"Too artsy."
"Too deranged."
"Too petty."
"Too lanky."
"Too independent."
"Too mouthy."
"Too much."
I took the insults and inhaled them as if they were

compliments, swallowing each and every one with a cupidity that suggested they made me happy.

And they did.

I liked being too much because it meant I was never too little. I never held back. I never bit my tongue. I never pretended to be someone else.

My critics were right. I was out there, artsy, deranged, petty, lanky, busty, independent, and mouthy.

And for the most part, I liked myself.

There.

I said it.

But I didn't like myself tonight.

Hank Prescott's death had been preventable. Reed had kept that from me. Betty had kept that from me. Nash had kept that from me—and *hated* me.

And me?

I smelled like Nash did before he hated me.

A thief cloaked in a tiger's scent.

The first thing I should have done when I ran back to my closet—barely remembering to shove my towel and shower caddy into my knock-off backpack that read "Jana Sport" rather than "JanSport"—was call Reed or Betty. Better yet, I should have tendered my resignation and gotten my ass out of dodge.

Instead, I sprawled across my sheets, spraying water everywhere because I hadn't even bothered to dry my hair. Flashes of Nash moments ago rattled me.

Steam licking his bare chest.

His sharp inhale at the sight of my breasts.

Wetness gathering between my legs as he glared at me like he wanted to hate-fuck me.

My shaky hands barely managed to hold my phone.

I pulled up the Eastridge United app and shot a

message to the one person who never judged me, my lust so thick it almost seemed tangible.

Durga: I need to come.

His reply came in seconds as if he'd had the app open to our chat when I messaged.

Benkinersophobia: I already have my cock in my hands. Strip out of your clothes, spread your legs, and tell me how much you want my cock.

I did as he asked, realizing I'd returned in my t-shirt and underwear, leaving my jeans hostage in Nash's bathroom. *Shit.* The other pants I owned were oversized sweatpants that would fit an entire cruise ship. Ones I reserved for laundry day.

Durga: If you don't make me come within the next ten seconds, I'm deleting this app.

Benkinersophobia: Cum not come. Say it correctly. Better yet, say it out loud. Beg me to make you cum.

I did, never backing down, even when my cheeks flamed as I panted to empty air, "Make me come, Ben."

It was Nash I pictured hovering above me. The vicious eyes. The messed-up hair. And now I knew what he looked like beneath his shirt. Vast muscles stretched the width of his body. A deep V led to what I remembered, all these years later, as a long, thick cock.

My lips craved the scars peppering his body.
I wanted to kiss them.
Bite them.
Trace them with my tongue.

I didn't believe in the word perfect. Never used it to describe anything in my life. But it was the only word I could conjure when it came to Nash's body. His personality might have left a lot to be desired, but his body and face left me aching.

Durga: Please, make me *cum*. My fingers are tracing my clit. Tell me what to do with them.

Benkinersophobia: I didn't say you could touch your pussy. Wrap your mouth around your fingers, imagine they're my cock, and apologize for disobeying.

Drawing my knees together, I kneeled and brought my fingers to my mouth, my heart threatening to escape my chest in the darkness. I could taste myself on my tongue as I slid three fingers past my lips and imagined Nash standing above me, feeding me his hard cock.

I whispered around my fingers, "I'm sorry for disobeying you."

Jesus.

I was so turned on. Relinquishing control drove me crazy. I wanted to feel dominated, overpowered, fucked so thoroughly I couldn't walk. Even with a knife to my throat and the threat of death dangling above me, I would never admit it was because rough, hard sex reminded me of how Nash fucked.

My first orgasm from sex.
My only orgasm from sex.

And I was so wet thinking about him, I could feel it sliding past my lips. I picked up my phone and squeezed my thighs together, trying to bring relief.

Durga: I can taste myself on my fingers.

Benkinersophobia: Describe the taste to me.

Durga: Light... Almost like nothing, but with a hint of citrus and vanilla from my body wash.

Durga: I like the taste.

Benkinersophobia: Pull out the vibrator I sent you, connect it to the app, lay on your back, and let me fuck you raw. Text me when it's inside you.

I reached for one of my boxes stacked in the corner, blindly fished out the vibrator Ben had sent me ages ago, and connected it to the company's app. Ben had full access to the app, which meant he could control it from wherever he was.

Laying on my back, I rubbed the tip on my nub before sliding the entire length inside me.

Durga: It's in me.

My fingers clenched the sheets as the vibrator came to life inside me. It pulsed to a steady rhythm, and just when I was close, Ben slowed the vibrations until I wanted to scream.

Benkinersophobia: Not so fast.

Durga: Ass.

Benkinersophobia: Beg me to make you cum.

Durga: Please.

Benkinersophobia: Please, what?

Durga: Please, make me cum.

He turned up the speed, the ribbed edges creating friction that had my eyes rolling back. I brought my hands to my breasts and squeezed, flicking each of my nipples, remembering how it felt to have Nash staring at me.

Staring at *them*.

My breaths fogged the tiny room. They came out in uneven pants. I came so hard, screaming Nash's name, too exerted to even feel guilty. My arms moved like jello, but I forced myself to slide the vibrator out of my body and turn it off.

When I came down from the orgasm, I shot Ben a text.

Durga: Thank you.

Benkinersophobia: Fuck, I needed that.

Durga: I'm sorry I came to your words with Nash's face on my mind. Nash's tortured faced with the fucked-up childhood, and the scarred body, and the dead Dad. Nash, who sacrificed himself for his family and was hurt because of mine. I'm sorry I love you but get wet for Nash.

I didn't send the last message.
It was too honest.
Too real.
Too raw.
Nash had it wrong.
I wasn't the broken.
I was the breaker.

chapter
TWENTY-THREE

nash

Emery's sudden reentrance into my life reminded me I needed to get more hands-on with my approach to revenge. Fika had disappeared, and I was no closer to finding Gideon than when I'd hired him four years ago.

Worse—Fika knew where Gideon was, and I had wasted four years trusting the wrong guy. Again. Who knew what else he had kept from me?

"Did you hire a private investigator?" I asked Delilah, pulling up my correspondence with a Singaporean diplomat on my laptop.

I'd never actually wanted Prescott Hotels. It was a responsibility I'd taken on because I needed the money to fund all my other projects. My penance. The charities. The revenge. I created Prescott Hotels with illegal money, building new hotels and buying and remodeling old ones across the world.

But this project—Singapore.

I wanted it.

Badly.

Two years ago, on a scouting trip in Asia, the plane made an emergency landing in Singapore. Delilah and I ate dinner on the top of the highest building. Feeling like a god staring at the specks of cars and buildings below, I decided I wanted it.

I wanted to buy the building and remodel it as a hotel. Even as a bidding war began against Black Enterprises and I knew it would get expensive, I didn't back down. We greased palms, exchanged emails with all the top contractors in Asia, and set up meetings with dozens of local vendors.

I felt the project within my grasp, and if I could feel happiness, I would have.

"Did you hire an investigator?" I repeated when it became clear Delilah had ignored me.

She paused in front of my desk, a small container of Greek yogurt in her hand and a biodegradable spoon in the other. "Yes, Master. He'll update you when he finds something, Master. Anything else I can do for you, Master? Massage your hands, Master? Spoon-feed you lunch, Master? Schedule your annual prostate exam, Master?"

"Point taken and ignored." I minimized the Singapore files and pulled up my folder on Gideon. My eyes skimmed the trade data for Winthrop Textiles, trying to pinpoint what didn't feel right.

Delilah returned to her desk, an oversized Parnian we'd had shipped here a few days after the design staff meeting. "Chantilly asked for a sit-down, and before you ask me to relay any messages, no. I am not your assistant."

Ignoring her last sentence, I ground out, "Tell her no."

I exited out of the document, knowing I'd find nothing if the S.E.C. couldn't. Before I could stop them, my fingers pulled up Emery's Insta account. She had three followers, @TheInaccessible as her handle, a feed full of words I was sure didn't exist, and a bio that read, *Scratch here to read my status.*

Other than that, no pictures of herself. The only twenty-two-year-old to roam this Earth without ever having taken a selfie.

Fucking perfect.

It occurred to me that I had nothing to gain from playing friendly with Emery. Nothing I could say or do would make her quit. She wasn't built to back down from a challenge. She would cut out her liver and sell it on the black market if it meant she'd win a bet.

Delilah snapped the lid off the yogurt and pointed her spoon at me. "I'm starting to think the words 'I', 'am', 'not', 'your', and 'assistant' are not in your vocabulary. Also, she's outside."

"At this point, I'm convinced you're making up words to fuck with me. Fucking hell." Scrubbing at my face, I eyed my watch and exited out of the dictionary disguised as an Insta account. "How long has she been out there?"

"Fifteen minutes? I wanted her to sweat." D shoved a spoonful of yogurt into her mouth with the grace of a hog.

"She's dressed like she wants something from you, and it isn't a promotion."

"Wait fifteen minutes and let her in."

"I am not your assistant," Delilah repeated with a smile on her face.

She set down her yogurt, walked to the door, and let Chantilly in without waiting the fifteen minutes I'd requested. She took a seat on her oversized wing-backed chair and didn't bother hiding her amused smile as she watched Chantilly flick her eyes back and forth between us.

Chantilly stood by the door, the smile slipping from her face when she realized I wasn't going to invite her in. "Umm..." She upped her smile until she resembled Jack Nicholson's Joker and snagged a seat on the chair in front of my desk.

(For the record, Heath Ledger played the best Joker, and I'd annihilate anyone who argues with me about it.)

"That chair's not yours," I bit out, sliding my phone out of my pocket to message Durga.

Benkinersophobia: You've been quiet. Everything good?

God, I was acting like a pre-teen tool who wanted to get his dick wet for the first time. Truthfully, Durga could be an artificial intelligence playing games with me for all I knew, but she was also the closest thing to a relationship I'd ever had.

Three years of late nights, intense conversations, and phone sex.

I cared.

Okay?

Sue me. Take out an ad. Shout it to the world.

I fucking cared.

Chantilly shot up from the chair, stumbling her way out of the leather. "Oh, I thought... it was empty."

"It's Rosco's. Rosco was just getting a sip of water." I turned to the rat in front of Delilah's desk, who had his hind leg raised. He lapped at his ass. "Weren't you, Rosco?"

Delilah snorted when Rosco didn't move.

Asshole.

I finally stared at Chantilly. "Who are you?"

Her expression reminded me a little of how I'd left Emery a few nights ago—mouth gaping like a whale shark's. "I lead the design team?"

"Are you sure?"

"Huh?"

"If you lead my design team, you lead my design team. For God's sake, don't say it with a question mark. I feel embarrassed for you."

"I-I... Yes, I lead the design team. I met you at the design meeting a few weeks ago. My name is Chantilly."

"Why are you here?"

She toyed with the spaghetti strap of her short dress. "We need to bring on an additional member. Sally retired a few months ago, and Mary-Kate will be on maternity leave for the duration of this project. The workload is too high for two senior members, a junior member, and two interns. Our last project involved six people, and that location had less than half the square footage."

"Fine." I waved a hand to shoo her and returned to an email from a Singapore supplier. "Hire another junior associate."

Chantilly still stood in front of me, unable to take a hint, reminding me of the idiots who responded to my one-word emails with paragraphs. "We ordered statuario flooring for the entire lobby and elevators. The tariff increase was more than we'd been expecting, so the budget is tighter elsewhere."

I attached a jpeg of a middle finger to the email and replied to the supplier's offer with one word—no. I'd sooner soak my dick in Icy Hot and visit a two-for-one brothel than pay triple the industry standard for subpar steel.

Durga messaged back. Finally.

Durga: It's not you. There's this guy.

I bit back a curse, aware of the audience. It wasn't like Durga or I had been celibate these past three years, but it didn't mean I liked to hear about another guy.

Benkinersophobia: He's a pussy. Lose the guy.

Durga: You don't know what I was going to say... -_-

Benkinersophobia: Don't care. Don't like him.

Durga: For the record, he's a jerk.

Benkinersophobia: But you want him.

Her silence bugged the fuck out of me.

Benkinersophobia: There's an obvious answer.

Durga: Yeah? What's that?

Benkinersophobia: Hate-fuck him. Get the douche out of your system. Move on to a guy who deserves you.

Durga: Who deserves me?

Benkinersophobia: Not him.

When I glanced back at Chantilly, she was still talking. I tapped my Graff Diamonds watch and said, "Get to the point faster. You get one more sentence."

She shifted from foot to foot, choosing that sentence wisely. "We don't have it in the design budget to hire another designer."

I needed Mary-Kate back. Mary-Kate didn't talk. Where the fuck was Mary-Kate?

"Go above budget." I pointed to the door. "Close it on your way out."

"No," Delilah cut in. "We need to stay on budget with this one. The Singapore contract may need more... leveraging."

Bribes.

She meant bribes.

I fucking hated everyone.

I sighed, leaning against my chair to look at Delilah. "Hire another intern."

Delilah didn't bother returning my attention as she stated, "No."

"Are you saying you won't do it or I don't have enough money to hire another intern?" I added a tab to my browser and double-checked my bank account.

Yep.

Still filthy rich.

"You pay your interns like they've been loyal employees for a decade. It's basically like hiring an experienced employee," her brow arched, "only you're not getting an experienced employee."

"You're exaggerating," I said, pulling up Emery's employee file to verify.

Yearly salary—forty thousand, one-hundred, and forty-five dollars. Not exactly a windfall, but about two-and-a-half grand a month after taxes and withholding. Still, more than what Dad and Ma made working for the Winthrops.

Also, she had a trust fund that could make her overly-Botoxed mother weep, and Virginia had more plastic in her face than a delivery truck of Lean Cuisine trays. Just by working for Prescott Hotels, Emery had stolen a job that could have helped someone else.

Maybe I could pay my interns less, but maybe I could also become a corporate welfare shill that contributed to problems like my parents'.

No, thank you and fuck you very much.

Delilah scribbled her signature on the bottom of something and added it to the mountain of papers on her desk. "I'm not exaggerating."

Chantilly's head ping-ponged between the both of us.

I asked, "What's my net worth again?"

Delilah dropped her Conway Stewart pen and spooned yogurt into her mouth, not bothering to wipe it when a clump fell to her desk. "Not as high as you'd like to think, considering how much of it you give away. I shudder to think of a world run by you. Is fiscal responsibility in your vocabulary?"

Yes, and so is penance.

I bit my tongue.

This fight was a long time coming, but I wasn't having it in front of Jessica Rabbit's desperate long-lost cousin.

"You do charity work?" Chantilly fluttered her lashes at me and fingered a strand of hair. "I donated blood to the Red Cross a few years ago."

I spared her a glance. "Chasmophile, you're embarrassing yourself."

Spiky nails the color of blood dug into the upholstered back of the three-thousand-dollar cantilever chair she'd tried to sit on. "It's Chantilly."

Delilah set her pen down and watched us with her full attention, amusement lighting up her eyes. "Who confuses Chantilly for Chasmophile?"

Good question. I had no answer.

"If anything," she continued, "you'd think it would be Chartreuse."

"Oh, you're so funny, Delilah. Chartreuse." Chantilly paused mid-laughter, fingers indenting the chair's upholstery. "What does chasmophile mean?"

Delilah mocked a patient smile that reeked of condescension. "A lover of nooks and crannies."

Oh.

Emery.

Always Emery.

She'd worn a shirt that said 'Chasmophile' when she went through her Twilight phase, reading in every corner of the house, migrating with Virginia's movements. Wherever Virginia was in the mansion, I'd always bet Emery sat in the exact opposite end of the house, legs curled up against her chest as she read in a little nook.

And I was about ready to donate my brain to science

to cure whatever ailment made it continually think of Emery.

"Delilah," I began.

"I know that tone enough to know I'm not going to say yes." She turned to Chantilly. "Cover your ears."

"What?" Chantilly's eyes begged me to save her.

I didn't. "Cover your ears, Chartreuse."

Delilah talked back to me. I let her. Enjoyed it, even. But she knew not to do it in front of others.

"Relocate a temp from your office to design," I said as soon as Chantilly covered her ears.

"I don't think so." Delilah stapled a stack of papers together with the vigor of a running back diving into the end zone. "We're busy enough as is."

"You, perhaps?"

"Ha. Ha. You're so funny. You have a career in stand up if your hotel fails—and it will if you continue to pay employees more than their positions call for and exceed project budgets."

For the record, I paid well because the company had started out hiring from a pool of the poor half of Eastridge. The half that suffered most from Gideon's betrayal. What was I supposed to do? Pay every non-Eastridge employee less?

Delilah leaned down to pet Rosco when he pawed at her shins and continued, relentless, "And in case you're not joking, and I know you're joking because you cannot be serious, I can't afford to relocate one of my temps. I'm already working remotely here, which is a hassle that cuts into my time. Plus, I am busy renewing my contract with my husband."

"You mean your wedding vows?"

"No, I mean my *contract*." She dragged the word out like I was an idiot for not following.

"You have a relationship contract with your husband? Who does that?"

"Lawyers. The asshole wants anal written into the contract this year."—Chartreuse choked on her Evian. I'd forgotten she was even here—"I want two kids." Delilah turned to the redhead. "Chartreuse, honey, I said cover your ears. I won't repeat myself." She turned back to me. "We're entering negotiations."

"How about no anal and no kids?" I suggested, returning to my mounting to-do list. "It's a win-win situation. He doesn't have to wipe baby asses, and you don't have to take anything up your ass."

"You're saying that because you don't want me on maternity leave."

"You're the head of an entire department." I pulled up a folder on my laptop, opening Mary-Kate's employment file. "Come to think of it, so is Mary-Kate." I swore as I read. "A year of maternity leave? Are you fucking serious?"

Standard maternity leave in the states ranged from zero to twelve unpaid weeks. Paid leave if you lived in California, Rhode Island, or New Jersey, but we didn't, so what the fuck.

"You told me to write up the company's employee contracts. So, I did." She rested her smug-as-hell face on her knuckles as if she hadn't just told me the company overspent on employee salaries earlier. "Do you expect women to pop out babies and head back to work, milk leaking from their nursing bras?"

"I knew I should have hired Earl Haywood." I tucked back a smile, knowing the mention of Earl would piss her off.

"Earl Haywood has a beer belly from drinking at work." She mimicked his permanent drunk sway. "Plus, his name is Earl. Hay. Wood. But by all means, hire him and watch your company crumble."

"Um," Chantilly raised one hand, waving it a little like a preschooler who needed to use the restroom. "Can I uncover my ears yet?"

"No," I said the same time Delilah said, "Yes."

Chantilly dropped her hands and shook them a little, like pressing them to her ears had caused an ache. "So... can I hire someone new?"

Delilah arched a brow at me before turning to Chantilly. "No need. Mr. Prescott has agreed to become more hands-on with the project."

I should have said no.

I should have hired someone else.

I didn't.

Instead, I nodded because Emery worked in the design department, and I needed Gideon's location even if I had to pry it out of her unwilling fingers. Plus, I wanted her miserable, and nothing made her more miserable than my existence.

"See you bright and early tomorrow, Chasmophile."

chapter TWENTY-FOUR

nash

The cafe across from the hotel served chicken and dumplings that reminded me of the ones Ma made. So, even though I preferred unclogged arteries at seven in the morning, I indulged myself for sentimentality's sake.

Chicken and dumplings used to be Dad's favorite. We had it every holiday and for all three meals on his birthday. These didn't hold a candle to Ma's, but the dumplings had been cut into the same shape, and if I squinted my eyes and medicated myself enough, I could probably convince myself they were Ma's. Add in some hallucinogenics, and I'd be fighting Dad for the leftovers.

I sat in the cafe, at the table nearest the window, my eyes fixed on the sight across the street. Leaning against one of the red maples at the hotel entrance, Brandon Vu checked his watch twice before pulling out his phone and dialing a number.

He dressed in a suit he'd had tailored to fit him, but the polyester-rayon screamed, "I live on a government salary! Please, don't ask me to pay for this date." His suede loafers tapped twice on the sidewalk. He beat his fingers against his thigh.

I'd taken my time eating as soon as I'd clocked him half an hour ago. The waitress had set down my food, and I could have left a big tip and dipped out the back, but I reveled in watching Brandon wait.

He had the patience of dog waiting to piss. His thumb and pointer fingers twitched, like someone kicking a smoking habit. With his free hand, he reached behind his ear but came up empty and patted the front and back pockets of his suit slacks.

Empty, also.

He paced a few steps, pulled out his phone, and begun shouting at the poor schmuck on the other end. I couldn't hear from here, obviously, and reading lips was a myth television shows made up, so I watched impassively as Brandon hung up and stopped his pacing.

He was staring at something.

I followed his line of sight to Emery. She wore the same black hoodie, unzipped, with a pair of oversized sweatpants. Something that resembled a shoelace—if it'd been chewed up by Rosco—held the sweats up at her waist, but she still found herself adjusting them every ten steps.

She was beautiful in a way that disgusted me. The type of beautiful nothing could conceal. Not sarcastic t-shirts that made no sense to anyone but her. Not that dollar store crap she called makeup on the days she even bothered. Not the oversized sweats she had to pull up every five seconds.

Just. Fucking. Beautiful.

Period.

End of statement.

Delilah spent hours at the hair salon, perfecting her balayage so it looked natural. Virginia still bore scars from a Brazilian Butt Lift she swore never happened, even after she came back with a new ass and a figure the shape of a violin, claiming to have caught mono for a month. Chantilly caked herself in makeup, scanty dresses, and desperation that screamed for attention.

Meanwhile, Emery didn't care.

She simply gave no fucks.

It made no sense because she was a *fashion* design major. She'd grown up in a world that told her appearances mattered and pursued a major that enforced the idea, yet she possessed no interest in succumbing to societal expectations.

So authentic.

So fresh.

So fucked up, I reminded myself.

The hood of Emery's hoodie had been pulled over her head, but I knew it was Emery because her shirt read, "Selcouth," this time in a sans serif font that took up the width of her chest. The chest I'd stared at a couple of nights ago.

So perky, her tits begged me to slap them and watch them bounce.

She's twenty-two. Don't give in, asswipe.

I did.

Tugging my phone out of my inner pocket, I opened up the dictionary app and typed in, "Selcouth."

Adjective.

Unfamiliar, rare, strange, and yet marvelous.

She was selcouth like I was a rainbow-riding unicorn. For the record, I was well aware I was lying to myself. I knew I wanted Emery, but on account of her being a Winthrop and twenty-fucking-two, my dick could sit this one out.

When I glanced back up, Emery had pulled a full-body coat out of her bag. With a quantity of pockets that veered more on the side of functional than fashion, it had a cotton hood popping out of the thick wool.

She continued walking, and before I could stop myself, I placed two hundred-dollar bills on the table and left the diner out the front with my head down, hoping Brandon wouldn't notice me.

Sanity, it turned out, was a deadbeat dad—it fled when you needed it the most.

When Emery turned left, I followed but kept my distance as I realized Brandon hadn't been waiting for me. He'd been waiting for Emery, and now he was trailing her to wherever she was headed.

About four blocks from the hotel, which I walked in a suit not intended for walking in, Emery stopped in front of the tent city the Haling Cove city council had been trying for years to eradicate.

The suit pinched my skin. I watched Emery weave through tents like she owned the place. She didn't. I knew this because, *I* did.

Rows of homeless men and women lived in tents in a vacant lot owned by yours truly. (Through a shell corporation, because making enemies of the city council wasn't on the top of my to-do list, thank you very much.)

I knew many of these people first-hand from volunteering at the soup kitchen a few doors down. Since I'd arrived in town, I donated money for groceries and volunteered five times a week, usually during peak hours.

Maggie squeezed Emery in a tight hug. She had a smile on her face despite the fact that she'd married young, lost her husband to an IED, and lost her home a few months later. Emery handed the coat to Maggie, making a show of popping the hood on and off before she bent down to hug Maggie's twins.

Harlan dug inside the bag, pulling out smaller, kid-sized coats. Stella jumped on Emery's back, the teddy bear I'd given her last week dangling from her fingertips. Emery spun Stella in a circle before she checked her phone and grimaced.

They parted with drawn-out hugs, Maggie swaying Emery side to side like she was a sister she hadn't seen in years. At this point, we were both late for work, and I had no clue why I even bothered to follow her, except my eyes continued to trail Emery even when I told my legs to cut this shit out and return to the hotel.

Work, Nash. Remember that? The thing that keeps a roof over your family's head?

As Emery walked out of the tent city, Brandon grabbed her upper arm, pulling her into a secluded area of the street. She fought him, clawing at his fingers. I almost intervened until she glanced up at him and stopped fighting.

She knew him.
She knew Brandon Vu.
She knew the damn S.E.C. agent investigating me.

Worse—she took whatever he handed her, glanced around the street, and shoved it deep into her pocket.

I'd seen enough.

I made my way back to the hotel, firing a text at Delilah to have the P.I. look into whatever connection Emery shared with Brandon.

Before I could send it, I deleted the fucking text, because I wasn't stupid enough to leave an electronic trail. Instead, I pulled up the Eastridge United app, releasing a centimeter of my frustration at the sight of a message from Durga.

Durga: Is poison a discreet way to kill someone? Asking for a friend, who may hate her boss. (FYI—That friend is me, so I expect a useful response.)

Benkinersophobia: Tell your friend she can always work for me. With her mouth. Beneath my desk. The hours are long and hard. Consider yourself warned.

What I really wanted to do was to ask Durga if she'd fucked the douche nozzle yet, which if you thought about it, was hypocritical of me considering I'd spent the past few nights jerking off to the memory of Emery's tits pressed against my shower door and how tight her pussy had been when she'd snuck into Reed's room...

Damn, you are a special brand of douche.

I released a breath, leaning against the entrance to the hotel. Emery stopped as soon as she saw me blocking the door. It hadn't been my intention, but I took advantage of the situation, crossing my arms against my chest—the message clear.

Do. Not. Cross. Me.

Too late.

She looked thrown off-balance at the sight of me. Her recovery came quickly, and she tried to move around me, but I shifted with her.

"I have work, Nash. Chantilly will dock my pay if I'm late."

You're already late. I wonder why, my Trojan horse.

I didn't budge. "Considering I'm your boss, I'd say I'm more important."

"Consider this—Bieber bangs would hide that overinflated head of yours."

I nodded my chin at her chest. "Speaking of inflated things, are your nipples patriotic, or are they saluting me for no reason?"

Douche.

I shouldn't have brought up her nipples, but one—did she even own a bra? and two—I hadn't had sex in ages (unless phone sex with Durga counted), and now it seemed like the only thing I could think of, along with exactly how flexible twenty-two-year-olds were.

Stop it, creep. You finished college and knew the ins and outs of anal while she still thought she pees and fucks from the same hole.

Emery's arms wrapped across her chest, because no, I hadn't been lying. Her nipples were hard as fuck, and they pointed right at me like two tiny sorting hats choosing my lips as their Hogwarts House.

(Yes, I'd watched *Harry Potter* after Durga mentioned it.)

Wishful thinking was a real thing, and I had a bad case of it when it came to Emery Winthrop. But I would never give in.

I'd broken Emery, whittled her will down to nothing but rage.

She battered her way past me, ramming my arm.

I latched onto her elbow, buried my face into that wild mane of black hair that smelled like me, and whispered, "Watch yourself, Winthrop. I am the king in this palace, and Prescott Hotels is my empire. If you think you can stand toe-to-toe with me without a fight, an hour of docked pay will be the least of your concerns."

She needed to realize life was not a game of Chess. It was a game of Battleship, and the last person to sink wins.

chapter TWENTY-FIVE

Emery

I had two assholes following me.

First—Brandon Vu had stalked me to the tent city, shoved a card into my hand, and demanded I take it. Afterward, I realized I still hadn't shaken the feeling that I knew him from somewhere. Even the way he'd said, "We need to talk," sounded familiar.

Second—Nash Prescott and his relentless jabs.

If I were being honest, I would have taken an S.E.C. agent—who was probably gunning for Dad and taking it out on me—over Nash any day of the week.

Nash had stood in front of his building in ripe shape, always looking goddamn near murderous. Any resemblance between his behavior and civility was completely coincidental. In fact, I wondered how he conducted business with anyone who wasn't a rabid wolf.

This morning, I'd convinced myself that it would be a good day. For starters, I managed to avoid Nash after the unfortunate shower incident. Then, the gym opened a day sooner than expected, so I showered before work.

I was finally clean, but the second he came near, I felt dirty again.

Evidently, this wasn't a good day.

I should have remembered that good days didn't exist at Prescott Hotels. Not when its "king" was a tyrant with an ego so fat, it could break a dollar into change just by sitting on it.

"Why are you following me?" I hissed.

He trailed behind me in the lobby, his threat still ringing between my ears. The man made washed-up child actors look sane.

"I work here." His offhand comment needled its way beneath my skin.

"Take the next elevator." I stabbed the elevator button, pulled up my sweats when they slid down again, and turned my nose up to inhale, hoping he read it as defiance.

Did the cleaning products smell like cinnamon rolls or was I actually that hungry?

"You're having a hard time understanding the employee-boss dynamic." Nash's arm shot out, blocking me from entering the elevator. He crept forward, but I felt his presence tumbling toward me at the speed of an avalanche. A cloud of frost and wrath descending on my sanity. "I could give you a refresher course."

"I don't need anything if it's from you."

Other than money.

The thought tasted bitter. Oh, how the tables had turned.

I dipped under his arm and sliced through his overwhelming scent, clutching onto my sweats so they wouldn't slip off. I needed my jeans back from his bathroom floor, but A—he had probably burned them and B—on the off chance he hadn't, asking him nicely would bring attention to that night.

No, thank you.

I continued from the elevator, "Why don't you take your lessons elsewhere? I'm sure Stalin, Mussolini, and Hitler are begging to learn a thing or two from you." I pivoted to face him, pressed the *close* button, and added, "In hell."

He left without a word. I waited until the double doors shut and jabbed the button for level sixteen, hoping to drop my bags off in the closet before work. Except the doors opened on level two. Nash stood in front of the elevator, so fucking smug, I couldn't take it much longer.

He must have run up here in order to press the button on time. What kind of person did that?

Devious intent glinted off his eyes. Trouble had found me, disguised as a gentleman in a Westmancott suit and Brioni loafers. He was a gentleman like I was a fairy tale. As in, not at all.

I couldn't shake Ben's texts.

Hate-fuck him out of your system.

Could I?

Did it work like that?

A little Vitamin D, and I was suddenly cured of my Nash fixation?

No. Even I didn't buy my bullshit. It felt like an

excuse to scratch the permanent itch that was Nash Prescott.

"See, the thing I can't quite shake is why you're even working here," Nash drawled, blocking the elevator doors from closing with his body. "You're filthy rich. You were born with a spoon in your mouth, and it fed you opportunity after opportunity. It's almost as if you have an ulterior motive for working here. Maybe someone asked you to?" He cocked a brow, crossing his arms. "Maybe you're working here to get close to me?"

Confusion tipped my brows together. I had no idea what he was talking about, but he was high if he thought I would admit how far I had fallen.

Needing a job didn't shame me.

Needing one from Nash?

That was a knife in my gut.

One I couldn't pull out.

It kept twisting, the wound festering with each passing second.

I stepped closer to him, forcing him out of the elevator's trajectory with my movements. The doors began to shut behind me, but I ignored them. "Is this the part of the day where we make up conspiracy theories and accuse each other of ridiculous things? Fun. I would grade yours a D at best."

My sweats slipped lower, showcasing the top of my panties. I didn't move to lift them.

He took a step toward me, but I met him head-on. We stood foot-to-foot. Nose-to-chest. I could feel his breaths on me. Could smell him all over me.

It was like that night in the shower, except no glass separated us.

And I wasn't naked.

But fuck, I wanted to be.

Do it, Emery.
Hate-fuck him out of your system.
He's a poison, and the only cure is to suck him out.

"Don't stare at me like that." Nash's voice caressed my face and lured me in like a fishing reel.

"Like what?" Somehow, we had reached an unspoken agreement to speak softer, cocooned in the privacy of this unfinished floor.

No doors on the frames.

No paint on the walls.

No furniture on the carpet.

No witnesses.

"You're staring at me like you want to get fucked. It's not happening." He edged closer, and it was just enough to make contact. My chest pressed against hard abs. Despite my height, he towered over me. "In case you haven't noticed, Jailbait, I don't like you. I don't even hate you. You are as insignificant as your teenybopper friends."

"Hide behind your words, Nash. Use them to feel good about denying you want me, but this is happening." I inched closer, a tiger tracking her next meal. "You look like you want to touch me, Nash. Do it," I dared him. *Let me ruin your reputation.* "Take off that leash."

Inside, I shook.

I hadn't considered the consequences of an unleashed Nash. Ire darkened the moss-colored flecks in his eyes. Two storm-struck irises punctured my sanity. If he wanted, he could snap me in two and leave my body for the construction team to discard.

They wouldn't say a thing because fear and power are conjoined twins—unable to travel without the other.

Nash didn't move.

Didn't blink.

Didn't breathe.
I needed to him to fuck me.
I needed to ruin him back.

My bags slipped from my fingers, and I jumped on him before he could respond.

He caught me. Probably on instinct. Two large palms gripped my waist. I wrapped my legs around his back before he could second guess this. I needed him out of my system. I needed to scratch this itch until it bled and bruised and scarred.

Until I had something inside me that matched the battle scars on his torso.

Nash could say I didn't matter to him, that he hated me, or even that I wasn't important enough to hate, but it didn't change the pesky little fact that he wanted me.

His erection hit me through my clothes, proving my point.

Had he been hard this whole time?

I rubbed against it, my fingers digging into the hair at the nape of his neck as I panted against his lips.

"Fuck." He pushed me down harder on him, grinding his cock between my thighs. "I can't figure out what's worse—that you're twenty-fucking-two, that you're my brother's best friend, or that my mouth has never touched your pussy."

I leaned forward for a kiss, but he pulled his head back, eyes hard.

He enunciated his words. "I. Don't. Kiss."

It occurred to me that he hadn't kissed me that night in Reed's room either. Suddenly, all I wanted from Nash was a kiss, but it couldn't happen.

He towered over me like a villain. Scathing eyes. Midnight hair. Locked jaw.

I hated him for being right. Kissing him would be too

intimate for what we were. I needed a dirty fuck. Filthy. Raw. Something I could remember ten years from now as I laid beside a man I loved.

My lips tingled with need, lusting to be traced by his tongue, but he never would.

Didn't mean I had to take it lying down.

"You also said you won't fuck me, but here we are." I jutted my chin up, refusing to show him he had dug beneath my skin and affected me. "Our second time."

"I'm not fucking you." He palmed my ass, gripping it tight. His nails dug into it. "I'm about to ruin you. If you know what's best for you, you'd take your vanilla ass to the elevator and go to work like a good girl. If you stay, you will never recover."

"Ruin me, Nash. Do your best."

I'll ruin you back, and you won't see it coming.

I bit my lip until it bled, holding back a whine as he set me down. When I looked around, I realized he had walked us past a doorless threshold and into an unfinished suite. Construction materials bunched on a table in the corner, fresh low-pile carpet covered the floor, and unassembled cabinets laid stacked in the far corner.

Nash slipped his suit jacket off, tossed it onto the carpet, and slid off his belt. "In ten years, when you're laying in bed next to your boring husband with the cookie-cutter day job, fingering yourself to the memory of how fucking hard I made you come, remember you begged for it."

He stalked toward me with the long strap of leather between two tightened fists.

Nash was the sky moments before a storm.

Daunting.

Dark.

Beautiful.

I backed up until my butt hit the wall-to-wall, floor-to-ceiling windows. Behind me, dozens of people lounged on the beach—laughing, reading, unaware. If they looked up a level, they'd see our dance, a princess and her dragon. The idea of getting caught left me soaking wet. I wanted to dance in Nash's fire until I burned as hot as he did.

My fingers fumbled against the window, remembering the privacy coating still sat in the warehouse. "They can see us."

He didn't budge. "Nice view."

"*Nash.*"

"Strip and hold out your arms... or we can leave."

Heat pricked my cheeks. I kicked my shoes off. They flung across the room, clattering against the table of tools. My socks went next, followed by my sweats. I stood in front of Nash in my panties and t-shirt.

No bra.

Just false bravado and my *selcouth* shirt as my armor.

It wasn't desire that led me to obey him. It was defiance. I refused to back down, refused to show him I feared the reaction he garnered from me. That this would be done, and I would still want him.

Nash cupped his erection through his pants, rubbing at it as he nodded at my panties. "Those, too."

I slid them down my legs until all I had on was my shirt. The breeze felt cold against the lips of my sex. I crossed my legs but stopped when he *tutted*.

"You go first," I managed. My voice sounded hoarse. Unused.

He laughed at me. Actually laughed. "You're not in a position to bargain for what you want."

He was right.

I had initiated this, and if I wanted it to continue, I needed to hand him control and suffer the consequences.

Why do you want this, Emery?

Morbid curiosity.

The type that kills.

I needed to confirm our connection the first time was a fluke. Then, I could move on with my life in peace.

Itch scratched.

Problem solved.

Nash undid his tie and loosened his collar. "Part your pussy lips and ask me if I like what I see."

Jesus.

I knew immediately this was a bad idea. There was no purging Nash out of my system. I was an addict being given her next fix.

I did as he asked, my insides clenching as my nails brushed against my clit. "Do you like what you see?"

His eyes fixated on my slit. Taking his time, he approached me, reached a finger out, and traced the lettering on my shirt. "Selcouth. Do you think you are wondrous, Emery?"

I didn't answer, but my hips jerked forward at his words. He knew what selcouth meant, and I didn't think I could be more turned on.

"Or," he continued, his fingers brushing my nipple over my shirt, "perhaps you think you're rare."

"I think no one is rare." I shook my head, unable to focus on my response. He took turns teasing my nipples. "No one is special. Everyone just wants to be."

It was perhaps the realest thing I had ever said to anyone but Ben in a while. Too real for this moment. This was supposed to be raw, ugly, filthy, fuck-it-out-of-my-system sex. This was not supposed to be an interview with Oprah.

Part of me wanted to demand that he fuck me already, but I wouldn't. I refused to play into his hand.

He wanted to draw this out.

Tease me.

Make me beg.

Prove to me I wanted him and not the other way around.

And at the end of the day, after we finished worshipping each other's bodies, both equally panting, both sweaty, both spent—he would somehow come out the victor. I knew this, but I wanted him anyway.

"Tell that to the millions of dollars in revenue Prescott Hotels brings in annually from birthday events alone." Nash's fingers drew mine back to my pussy when I tried to remove them. Together, we trailed a path down the slit. "Open them. Hold your fingers still. Beg me to run my tongue from your pussy down to your ass."

"Birthdays are a lie," I said, ignoring half of his orders. I held myself open for him, feeling too naked in front of his perusal, but I refused to beg. I wouldn't give him that satisfaction. The room had no door. Anyone could walk in and see Nash fully clothed as I spread my lips for him. "Society gives you this day to celebrate, and you're supposed to feel special and unique on it, but the truth is, statistically, you share your birthday with twenty-one million other people, and *that* is what's special. The threads that tie people together are what should be celebrated."

He agreed with me. I saw it in his ticked jaw and the way his fingers paused at my hipbones, skimming just beneath my shirt. They dug into my skin for a second before releasing. Tiny indents marked the flesh.

"Selcouth..." He tore my shirt down the middle until

the two halves hung loosely on my frame. "Your shirt is a lie, and I hate lies."

He didn't give me a chance to respond.

He whipped me around, pressed my front against the window, and bound my wrists behind my back with his belt. My breasts were on display for everyone at the beach.

I prayed no one would see.

I prayed everyone would see.

Desire played tricks on my mind. I didn't know what I wanted, but I knew I would go crazy if he didn't make me come now.

His palm landed on my ass. Twice. Not giving me a second to collect myself. "I told you to beg me to run my tongue from your pussy down to your ass, Emery."

He was a storm, chaotic and volatile.

But I never ran from storms.

I chased them.

"Stop pretending I'm the only one who wants this," I ground out, hating myself for arching my back, giving more of my ass to him. "I won't beg."

"Fine. Then, you won't come."

My wetness trickled a path down my thigh. I couldn't see him, but I knew he saw it. The awareness pricked at my cheeks, coloring them. He dipped a finger between my legs from behind, ran my wetness up and down my slit, and dragged it to the hole no one had ever touched before.

I instinctively clenched at the contact. "What are you doing?"

Nash stepped back, not answering. I turned my head, tracking his path to the unfinished cabinets in the corner. He picked up the cabinet knob, the one Ida Marie and I had insisted resembled a butt plug.

Anticipation filled my stomach, but I felt compelled to refuse for my dignity's sake. "No. Whatever you're thinking of doing with that, no."

Would he really slide a cabinet knob up my ass? The prospect drew deep breaths from me until they fogged the glass.

"Are you telling me you don't want this?" He approached me from behind, tilted my chin until I stared out at the crowd on the beach, and traced the knob's cold metal down my slit. It slid across my skin easily, so wet and smooth and cold.

Goosebumps peppered my arms. My heavy pants pressed my nipples harder against the glass. I needed to slip my fingers between my legs and relieve the ache, but my bound hands refused to budge.

"This isn't a boardroom, Emery. You're in no position to negotiate. You either want me as I am or you don't. Make your choice, because I won't offer you a second chance."

I swayed a little, running my nipples along the glass as I considered this. He stepped closer to me, his breath fanning my neck.

"Now or never, Jailbait." Nash pressed the pad of his thumb on one of my asscheeks and pushed, inviting air against my hole.

I knew the moment the game ended.

He won.

I lost.

Tale as old as time.

Nash didn't play fair.

Never had.

Never would.

"Now," I whispered, but it felt like a death sentence.

My body didn't get the memo.

I tingled in anticipation, every nerve ending alert. Like most things involving Nash, I expected to hate it as much as I loved it. I expected to toss and turn over it at night. To recall every touch, every moment, every breath.

I expected to *obsess*.

"Good girl." He palmed my ass. "Arch your back and give me your ass."

I pushed it out, pressing my breasts so hard against the glass that my nipples stung. The heat of the sun warmed my skin, yet my nipples formed pebbles against the window. I startled as he trailed the knob up and down my slit again.

Nash bent behind me, not giving me a second to recover before he ran his tongue from one entrance to the other.

"I wonder how all your lies will taste," he whispered against my slit before burying his tongue inside me.

I fought against the belt and screamed out his name. "Nash!" I was moaning. Shaking. Coming apart for a villain who had buried his soul in my past. "Oh, God. I'm so close."

We had barely begun, yet I was near completion.

So needy.

So innocent.

So inexperienced.

His jailbait.

Nash *tsked*. "You don't get to come on my tongue."

I almost whimpered when he pulled back, but he replaced his tongue with the knob, using my wetness to coat it before he slid it slowly into my backside. My breath sucked in at the intrusion.

It felt cold.

Full.

Tight.

He eased it out a little before sliding it back in, a little further this time. Again, and again, and again, until he filled me up, a devil fixated on ruining me.

"Straighten up," he ordered.

I released a breath and obeyed, gasping at how full my ass felt. His palm landed on my ass with a smack.

"Nash," I managed, clenching around the knob, panting for him.

"Turn around." He stepped back from me, waiting as I obeyed.

My movements dragged. I took my time turning. Nash's fingers dipped between my folds again, brushing against my nub before he slid three fingers inside me at once. My head sloped down to rest on his chest, finding refuge against an immovable mountain.

He surrounded me.

His body.

His scent.

His lust.

Just pure *him*.

And I was close as he slid in and out of me, curling his fingers at a spot I could never find myself. "Please, Nash."

He halted at the sound of my pleas, ignoring my desperate whimper. "Tell me what you say when you mutter under your breath."

Lust fogged my thoughts, or I would have marveled over him noticing my quirks. Noticing me.

"Nash, I need to come. Please." I wasn't here for a heart-to-heart. I was here to purge him from my soul.

Nash slid his hand in and out, so slow, occasionally pressing against that spot. "Tell me."

He was ruthless, and I was silent.

Then his palm pressed against my clit, and I'd had enough. "I don't know! Okay?!" I shouted, wishing I could grip his shirt and beg him to end my suffering. "It's different each time. Magic words. Words that make me happy. Words on my shirts. Words on my mind. Words that matter. Words that don't. Satisfied? Make me come, please."

He did, lowering his mouth to my neck and sucking so hard I knew he would leave a mark. His fingers went crazy inside my pussy. They twisted against my walls, thrusting in and out. He curled them into a hook and pressed exactly where I needed him.

I moaned loudly as I came, not caring if the whole office heard me and rushed down from the fifth floor. I was late to work, exhausted, irresponsible—and so, so satiated that none of it mattered.

Nash pulled out as soon as I shattered around his fingers, leaving my body aching at the emptiness. The echoes of the orgasm forced my walls to clench emptiness, throbbing against the knob that filled my ass.

"Get on your knees," he demanded, not waiting for me to recover. "Beg me for permission to suck my cock and swallow my cum."

The post-orgasm euphoria fogged my mind, reducing me to nothing but need.

I forced myself to stare him in the eyes as I knelt. He looked lethal. A dangerous fantasy confronting reality. Every death-defying moment condensed into a single person. Something that sounded like a human, breathed like a human, but couldn't possibly be human. He was so much more.

With my knees on the floor, I squeezed my thighs together, desperate to find relief. The movement made the knob feel tighter in my ass, drawing a tiny moan from me. It had been so long since I had been touched, and he was torturing me for the hell of it.

"May I suck your cock?"

My tone suggested he could go to hell. I sealed it with a taunting smile, unbelieving of how wet I was. He narrowed his eyes and waited for me to continue.

Shit.

Was I really going to ask this?

Was this really my kink or was I just desperate for Nash?

Both, I decided and submitted to his will.

"May I swallow your cum?"

"Fuck."

A mutter.

He looked like he couldn't believe he had let it slip out.

Or maybe he couldn't believe I had actually asked that.

Neither could I.

His face remained frozen in a scowl, like he was fighting himself. Two hazel eyes glistened with irritation. That defined jaw clenched. Our eyes met and held, his defiling mine, stripping me down to nothing.

Nash recovered first, unzipping himself. Instead of removing his shirt and sliding the suit pants down, he pulled his erection out and ran his palm down the long, thick length. "Open."

I parted my lips, slipping the tip of my tongue out. He traced my lips with the head of his cock. Pre-cum smeared across the sensitive skin before he suddenly slid in as far as I could take him.

"Shit," Nash cursed.

My wrists bit against the belt, needing to place two palms on his thighs and steady my body.

He slid out slowly. His eyes fluttered shut before they popped open, meeting mine. He thrust back into my mouth and hit the back of my throat. I struggled to take as much of as him as I could, but I wanted to prove to him I was more than he thought I was.

It shouldn't have mattered, but it did.

"So fucking good." He ran a palm through my hair, clutching the messy strands and gripping onto them in a way that hurt so nice. "That's it, baby. Take my cock."

His groans lit me up. I hollowed my cheeks, sucking as hard as I could, pushing as deep as my body allowed.

When I moaned around his cock, he growled, "You only ever get wet for me, don't you?"

Yes.

But he couldn't know.

Even when I spoke to Ben, it was Nash I pictured as I'd touch myself. Nash I'd imagine as I came.

Nash, Nash, Nash.

He invaded my mind, all because of one night I couldn't wipe from my memory.

I hated his control over me. He didn't need it. Probably didn't even want it. But he had it. A gift I couldn't pry out of his fingers even if I tried.

So, I shook my head—or tried to, but his thrust stopped the movement.

"Such a liar." Two palms pressed the back of my head until my nose dug against his skin and he slid down my throat. Nash thrust into my mouth again, deep and long, before he pulled out and stroked his length. "Open your mouth, my devious liar."

He gave me half a second before jets of cum shot out at me. I barely parted my lips in time to catch them. It fell down my chin and dropped onto my chest.

"Don't swallow yet." He stepped forward to trace the cum on my chest around a nipple. "Let me see."

I opened my mouth. His essence still filled it, the taste something I savored. Nash's chest rose as he took in the sight. Disheveled hair. Harsh eyes. Defiant stance. He looked like he felt—a nightmare disguised as a dream.

Leaning down and reaching behind me, he released me from the restraints and nudged my jaw closed with a single finger.

"Look at me as you swallow."

I tilted my chin up to face him. We held eye contact as his cum slid down my throat. My poor heart battered my chest at the look of satisfaction unfurling across his face.

"Tell me how I taste, little Tiger."

Like a god.

"I've tasted better."

"Pretty little liar." His thumb traced the length of my jaw and tilted my chin up until I couldn't look away. "You suck cock like a good girl, but everything else from your lips is so, so bad." Full lips met my temple and dragged down until they pressed against my ear. "Do you want more?"

My palms fell to his chest, yearning to scratch away his shirt and dig into his smooth skin. "Yes."

So quiet, I wondered if he had heard it.

I didn't want to repeat myself. He had carved my resistance. A rose without her thorns, naked and yielding.

Nash dragged a finger past my collarbone, between my breasts. "Do you want my cock inside you?"

"Yes."

Another whisper.

"How badly? Tell me how badly you want my cock. Tell me how you want me to fuck your tight, little pussy."

I should have processed the glint in his eyes as he said it. It reeked of ulterior motives. The face a grandmaster made seconds before he said, *checkmate*.

Instead, I latched onto Nash, cursing the fact that everything with him was a challenge.

A test.

I refused to lose.

"Rough." I dug my nails into his chest and scraped. I wanted to leave a mark, like the scars that adorned his torso. Mine would be shaped like me—wild and unforgettable. "Hard. Like it's the first and last time you'll ever touch me."

He laughed then, the sound deafening so close to my ear. "I told you we're not fucking. And unlike you, I'm not a liar."

In the time it took to exhale, I had already lost. He was past the doorway, leaving me in my ripped shirt, cum dripping down my thigh and a knob in my ass.

This was supposed to cure me of my fixation.

It had only made it worse.

chapter TWENTY-SIX

Emery

My mood worsened as the day progressed. I told Nash to go to hell, and by the time I cleaned up, changed, dropped my bags off in my closet, and arrived to work two hours late, Nash was typing away at his laptop with the rest of my coworkers.

Apparently, hell was my office.

He cocked a brow as if to say, *and where have you been?*

I had been joking when I accused him of stalking me.

but maybe he actually was. He had made himself at home in the office, replacing one of the computers with his own laptop, taking up the entire desk as if he owned it.

He does own it, Emery. Given the state of your trust fund and how desperate you are for work, he basically owns you, too.

God, trying to screw Nash had been a horrible idea, like taking on the Avengers armed with an unloaded gun. I pulled out my phone and typed a message to Ben.

Durga: Newsflash—you give horrible advice.

I deleted the text without sending. Guilt gnawed at my stomach. A—Ben usually nailed every piece of advice he delivered. B—screwing Nash out of my system would have worked if he were anyone else *but* Nash, the one guy on Earth to take more pleasure in turning down a no-strings-attached hook up than wild sex.

Pocketing my phone, I eyed everyone. Cayden's desk was too messy for anyone to justify booting him from it, so Chantilly sat on the couch I normally shared with Ida Marie and Hannah.

No one explained why Nash was here as I entered, the silence so opposite of what this place resembled sans dictator Nash.

I dropped my Jana Sport at the foot of the couch and leaned down to hug Ida Marie. "Sorry that I'm late, y'all. Some asshole wouldn't let me into the elevator, and then I had to stop by the, um, restroom."

Lame as far as excuses went.

I was off my A-game, stealing glances at Nash every few seconds and trying not to be obvious about it. He didn't look up at me. In fact, he typed away at his laptop as if nothing had happened.

"Pay dock." Chantilly pointed to the coffee table with her chewed-up pen, not bothering to offer me her attention.

I took a seat on the floor, wondering if I had stepped into the Twilight zone. I pulled out my sketchbook to begin drawing portrait ideas for the C-level suites. As soon as my sketchbook hit the coffee table, a stack of folders fell above it like Jenga pieces collapsing.

I counted down from ten, bit my tongue until it bled, and finally looked up at the jackass who had thrown the papers down. "Yes?"

Nash wore the same bespoke suit. His hair no longer stuck up in several directions, but his eyes remained wild, caged by a thinning veneer. I studied him for signs I had company in this lust.

How easy it had been for him to leave me etched doubt into my brain.

His tongue against my collarbone.

His fingers curled inside me.

His cock pressed against the back of my throat.

None of it seemed to faze him.

But to me, touching him was a song on repeat you couldn't forget. Each touch—the beat. Each orgasm—the bass. Each demand of his—the lyrics.

Beg for me.

Suck my cock.

Swallow my cum.

A song that never got old.

"I need copies of these." His eyes snapped to the Bvlgari watch he never would have been caught dead wearing four years ago. "Two each."

I skimmed the papers. Half of them had been typed

in a foreign language. The word Singapore stood out to me, along with Delilah and Nash's names.

"I'm not your assistant." When I swiped them off the table, the papers floated to the carpet like dead leaves. I wanted to step on them and watch them crumble. "Do it yourself."

"Check your contract."

Nash didn't bother to pick up the papers. He pulled out his phone, and I just *knew* he was playing Candy Crush. I doubted he played for the game, but for the pleasure of pissing people off. Another tool in an arsenal that resembled the U.S. Army's.

He continued with his game, adding, "You'll notice clause forty-two, subsection C clearly states each employee may have added job responsibility in the company's time of need. I am the company, and I am in need."

I waited for a sign he was bluffing.

Wishful thinking.

He could bluff, but he'd never break.

The contract had been ridiculously long, and it would have taken me a month to go through it in detail. I skimmed it as best as I could, but it had been lawyer-speak, and Reed assured me it was a standard form every employee had to sign.

Fuck. Me.

We didn't have printers in this temp office. Where did he expect me to go? Did Kinko's still exist?

Nash continued, "There's a coffee shop next to the printing center on third street." Fishing out his all-black credit card from *my* wallet with fingers that had just been inside me, he tossed it onto the stack of papers. "I'll make it easy for you this time, seeing as your level of competency sits somewhere between a lobotomized pigeon and the dip-shits who wrote *Disaster Movie*. Dark roast. Black. Largest size."

Picturing his torture, I collected the papers from the floor and the company credit card, taking my sweet time. I used his company card to buy everyone at the tent city Chipotle, myself new jeans to replace the pair I'd left in his room, his damn paper copies, and the coffee (decaf because he didn't deserve to be caffeinated).

I shot a text to Ben on my way back.

> **Durga:** Does North Carolina have the death penalty for murder?
>
> **Benkinersophobia:** Yes, but you can take out your aggression through angry phone sex tonight. My balls are bluer than a whale's.
>
> **Durga:** Whales have pink balls, and they weigh, like, one ton. At the very least, I hope you're proportional.
>
> **Benkinersophobia:** Durga?
>
> **Durga:** Yes?
>
> **Benkinersophobia:** Shut up and fuck me tonight.
>
> **Durga:** [GIF of Chris Pratt thrusting]

Nash was still in the office when I returned after changing into the new jeans and dropping my sweats off in my closet. Except this time, he had begun a meeting without me.

I snuck in and sat next to Ida Marie, resisting the temptation to crawl my way there on the zero-point-zero-zero-zero-one-percent chance he wouldn't see me.

No such luck.

Nash glanced at his watch before ignoring me. I set his copies and coffee down on the table, took my seat, and whispered—in my defense, discreetly—to Ida Marie, "What is he doing here? I thought he wasn't supposed to show up until we had the 3D renderings done and ready for his approval."

That should have given me at least a week without seeing him.

Ida Marie scribbled across her notepad in indecipherable strokes. "Chantilly just announced that he'll be helping with the workload."

"Couldn't he hire someone local for this project?"

My notebook sat at the bottom of my Jana Sport. Rather than fetch it, I leaned back and studied Nash. He ran a hand through his hair, messing it up. Fifteen years of knowing him, and that was the single habit I ever noticed.

Ida Marie dipped her shoulders and fidgeted with the notes she'd been taking. "Maybe he's one of those involved C.E.O.s?" Even she didn't sound convinced, and a felon dressed in a bright orange jumpsuit could swindle her out of her wallet. "I'm sure there's a good reason. You don't think we're in trouble or anything, right?"

"No."

But there had to be a reason. I remained on high alert. Nash plowed through request after request, ordering us around like a drill sergeant. He held up the fabric swatches and sorted through them before settling on the one I liked the least.

I mean, I disliked all of them. I thought this make-the-hotel-as-bland-as-possible thing was a huge mistake, but what did I know? I only had a major in fashion design and a minor in interior.

"This color contrasts with the flooring." He seemed hollow as he spoke, almost detached in a way that made me question why he had chosen the hotel business in the first place. "We had a similar color scheme in our Beijing location, which was featured in an hour-long *Hotels Digest* film. It's also a AAA Five Diamond Award recipient."

Somewhere in the past four years, the passion had seeped out of him, a leaky faucet of enthusiasm. This wasn't the Nash Prescott who walked around with bruised knuckles and a look in his eye that suggested he knew something I didn't.

Working at Prescott Hotels bored him. A daily chore. I never thought Nash Prescott would be the type to sell out.

I must have been making a face, because he asked, "Is there something you'd like to say, Miss *Rhodes*?"

I mulled over an answer before settling with, "Oh, I don't think that's a good idea."

Translation: you're not gonna like it, so let's not continue this war in public. Blood is a bitch to get off low pile, polypropylene carpet.

Say it. I dare you, his eyes challenged me.

Chantilly's eyes, on the other hand, screamed with warning, and if she could have strangled me without ending up in a six-by-eight cell, I was sure she would have... but because I had never been one to pass up a good dare, I spoke my mind.

"Your 'vision'—and I use that term loosely—feels like a sell-out. Yeah, your company's brand is this bougie, ritzy bullshit, but you've never been." *Fuck.* That sounded like I knew him. "I mean, your brand originally wasn't," I corrected, my voice sharper than an ice crusher. "Your first location in Bentley, South Carolina had style. It screamed class without the side of boring. Haling Cove is a college tourist trap. Your clientele may be wealthy, but they're also young. This is your opportunity to finally do something that isn't total Arnault-Koch-and-Mercer-style bullshit."

Silence.

Would have been blissful had my heart not been pounding so hard, I swore I was seconds away from a heart attack. Horrible figure of speech, given the audience, but I felt no sympathy as Nash stared at me like he wanted to storm over here and...

I didn't know.

Strangle me?

Bend me over his knee?

Seems legit.

"You're right," he began, his eyes finally, *finally* alive. It thrilled me to bring the spark there, which should have been a sign to back off. He'd already made me beg him to fuck me then left me hanging. What more could he do? "This is North Carolina. Maybe hotel guests will be turned off by the aesthetic. We want less Winthrop Scandal and more friendly neighborhood billionaire. Any suggestions?"

I could have killed him, picked apart his eyes, and fed them to the coyotes. "We need a focal piece for the lobby. It needs to be large enough to take up the entire center of the lobby. It also needs to be something that draws attention to justify the minimalistic design points. We want it to be a conversation starter, too. It's the only thing that will save this hotel from being a total snooze fest."

Chantilly raised her hand before speaking. "We can't afford a focal piece. We have to stay on budget. We already bought some of the fixtures, flooring, and paint in the current color scheme," she slanted her gaze my way, "so I strongly suggest we ignore Emery's idea."

Nash twirled a pen in his fingers, so uncaring about this hotel, it bothered me. "I guess Winthrop Scandal it is."

Chantilly droned on about her overpriced ideas.

Ida Marie leaned into me and whispered, "What's the Winthrop Scandal?"

"Just another case of an asshole stealing from the little guy," I replied, thankful none of my coworkers came from the South or had picked up a Financial Times article ever.

Not that I had been the face of the scandal.

Dad had.

Still.

I couldn't control my heartbeats. They consumed my poor chest, thudding a fierce rhythm worthy of a Carnegie Hall drum solo. It felt like Big Foot had laced up his Nikes and started running a marathon inside me.

Keep your shit together, Emery. Small minds come attached to big mouths. Look at Chantilly's flapper go. Does someone who spent a chunk of the dwindling budget on cabinet knobs that resemble butt plugs seem like the type of person who could piece together your identity?

"Oh." Ida Marie doodled on the margins of her notebook as Chantilly wrapped up her bullshit defense of her design. "I hope he went to jail."

Nope, just living in a beach-side cottage in a small North Carolina town. Dad emailed me postcards once a week. I never replied, but sometimes, when I felt particularly masochistic, I would stare at the pictures and wonder how he fared living somewhere that couldn't fill a high school gymnasium. Eastridge's population nearly doubled Blithe Beach, and still, gossip in town moved like a cheetah prowling for prey.

I wondered how far Nash would take terrorizing me. I had figured out his game. Reed hated Nash, but Nash didn't hate Reed. That had to be the reason I still had this job. I threaded Reed and Nash together, and to cut me would be to cut their already strenuous relationship.

Nash continued, ignoring me, "I expect the 3D renderings to be done by the end of the weekend, so we can begin finalizing purchases and move on to the artwork for the suites. This is not some cookie-dough-latte and chocolate-jalapeño-croissant-serving coffee shop you can smoke a joint behind. Slow and mediocre work will not be tolerated."

"Chocolate jalapeño croissants. So gross, am I right?" Chantilly stepped beside him, her knee bumping into the back of my head as she scrambled off the couch. Two palms clapped together, rally girl style. "We'll begin with your penthouse suite first, Mister Prescott, then the presidential suite Mrs. Lowell is currently staying in. Do you have any requests?"

"Keep the same color palette for the penthouse and presidential suites. The presidential suite should stay in line with the aesthetic of the hotel, since it will be booked by guests." Nash pulled out his phone, his wandering attention further confirmation he gave no fucks about this project.

"I think I have a good idea of your tastes." Chantilly crept closer to Nash and tried to peek at his phone. "I was on the team that designed your New York City penthouse. Mary-Kate let me lead that project."

"Right." The light of the screen lit up his bored features. "My least favorite penthouse. Actually, second. The one in Kuala Lumpur looks like Barney threw up in it, hosted an orgy inside the bedroom, then jizzed all over to reclaim his dignity."

Accurate.

If I liked Nash, I would have fallen back into the couch, laughter tickling my stomach. The pictures of Kuala Lumpur in the online design archives showed a magenta-themed living room and a bedroom with streaks of cum-like white in the bay oak flooring, milk wall paint, and brocade sheets.

"I didn't lead that one in Koala Limper." Chantilly toyed with her hair.

When she smiled, the makeup caked on her face crumbled around the eyes. For a moment, I wanted to draw her in for a hug and tell her she's unbelievably gorgeous where it matters... but then I remembered she had put me on actual time out yesterday for trying to share the elevator with her while she talked on the phone, and the best condolence I could offer her was that she's pretty on the outside.

(For the record, eavesdropping on Chantilly gossiping sat on my to-do list somewhere between skydiving with a broken parachute and swallowing a brain-eating amoeba.)

"Kuala Lumpur," Nash enunciated, lashing us all with his irritation. "It's a city, not some cane-wielding marsupial, Chartreuse. For what I pay you, I expect competence."

So this was what blue balls did to you. Turned you into an insufferable bastard. Nash wore impatience like a second skin sheathed around him. He hadn't glanced at Chantilly once, but she jumped back at the scorch of his wrath.

Maybe after this, she would finally stop whining to Hannah about how much she wanted to be the next Mrs. Prescott. Her dreams included marrying Nash, having his babies, and swapping her design job for a life spent in spas and country clubs.

"Right." Chantilly nodded once and mouthed the city name. "I'll get it next time. Second time's the charm."

"Romanticizing failure." He slid his eyes my way. "The hallmark of the participation trophy generation."

Anyone else, and I would have stood up for her. Even Hannah and her general disdain for poor people would earn my defense. I bit my tongue. Chantilly glanced between us and Nash, her lips downturned. She read the room and swallowed her retort.

Nash pocketed his phone. "If we're done with today's attention-seeking antics, I'm continuing with the aesthetic. The penthouse will not be rented out, so there's more leeway there. I want earth tones in the living room and suite, minimalist furnishings, and a sculpture against the North-facing wall."

Chantilly fidgeted with the hem of her dress and pulled it away from her body. The sequins caught the lighting, reflecting a kaleidoscope of reds across Nash's face, yet he didn't look at her as she asked, "Of?"

"Sisyphus."

"Sisyphus?" It escaped my lips as less of a question and more of a gasp.

Nash's head snapped to mine. He studied me, a dip in between his brows as if he had tried and failed to figure me out. "Yes, Sisyphus. The thief."

"The king," I corrected, feeling defensive for Ben, who for some reason saw a part of himself in Sisyphus.

"No." His face didn't budge. He stood there, an immovable boulder, much like the one Sisyphus had been forced to carry for eternity. I wanted to be the one that chipped at its edges until it cracked and crumbled to dust. "The liar. The grifter. The con."

My dad was a liar.

A grifter.

A con.

He had hurt people. Most importantly, he hurt Nash's dad, and I would always suffer the guilt. Was that what Nash wanted me to know? He saw me the same way as he saw my dad? Was my punishment to search for a sculpture that had somehow become a slur against me?

Worse—the knowledge that Nash considered me a liar, too, chipped away at my sanity.

I raised my chin and didn't waver as I argued, "Sisyphus is a king. A human who rules the winds. Cunning. Intelligent. Brave. A savior, who captured Death and freed humans from his clutches. All things you are not. I can understand why you'd want him as the focal piece of your penthouse, seeing as he is a reminder of the areas in which you are lacking."

I'd gone too far. Broaching the subject of death reached a level of taboo that exceeded the idea of screwing him at eighteen while he'd been nearly thirty. It even surpassed the wrongness of showering in front of my boss and skipping work to fuck him.

"Sisyphus is a symbol of punishment," Nash said easily, fixing his collar. Always adjusting his collar around me. I wondered if he smelled me on his fingertips or if he had washed me away the first chance he had gotten. "Of penance. Some people would do well to remember that, especially before stabbing others in the back."

The dig hit harder than perhaps he had even intended. I had learned long ago that there was no such thing as a truly selfless act. People are hardwired to believe charity is selfless. In reality, charity is giving to yourself by giving to others. That's not selfless. That's penance.

I could make coats for the homeless, spend my free time volunteering, and give every inch of myself until I had nothing left, but there would always be a motive.

To feel better about myself.

To not hurt so much.

To right my wrongs.

To ease the guilt.

I wasn't a good person, and I had fooled myself for too long, trying so desperately to be something my father and mother weren't.

Nash waited for me to answer.

When I didn't, he added, "Sisyphus will be your task. Find me the sculpture and have it placed against my wall. I want Sisyphus carrying the boulder on his back, pushing it up the wall, his expression anguished and the task Sisyphean."

I didn't know what he was trying to tell me, but his eyes showed me all I needed to know.

You are beneath me, they screamed.

And for once, I didn't argue.

Not because I agreed, but because I saw beyond the scathing veneer. Nash was so broken, it was almost beautiful how he had erected walls of thorns and poison ivy around himself.

A haunted castle armed with insults as cannons; two staggering, hate-filled eyes as guards; and a lonely king who never abandoned his throne for fear it would collapse.

And me? I was the fallen princess destined to never step inside his fortress.

For some stupid, foolish, self-destructive reason, I ached at the thought.

chapter TWENTY-SEVEN

Emery

A motor had gone off in my stomach. At least, it sounded like it. A symphony of growls rumbled again, detonating a chain reaction of head turns on the public bus. I wanted to care, but another long day of scouring an art gallery for a Sisyphus statue left me too drained.

I found two statues today at the same gallery. Both possessed the anguish Nash required and the boulder on top of Sisyphus' shoulders, but whereas one depicted defeat, the other depicted success.

My legs had carried my way to an empty corridor as soon as I'd seen the last one, aware I should have reserved the defeated Sisyphus after the hell Nash had unleashed upon me, but knowing I wouldn't.

I hid in the shadows until I collected myself, surprised by how much the statue had affected me. Autopilot led me to the curator. I requested a five-week hold on the statue. Waterboarding couldn't get me to remember my walk to the bus stop, climbing the steps, or taking a seat. Even now, I remained affected by the sheer art.

The bus careened to another stop. I let my body sway with the movement. The four-year-old in the lavender tee peppered with yellow hearts barreled into my body like a bumper car. She readjusted herself into the bright blue plastic chair beside me, dredged a granola bar from her yellow Snow White backpack, and offered it to me.

"Your stomach is loud." She wagged the bar in front of my face with pudgy fingers. It resembled a dog's tail whipping back and forth. "It's my favorite kind."

This is what your life has become, Emery. Twenty-two years of fine etiquette, prep schools, and higher education has led you to the pity and charity of a four-year-old wearing her shirt backward.

"Thanks, sweetheart."

"Lexi."

"Thanks, Lexi." I accepted the granola bar but slid it back into her backpack along with one of the plaid teddy bears I had stitched for Stella.

Relief inched its way across my body. I leaned back, finally free from Nash's Sisyphus task. The past two weeks had been spent traveling from art gallery to art gallery, searching for a statue that fit Nash's description.

This trip placed me too close to Blithe Beach, where Dad lived. Visiting him tempted me, but I didn't cave. I would never.

Still, I yearned like I shouldn't and pretended I didn't, because above all else, I was a talented liar. The email from Virginia idled in my inbox, unread for the past six hours. The alert taunted me each time I checked my phone for messages from Ben.

Hunger pains continued their relentless assault. I watched the girl share the granola bar with her mother. I pretended I was back in elementary school. Reed once tattled to Nash that Virginia never gave me lunch money or packed me food.

Lunches give pretty girls spare tires until they're no longer pretty, she'd say. *Don't you want to be pretty, Emery?*

Nash stopped by our table every day with the brown lunch sacks Betty packed him. He never said anything as he gave up his lunch for me, but he always scratched out the I-love-you notes Betty left him, scrawled something ridiculous on the back, and tucked them back inside the bags.

> *If multi-player dreaming existed, whose dreams would you play in? Yours or Reed's?*
>
> — **NASH**

> *Ma bought an eighteen-pack of socks yesterday. Dad said he didn't know why anyone needed eighteen pairs of identical*

socks. I told him they reincarnated into Tupperware lids every time Ma lost one.

(Then, I asked myself why we have more lids than containers. I know you stole them to paint stories on. Give me one to gift Ma for Mother's Day, and we'll call it even.)

— NASH

❝ Do you ever get more excited about being uninvited somewhere than invited? Like, if Virginia ever asked you to go to a charity gala with a hundred of her closest enemies then uninvited you, wouldn't you be celebrating that ~~shit~~ with a ~~fuck~~ ton of ~~alcohol~~ juice pouches?

— NASH

❝ People get surgery to change the body they were born into, but what if we could change our personalities? If some surgeon walked up to you and said, "I can operate on your brain. Recovery time is about the same as a tonsillectomy, and it's totally safe," would you?

No offense, dude, but I'd give Virginia a personality transplant—along with new *batteries for her heart. Think she'll let Ma take a break after her tonsil removal? Yeah, me neither.*

— **NASH**

> *I saw a cat and his owner playing with a laser yesterday. Think about that ~~shit~~. Lasers used to be this huge ~~fucking~~ scientific breakthrough, and now some ~~dumbass~~ cat lover in a designer knit beanie is using one to drive his cat nuts. If I invented the Tide Pod and had to watch someone swallow it, I'd probably haunt them from the grave.*

— **NASH**

> *Saw some ~~douche jackass~~ turd berate a worker at McDonald's the other day. Could you imagine if Virginia had to work a year at McDonald's? She'd either be more insane or more tolerable. Now that's a thought.*

— **NASH**

I never answered Nash's questions. He never asked me to. But I kept the notes, tucked inside my box in my nightstand at the Winthrop Estate. I hoped whoever bought the house hadn't tossed my things.

The idea of my memories lying in a dumpster frayed my heart. I hadn't realized it back then, but small moments matter most. Millions of raindrops dance together to form a storm, but a single drop is just a tear.

Lonely.

Tiny.

Insignificant.

I couldn't watch Lexi eat her granola without wanting to snatch it and swallow it whole, so I opened Virginia's email as a distraction.

From: virginia@eastridgejuniorsociety.com
To: emeryrhodes@cliftonuniversity.edu

Subject: 4th of July Brunch

Emery,

Allow me to prelude this email by informing you your response is unwanted. I am writing to remind you of the details for the Fourth of July brunch. We'll be celebrating at the country club at ten in the morning. Be on time.

Able Cartwright is dining with us. Remember him? He is lovely, that boy. Last week, he started up at his father's law firm while he continues with his Juris Doctorate. The talent in that family is remarkable. I am sure you would agree if only you'd consider a date with sweet Able.

I will be at brunch, accompanied by your Uncle Balthazar. Unfortunately, Eric Cartwright has left for the South of France with his wife, but every other important Eastridge family is attending. Please, do not embarrass me with your dramatics.

I strongly urge you not to wear that horrible dress with the dead flowers. If you would like, I can have a wonderful Oscar De La Renta dress shipped to your dorm room by sunrise. My team of stylists are mobile and can get your hair back to the shiny blonde halo in under an hour.

Allow me to remind you I control whether or not your trust fund is dispensed to you in a timely manner—or dispensed at all. That said, I expect you to be on your best behavior. Don't be late for tee time.

Sincerely,

Virginia, Chairwoman
Eastridge Junior Society

My head fell against the window with a thud. Virginia still didn't know I had graduated, and she thought I lived in the overpriced dorms. That alone made me want to wear the dress she hated, not to mention the trust fund threat.

With Dad off the grid, Virginia controlled my trust fund payments. Meaning, unless I obeyed every single demand of hers, I wouldn't see a dime of it. I wouldn't blow through the trust fund money if I had access, but at the very least, I would donate most of it, pay off Wilton University and my Clifton University student loans, and spend just enough to keep myself fed and sheltered.

Each time I visited the soup kitchen, I felt like I had taken a meal away from someone who needed it more. But the scholarship fund hung over my head. A parrot who haunted me with the same line.

Squawk! It's the right thing to do.
Squawk! It's the right thing to do.
Squawk! It's the right thing to do.

It would be over soon. One more year, and Demi graduated. I would survive another year of this.

Lola waved at me when I heaved the Jana Sport over my shoulder and bounded down the bus stairs at the next stop. It let off in front of the soup kitchen, a little earlier than I had planned. I tried to avoid peak hours because hungry families came in crowds and caused food shortages.

The crowd lived up to the rumors, filling every table in the cafeteria-style hall. I spotted a familiar flash of color and took a spot in line near Maggie and her kids. She allowed the couple in front of me to cut in line.

I plucked a tray and plate from the rack and slid it down the buffet. Another notch in the conveyor belt.

"Is it always this crowded during peak hours?" I held out the plate to a volunteer.

She dropped a quarter-slice of buttered toast in the middle.

"Always." Maggie helped Stella lift her plate while Harlan waved his around like a flag. "Come to think of it, I've never seen you during a dinner rush. First time?"

My nod tussled my hair until it covered the *atelo-*

phobia printed on my tee. "I try to avoid them, but I had a long day at work and needed sustenance."

"You're in luck. It's turkey today, and they would have run out if you came any later. Plus, the guy serving it is some serious eye candy." Maggie slid her tray down and covered Stella's ears. "I actually think the dinner rushes have been more crowded since he started volunteering because every woman wants an extra side of meat with their protein if you catch my drift."

I craned my neck to see this guy, but the line that snaked around the meat station extinguished any hope of catching him. "Is he nice?"

"He's not very talkative, but the kids love him, Stella especially." She held out her plate for my favorite cheap carbs—canned creamed corn and mashed potatoes. "He's nice to everyone when he does talk, though. It's infectious, like the world waits for him to smile before it can work again."

"So, he's a nice guy." It came out harsher than I'd intended. Bitter didn't suit me, but neither did hunger, a fucked-up boss, or North Carolina. I helped Maggie offer Stella and Harlan's plates before holding up my own. "Doesn't sound like my type."

Maggie laughed at my sly grin, hip-checking me. We moved down the line at a snail's pace. By the time we reached the meat station, my food had grown cold, yet my heart grew colder at the sight of Nash carving a turkey before delivering a generous portion onto a kid's plate like the Food Network's answer to plummeting ratings.

He wore his signature button-down, though the sleeves had been rolled up until the edges of his penance tattoo peeked out. The one I wanted to bite down. To hurt him like he hurt me. His presence consumed more space than his body, and for once, he didn't look ten seconds from killing someone.

Either way, I wouldn't take my chances. My heel inched back, desperate to help me flee before he caught sight of me, but I stumbled into the person behind me.

The noise drew his attention. His eyes landed on me with a precision that scraped goosebumps from my arms. An inquisition in his eyes I couldn't escape. The First through Sixth Crusades compiled in one defeating glare.

I was a Matryoshka doll. He kept peeling at my shells, and I wanted to stop him before he reached the center and realized nothing existed inside of me but air and things that vanished.

One.

Two.

Three seconds was how long it took for him to sneer at me, then turn back to the kid he had been serving as if he didn't know me.

"That was odd," Maggie whispered before Stella skipped in front of Nash, taking the kid's place. "I've never seen him do that. You don't know him, do you?"

"No." I couldn't muster up the guilt that usually accompanied my lies. "Never met him in my life."

"Hmm..." A hint of a smile ghosted her lips. She watched Harlan tell Nash about the dog he'd witnessed peeing all over someone's leg this morning. Humanity suited Nash, but so would a trash bag. "I think he's hotter when he looks angry. I swear, I have goosebumps all over my body."

Me, too.

That was the worst part.

I always had goosebumps around Nash. I didn't know when that had started, but I needed it to end. For starters, he had seen me naked three times and hadn't wanted me any of them.

Nash had turned me down so many times, I had no clue why I still craved him like an addict. He boasted the personality of a rabid dog in heat. And if that wasn't enough, he was probably getting head in the back of a crowded movie theater around the time I learned to brush my teeth.

"Hi, Nash!" Stella reached a hand out toward Nash, wiggling her fingers. "Where's my toy?!"

"Stella!" Maggie clutched onto her shoulder and crouched down. "You can't demand things from people like that!" She glanced at Nash, an apology in her baby blues. "I'm so sorry. I don't know where she learned that."

"But Mommy!" Stella swung side to side, flicking her attention between Nash and Maggie. "Nash says if I want something, I have to demand it. I don't want to be a little britch about things."

"Bitch," Nash corrected, and I wondered if he was born without any tact or if it had abandoned him after his first birthday. "Not britch."

"Oh," Maggie breathed out, her nosed bunched up like she had caught a whiff of something bad. "One—we don't curse. At all. Ever. Two—that is not true. We don't demand things from people. If it's a reasonable request, we ask politely or we don't ask at all. Three," she shifted her focus on Nash, "that's all on you, Nash. I rescind my apology. In fact, I think I might expect one."

Nash smiled at Maggie.

Actually smiled at her.

As in, that nice thing civilized humans did.

Something I refused to call jealousy lashed at my throat, making it difficult to breathe.

Stop, Emery. You don't own him. You don't even like him, and he definitely doesn't like you.

As Nash smiled at Maggie, I decided I didn't like his smile.

I liked his scowl.

His sneer.

His scars.

Even his indifference.

I liked his ugliness.

The slash of his words.

The pain infiltrating his bloodstream.

I liked the parts no one else but me could see, because against all odds, I had fleeced secrets out of him, and now they were mine, too.

I've seen your scars. I'd taste them if you'd let me.

But there Nash was, displaying a human emotion for Maggie without looking human.

He looked like a god, descending upon Earth.

An angel seconds before becoming a demon.

I wanted to scratch my fingers down his face until he lost that smile, then rip his shirt open, point at the constellations of raised skin, and shout, "There! That's the real Nash. Scarred, and broken, and permanently damaged, and definitely not smiling at a woman who deserves a smile from every man."

I also realized I had completely lost my mind, because Nash Prescott gave Freddy Kruger a run for his money in the terrorizing department. He had also made it clear how little he wanted me when he'd walked away.

Nash carved up the rest of the massive turkey and distributed all but one tiny sliver between Maggie, Harlan, and Stella. "Just saying it how it is, Mags."

Mags.

I was going to vomit. Maybe Nash did inspire my gag reflex.

"You are so bad." Maggie shook her head before squishing the three plates onto her tray. "Thank you for the extra portions."

Nash snapped his gloves off, reached into his back pocket, pulled out a crudely wrapped present, and offered it to a squealing Stella. She hopped up and down, doing a happy dance I wished I could enjoy.

"What about me?!" Harlan edged forward on the tips of his toes to get closer to Nash. A rocking chair near its tipping point. Five little fingers gripped onto the edge of the sticky buffet countertop.

"I've got the good stuff for you, Harlan." Nash pulled out *my* wallet, sifted through a bunch of bills (not mine on account of me being broke), and plopped ten hundred-dollar bills onto Harlan's tiny outstretched palm. "Buy whatever you want and give the rest to your mom, so you don't lose it. Alright?"

That money wasn't for Harlan.

It was for her.

For *Mags*.

Morosis.

Solivagant.

Drapetomania.

Magic words that fizzled and died on my tongue.

"Sweet!" Harlan jiggled the bills a little before sliding them into his mom's purse. "Thank you!"

"Nash..." Maggie's voice dipped, her cheeks turning a shade of scarlet I marveled at. "It's too much."

"It's for the kids. Don't worry about it, Mags." Nash slid the wallet back into his back pocket. Civility. Who would have thought he possessed it? "In fact, I don't want to hear any more about it. There's a line."

"Yeah, okay." She nibbled on her bottom lip, peered up at him beneath a curtain of long lashes, then glanced at me. "Will you sit with us, Emery? We'll save you a seat. I'm gonna grab a table before they're all taken and the kids run wild around here."

"Yeah," I promised, reminding myself I was not the person who hated another woman out of jealousy.

Mags.

Maggie left me alone with Nash, the silence enough to undo me. I stared at him. He stared at me. The woman beside me tapped her foot and coughed a few times, probably pissed off about her cold food.

Nash broke the silence first. "Those ten minutes of adulting really took their toll on you. You are a mess."

"Excuse me?"

He ticked a finger, not bothering to keep his voice down. "You snuck into my parents' house and fucked the wrong brother." My face flamed, but I was shocked into silence. He spoke so loud. "You turned down a full ride to Duke with no valid reasons."

Another finger.

"Do you understand how worried my mom and Reed would be if they saw you right now? Or do you simply not care about anyone but yourself? You look like you've spent the past century starving, and newsflash—it's not hot, so you can stop now, Anorexia Barbie. That model has been discontinued. Virginia isn't here to monitor your mouth. Act like an adult. Eat a fucking cheeseburger or ten."

Three fingers.

"On top of being mouthy, you lie to your boss constantly."

Four fingers.

"You took a job at Prescott Hotels that could go to someone who needs the money."

Five fingers.

He ran out of fingers on the hand, but he kept going. Ruthless. "You are so starved for attention that you broke into my penthouse for a shower. You are untrustworthy. A Trojan horse determined to raze my empire to the ground. And now, like a silver-spooned, selfish princess, you are stealing a meal that could feed someone who actually needs it. I'd ask you why, but it would require caring enough to hear your excuse."

If murder was legal, he'd probably strangle me right here. In front of everyone. Or maybe slice me open and hang me upside down to bleed out. He seemed like the type to take pleasure in slow torture.

And still, he had more to say. "I can't even fathom how entitled you must feel that you—"

I cut him off, dipping my voice low, because unlike him, I understood civility, "I don't recall signing up for this TED Talk. For your information, my trust fund gradually pays me. I get one million dollars a year until I turn thirty-one. Then I get two-hundred and fifty-six million dollars in a lump sum."

He picked up that sad sliver of turkey with his bare hand—the same ungloved hand that touched the filthy money he gave Harlan—and tossed it onto my plate. Half of it landed on the counter, absorbing those germs. The other half landed on the mashed potatoes and gravy, splattering my shirt.

"How sad," he bit out, no fucks given. "Only one million dollars. I feel so bad for you, sweetheart. Allow me to make a donation to the Billionaire Heiress Charity Foundation. I'll address it to your nine-figure trust fund.

Be sure to spare a few cents to someone who needs it more—literally anyone else in the world."

Fumes trapped themselves inside my head. The type of anger that gripped my throat and shook the cords until I couldn't speak a word. I swallowed the frustration and counted down from ten.

"You didn't let me finish, asshole. Virginia is holding it above my head, blackmailing me every ten seconds and changing the stipulations of my trust."

My hands shook. I clenched them together and hid them under the counter, because showing him he rattled me was absolutely not an option.

I didn't care if money had always been a sore subject for him.

I didn't care that his parents struggled to put food on the table.

I didn't care that he hated overprivileged Eastridgers who possessed no gratitude for the security their wealth afforded them.

I didn't care that poverty, my dad, and lack of healthcare killed Nash's dad.

I wasn't thinking of that.

I thought of my pride.

Of wasted nights spent tossing and turning over his touch.

Of the delicious lash his words formed against my skin.

Of the way he treated me like I was less than human for being a Winthrop.

Of the way I used to worship him only to be disappointed when he turned out to be a villain.

Of the way I still craved him.

Nash consumed me like the heart of a storm. I was trapped outside with no shelter, forced to endure the relentless battering with no control over when it would stop.

I didn't choose my parents, but I could choose whether or not to bite my tongue, and I sure as hell would not.

Nash's tone was tighter than a coiled wire. "Last I checked, you have two parents, and your excuses are less entertaining than an episode of *Keeping Up with the Kardashians*."

"I haven't talked to my dad in four years."

This made him pause.

For all of two seconds.

Then his face hardened like he didn't believe me, and he finally, *finally* lowered his voice. It made his words sound like a hiss. "And I pay you over forty grand. I understand that's nothing to a spoiled princess who has lived in a gilded castle all her life, but do you have one responsible bone in your body?"

"Yeah. This one." I flipped him off, waving my middle finger in front of his face. I raised my voice, so everyone could hear, "And for the record, it's bigger than your dick and feels better, too."

I pivoted, clutching onto my mustard-colored tray like it was my lifeline. My tongue hurt from biting it, coated in blood and frustration. So many eyes stared at me, but I had never been the type to be humiliated by mass judgment.

No, only hazel eyes and a whip-fast tongue snuck under my skin and unsettled me.

When I glanced down at my food, it felt pathetic.

I felt pathetic.

The turkey taunted me.

It looked dry.

Shriveled.

Lonely.

My spirit animal wasn't even a chihuahua named Muchacha anymore.

It was a dirty, sad slice of turkey that I still intended to eat because I was hungry and desperate and two heartbeats away from calling it quits and running to Virginia with outstretched palms and a leash for her to handle.

But Nash was right about one thing.

I was a princess, and I had traded in my ballgowns for battlefields.

He had started the battle, but I would win the war.

chapter TWENTY-EIGHT

Emery

N ash's taunts stung me, but I ignored him because he didn't deserve mine. He stared at me from his seat at the couch.

Watching.

Waiting.

Never saying a word.

A hunter content to stalk his prey.

My pursuit for the Sisyphus statue had been less of a punishment and more of a reprieve from Nash. Now I was expected to sit in this office all day as he glared at me like he wasn't sure what method he wanted to use to kill me.

I made sure to avoid the soup kitchen during peak hours in the week since our run-in, but I still had to sit in the same room as him during work.

"I'm just saying that you and Nash are always at each other's throats, and I've never seen anything like it. No one stands up to him." Ida Marie's voice was a whisper.

She adjusted her sewing machine. We had taken over Nash's desk to redo hemming on hundreds of textured gray curtains that came cheaper at this length.

"Everyone should," I muttered back. "He's a tyrant."

I'd been born with a spine, and I fully intended on using it. Flowers wilted. Girls didn't.

"A tyrant no one has the guts to stand up to except you." She slanted her head my way, for once looking sharp-eyed. "You either have a death wish or... I don't know. Something."

I fed the thick fabric to the machine, increasing the pressure on the foot pedal, feeling in my element for the first time in ages. "I think you're looking too much into this. I hate bullies, and he's the biggest one I've ever met."

Understatement.

Nash made Hannibal Lecter look like the second coming of Jesus.

Ida Marie had the decency to seem ashamed. "Sorry. I thought maybe... you liked him? He certainly seems taken with you." She released her hands from her curtain for a second, causing the stitch to veer left. "I mean, I sound like I'm five, talking about preschool crushes, but you two are always staring at each other—"

"Yeah, that's a hard no."

In fact, I had done a good job of avoiding one-on-one situations with him since he left without sex.

With the exception of the Soup Kitchen Incident.

I couldn't see the bruises around my neck, but they existed, rearing their heads every time I remembered what it felt like to be judged by someone I'd once respected. Someone childhood Emery considered a savior.

"—but I was reaching," Ida Marie continued. "He's always with Delilah anyway."

I had never talked to Delilah, but I saw her long enough to know she wore a wedding ring on her finger the size of a small country. Nash was a bastard, but he was a loyal and proud one. No way did cheating or being the other man interest him.

Mags, on the other hand, was fair game.

And why the hell did it matter?

Answer—it didn't.

The only use Nash provided me was getting off, and I had Ben for that. Our phone sex the past few weeks had been more intense than usual, like we both needed to exorcise our frustrations by way of orgasms.

Ida Marie peeked at my stitches. Her eyebrows crept up her head. "How are you doing that?"

I lifted my foot off the sewing machine pedal and hovered over her machine, skimming my eyes across her set up. "Your feed throw timing is off. You actually might want to adjust your hook timing." I fiddled with a few buttons, my ass bent over—and I could feel Nash's glare scorching it. "Here. Try that."

"Thank you." She inched her foot onto her pedal until she accustomed herself to the new settings. "I should have minored in fashion, too, instead of going all-in on interior."

"I actually majored in fashion and minored in interior."

"Huh. Why are you working interior then?"

I sat back down at my station, working the fabric under the needle. "No market for fashion designers in this part of town."

I tucked my chin down and focused on my curtain, not bothering to elaborate. Talking about the way I had entered college with stars in my eyes and a dreamer's mentality enforced Nash's accusations that I had fucked up my 'ten minutes as an adult.'

Fashion design made no sense to Virginia. Her argument hinged on my lack of style, but it never was about style for me. Fashion is showing people who you are on the inside because most of them never bother to look past the packaging.

Tell me another way to speak without speaking, and I'll learn it, live it, breathe it.

From Cayden's desk, Chantilly turned off her machine and stalked over to me. "Coffee, Miss Rhodes."

"I'm in the middle of a stitch, and—"

"Coffee. I'm not asking."

Unbelievable.

Chantilly had taken Nash's demands as an invitation to order me around—more than she already had been. Yesterday, I dropped her dry cleaning off and picked the purple Skittles out of her family-sized bag.

"Actually, I think it's time for lunch." Cayden stretched his arms above his head before standing. "Anyone want to grab a quick bite to eat with me?"

Hannah and Ida Marie left with Cayden, but I stayed because I was even broker than usual. This morning, I had sent in the twenty-five-hundred-dollar donation to the Winthrop college fund.

I also didn't want to chance leaving for the soup kitchen only to have Nash head there, too. Safer to suffer in hunger than risk another fight and be banned for life. Turned out, Nash funded most of the meals served there, which meant he owned me in more ways than I knew.

Chantilly hung around the office, waiting for Nash to invite her to lunch. He didn't. She left soon after him, her head dipped down like a five-year-old who didn't get the toy she wanted for Christmas.

My mind shot into overdrive. I fired a text to Reed once I was alone.

> **Emery:** I have to be in Eastridge for the fourth of July. Please gag me and drop me off in the middle of the ocean.
>
> **Emery:** Kidding
>
> **Emery:** Sort of.
>
> **Emery:** I need a ride... Haling Cove is sort of on

the way from Duke, and I happen to know a blonde-haired, blue-eyed best friend who owns one hell of a Mustang...

Maybe Reed could come and be a buffer between me and Able. That scar on Able's head had never faded. Our presence would probably throw him off balance.

Reed: Sure. I'm headed to Eastridge to go yachting with Basil and her family. We leave a few days before the fourth.

Fuck.

I had to go to the art gallery with Nash to view the Sisyphus sculpture and get his final approval. Another thing I dreaded. No way would I show him the triumphant Sisyphus now. He'd get the defeated, depressing one whether it'd been sold or not. I'd make sure of it.

Emery: Gahhh, no. I have something with work.

Emery: I'll figure out another ride. Don't worry about it. Hope you're giving them hell in Durham, Reed.

I set my phone down when a wrapped lump fell to the desk in front of me. A sandwich. The label read Tuccino's, the overpriced delicatessen a block over that catered to women of the Range Rover-driving, toy poodle-holding, flawless-credit-history variety.

Nash stood in front of me, that perma-bored expression glued to his face, staring at me like he expected a thank you.

I didn't touch it.

Didn't thank him.

Didn't do anything but stare at him, face blank, a half-smile on my lips that I knew would taunt him.

In reality, I was flexing the hell out of my stomach, praying it wouldn't growl at the scent of what smelled like pastrami on rye.

Holy crap, I wanted that sandwich.

I also wanted to not be poisoned sometime this century, and I trusted Nash Prescott like I trusted the phrase, "just the tip."

"Eat the fucking sandwich, Emery. You look like ninety-nine percent of your weight is in your tits, and a half-starved preteen under my employment is bad PR."

My fingers pried open the wrapper, holding eye contact with him and loathing that smug expression. I took a slow bite of the sandwich, chewing with an open mouth before I spit it at his foot.

The second it left my mouth, I regretted it.

One, I was hungry. Real hungry. The type of hungry where it felt like my stomach was trying to eat itself.

Second, wasting food made me feel like a shit person. Everyone I knew at the soup kitchen would kill for this sandwich, but my pride never let me back down.

Funny that Nash's mom had been the one to tell me that pride changed angels to devils, and here I sat in front of her devilish son, turning into something that reminded me too much of him.

Nash ground his teeth together, his jaw so ticked, I couldn't help but notice how defined it was. I had it in me to feel bad about wasting the food, but not about spitting it at his foot. He treated me like dirt, second only to Basil Berkshire.

I would not cower in front of him.

Not be his charity case.

Not walk into whatever trap he thought he was setting.

I. Would. Not. Lose.

"Thank you for the sandwich, Mister Prescott." With a smile on my face, I took care in wrapping the sandwich up so the paper covered every inch and tossing it into the trash. "I enjoyed it very much."

I'd enjoy it more if you'd bend me over this table and make me scream or turn around and leave. My grin never wavered. *Take your pick, asshole.*

Nash was wordless as he pivoted and left. As soon as I was sure he was gone, I fished the sandwich out of the trashcan, unwrapped it as carefully as I could, and scarfed it down my mouth in five giant bites.

I would rather choke to death swallowing this sandwich than swallowing my pride.

chapter
TWENTY-NINE

nash

According to Greek mythology, King Sisyphus betrayed Zeus. In return, Zeus ordered Death to chain Sisyphus in the underworld. Sisyphus asked Death to demonstrate how the chains worked, then seized the opportunity to trap Death in the chains.

When he was caught, Sisyphus' punishment was to roll a boulder until it reached the top of a steep hill. Zeus had enchanted the boulder to always roll away from Sisyphus before he reached the top. That condemned Sisyphus to an eternity of useless efforts and unending frustration.

The moral of the story—no one is above penance. Even kings can't escape punishment.

Sisyphus' eternal punishment is also why pointless, difficult, or impossible tasks are described as Sisyphean.

I imagined Sisyphus carrying a boulder in front of me, like I often did when I needed to remind myself penance required delivering. That I would be trapped in this Sisyphean task for life, and even when I accomplished it, I would always suffer knowing I could have prevented all this.

My penance was to deliver punishment to those involved in the Winthrop Scandal.

Gideon Winthrop for embezzling money.

Balthazar Van Doren for co-owning Winthrop Textiles and helping Gideon.

Virginia Winthrop, Eric Cartwright, and Emery Winthrop for knowing or worse—being involved.

The second Dad died, retaliation fueled my nights, turning dreams into revenge fantasies and plotting into an obsession. The first nail in the head would be Gideon. He had been the ringleader, the main owner of the company, so he would be the first domino to topple.

I planned to acquire access to his fortune, then sit in front of him as he watched it bleed dry, knowing the son of a gardener had brought his deliverance. And like a sudden windstorm, he would never see it coming.

The others would suffer after, their penance easy to achieve. Virginia thrived on a life of luxury. Without money, she would wither to nothing. Balthazar and Eric deserved to suffer in six-by-eight cells, which would happen once I turned over the ledger to the F.B.I. or S.E.C. and testified to the two conversations I had heard the night of Emery's cotillion.

The one before—where Gideon and Balthazar

discussed embezzlement and the downfall of Winthrop Textiles.

The one after—where Gideon, Eric, and Virginia argued in the office, Virginia yelling that Emery already knew.

And Emery's penance was supposed to be dismantling her trust fund... If she was to be believed, however, she had no trust fund. I believed her like I believed Mariah Carey sung without autotune.

I considered her involvement. She'd been young at the time, which was why I only intended to relieve her of her trust fund. But she was old enough to know better. To, at the very least, warn Reed, Ma, and Dad. That was all I expected. Instead, she'd kept her mouth shut, my parents lost everything, and Dad lost his life.

No, Emery Winthrop didn't deserve my pity nor my futile attempts to feed her.

I chalked it up to habit. With Virginia forgetting to give Emery lunch money so often, it had become a habit to stop by Reed and Emery's table at lunch and hand her the brown lunch sack Ma packed me.

Now, she was hungry again, and habit had taken over. Worse, she had met with Brandon Vu outside the tent city. A gilded snake in my stolen kingdom.

Maybe taking me down was *her* penance.

After all, she had led an S.E.C. agent to my family's cottage the day of the F.B.I.-S.E.C. raid on the Winthrop Estate. I'd only seen the back of his head, but he wore a windbreaker with S.E.C. printed on it.

Either way, Dick Kremer, the private investigator Delilah hired for me, needed to deliver, or I would level the state searching for answers.

Dick popped a sugar-free Jolly Rancher into his mouth, and I already knew I would dislike him and anything he had to say. I pulled out my phone and shot a text to Delilah.

Nash: Where did you find this guy? Last I checked, Craigslist shut down personal ads.

Delilah: Haling Cove Flea Market. He came with my used tea set. Be gentle. Neither is refundable.

The pad of Dick's thumb swiped at his nose. He clutched the chair handles with that same finger before drawing his eyes away from my penthouse view. "Emery Winthrop has taken out, like, a ton of student loans. Before this, she had a job at a diner in Alabama near Clifton University's campus."

Fika hadn't told me that.

Fika hadn't told me a lot of things.

Dick continued, "She used all of that diner money to pay a company called Atgaila. It's Lithuanian for penance. The company is registered under her name in Lithuania, and other than that, it's like it doesn't exist."

Student loans.

Diner job.

Shell company.

Penance.

I had been given a puzzle with a million pieces, and the biggest one had been hidden. What I did know was, the word penance implied she had done something wrong to atone for. I latched onto that like fingers gripping the edge of a cliff.

"What does the company do?" I finally asked.

"Dunno." Dick scratched his belly, the one he had shoved into an Ed Hardy tee two sizes too small, the gym rat muscles peeking out in a way that was very much obscene.

I rarely raised my voice. Speaking threats at a level volume always worked better than shouting them, but I upped mine a notch or two, because Dick was that type of person. The type that mistook aggression for strength. "How much is it worth?"

He withered in front of me. The two-hundred-and-seventy-pound boxer in the distressed True Religion douche jeans and hot pink Tap Out briefs peeking out actually *withered* in front of me. "I don't know."

"Where is its headquarters?"

"Um, I don't know?"

I wanted to strangle him. "Dick—"

"It's Richard."

"*Dick*, take a break from your Jamba Juice green smoothies, extra-strength steroids, and failed super heavyweight career, and teach your concussed ass how to do its fucking job."

First Fika.

Now Dick.

Un-fucking-believable.

Competence, it turned out, was the Lochness Monster—it never existed in the first place, but people sure as hell liked to say it did.

I pointed to the penthouse door. "Get out."

"But—"

Sliding Emery's wallet out of my pocket, I tossed a few hundred-dollar bills at Dick's stunned face. "Buy yourself a new fucking brain, and get out."

I ran a palm down my face as Big Dick scrambled out of the chair. The door opened but never closed. When I looked up, I caught Fika hovering near the entryway like a confused puppy unsure how to use the stairs for the first time.

Delilah Lowell.

She could never mind her own business.

"Delilah sent you here," I stated, taking in the newfound weight Fika carried.

His tan had returned since I had last seen him. I'd never seen his eyes this crystal clear, too. He wore a fitted purple Henley sheathed over scraggy muscles, but his skin no longer glowed a shade of death.

He paired the same distressed jeans he always wore with Nike slides and red and gold tube socks with the number seven stitched on the sides in white. Even the sallow cheeks I'd gotten used to had filled out.

"Delilah called me last night and said I might wanna make a day trip to Haling Cove." Fika rubbed the top of his head, brushing four strands of stringy blond hair to the side. The Jonas Brothers wig no longer covered his scalp, but he had the same amount of hair as Rosco. He also didn't look tired. "Not much to do for me in Eastridge, so I said, yeah, I'd make the trip. Saw your Ma at the supermarket the other day. She said Reed is coming back to town soon."

I ignored his last comment, slid Emery's wallet back into my pocket, and gestured to the chair opposite of mine, wondering if I had any cigarettes in my desk. I didn't smoke, but I used to keep them around for Fika's visits. "You look like shit, but less shitty than usual."

"The tumors in my lungs are basically gone." He rubbed around his ribcage before taking a seat. "Hopefully for good this time."

I booted my laptop up and searched for Emery's shell company. "Why are you here?"

"I know you paid off my medical bills."

Fika looked two seconds from thanking me, so I cut him off, "It was anonymous."

If I wanted his gratitude, I would have cooked him dinner and complimented his eyes. Never happening in the next ten lifetimes.

"What do you know?" His shrug emphasized how much he had filled out since I'd last seen him. "I'm a good P.I. I'm good at following clues."

"Funny, considering you haven't clued in on the fact that I want you out of here."

I didn't.

Not yet.

I had questions.

He had answers.

"Fine." Fika held up both palms in the universal sign for surrender. "I was only here to say thanks."

I let him walk to the door, searched for any signs of exertion, then stopped him. "Wait."

He did. "Yeah?"

"Emery Winthrop—"

The few wisps of hair on his head flopped forward as he shook it. "I already said I ain't sharing more about the Winthrop family, Nash."

"Let me ask the fucking question first," I bit out.

In front of me, my search for the shell company had come up empty. It would always. Unlike her pigeon-brained mother, Emery had a head on her shoulders. Fika, on the other hand, possessed answers. I needed them.

Fika heaved a sigh before returning to the seat and crossing his legs at his ankles. "Fine. Make it quick."

"Look at you, Fika." I toyed with the business card Brandon had left me a while back. It laid at the edge of my desk since. "Did your doctors swap your chemo drugs with something to grow your spine?"

"You're an ass. You know that?"

Original. *I've only been asked that by literally everyone I've ever met.*

"Shocking revelation. No wonder you're a P.I." I cut to the chase, "Emery Winthrop is paying a Lithuanian shell company around $20,000 a year." My eyes inspected his face, taking the time to search him for signs of distress, a spark of knowledge. Anything. "Do you know where the money is going to?"

He did.

It was obvious.

Stiffened shoulders.

Heavy sigh.

Resignation written between the grooves of wrinkles across his face.

"Yeah." He paused and scrubbed his eyes, aging again before me. "It's for a scholarship fund at Wilton University. The only recipient is this kid. Demi Wilson."

"Who is she?"

"Angus Bedford's daughter."

I leaned forward in my seat until the edge of my desk pressed hard against my abs. "Angus Bedford didn't have any kids."

"He did with his first wife. They divorced while she was a couple of weeks pregnant. She put her last name on the birth certificate over his. He didn't learn until later in life. His ex-wife passed away, and the kid lived with her uncle but went searching for her Dad."

"She find him?"

"When Angus figured it out, he started making trips to New York every weekend to meet with Demi and help pay the bills. Had to stop after he lost everything he invested in Winthrop Textiles. Didn't have the money for the trip or the bills. Life kinda spiraled for him. Then, he..."

"Killed himself," I finished.

The newspapers blamed it on the Winthrop Scandal. I had, too.

Still did.

Emery's involvement, on the other hand, remained fuzzy. Mostly, I couldn't pinpoint her motivations. She reminded me of time—out of reach, always changing, never conforming to my needs.

"Yeah." Fika clutched the chair handles, the same exact spot Dick had after picking at his nose. "Yeah, he did. Shit, this is depressing."

"And Emery is paying for his daughter to go to college?"

"Yeah, Demi's a good kid. They both are. Don't go after Emery, Nash." His hesitation invaded the space between us. "She has no money."

I could list Emery's sins, but I locked my jaw, counted down from three, and said, "She has a massive trust fund."

"She doesn't touch it." He leaned forward until the only thing that separated us was the ebony-stained desk. "I know that makes her an easier target, but don't you dare touch her. You get away with a lot of shit when it comes to me, but I wouldn't be okay with it if you hurt her. Not one bit."

"She knew about the embezzlement while it was happening."

"No way."

"I heard Virginia say it."

She already knows. Why do you think I sent her to that shrink to set her straight?

Word for word, I remembered it.

"Well, you heard wrong." A sigh laced his words, along with a determination I recognized but not on him. "Poor girl can't even afford a damn meal."

My eyes snapped to his. I searched his face, didn't find what I wanted, and searched it again.

I didn't hear wrong, Fika. She met with a fucking S.E.C. agent.

I left that argument out, because if she had, I definitely deserved it.

My brain kicked into overdrive, recalling all the fucked-up things I had done to her because I had thought she was complicit in the Winthrop Scandal.

Being a general dick.

Laughing in her face when she accidentally screwed me instead of Reed.

Stealing her wallet.

Making her buy me coffee with her twenty-dollar bill.

Forcing her to give me the change.

Ripping her photo of Reed in half.

Watching her shower.

Threatening her.

Getting her off when she was barely older than half my age.

Ripping her clothes.

Leaving her naked when we both wanted to fuck each other's brains out.

Embarrassing her in front of her coworkers.

Giving her grunt work.

Depriving her of a meal.

Shit, the list went on, flashes of scenes I'd been able to justify at the time.

Fika's revelation haunted me.

She can't even afford a meal.
And I'd taken one from her.

The thing about revenge is, people feel entitled to it. Being wronged is an invitation to retaliate, but the cycle never stops. I had justified everything I did to her at the time with one sentence—Dad died. My morals didn't exist, though I told myself I thrived on them.

I tried to fix myself by breaking her.

Fika made me promise to leave Emery alone before he left. I didn't remember what I had muttered back, but it must have pacified him because he placed a palm on my shoulder, said something I didn't hear, and left right after.

My new phone hit the wall as soon as the door shut behind him. It clattered to the floor, chunks of glass flying off, the screen looking eerily similar to the one Emery had crushed to pieces.

She can't even afford a meal, and you took her money and publicly shamed her for eating a pathetic slice of turkey. She can break all your damn phones until you die, you miserable bastard.

I stepped on the glass, uncaring that the shards dug into my heels and drew blood. Kicking my broken phone to the side, I stripped off my suit, scattered it to the ground like littered trash, and stood under the shower head. It hammered scalding-hot water onto my scalp and shoulders.

My skin turned red beneath the blaze, but I didn't let myself move. I ground the glass deeper into my skin. Blood drifted from my feet. The dark red faded into the water, diluted to pink, and swirled down the drain.

Two palms pressed against the wall, I studied the floor, placing my feet exactly where Emery had stood when I'd watched her finish her shower. My dick instantly hardened, and I was so fucked up for grabbing it.

Stroking it.
Picturing her.
For the first time in my life, I accepted the truth.
I am the villain in this story.

chapter THIRTY

Emery

Freshman year of college, I realized I would forever spend my life chasing redemption. Finals week came to a conclusion, the winter frost biting my cheeks until they turned a bright scarlet. The paper clenched between my fingers bore a capital A in red marker. It had taken me all semester to write it, the grade a culmination of an entire semester of effort.

I should have been happy.
I should have been a lot of things.

Instead, I walked like a hollowed-out tree, arms swaying with life, but inside a gaping cavity. Dad would have thrown a party and shouted my accomplishments until I hid my face into his side and begged him to stop embarrassing me.

Virginia would have scoffed at our loud, uncouth behavior, but when cocktail hour rolled around, she'd brag about my grades to her friends, tittering when one of them complained about their child's failures.

With the essay clamped in my palms, the weight of loneliness struck me until I ran to the nearest trashcan and dry heaved. Nothing came out. A semester with minimal food had turned my corpse to skin and bones.

Spit flew past my lips. I fell to the concrete and leaned against the sticky can, trying to get ahold of myself. Magic words didn't work. They evaded me, my brain suddenly feeling like a dangerous place to be trapped in.

Ironic that I sought reality on my phone, pulling up Instagram as if it was my sole tether to the real world. No new pictures from Reed. I talked to no one else. Told myself I needed no one else.

Pictures of book spines kept me company, my heart almost seizing at the incoming message alert.

"Die. Just die."

I remembered the words, often rolling them around my tongue, feeling how they formed on my lips with so little effort.

I had gotten death threats in the past, but something about this one felt different.

Two words.

Just and *die*.

The threat shouldn't have given me pause, not after the long paragraphs and soliloquies I had received, creative fantasies of my death that, honestly, deserved to be featured in some Chris Mooney thriller novel.

Blaming Reed seemed like the perfect route whenever I scrolled through a series of messages that should have struck me with their brutality but didn't. I had never been a fan of social media, but one night, Reed had posted a picture of his lips locked with Basil's, and I had caved to masochistic needs.

Basil had always been the one to post pictures of herself with Reed, captioned with hashtags like #Forever, #Soulmates, #DatingTheFootballCaptain, #QB1, and #MineAlways stamped on each one.

But Reed? His feed consisted of the three Fs—food, family, and football, an endeavor to impress college scouts with his dedication. Posting this picture equaled some stamp of approval, a sign of commitment I couldn't ignore no matter how much I wanted to.

I stalked them both for months, following Reed and a few logophile accounts to cover the fact that I had opened a social media account for the sole purpose of stalking my best friend. I posted quotes twice a month, the occasional t-shirt, and one time, a potato from the garden in the shape of Abraham Lincoln's head.

The day after the Eastridge Daily published an article on the F.B.I.-S.E.C. raid, I had woken to death threats scattered across my posts. They ebbed and spiked with the news cycles, reappearing each time something about the case came up.

When the site wrote about the lack of conclusive evidence, I laughed at the names people called my dad, Virginia, and me. Most of them didn't even make sense, proof conspiracies about the case ran rampant or people just plain hated us.

Overprivileged red necks. (Virginia tossed a 14th

century Ming dynasty vase against the butler's pantry wall at that one.)

Succubi of the South. (Virginia dumped her fresh-squeezed kumquat juice into the pool and booked a four-hour-long, deep-tissue massage at an overnight spa.)

Stock Fraud Barbie. (Virginia legit flipped her shit, binge eating her way through a thousand grams of cheap carbs.)

By the time Hank Prescott had died and the threats grew to the worst they had ever been, I had long since abandoned checking my comments and messages. I still refused to delete my account or set it to private because it felt like admitting defeat.

Didn't matter either way.

The threats didn't get to me. Not until Hank died, and I had felt the real-world impact of Dad's theft and the accusations finally held merit. Angus Bedford's death came next, and that brought more nasty comments.

I accepted them all as my new normal, occasionally logging on to Insta and searching for pretty words to pass time. But this message took me by surprise. Not because I felt lonely but because her words felt lonelier.

DIE. JUST DIE.

The sender hadn't bothered to put her feed on private or create a fake new profile like some of the others. It was so simple a threat on a rare moment the Winthrop family had left the news cycle, so it made me curious.

Demi Wilson.
18.
Dog lover.
Car lover.

People hater.

A kindred spirit.

I browsed her feed, learned her life, and found one picture I couldn't forget.

She had her arm around Angus Bedford's shoulders. They stood in front of a classic car with tools sprawled all over the floor. Rain plastered their hair to their foreheads, but it didn't faze their goofy smiles.

The caption: I miss my dad something fierce on rainy days. #RIP

The next day, she apologized, told me she'd been drunk, and said she didn't blame me for my dad's mistakes. I messaged back a cheesy meme of two stick figure eggs hugging that read, "Apology Egg-ccepted."

What I really wanted to say was—Forgiving others is a myth. The only prisoner freed when you forgive someone is you.

It didn't matter if the Winthrop haters ever forgave me, because I would never forgive my family and the way I'd lived a life of privilege, oblivious to the sins that funded it.

I never talked to Demi again, but I checked on her like you would a wild animal in your backyard.

From afar.

Never speaking a word.

Just watching.

Waiting.

Wondering.

Months later, Demi posted her acceptance to Wilton University on her Insta feed. Two weeks later, she added to her Snap story when she received a full-ride scholarship from Wilton, then again when she got a C in Art History and it was rescinded.

I signed her change.org petition, which begged

Wilton to change its mind. She had thirty-six signatures excluding my own, none of which did a thing. What she really needed was a wealthy father like mine, or at the very least, Angus Bedford, who had invested a decent chunk in Winthrop Textiles's college fund before his death.

Each dollar put in would be matched by the company for use on college tuitions of employees and their families. When the company fell, so did the college fund.

My freshman year of college, I barely left my apartment, pigging out on packets of ramen I bought four for a buck at the dollar store down the block. My books landed on the iPhone Dad gifted me ages ago from my library scans. I paid my tuition and a small stipend with the crazy amounts of student loans I had taken out.

Virginia held my trust fund over my head, which meant I was broke, spending more money than I had each year, and taking out student loans to sustain the costs. Broke as I was, I couldn't let Demi skip college.

I asked Dad's old fixer to set up the anonymous scholarship fund and applied for a full-time job at the diner.

The double shifts gave me feet and back pain, but they didn't kill me.

The inflexible work hours forced me to take classes I hated, but they didn't kill me.

The extra responsibility racked me with anxiety, but it didn't kill me.

The sleep deprivation made paying attention in class close to impossible, but it didn't kill me.

The hunger pains bothered me, but they didn't kill me.

At the end of the day, I didn't regret paying for Demi. It was the right thing to do.

I was a hollowed-out tree, long past death, and I had found a way to grow a leaf.

chapter THIRTY-ONE

Emery

Nothing made me more agitated than talking about Sisyphus with Ben.
  Not hunger.
Not poverty.
Not Virginia.
Not Dad.
Not even Nash Prescott.
  Ben saw Sisyphus as having been punished, but I knew Sisyphus was smart.
  Cunning.

A planner.

Here's my take: Sisyphus created an empire. He was a human, yet he ruled the winds. He tricked gods and goddesses. Even Death feared him.

Sisyphus wanted his punishment; otherwise, he would have escaped it, too. Sisyphus *chose* not to, and each day, he got to reach heights no other mortal man could.

Through his punishment, he was the never-ending battle of the sea, the constant rise and fall of the tides, the cycle of the moon and the sun. His punishment immortalized him. Placed him in the company of gods and goddesses. Gave him the power of a god, too.

Ben didn't see it that way, and no matter how much I wanted to shake him and demand he wake up, I couldn't. I scrolled through our messages, resisting the urge to run out into the rain and let it drown my screams.

Benkinersophobia: What do you think about regret?

Durga: Regret is endless. That's why it's life's longest punishment. There's no way to fight it. You just learn to live with it.

Benkinersophobia: Like Sisyphus, destined to carry the boulder for eternity.

Durga: He could stop it if he wanted.

Benkinersophobia: It wouldn't be a punishment if you can choose when it ends.

Durga: It's not a punishment. It's a test. Sisyphus has to prove he is worthy of the gods. By continuing to roll the boulder uphill, he is immortalized, a never-ending cycle, experiencing heights no other mortal has, in a place built by gods for gods. If he beats the test and levels the mountain by chipping a piece off each trip, he tricks Zeus once again. Either way, he has won.

Benkinersophobia: So, why would he choose to roll the boulder instead of leveling the mountain?

Durga: Sometimes, the struggle is important. Struggle changes people more than success.

I'd spent the past two days trying to explain this to Ben, but it was useless. He'd set his mind on condemning himself. I didn't understand why, and I felt powerless to help him.

I rolled my bottom lip into my mouth, scraping my teeth against it just to feel the bite, wishing I could distract him from his demons. I hoped Ben considered me his escape as much as I considered him to be mine.

Durga: Tell me what you would do if we met in person.

Benkinersophobia: You're changing the subject.

Durga: Am I that obvious?

Benkinersophobia: Nothing about you is obvious. But I read you well, Durga, and often.

I would take that any day. Two giant wings expanded in my belly, flapping their way to my chest. They weren't butterflies. They were powerful tsunami waves, consuming me each time I spoke with Ben.

He's a fantasy, Emery. You will wake up one day, and he'll be gone. Keep your distance. Save your heart. Nothing good lasts.

Like always, my warnings didn't deter me. I typed out a reply, hoping I was Ben's fantasy, too—a warrior princess who fought his demons beside him.

Durga: I love you.

I'd said it before.

After he'd talked me down a ledge caused by a failed finals exam.

Or when I got evicted from my apartment sophomore year, and he offered to break the rules and help me in person.

And that time I nearly caved and answered Dad's postcard, where he told me he loved me, missed me, and would always be here to balter with me.

Probably a dozen times after, too.

Each time felt different.

This time, the declaration came from comfort. I needed him to know someone cared about him, was there for him, and would always be there for him. Because at the end of the day, that's all any of us really need. Someone who shares their sunshine no matter the weather.

Benkinersophobia: I don't deserve it.

Durga: Just tell me what you would do if we ever met.

Benkinersophobia: I'd say, "Hi. I like your ass. Would you like to fuck?"

Durga: Romantic.

Benkinersophobia: I thought so.

Durga: You don't know what I look like. You may not like my ass.

Benkinersophobia: I like you, therefore I like your ass.

I never stopped smiling when I talked to Ben. I hoped, wherever he was, I made him smile, too.

Durga: Have you heard of the Maasai?

Benkinersophobia: From Africa?

Durga: Yes. About four hundred years ago, a Maasai leader had a daughter named Naserian. She dated a village elder's son, who eventually broke her heart. Naserian's father banished him. When he left, he took his elder father, mother, sister, uncles, aunts, and cousins.

Durga: A month later, Naserian dated another

man who broke her heart. When he was banished, he took with him his father, mother, sister, uncles, aunts, and cousins. The Maasai numbers began to dwindle, which left them vulnerable.

Durga: See where I'm going here?

Benkinersophobia: The Maasai have a shit ton of family members?

Durga: Ben.

Benkinersophobia: Naserian needs to chill with the assholes?

Durga: Ben.

Benkinersophobia: The Maasai need separation of state and daughter like ninety-year-olds in Congress need retirement?

Durga: BEN.

Durga: Stop.

Durga: OMG. You're impossible.

Durga: Moral of the story—when you act in vengeance, everyone around you suffers.

Benkinersophobia: I'm not talking about revenge. I'm talking about regret.

Durga: Revenge and regret are cut from the same cloth. Both are infectious. Both are cured by forgiveness and forgetting. The last thing I want is for you to suffer.

Benkinersophobia: You worry too much about me.

Durga: Because I care.

My grin splintered as I waited for a response. Not because I didn't think Ben loved me. I knew he did—just like I knew I made him smile and the real reason we refused to break the barrier and meet each other had nothing to do with the rules.
We were geode crystals.
Beautiful.
Tough.
Shiny.
Resilient.
Destined for a life sheltered inside an ugly rock.
My worry for Ben egged at me to press harder, to beg him to see himself the way I saw him, but I wouldn't, because even geodes shattered. If we shattered to pieces, I would lose my compass, my refuge, my sanctuary.
Selfish, selfish, Emery. Tell me all about how you're a good person.
I whispered magic words into the empty office air, even though I knew magic words wouldn't save me from this.

Benkinersophobia: How do the Maasai still exist if they banished everyone?

Durga: Well, the story ain't true, but it proves my point.

Benkinersophobia: You made up a story about the Maasai for me?

Durga: I know you're laughing. Stop judging.

Benkinersophobia: Durga?

Durga: Ben?

Benkinersophobia: I love you, too.

My cheeks still stung red when Nash walked into the office ten minutes later. He held out a to-go bag of overpriced food from a local steakhouse. Everyone else had gone out for Taco Tuesday lunch, so nothing but silence filled the room.

He gave me a solid thirty seconds to grab it before he plopped it on the coffee table in front of me and studied my flushed cheeks. "It's lemon herb salmon with the little green things Ma makes that you're obsessed with."

"They're capers, Nash, and people don't make them. They cook them." I tapped my naked nails on my phone screen, breathing from my mouth so I couldn't smell the food. My stomach continued its relentless growls. "How do you know I like capers?"

"Is that a serious question? You and Dad would fight over them whenever Ma made Chicken Piccata." Nash sat next to me on the couch, making it feel a hundred times smaller. He dragged the bag closer to the edge of the table and pulled out a black plastic container with a transparent lid. "You spilled the entire serving plate one year while trying to steal the capers from Dad and Reed's plates." It looked like the memory made him happy, which did uncomfortable things to my chest, even as I did my best to ignore him and the food. "Ma ended up doubling the capers in the recipe. Every time she makes Chicken Piccata, it's like eating green shit with a side of chicken and pasta."

My eyes dipped to the dish as he pulled off the lid.

Fuck.

Was I drooling?

"Betty still makes Chicken Piccata?"

"Yeah. Once a month."

His words pulled me out of his orbit.

Out of the tussled hair that made me think words like *cafune.*

Out of the full lips that parted every time he spoke.

Out of the scent of him I loved to steal.

"You see her once a month?" I stumbled over the words, not quite believing them. It fought the villainous archetype of Nash I'd built in my head.

The one that kept me safe from pesky attachments and reminded me this was not the same guy that packed me lunches and steadied me after the Able incident.

Nash pierced the salmon with a fork at the same time my stomach let loose an obnoxious growl. "I see her nearly every weekend." He waved the salmon in my face, showing off its flawless medium cook. "I'm eating this if you don't, and your stomach sounds fucking pissed at you."

I ignored the food, latching onto a piece of my past that didn't feel tainted. "How does Betty look?"

He shoveled the fork into his mouth. "Strong."

"What does that mean?"

"It means she's keeping herself fed and smiles when I'm looking."

"And when you're not looking?"

"She stares wherever Dad should be, eyes leaking like a broken faucet. If we're at the dinner table, she eyes the empty chair. If we're in the living room, she eyes the La-Z-Boy. If we're in the car, she stares down the steering wheel at every stoplight like it should be him driving instead of me."

"Why are you telling me this?"

"Because you asked, and maybe you care."

"Maybe? Of course, I care about Betty. I love her."

"Are you eating or what?"

Why do you keep trying to feed me, you confusing, fucked-up villain?

The words sat at the tip of my tongue, begging to be unleashed. I had no energy for a fight, so I swallowed them. They tasted like poor decisions and a forlorn appetite.

My eyes tracked each bite of his. I allowed myself two and half seconds of misery before I turned away from the food and clutched my phone like it was my only connection to Ben. (It was.)

"No," I forced myself to answer. "I'm not your charity case."

Ben loved me.

Nash confused me.

And at the end of the day, lust was just a consolation prize for love.

chapter THIRTY-TWO

Emery

For someone who thrived on confrontation, I could list avoidance under the "skills" column of my resume.

The construction worker glared at me beneath the sun's harsh rays. "Again?"

I swiped the hair out my face, wishing I could flick some guilt off with it. "Last time. I swear."

I'd said that the last four times I asked him to move it.

"A little to the left."

"Maybe slightly lower."

"Ohh... that's too low. Higher?"

"To the right."

Ninety percent sure the Prescott Hotels sign currently sat where it had started.

"Like this?" He shifted the hunk of metal higher above the entrance.

"Yes. We're good."

His relief slithered across his body. He took the opportunity to dismiss me with his back. Loitering by the double doors, I wished for a cigarette habit or something to keep me outside and away from the office, where the feeding saga continued in full force.

Nash brought me decadent dishes every day, and I declined every day.

My willpower resembled a starving puppy's, jaw snapping open at the slightest whiff of food.

The sun brought spots to my eyes. Two delivery men jostled me out of their way. A giant chrome refrigerator sat on a trolley between them, Nash's persistency written all over it.

What. The. Fuck.

My eyes fluttered with rapid blinks. I pinched my forearm—twice—to assure myself that I hadn't hallucinated a damn fridge. Not just any fridge. One of those smart ones with a tablet built into the door.

Turning to the construction worker, I rubbed at my eyes and squinted at him. "Did you see that?"

He dipped his head down as if that would spare him my attention. "See what?"

"Never mind."

Palming my phone, I pulled up the Eastridge United app.

Durga: What's the number for a good shrink? I think my boss needs psychiatric help.

Benkinersophobia: Funny. I feel the same way about one of my employees.

Durga: Fire them. Let me work for you instead.

Benkinersophobia: Consider this your job offer—forty hours a week, easy access clothing only. I'll allow kneepads given the labor requirements.

His next text came right after.

Benkinersophobia: Really, though, you good?

Durga: I will be.

Durga: I missed you this weekend.

Benkinersophobia: I spent the weekend with family. Usually, I can message you fine, but my mom's hiding something from me. I spent the past few days trying to figure it out.

Durga: Did you?

Benkinersophobia: No, but I will. I always get what I want. You should know this by now.

Durga: You sound like my boss.

Benkinersophobia: Fuck your boss.

I already did.

Benkinersophobia: (The curse not the verb. Don't actually fuck your boss.)

Too late.
My fingers flew across the keyboard until a shadow darkened the screen. Two shiny chestnut loafers entered my vision. I trailed them to their owner.
Not again.
That same déjà vu tickled my head, begging me to listen to it.
You know Brandon from somewhere. Figure it out. This is important, Emery.
Still nothing.
"I'm not interested." Rough heartbeats ate their way up my throat. Pocketing my phone, I quirked a brow and played it cool. "Can't take a hint, Mr. Vu?"
"Mr. Vu is my father."
"Mr. Vu is also you. Great conversation. Let's never do it again." I feigned left and swerved right, feeling like the next Odell Beckham when Brandon fell for the juke.
"Miss Winthrop, we have to talk." His fingers curled around my wrist, releasing when I jerked it away. "This is important. You're not in trouble."
"No shit." I swiveled and snapped my glare to him. "I'm well aware I didn't do anything wrong. I didn't break any laws. I don't care about whatever three-lettered government agency you came from. It means nothing to me. *You* mean nothing to me." A bruise would form around my wrist, but I refused to cradle it. "You're looking at the wrong Winthrop, and newsflash, I haven't

seen my dad in years. I have work to do. Have a shitty day. I know I will."

The metal door handle cooled my palm, but I still ran thirty degrees hotter inside. I pivoted and staggered back when my eyes caught and held Nash's through the door's reflection. His narrowed eyes flicked from me to Brandon and back to me.

Two fingers toyed with the cuff on one hand, like he was gearing for a fight. Being his victim appealed less to me than a conversation with the S.E.C.'s lapdog, so I swung the glass door open and shouldered past him.

"Tiger."

I didn't stop.

"Emery."

Still didn't stop.

The daytime security guard nodded at me as I strolled past him, his opinion of me suddenly more favorable now that I kept him fed. Pride made accepting food from Nash impossible, even if it meant hurting myself in the process.

My vision blurred from the hunger, colorful spots dancing at the corners. I could put myself out of my misery by taking the meals. Instead, I let Nash eat them or gave them to the security guards.

I thought I had hallucinated the fridge, but when I entered the office, an Insta Cart deliverer stood in front of it, cramming a spread of frozen meals, expensive protein, and yogurt inside.

Falling to the couch, I considered my options with Brandon. Really, I had none. He could keep showing up, but I didn't have answers for him, except my dad's location, which wouldn't help. The S.E.C. and F.B.I. hadn't found anything on Dad the first time around.

The Insta Cart guy turned to me every ten seconds

like he thought I would attack him. I spared him my resting bitch face and sloped my head to face the ceiling, toying with a pen as I considered ideas to make the hotel design less of a bore.

The one true save would be to scrap it entirely, but we didn't have the time or budget for a drastic change, and Chantilly would find another way to run a second budget to the ground. She came from a poor family. While poverty sometimes bred thrifty spenders, it had turned Chantilly into a fiscal nightmare.

She thrived on spending every dollar she owned and then some. Appointing her as the temporary department head was like taking a five-year-old to Toys 'R Us and telling him to have at it. The Haling Cove budget would make a hedge fund manager weep, yet she'd managed to exhaust it.

We needed a conversational focus piece, but we couldn't afford one. The snobby hotel crowd would treat D.I.Y. projects as trash, and high-end artists never worked for free. I'd toyed with this puzzle all week. A knot I couldn't untangle, and I felt like the only one trying.

"You look like you're deep in thought." Ida Marie plopped her bag at the foot of the couch and sat next to me. She smelled like *Shakshuka* from the Tunisian place nearby.

What did it mean that I didn't get jealous of how pretty or smart or well-dressed people were but rather of the food they ate? I wanted *Shakshuka*—and *Brik a L'oef*, *Fricassé*, and *Bambalouni* for dessert.

Now, what did it mean if I could have all of that just by asking Nash, yet I refused?

"I'm trying to figure out what to do with the design." I tossed the pen up and caught it.

"There's nothing to figure out. We don't make the decisions."

No, but Nash did, and he cared. He wouldn't show it. Probably wouldn't even admit it to himself.

How would you know that, Emery?

Ugh.

Good question.

I knew Nash cared like I knew Reed muttered under his breath when something irritated him, Betty had a favorite prayer, Hank wiggled his toes each time he laughed, and Nash ran a palm twice through his hair when he thought someone was an idiot and three times when he was somewhere he didn't want to be.

"I'm not gonna have my first project for Prescott Hotels be one I hate." I watched the Insta Cart shopper unload the rest of the groceries, wanting to help him but knowing I'd be too tempted to eat something from the fridge if I did. "At this rate, none of us will be invited to work on the Singapore location."

Everything about the Singapore location rubbed me wrong. Maybe the way Nash seemed too invested in it. Office rumors placed the likelihood of Prescott Hotels winning a bidding war against Asher Black pretty low.

If Nash did win, it would be at a steep cost that wouldn't be worth the location.

Why go through that?

Why not find another location in Singapore?

Why that property?

My pride crippled me; Nash's didn't. If logic dictated he find another location, he would have. Something kept him there, and my thirst to understand him didn't allow me to ignore it. As with everything involving Nash, my curiosity would remain unanswered like a light switch that refused to flick on.

Ida Marie waved at the Insta Cart shopper when he left, escorted back to the lobby by a security guard I didn't recognize.

"Singapore is probably going to the design team that did Dubai and Hollywood." She chewed on her gum and popped a bubble. "I don't think we had a chance from the start. You ever notice how stunning all the Prescott Hotel locations are compared to the North Carolina ones?"

Her arms swung as she spoke, "It's like these are the throwaways. They're still better than everyone's except maybe Black Enterprise's, but they're just... less. You'd think, being from North Carolina, our boss would spend extra attention on these."

Nash hated North Carolina because he hated Eastridge. I read between the lines in his notes. It seemed like he warred with himself, and the only way he could get his thoughts settled was to put them down on pen and paper.

When he graduated high school and Betty took an extra job doing morning house chores at my neighbor's, she asked Nash to make Reed's lunches. He continued to make mine, too. Notes and all.

Some of them spoke of leaving, especially once Nash got accepted as a transfer to a few Ivy League schools and never told anyone except, I now realized, me.

> *Do you think you're in anyone's favorite memory? I think I'm maybe in Ma's or Dad's. It's one of the reasons why I stay in North Carolina. You can't leave someone who has a favorite memory featuring you, ya know?*

— **NASH**

> Dad lost the T.V. remote last night, and Ma yelled, "Ain't nothing lost until I can't find it." I asked her if she could find my ~~fucking~~ hope. I was kidding. She didn't find it funny. She begged me not to say anything like that again.
>
> I was gonna ask her what she thought of me leavin' for Harvard or Wilton, but I didn't after that.
>
> I got into Harvard, Yale, and Wilton.
>
> (Fuck Yale.)
>
> Can you believe it? The Eastridge Prep scholarship kid at Harvard. Probably won't go, but still... Some things you've just gotta say out loud to make sure they're happening.

— **NASH**

> You know how they say money can't buy happiness? Everyone on this side of Eastridge is so ~~damn~~ rich, and I have a theory. I think they've managed to buy themselves different degrees of misery.
>
> The Kensingtons are both richer and less

> *miserable than the Abbots, but the Abbots are richer and less miserable than the Grimaldi family, who is richer and less miserable than the Stryker family. I wonder if it's like that anywhere else. Norway? Côte d'Ivoire? Trinidad and Tobago?*
>
> — **NASH**

It occurred to me that I knew parts of Nash no one else did. I didn't know what to think of that except to exorcise it from my head.

I cut off Ida Marie's complaints about being assigned the North Carolina location, "Giving up sets you up for failure. It's like saying you want something, but not hard enough to work for it."

"Being assigned the Haling Cove branch set us up for failure." Ida Marie perched a fist on each hip. "You know it only happened because we're on Mary-Kate's team. They're not going to let Chantilly take over a project that actually matters to Prescott Hotels. She doesn't have the experience."

"Every project matters to Prescott Hotels," I argued, except doubt trickled in.

This all started to feel like fate—as if so many events clicked into place to land me this job.

Mary-Kate's Tinder one-night stand led to a baby.

That baby led to her maternity leave.

The maternity leave led to Chantilly's promotion as the interim head of the design team.

Nash's need to dominate North Carolina led to a branch opening in Haling Cove.

Chantilly's inexperience led to the team being assigned to Haling Cove because Ida Marie had been right—Nash did treat the North Carolina Prescott Hotels as throwaways.

A gazillion events led to me needing a job.

Something Reed did for Delilah led to Delilah owing Reed a favor.

That favor led to Prescott Hotels hiring me.

Someone retiring on Chantilly's team led to me being assigned to Haling Cove.

Being assigned to Haling Cove led me to that elevator and my work with Nash.

How many moving pieces was that?

Eleven.

More, actually, if you broke down my dive into poverty. What more could Fate throw at me? Hell, what was it trying to tell me?

Ida Marie stretched her arms above her head instead of answering and nodded to Hannah and Cayden as they entered with Chantilly. The three of them eyed the fridge before Cayden walked up and studied the contents.

"Neat." He pulled out some cold cuts and a can of soda. "It's the good stuff. Perhaps the king has a heart after all."

Ten years ago, maybe. It's long gone now—buried so deep, he has forgotten it ever existed.

"You just ate!" Hannah joined Cayden and grabbed an apple juice. "Whoa. These are, like, ten dollars a pop at the juice bar. Nash bought this? For us?"

Chantilly and Ida Marie followed suit, riffling through the fridge. Meanwhile, I sat with my hands tucked under my thighs, knowing if I allowed myself to indulge, Nash would probably walk in ten seconds later to witness the moment of weakness given my luck.

I avoided the heavy stares from my coworkers when

my stomach conjured a growl that resembled two dogs fighting over a bone. "What? We don't have time for food."

By the time Nash stepped into the room, everyone had settled in and begun their afternoon sketches. He eyed the Coke can in Cayden's hand, the yogurt in Chantilly's, the string cheese in Ida Marie's, and the organic juice pouch in Hannah's.

Then he clocked my empty palms, ran his hand through his hair twice—which implied he thought I was an idiot—and stalked to the refrigerator. Swinging the door open with the grace of a drunk sumo wrestler, he skimmed each row as if to double-check they had been stocked and eyed my empty hands once more.

His fingers hovered over the fridge, almost curled around the handle. My face flushed at the memory of them inside me, then hardened at the reminder he'd left. Civility should have been a foreign concept, but it felt weird to hate him over the way he spoke to me in the soup kitchen.

Not because he didn't deserve it—he so did—but because I had touted forgiveness and moving on as a lesson to Ben. If I didn't lead by example, I would be a liar. I could do that to Reed, Virginia, and Nash, but I couldn't lie to Ben.

The stare-down with Nash lasted nearly a minute. The questions simmering inside Ida Marie and Chantilly lashed at me, but I didn't dare look away. I would deal with the consequences later.

"Have you eaten?" Nash spoke as if no one else was in the room. His eyes dipped to my stomach like they would give him some answers.

"No."

I didn't elaborate.

Didn't waver.

Didn't tell him that it had been fourteen hours since food last touched my lips.

Didn't tell him I used his app to talk to Ben.

Didn't tell him I couldn't stand the idea of his dad's death on my dad's hands.

Didn't tell him it gave him no right to be cruel to me.

Instead, we communicated with our eyes.

Mine said, "I'm not built to lose."

His said, "I'm only built to win."

Another minute.

Two.

Chantilly approached Nash on the third.

He ignored her, speared one last glare at me, and left.

I released a breath with him gone.

Victory felt as hollow as an aluminum baseball bat.

Cold.

Hard.

Never permanent.

chapter THIRTY-THREE

nash

If I had to watch Chantilly wiggle her ass for me one more time, I deserved a monument in the fucking Smithsonian.

She parachuted a tablecloth in front of her, letting it float to the office carpet. It laid flat on the floor, but she took her time bending on her hands and knees. Ass in the air, she smoothed out the wrinkles.

Our new office lunch ritual, ladies and gentleman.

If this is hell, I'll change my ways. Fucking promise.

"Will you help me, Nash?" She peeked back at me, her body arched doggy-style.

My eyes remained glued to my phone.

Candy Crush again.

Full volume.

Victorious *dings* filled the air.

"Unless capitalism has changed in the past twenty minutes, the whole point of paying people money is so I don't have to waste my time with pointless shit." My thumb ran miles across the screen. The light cast a shadow from my lashes to the phone. Candy wrappers crushing echoed in the room. "Did I miss a memo?"

Cayden eyed Chantilly's ass as she ran a palm along the polyester fabric. He had two working eyes and a healthy libido, and Chantilly bore the body of a Sports Illustrated model. Yet, I didn't glance.

Not once.

Definitely not in the past ten days, as each attempt grew more desperate than the last.

You'd think she'd take the fucking hint.

Office picnics for lunch had never existed before I started my feeding attempts, and Chantilly caught on.

If Emery—*fucking Emery and her stubborn ass*—would cave, everyone in this office could go back to ignoring each other, please and thank you.

Chantilly spread five sets of silverware across the cloth—one for everyone but Emery. "It's just lunch, Nash."

"It's Mr. Prescott to you, and because you have such difficulty understanding boundaries, allow me to teach you a lesson in them." I pocketed my phone, stepped on top of the cloth, and rattled the silverware, shattering a crystal plate with my three-thousand-dollar dress shoes.

I continued, "This is what happens when people overstep my boundaries." My heel dug into the crushed plate and twisted. "They become as useless to me as a broken plate. People are expendable, including you. Clean this mess and clear the office. In the future, Chartreuse, do not overstep if you'd like to keep your job."

Problem was, Chantilly cared about her job as much as she cared about melting ice caps in the Arctic. As in, not at all. I'd become her goal the second I'd stepped foot in this office and introduced myself to the team.

Perhaps earlier, considering her behavior at the corporate party she'd crashed. If it weren't for her uncle, I'd fire her. Easily.

Cayden left with Ida Marie and Hannah, his phone pulled up to his Uber app. Cheeks the same shade as her hair, Chantilly folded the edges of the tablecloth to the center, bundled up the mess in the middle, and shoved it under Cayden's desk.

Emery slid her sketchpad into her Jana Sport and flung it over her shoulder. Her toe hit the door's threshold when I stopped her.

"Not you, Miss *Rhodes*."

A mouse squeaked.

Or Chantilly.

They sounded the same.

"Yes, Mr. Prescott?" She pivoted, rested a hip against the frame, and studied me.

I eyed Chantilly, who took her time gathering her belongings into the Birkin bag she wore—something her salary did not afford her, but her family did. The silence allowed Emery to scrape her eyes down my body, trying to satiate her curiosity.

Good luck, Tiger.

That ember between us never extinguished. Proximity drew sweat from her palms. She rubbed them on her jeans, staring at me like she needed to taste me, fuck me, use me. To affirm our one-night stand meant nothing.

A fluke orgasm that would have happened if anyone experienced touched her.

Yeah, right, my lifted brow told her. *Keep fooling yourself.*

She muttered something under her breath. Not weird words this time. Actual sentences. I edged closer, trying to hear them.

Something along the lines of, *"It felt worse than the first time, which makes sense, considering I mistook you for the better Prescott."*

"Thank you for the fuck. I have no intention of doing it again. No desire to either."

"I liked who you were, but I hate who you are."

"Bye, Nash."

I popped a brow up and watched her watch me, leaning against my desk. The same desk I worked from everyday, efficient and diligent. I offered input when needed and minded my own business if I had nothing to contribute.

Exactly what I wanted everyone in here to fucking do, but Chantilly seemed incapable.

When dinnertime approached, I would look at Emery, read her unwillingness to accept my food offers, and order her takeout that ended up in the palms of the night guard.

By the time the furniture orders had been placed and shipped, everyone else began ordering in, too. Hence Chantilly's newfound picnic fetish, where she dished out mood candles and heavy silverware like an overachieving mom handing out healthy Halloween candy no one wanted.

"What?" Emery snapped as soon as Chantilly left, whipping the hair out of her face with a rough swipe.

"Woke up on the wrong side of the bed?" I eyed her

hair like it supported my theory. It did. Wild and crazy as ever.

Irritation masked her lust.

"Is there a point to this?" She patted her stomach just below *latibule* on her shirt. "I'm hungry. It's my lunch hour."

"Anyone ever told you that you need a Snickers? You're as pissy as a toddler when hungry."

"For the record, this is the reaction you inspire from everyone who has ever met you. And if you were hungry and couldn't feed yourself or talk, you'd throw worse tantrums than toddlers. In fact, your daily setting seems permanently stuck on tantrum."

I pretended to ignore her—*of fucking course, I couldn't*—fetched something from my desk drawer, held it up, and shook it. "Ma made these for you."

Check. Mate.

Emery

I RECOGNIZED the neon pink as soon as I saw it. A surge of homesickness throttled through me like an earthquake. My fingers twitched with the need to pry it from Nash's fingers and claim it as mine.

I played it cool. "You saw Betty this weekend?"

"We've been over this. I see her almost every weekend."

He ate the distance between us in two strides. I loosened my grip on my shirt, leaving huge wrinkles above my belly button. When he plopped the Tupperware container onto my palms, I latched on.

A koala clinging to a eucalyptus tree, except my home was a one-hundred-and-forty-pound, five-foot-two woman with graying hair and two hazel eyes that matched Nash's.

"You have your mom's eyes."

The words slipped past my lips before I could swallow them. An accidental gunshot wound to the gut, fired from my own weapon. Embarrassment mixed with a shit ton of pain. I mouthed magic words and cataloged my body, searching for a wound.

Nope. Just inside, you dolt. You are the reason guns come with a safety latch.

Those hazel eyes studied me and drew me into their current. I refused to look away or explain myself. Breaking the silence would be tantamount to losing, so I suffered in it. Not masochistic. Just stubborn.

Why is being near you always a series of lose-lose situations, Nash?

"I know, considering they're in my eye sockets." He threw back my words like a Major League pitcher, striking me out while I failed to consider why either of us remembered them. "Ma baked those yesterday." Nash flicked his attention to the container I refused to loosen my grip on. "White chocolate macadamia nut. Your favorite."

"Snickerdoodles are my favorite."

"Liar. Snickerdoodles are your least favorite." He gave me the stare people gave crying babies. Irritation hidden behind a patient smile. "You once faked a cinnamon allergy, so Ma would stop making them instead of the white chocolate macadamia."

"Until she told me she mixed cinnamon in the white chocolate chips, too." I kicked at one of the tablecloth packages on the carpet, digging this trip down memory lane, even if it was with my least favorite Prescott. "Betty's secret ingredient for every damn dish she cooks."

"She made you watch us eat white chocolate macadamia nut cookies while you ate the snickerdoodles." Nash leaned against the doorframe, kicking one ankle over the other. His suit pants tightened around his thighs, but I. Would. Not. Stare. "Ten years later, you still haven't learned your lesson about lying, have you?"

I didn't want to reminisce with him. It delved too close to a line I wouldn't cross—focusing on better times. Forget the past, and it can't haunt you. That included forgetting the good stuff.

"I don't want food from you."

Another lie.

Betty stacked her Tupperware in a cabinet next to the sink. I'd sneak a few out of the cottage and repaint them black with lilac-colored Northern Lights and white stars in the shape of magic words.

I not only wanted the food, but also the container.

"They're not from me." Nash's North Carolina accent sounded more pronounced as he folded his arms across his chest. "They're from my mom. Would you really deny my mom's gift? She spent hours baking them."

Indecision ran laps around my brain until I heaved a

breath and distanced myself from him. My shaky hands stretched out, offering the Tupperware to him.

If he grabs it, y'all better let go, Fingers. Don't embarrass me.

Nash eyed the container, taking his time to examine the way my fingers clenched around it. "Stop." Harsh. Gruff. Loud. A command I felt above my neck and below my waist. "Just stop."

"What?"

"This." He gestured to me like he meant *all* of me. My entire existence. "You're lucky pride doesn't come armed with a dagger, because yours would kill you if it could. Stop being embarrassed. It's not embarrassing to need help. It's not embarrassing to be poor. None of this is embarrassing."

I edged back an inch at his words, knowing he had a point, but not wanting to address it.

He continued, ruthless, "You know why I call you the tiger?"

No, but I had a good idea. A statue of Dionysus riding a tiger consumed the expanse of the foyer at the Winthrop Estate. Virginia used to pet the tiger each time she passed it. Right along the jugular vein.

"Because Dionysus rides the tiger." I hitched a shoulder. The outstretched Tupperware stilted the awkward movement.

"No." Nash pushed the container until it shotgunned to my chest, still squeezed between my palms. "Because the tiger cannot be tamed. The tiger rules the jungle, and only a god can worship the tiger properly. Your mother is an uncultured idiot, who mistook a tiger for a panther." His scathing laughter tasted like candy against my lips as he leaned close. "Dionysus doesn't ride a tiger. He rides a panther. The tiger is his sacred animal."

And gods worshipped sacred animals.

It's why I'd chosen Durga as my username.

A goddess known as The Inaccessible.

The Invincible.

Her sacred animal is the tiger, and I wanted to feel sacred.

"What are you saying?" I asked, hoping Nash would give me an answer that would make me hate him more. I clung to the container, the only thing separating us.

His breath fanned my cheeks.

Actually, it also sounds fucking cute.

"I'm saying eat the cookies, Tiger."

chapter THIRTY-FOUR

Emery

Saudade.
　　Sciamachy.
　　　Thanatophobia.
Useless words.
Nothing could tamp my frustration.
"We need a centerpiece!" I waved a picture on my phone of a giant abstract monstrosity we had no budget for.
This had become my hill to die on.

Destined to perish from a wound in the shape of Chantilly's indifference, and my tombstone had better be a damned centerpiece.

Ida Marie flicked her eyes between the two of us, lips pressed together. She swallowed her saliva every ten seconds.

She agreed with me. So did Cayden and Hannah... but they also agreed with Chantilly's point—we didn't have room in the budget.

"We're done talking about this." Chantilly shut the meeting books and shoved them inside Cayden's desk.

I shot up from the couch. "It has to happen," I said, wondering why I even bothered. We'd all die eventually, and none of this would matter.

You are dust. Small and solid, but destined to vanish.

"We don't have it in the budget!" Chantilly tossed both hands in the air. "And even if we did, it's not happening. It's all useless. Mr. Prescott doesn't care about this location. You're supposedly chummy with him," she spit the words out like she wasn't sure whether to be confused or disgusted. "Can't you see that?"

Would speaking slower help this seep into Chantilly's skull?

I wondered whose side Nash would take if he were here. Chantilly's, most likely. His priorities laid with the Singapore location. Even now, he'd left for the penthouse to go over offers with Delilah.

"He may not care, but I do." I jabbed my chest with my pointer finger. It hurt, but so did everything.

"Why?"

She could send me to Guantanamo Bay, and I still wouldn't tell her. Not when it meant revealing just how much I knew Nash and the Prescotts.

"Because," I began, forming my lies as I spoke, "this

location is my first job, will go on all of our design portfolios, and should matter regardless because it's our damn jobs to care. Why am I the only one who cares?"

Security interrupted our argument with Chipotle catering trays. My eyes swung to the door, but I already knew Nash wouldn't be there. I didn't feel him in the room. No heavy air. No heat around my body. Nothing.

The giant servings of chicken, steak, and barbacoa consumed most of the tablecloth Chantilly laid out, so Cayden opened another one next to it. I helped the guards fan out the containers of tortillas, cheese, rice, beans, guac, and salsa, but I didn't dare grab a plate.

It looked good.

It smelled better.

I hadn't eaten all day, and if we continued through the night, the soup kitchen would be closed by the time I clocked out.

Logic told me to eat.

My body told me to eat.

Even Ida Marie turned to me and told me to eat.

My heart refused to.

That same dumb organ jostled inside my ribcage as soon as the elevator pinged in the hall. This is why ribs form a cage around the heart. It's an untamed animal, and wild animals can't be trusted.

If my coworkers thought I had a serious eating disorder, none of them bothered to suggest I seek help. They dug into the food, piling glutinous layers onto their paper plates. I envied the hell out of them.

Grateful I hadn't succumbed to the temptation, I pulled out the sketchpad and continued with my shading, knowing this one-hundred percent would end up at the bottom of the trashcan.

"Are you sure this is from Nash?" Ida Marie frowned

at the food, eyeing the beans like they might be poisoned. "It doesn't seem like something he would do for anyone, except maybe…"

Her voice trailed off, but we all knew what she meant to say.

Anyone except Emery.

The divide deepened. I stood stranded on one side of a canyon while Cayden, Hannah, Ida Marie, and Chantilly stood on the other. Except Chantilly refused to see it like it was. She'd sprint over to my side on a tightrope if she could.

Her nose scrunched as she shook her head.

"Don't be ridiculous, Ida Marie. It's definitely for us. I've been working late. Putting in so many extra hours." She loaded extra meat onto her tortilla, and I. Was. So. Jealous. "I deserve it—and the fridge. Totally. Plus, I think he really likes me. I caught him staring at me this morning."

"I can assure you, I do not like you. You remind me of a dog begging strangers to pet her, and as far as kinks go, bestiality isn't mine." Nash rested a hip against the door frame, staring me down without paying a lick of attention to Chantilly. "I was staring at Emery. You kept getting in the way."

My heart hiccupped before chasing its normal pace. Cue the awkward silence as everyone and their mothers misconstrued Nash's words. The stare-down had lasted five minutes over the extra white chocolate macadamia nut cookies he'd slipped into my Jana Sport when I wasn't paying attention.

One—he was right. I loved them. Everyone who knew me knew I loved them. Not exactly a national secret.

Two—I couldn't hand them back without drawing attention to Nash's fixation on feeding me. They still sat at the bottom of my Jana Sport, taunting me each time I pulled out a different charcoal pencil to sketch with.

Three—I hoped he never found out that I'd eaten the ones in the Tupperware container he gave me days ago.

Ida Marie's cheeks turned pink for me. She tapped my shoulder and held a paper plate in her outstretched hand. "Are you sure you're not hungry?" Her wide eyes avoided Nash. "There's so much food here. One of us will end up taking a feast home."

Nash had approved our 3D rendering with minor changes, which meant flooring, cabinets, and finishes were already installed with furnishings ordered and arranged soon after. It also meant I would be here even later today. The soup kitchen might end up closing before I left.

Stop letting your pride eat at your sanity, Emery. Nash is right. It's okay to accept help. It doesn't make you any less of a person. Maggie lets you make coats for her and the kids. You allowed Reed to hook you up with a job. Getting food from the soup kitchen never deterred you. It's starting to sound like you only have trouble accepting help from Nash.

Nope, the pep talk did nothing.

I'd sooner step in a bear trap than accept Nash's help. Because I preferred him cruel. At least, I knew what to expect.

"I'm good." I plucked my eraser from the Jana Sport. "I have dinner plans tonight."

As in, the soup kitchen if I'm lucky.

Nash narrowed his eyes at my words. I had screwed myself when I agreed to civility for Ben's sake, because each time I didn't fight Nash, I got more and more comfortable justifying our proximity.

This did nothing for my lust. He still looked like womenkind's answer to dry spells, and I still had the memory of his fingers inside me and my lips wrapped around his cock to keep me warm at night.

"Emery." Nash lifted his chin toward the hallway. He had managed to turn my name into a demand. As soon as we reached the elevators, he fired at me in rapid succession, "Make no mistake—I'm not a nice person. I don't do nice things. If I hold the door open for you, it's to look at your ass. If I do you a favor, it's because I expect one in return. If I feed you, it's because I'd rather deal with your scrawny ass than Ma's wrath. The sooner you get that, the better."

But the words held no real bite to them. A toothless husky gnawing his favorite toy. He seemed so uncomfortable with the idea of feeding me, it almost made me laugh. Dip below that, and all he'd done was throw money at my problems with a hint of his signature tenacity.

The exact opposite of the younger Nash who used to give me lunch at the cost of his own, who didn't speak as if he owned me, and never made me feel like accepting his generosity would come at the expense of my soul.

The slow shake of my head offered me time to summon an adequate response. "My refusal to accept your food has nothing to do with an aversion to niceties and everything to do with the fact that I don't need your hundreds of dollars in catering, your fancy salmons, or forty-eight-ounce porterhouses that can feed ten families." My Chuck-covered feet clambered closer to his Salvatore Ferragamo loafers. "Money doesn't solve all problems, including mine. Sometimes, I don't recognize you, Nash. Doesn't that scare you?"

I'd struck him.

Lightning straight to the hollowed-out cavity where his heart should have been.

Old Nash used to go without food so the overprivileged Winthrop could eat lunch. He never asked for a thank you, never made me feel bad about my crappy mother, and never forced me to accept his charity.

He left me notes because my longing eyes would track Betty's every time Reed flicked it into the trash after a cursory glance. Once, I even hijacked one from the trash, brought it home, and pretended Betty was my mom and she'd written the words for me.

Nash found me hiding it under the bench in the center of the maze, paranoid Virginia would find it and tear it in half. Leaning against his dad's iron shovel, he eyed the guilt etched on my face and held out a gloved hand.

My shaky fingers dropped the note into his palm. I prayed he wouldn't toss it. Instead, he offered me a look I didn't understand and told me the gap beneath the Hera statue made a better hiding spot.

If that Nash walked up to me now with a brown paper sack and a handwritten note, I'd gobble the peanut butter and jelly sandwich with a smile on my face and recite the note over and over until the words etched themselves in my soul.

This had everything to do with pride, but it also involved self-preservation.

I refused to taint my memory of Nash.

His phone rang, sparing us both. Otherwise, who knew the lengths he would go to in his quest of feeding me? He muttered something about Singapore and left me to sketch while the others ate. An hour later, he still hadn't returned, but everyone had joined me in drawing portrait mockups.

"What did he say to you?" Ida Marie's hands flew across her pad. She hounded me, for the eighth time, over one of my many arguments with Nash. Except, she didn't know it had been an argument.

Plus, so much time had passed, and we hadn't gotten in each other's faces in a while. Come to think of it, the last time was the Soup Kitchen Incident. Or when I spat the sandwich at his foot if you counted that, which I didn't on account of A—the distinct lack of witty comebacks on my part and B—my embarrassment over rummaging the sandwich from the trash and devouring it.

A secret I'd take to my grave.

My coffin had better come padlocked.

Who are you trying to fool? You fight him every time he tries to feed you.

"I already told you. He basically told me not to step out of line again," I lied.

Sort of.

Was it a lie?

He had screamed it with his eyes the whole time, and I was almost certain he had said it, too. I didn't even remember what the argument had been about. Just that he looked like he wanted to bend me over his knees and teach me a lesson, and my body hadn't exactly been opposed to the prospect.

Ida Marie handed me a 4B charcoal pencil to fill the palm. I kept the pencil loose and slanted in my fingers as I shaded. Chantilly had us creating mockups for exclusive artwork to be placed in the upper-level suites.

None of us were well-known artists, but she had wasted a ridiculous amount of the budget on importing bamboo panels from China with a tariff that made me want to pull out her teeth and feed it to the gap-toothed Rottweiler that hung around Maggie's tent city.

Mags, I corrected.

She loved me for slipping Stella my extra bread roll and our mutual obsession over murals. If she knew what I thought of Nash's nickname for her, she would probably forgo the extra hours of sleep on the weekends and stop allowing me to babysit Stella and Harlan. Not that the tent city posed any dangers, but real mothers worried.

Virginia, on the other hand, never had.

I swapped the 4B for the 9B to color in the middle finger.

Ida Marie set down her sketch and scrunched her nose at it. "It's awful." She sighed, tore the sheet of paper from the sketchbook, crumpled it, and started again. Between us, a mountain of discarded sketches towered like a forgotten game of Jenga. "It's just that Nash Prescott looks at you like—"

Chantilly walked up to us. "He looks at her like what?"

"Like he is disappointed in the entire design department," Ida Marie lied. "You know, for going over budget on the furniture we ordered. Emery picked out the rugs."

I bit my tongue before I blurted out the rugs had been on sale, and with the exception of me, everyone had exceeded the furnishing budget. We both knew Chantilly possessed the nose of a shark, and she sought news of me and Nash like a shark sought blood.

"Nash is right." Chantilly straightened out Ida Marie's balled up sketch, rolled her eyes, balled it up again, and tossed it into the trash before returning her attention to me. "Do not embarrass me. You may have

Delilah Lowell's protection, but as C.E.O., Mister Prescott outranks her."

"Sir, yes, sir." I mocked a salute. If she wanted to treat Nash's company like it was the military, by all means, I would indulge her, but I would make her feel ridiculous about it.

"I mean it, Emery." She stalked off after Cayden called her name.

"She hates you." Ida Marie's unhelpful remark hung between us. A knife with a dull blade. "Antagonizing her won't help."

"I know, but I lack the impulse control to stop. She hated me before I even spoke to her, and I don't like bullies."

"She only hates you because you know Delilah Lowell, and Chantilly has been trying to work her way up the food chain for three years now. How do you know Delilah, by the way?"

I ripped off my middle finger sketch, laid it proudly on the coffee table, and returned to another sketch I'd started earlier. "I don't know her. I've seen her before, but I've actually never officially met her. She's just a friend of a friend."

"Hot friend?"

"Taken friend."

I'd been ducking Reed's texts and calls because I didn't have any proposal ideas for him except to say, *don't do it*. I never understood Reed and Basil. They shared nothing in common except the color of their hair.

Ida Marie peeked over at my sketchbook and let out an *ooooh*. "Definitely hot."

I glanced down at my picture, afraid I'd accidentally drawn Reed or worse—Nash. Instead, an outline of another man's face stared back at me. His card still burned in my pocket, the phrase "U.S. Security and Exchange Commission" close to hospitalizing me each time I looked at it.

I nearly choked on my spit when I realized where I'd recognized him from.

Brandon Vu came into my life the day it fell apart.

chapter THIRTY-FIVE

EMERY, 18; NASH, 28

Emery

Bad things seemed to happen when the world looked its best.

The red maples Eastridgers prided themselves for had begun to shed. Sanguine leaves painted the town vibrant shades. During this season, Eastridge could serve as a movie set, but we'd never taken too kindly to strangers, especially Hollywood folk.

The temperature sat somewhere between sweater weather and skinny jeans with a spaghetti strap, so I opted for a tee that read *ukiyo-e* and my black skinnies.

Virginia would lose her shit if she caught sight of me, but she'd been acting all weird lately, so I'd probably slipped her mind.

I came back from the grocery store with a bag of chips in my hand and rebellion stitched onto my face, my mother's black credit card hidden in my back pocket. The idea of Virginia catching me sent aftershocks through my limbs. Baby earthquakes I welcomed, because they meant something had rattled, shaken, *changed*.

The staff's strict orders to confiscate any junk food from me went ignored as I opened the door to dozens of unfamiliar faces. I recognized their windbreakers from the movies, bold yellow letters that spelled F.B.I. across the back.

Some had S.E.C. printed on them, and living in a town of sinners, of course, I knew those letters, too. I just never thought I'd see them in my house. The one Dad owned. Squeaky clean, all-around good guy Gideon Winthrop.

It had to be a mistake.

People came in and out of Dad's office, holding bagged documents and files, a few paintings, and his laptop. Even the wooden clock I'd made him with the crooked edges and the botched engravings went with them.

My eyes sought and failed to find Dad—or Virginia. I later learned the investigators had found nothing concrete, he hadn't been arrested, and they'd found enough light circumstantial evidence to launch a very formal, very public investigation. When Dad's company folded soon after, it might as well have been an admission of guilt.

But in the moment, I didn't care about the future. Panic sped my legs through the mansion. No one stopped me as I launched myself out the backdoor and sprinted to the Prescott's cottage.

The place looked deserted before I remembered Betty had gone with Hank to an annual doctor's appointment, Nash no longer lived there, and Reed left for an overnight tour of Duke with Basil. I couldn't hear the agents in the house from here. If I closed my eyes, I could convince myself they didn't exist.

The key in my pocket tempted me. I could let myself in, but I didn't want to bring the Prescotts into this mess they'd had nothing to do with. The idea of looking them in the eye mortified me, too. Not when none of us would ever be the same.

So, I folded my arms against my chest in front of the cottage, refusing to cross the invisible line past that ridiculous half-black, half-blue mailbox. Even when someone walked up and stood beside me, staring at the tiny house.

I didn't remember how long silence chilled the air before he asked, "Do you have a key?"

"No," I lied, refusing to stare at him, because if I did, it would make this more real than it already was.

This wasn't me. I wasn't the type to stand idly by as my world crashed around me. I was the type to fight back, digging into whatever flesh I could grab, diving headfirst into whatever abyss would take me, even if it tore my nails off and swallowed me whole.

But I knew whatever I did today would haunt me for the rest of my life. Something in the moment felt pivotal. If I sneezed wrong, I'd trigger a butterfly effect. I'd be smart about this. For me. For the Prescotts.

I wanted to walk in there, hug Betty and Hank, sit next to Reed at the spare dining room seat Hank had built just for me, and beg for an extra serving of chicken and dumplings one last time. Except, it wasn't a special day of celebration, and I knew I'd missed my chance as soon as I heard this man approach. That, and it was a rare day where the cottage had been emptied.

That itself should have been an omen.

The stranger shoved his hands into his pockets. "It's illegal to hinder a federal investigation." He sounded young, but I still refused to look at his face.

"It should be illegal to be a dick." It slipped out of my mouth before I could stop it.

He laughed, the full-bellied type that traveled all over your body and left you warm. "It should be, but it isn't. I'm glad, because I'm not made for jail. Are you?"

No. Neither were the Prescotts, not that they were going to jail. Not even Nash, whom I hated for sleeping with me and acting like a jerk after.

"I'm not going to jail." I kicked at a loose brick on the path to the house. It wiggled a bit but remained an immovable force, reminding me I needed to plant my feet and stop this madness from touching Reed and his family. "The Prescotts have nothing to do with this. I don't even know what *this* is, but there's a family living inside that is completely innocent and does not deserve to have their belongings torn apart and searched."

"Who lives there, Miss Winthrop?"

Liar, my lips begged to scream. *You already know, you snake.*

Magic words couldn't heal this, but I mouthed one anyway.

Querencia.

Noun.

A place where one feels safe.

A place from which one's strength of character is drawn.

The Prescott cottage was my querencia.

"Who lives in the cottage, Miss Winthrop?" he repeated.

"You don't know?"

"I do. I want to hear you say it."

"The Prescotts."

"No, Emery." My name rolled off his tongue so naturally, as if we were friends. *Filthy snake.* "Their names."

Not a snake.

A fiery serpent.

It reminded me of the Book of Numbers, the story some of the nannies would tell to scare us into behaving. God had sent fiery serpents to punish people for speaking out against him. Moses built the Nehushtan as protection against the serpents. A staff in the shape of a cross, a serpent coiled around the wood.

My hands itched to wrap around one and brand it as a weapon against the world. A weapon against him.

Instead, I whispered their names. "Betty. Hank. Reed. Nash."

Maybe he wasn't the snake.

Maybe I was.

A weak one, raised in captivity, not meant to be wild.

"Tell me about Nash," he said.

"Why?"

"The way you say his name—"

"Is none of your business." Venom slithered up my throat. If I were a snake, I would poison this man before he touched my Prescotts. "He doesn't live here anymore. It's just Betty, Hank, and Reed. And before you accuse them of anything, Reed is just a kid, and Betty and Hank are good people."

"And Nash? Is he a good person?"

I considered it and realized I didn't know. As much as

I wanted to say no, I couldn't. Not as an attempt to protect him, but because Nash's actions always contradicted his words. I didn't think of him as a bad person.

He wasn't sweet words.

He was sweet actions.

The notes the agents had probably rifled through proved that.

Besides, Reed never talked about it, but I figured Nash was going through something, and everyone deserved a second chance.

It didn't mean the sting of that night had disappeared. It didn't mean my cheeks stopped flushing each time I thought of him. But it was a good type of flush. The way your cheeks warmed when you knew a secret that was too good to keep to yourself.

I'd taken too long to answer, and when I turned to my right, the stranger had already left. I pivoted, pausing when I heard a tree ruffling in the maze. Forcing the curiosity aside, I sprinted down the path to the house in time to catch the profile of the man's face before he slipped inside my house through the backdoor.

The same face staring back at me on my sketchbook.

Brandon Vu.

chapter THIRTY-SIX

Emery

THE PRESENT

I should have taken tonight's starless sky as a warning.
 Nothing good ever happened on them.
 I swung the hotel lobby door open and glared at the sky, sifting through some secrets I could offer it.
 Secret #1—I may shed a tear if I get to the soup kitchen and find it closed—then poison Chantilly for making us work so late without overtime pay.

Secret #2—I screamed Nash's name so loud when Ben made me come last night. You can't imagine the fear fueling my veins when I peeped my head out of the closet to make sure no one heard me.

Secret #3—I snuck a bag of pita chips and cold soda from the fridge when everyone went to lunch today and Delilah came down to grab Nash's signature on a few papers. I hid the wrapper and empty can under the couch cushions when he came back sooner than I'd expected.

Chantilly sat on the cushion above the can, and everyone went silent because they thought she farted. I said nothing, even when red flushed her cheeks and she looked at Nash like he'd throw on a knight's armor and save her.

Does that make me the dragon and Chantilly the princess in this story? (If it's any consolation, she'd join a league of Snow Whites, and you know how I feel about that.)

There you have it. Are three secrets enough for you, Starless Sky? Will you spare me tonight?

"Waiting for the sky to fall, Winthrop? That would only happen if you ever decided to act normal."

My legs jerked at Nash's lazy drawl. I tamped their reaction as best as I could, exhaling as if I'd run a marathon in the past second. My staccato heartbeat reached a climax before falling.

"Following me is pointless." I gave the sky another fifteen seconds to respond—a shooting star, a comet, anything—before I lowered my head and began walking. "I'm never going to accept your double portions. You may as well stop."

I didn't have to stare at him to know the corners of his lips curled up when my stomach protested.

Loudly.

"Hmm..." Nash's stride matched mine. "Do you really want to walk yourself to the soup kitchen alone in the dark only to walk back after you figure out it's closed?"

Translation: are you that stubborn?

I tipped a shoulder up in a half-assed shrug and catapulted to record-breaking speeds. "If the shoe fits, it fucking fits."

"That's not the saying." Nash's hand shot out and steadied me when a car rounded the corner too closely.

My heart punched at my chest, rendering me too useless to protest as he swapped our positions, so he walked on the street side.

When I finally collected myself, I should have thanked him. Instead, I continued my speed walk. "You must wear shoes that don't fit."

"That's not a saying either." He dug two hands into his dress slacks. We waited for the sign to turn white. "For the record, I'm not following you. I volunteer at that soup kitchen. Better—I basically fund it."

"We both know the soup kitchen is closed. It's—" I grabbed Nash's hand to glance at his watch, but the wild rhythm of his pulse against my fingertips distracted me. Definitely didn't think that one through. "Umm..."

"Ten forty-six."

Catching sight of his amusement might very well kill me, so I glared at the sky. We waited for the crosslight to turn green.

I gave you secrets.
You gave me Nash.
What the fuck, dude?

"Right." I lowered my head. "It's ten forty-six."

"If you know the soup kitchen is closed, why are you still headed there?"

"Hope, young grasshopper." I rounded the corner adjacent to the soup kitchen, recalling his note about asking Betty to find his hope. Had he ever found it? "That shit gets me full."

"Like magic words?"

I stopped and gave in, studying his face with the vigor of a straight-A student. He seemed pleased with himself. Too confident that he'd found a pressure point of mine. The real pressure points were the questions that threatened to spill past my lips.

The most important one being—*why do you even care about feeding me?*

I bit my tongue.

"What do you know about magic words?"

"I know you look batshit when you mouth them during meetings with suppliers." His arm crossed over my stomach as a car careened past us at the crosswalk. My abs flexed at his touch, my shirt suddenly feeling too thin. Meanwhile, he appeared unaffected. "People stare at me and wonder why the fuck I hired the lunatic in the ripped jeans and *selcouth* tees."

"I haven't worn the *selcouth* tee since—"

He cocked a brow. "Since?"

"Is there a point to this conversation, or can we eat— Wait. You're pressing me." My fists rested on each hip. I tipped my head up to glower at Nash. "If you think you can do some subtle ninja interrogation and find a way to trick me into eating your food, you're as stoned as you used to be."

"Doesn't matter." He gestured across the street. "The soup kitchen is closed. The lights are off. Unless..."

You hate me, don't you, Starless Night?

"Unless?" I curled my toes inside my Chucks, knowing I'd loathe whatever answer he offered me.

"Unless you know someone who donates a shit ton of money and has a key to the place."

"That sounds suspiciously like a set up." I retreated a step when I realized how close we stood. "Or worse—a favor."

"Come on, Tiger." His jaw ticked, gaze flicking upward in a way that made me wonder if he talked to starless skies, too. "Give yourself a break."

"If you tell me why you call me Tiger." I bounced on my toes, wondering what else I could glean from him. Nash hoarded secrets like the Kardashians hoarded cars. He could stand to lose a few. "No bullshit. None of that abstract answer thing you pulled the other day, too."

The pad of his thumb brushed his bottom lip. "I tell you why I call you tiger, and you go in?"

"It's that easy."

His curse rocked my heels back. "That's not easy."

The button-down he wore pulled tight when he shoved his hands inside his dress slacks. Solid stone sat beneath his shirt, and I wondered if it would ever crack. He reminded me so much of the Sisyphus statue I'd found. I almost couldn't wait to show it to him, but I remembered I'd called the gallery and asked them to hold the Depressing Sisyphus instead.

His eyes dipped to my stomach, which took its cue to growl. "Fine." He ran his hand through his hair—once, which I'd never figured out the meaning of.

"An actual explanation," I warned. "Be honest."

Waiting for him to answer felt like finishing a book and learning the next wouldn't release for a year.

"Remember when I first said it?" His jaw ticked at his words.

"When I ran into you at my cotillion."

"Yeah." The scowl unfurling across his face could

conquer lands and unseat kings. "After you kneed Able Small Dick Cartwright in the balls. Twice." He delivered the words like you'd deliver a bomb. No remorse.

I jabbed at the crosswalk button, harder than necessary. "Good times."

"I said it because you're fierce." Nash touched my elbow until I faced him and held eye contact. "You came out of that room looking like a warrior, ready to destroy anything that dared cross you, including me and Reed."

Some people accept criticism well; others, compliments. I fell into a third category—neither. Mostly because I didn't talk to many people and cared even less about their opinion of me.

It made accepting a compliment from Nash more difficult than it should have been, because it came accompanied by the underlying threat of luring me in.

I shoved my hands into my pockets, allowing them to curl into fists out of sight.

"It's not an insult?" I barely heard my words over my pulse.

"It was never an insult."

A hummingbird had replaced my heart, and it fluttered inside me, beating its wings to a rhythm I couldn't keep up with.

Shut up, Heart. I can't deal with you right now. Go hibernate.

I wanted to ask so many questions.
Why are you feeding me?
Why are you mad at the world?
Why are you mad at me?
Are you okay? Has anyone asked you that since Hank died?

Swallowing them all, I nodded across the street. "The

crosslight turned green." I dodged around Nash and made it to the door first.

He could have asked me to move, but he leaned over my body. His front pressed against my back. He reached around me and unlocked the door. I shotgunned forward at the first opportunity, making my way through the buffet with my phone's flashlight until I realized everything had been emptied. Not even the chip packets remained at the snack station.

"Fuck."

Nash flicked the light on from the door. "I'll make you a sandwich in the back."

"The deal was, I'd go inside. Not that I'd eat anything." I trailed him into the kitchen because it felt weird to be in the buffet area without supervision. "Good thing Delilah's your lawyer and not you."

He ignored me, washed his hands, and pulled out ingredients with ease, obviously familiar with the kitchen's layout. I set my phone down and studied him. His fluid movements disgusted me. No one deserved to make sandwiches with the grace of a professional athlete.

Two slices of sourdough.

Turkey.

Extra chipotle mayo.

Lettuce.

Watching him make me food felt surreal. Obviously, I knew he'd done it in the past, but seeing it was a different story. Like breaking the fourth wall.

Nash was the star quarterback who lived in his own fiery universe, and he'd somehow gravitated into my icy one. I wanted to share my starless skies and steal his scorching sun. I would never understand it, but it was my truth.

This is why happiness isn't permanent, I thought. *Life*

introduces you to fantasies, then makes you feel like you can't have them. You spend the rest of your life seeking that fantasy. When you realize it grew beneath your feet, it's too late.

I set my phone on the countertop opposite of him, leaned against it, and gripped it with both hands. When Nash added a layer of Cheddar & Sour Cream Ruffles inside the sandwich, my head jerked back.

My favorite sandwich.

He remembered.

How the fuck?

Never once did he look up to me. His attention to detail unnerved me. He sliced the bread diagonally, placed it on a rectangular plate, and set it beside my hand on the counter. My feet seemed less solid as I stared at it.

It occurred to me that we knew more about one another than we'd let on.

Getting to know someone is like gaining weight. Scattered bits acquired here and there. Next thing you know, you're twenty pounds heavier, wondering where the hell all of it came from.

"What?" he asked when I didn't touch it.

"Umm..." I tugged the hem of my tee.

"Jesus, Emery, spit it out." Nash shot me a look that suggested he didn't know why he was putting himself through this. "You've never been shy before. Don't start now."

I went with the first thing I could think of.

"There's no card..."

"Are you serious?"

"Do I look like I'm kidding?"

I expected him to ignore me, but he shook his head, grabbed a pen and paper from a drawer, and set it on the counter. His tongue swiped his lips as he wrote. Slowly at first, then quick scribbles I feared I wouldn't be able to read.

He folded the note and set it beside the sandwich. "Don't read it now."

"But—"

"Do you want it or not?"

I tucked the note into my pocket before he could take it back. "Fine."

My stomach growled. I eyed the sandwich and toyed with the bread.

"What now?" His lips pressed together. He ran his hand through his hair. *Twice.* "Just eat the sandwich. Fuck."

His persistence reached a point where I couldn't deny it. I didn't understand his motives, but I knew he genuinely wanted me fed, and that offered me leverage. It was a matter of how much.

"If I let you feed me," I began, taking my time, "I get to ask two things of you—a favor and a question. I expect the truth."

"You used up your honesty for the day."

I jutted my chin up, daring him to pull a Chantilly and argue. "Nash."

"What?"

My eyes peered at him. I hoped he saw how much I meant it. "Work with me. Please."

He took his time examining me. I thought he'd given up on feeding me until he grabbed the sandwich and held it in front of my lips.

"Take a bite first, then we talk."

Blood rushed to my cheeks. I leaned forward and bit into the sandwich, pulling back when my lips brushed against his finger. I hurried to chew, unable to enjoy the taste as his eyes fixated on my mouth.

"What's the favor?" he asked when I swallowed.

"I want a centerpiece for the hotel."

"Why?"

The door seemed further away.

I peeked at it and considered making a run for it. "Why what?"

"You know what I'm asking. Stop being cute." A fingertip met the bottom of my chin. The slightest touch turned me to face him. "Why do you want the centerpiece so much?"

"This isn't part of the deal." His touch burned my chin. I dislodged from it with a shake of my head. "I eat, and you do it. That's the deal."

"Fuck the deal. Answer the question."

"You can't follow rules, can you?"

"Rules are made to separate leaders from followers. I know which I am, and it seems you're not the one I thought you were." He set the sandwich down and folded his arms across his chest, studying my face like he didn't understand me and didn't fully understand why he wanted to. "You could ask for any favor. A centerpiece doesn't benefit you. Why this?"

I resented Nash for being so relentless. His conviction matched my own, which meant every time we spoke, one of us won and one of us lost. And I usually sat on the losing side.

What was that Robert Kiyosaki quote?

Sometimes you win, and sometimes you learn.

I swallowed my pride and took the L, wondering what the fuck it taught me. "You don't care about Haling Cove's location."

"Because you know me so well?"

"I do."

I fidgeted with my fingers, telling myself my words

wouldn't condemn me. So what if I knew Nash? He'd lived on my dad's estate for almost ten years. It'd be less normal if I *didn't* know Nash.

I continued, "I don't like that I do, but it doesn't change the fact that I know you. You don't care about Haling Cove, but Betty cares about you. Haling Cove is close to Eastridge. That means she'll be here during the grand opening."

My pulse leapt in my throat, nearly choking me, a reminder of what a pain in the ass it could be. Loving someone Nash loved seemed more intimate in the moment. As if it were a degree too close to him.

"And?" he asked.

I considered lying, but what would the point? He usually saw through it. Plus, lies cost more than truths, and I was broke with a capital B.

"And," I drawled, rushing out a breath with my words, "I want her to be proud of what I helped build."

His silence made my feet bounce against the linoleum. I waited for him to wash away that glint from his eyes. It made the room feel hotter, the floor less sturdy, and my stomach prick with little needles.

I broke first. "Will you do it or what?"

"Done." That glint never left his eyes. If anything, it grew, a balloon near its popping point. "Eat the food."

Beside us, my phone buzzed. I shot my eyes to it, praying it wasn't a notification from the Eastridge United app before I remembered I'd shut those off. Reed's name flashed on the screen.

I didn't move to answer.

Nash had picked up the sandwich again, but it hovered in his hands as he eyed the phone. "You're ignoring him?"

"He's proposing to Basil."

I didn't elaborate.

"I don't understand it."

"Neither do I." I automatically bit into the sandwich when he held it up to me, then stepped back after I realized what I'd done. His amusement didn't waver as I glared at him, chewed, and swallowed. "I don't like him like that anymore," I added since he continued giving me a look that suggested I did.

"Sure."

"I swear."

"I believe you."

"I mean it."

I swiped hair out of my eyes and frowned, realizing something. Reed never made me feel like I floated in the air while tethered to the ground. A feeling I only knew existed because it was the type of off-balance that engulfed me whenever Nash neared.

As if the memory of who he used to be made who he currently was that much more enticing. The fighter who fed me turned into the billionaire C.E.O. who fed me, and not a single person in this fucking world could guess why, but at least I came closest.

"Reed and I never would have been good together anyway," I added.

"I know."

I narrowed my eyes. "Excuse me?"

Nash tilted his head and scanned my body. "Did Reed ever make you come?"

"We both know he didn't. Either your point is flying over my head, or it's so meaningless, giving it my attention would be a waste of time. I could be listening to Danez Smith poems right now."

He ignored me, a glimpse of a smile forming. "Did he ever make you wet without touching you?"

I folded my arms across my chest. "Not everything in life is about sex."

Nash set the sandwich down. "Not my point."

That smile shined in full force, and it occurred to me that I didn't remember ever seeing it. His smile could cure cancer, abolish student loan debt, and bring world peace. I wanted to pocket it and save it for myself. World peace sounded boring anyway.

"Would you ever let Reed touch you like I have?" he asked, engulfing me with just his words. It was like we stood in the unfinished suite again, and I couldn't get the taste of him off my tongue.

I focused on my toes, wiggled them inside my Chucks, and counted each one to distract myself. "I can barely believe I let *you* touch me," I muttered.

Or that I'd let you do it again.

"Did you ever feel like fighting for him?" His eyes read my face, collecting all the answers he needed from the dumbfounded expression pasted on it. "If someone looked at him wrong, talked to him wrong, touched him wrong, you would pick up a fucking sword and dive into battle without remembering to grab your armor?"

"I'd fight for him," I protested.

I would.

Reed was my best friend.

If he called me up at four a.m. and told me he'd killed someone, I'd help him dig a damn grave outside a police station if he needed me to.

Nash shook his head like he found me sad and pathetic. His confidence punished me, because it meant he believed in his words, and when Nash believed, I did, too.

"You'd fight *beside* him, not *for* him. Two separate things. If he asked you to put down the sword, you'd listen because your stake isn't bone-deep, a reflex, an untrained instinct. You have a choice in it, and that is the difference between loving someone and being *in* love with someone. You can control one, but you sure as hell can't control the other."

"What do you know about love?" I spit out, hating the gap in our wisdom.

In ten years, would I say things like this?

Would I even know things like this?

He slid off his suit jacket and tossed it onto the counter, stopping only to loosen his tie. "Enough to know you were never in love with Reed."

"But *how?*"

"Because I know what love looks like. I had to watch Ma and Dad love each other, then lose each other. Your parents have the most money of anyone I've ever met, but mine are the richest people I've ever known." He tore off his tie, unbuttoned the top two buttons of his shirt, and folded his cuffs midway up his arms, stopping just when the *penance* tattoo peeked out. "If I tell you anything worth learning, it's this. Love is the most expensive thing you'll ever own. You pay for it with grief, tears, and a piece of your soul, but in return, you receive happiness, memories, and *life*."

"Why are you telling me this?"

"Words matter to you, yet you throw the most important one around without understanding what it means."

Yes, but why does that matter to you? Why does it bother you enough to correct me? Why, why, why? I don't understand you, Nash Prescott. Do you even understand yourself?

"It was fierce loyalty that tricked you into thinking you were in love with Reed," he added.

"Because you know me so well."

"I do. Let's cut the shit and stop pretending that we're strangers. You never belonged with Reed, Little Tiger. He is domesticated. You are wild. To tame you would be a travesty. The sooner you get that, the sooner you can move on."

He said it so casually, so matter-of-fact, I almost didn't process the weight of his words.

Almost.

If that was how Nash saw me, why—*fucking why*—were we always at each other's throats?

If Reed was the prince of peaceful forests and snowless mountains, Nash was the king of smoke, and ashes, and lies. He was the fire that ravaged those forests and the ashes that rained down on those mountains. I wanted to inhale his smoke, coat my tongue with his ashes, and bury myself in his lies.

But smoke ruined lungs.

Ashes tasted like death.

And lies blinded dreamers.

I was a dreamer.

He was a nightmare.

chapter THIRTY-SEVEN

Emery

War brewed within me, fueled by envy.
I blinked at Nash, wondering how he could stand there with a fucking Turkey & Ruffles sandwich held out to me like this was normal. He arched a brow as if to tell me my opinion of myself was built on a lie.

We stared at one another until he brought the sandwich to my lips again.

I let him continue feeding me, accepting another bite.

It gave me time to hide my uncertainty. Handling our proximity shook me, but handling his words crippled me.

After I finished the sandwich, he washed and cut strawberries, then set a bowl of them on the counter. Sliding the freezer open, he scooped vanilla bean ice cream into the bowl and finished it off with Torani white chocolate and marshmallow syrups.

Fucking hell, I felt like the Eastridge princess I used to be as I brought a spoonful of bliss to my mouth.

The same ice cream flavor and toppings I would eat when a busted-up Nash broke into the mansion for ice.

His eyes remained on my lips as I chewed. They followed a path down the column of my neck when I swallowed. I was a zoo animal, on display for a feeding show. Or maybe I was the prey getting prepped to be fed to the predator.

"What about the question you owe me?" My voice sounded hoarse. Dry despite the ice cream that coated it.

"This isn't Twenty Questions." Disdain dripped from him like the ice cream melting from the side of the bowl. "You overestimate my generosity. You already got a favor and free life advice. I'm neither a Magic 8 ball, nor Oprah."

Thumbing the falling liquid from the ceramic, I sucked it into my mouth, stopping when I caught his intensity.

"Humor me..." I thrust the bowl out, hoping he wouldn't take it. "Or I'm suddenly feeling very full and would appreciate it if you could finish this. We wouldn't want to waste this food, would we?"

"Why does this feel like a fucking mistake?" he muttered, but he stepped closer with each word, his movements pressing the bowl back to my chest. His breath grazed my forehead, tickling my cheek. "What's the damn question, Little Tiger?"

"Singapore."

"Surely, that overpriced education did better than this." Nash toyed with a strand of my hair. I wonder if he realized he was doing it. It might've been the first time he'd initiated contact with me. "That's not a question. Ask an actual question." His fingers paused. "Last chance."

"Why Singapore?"

"Why not?"

Slipping my hair from his fingers, I spooned more ice cream into my mouth. "An honest answer or I'm never eating another sandwich from you."

I hadn't intended to, despite my stomach's protests, but the trade-off was worth it.

Nash shelved the syrups and faced me. "I like Singapore."

I realized my mistake too late. I'd asked the wrong question. Irritation blossomed in my chest, but I tamped it when I realized his redirects meant there was a lie to unravel here, a secret to be fleeced.

I wanted it.

I needed to own all his secrets.

Craved it.

If not for proprietorship, then for the sake of leveling the playing field.

"Why that property?" I pressed, setting the finished bowl onto the counter. My breath tasted like strawberry, vanilla, chocolate, and marshmallows. I wondered what his tasted like.

He rinsed the bowl in the sink and deposited it into an industrial dishwasher. "That's a second question."

"It's an add-on to the original question."

Nash shook his head and returned to me with a napkin in his hand. "Always breaking the fucking rules."

When he offered it to me, I ignored it, darted my tongue to the corner of my lips, and swiped off the white chocolate. He tracked the movement, whereas I tracked him.

His throat bobbed. The napkin crumbled in his grip. I imagined he wanted to loosen his collar or run his hand through his hair. Three times, because I made him uncomfortable. I made him want to leave.

"Always trying to make the fucking rules," I volleyed back and cleared my throat, unsure how to feel about our proximity. The laps my blood raced didn't feel very healthy. "No one made you king, Nash."

He spread his arms like an eagle in flight, taking up so much space he consumed me. "You're standing in my kingdom, Winthrop. I own the air you breathe, the land you walk on, the company you work for. I own North Carolina."

I didn't doubt his words for a second. It struck me how much the tables had turned. The fallen Winthrop princess. The unrelenting king who had taken her place. My heart rattled my chest as our fairy tale sunk in.

Not Disney.

Brothers Grimm.

In which a cruel king rules over a stolen kingdom, and a poor servant lives in the tyrant's line of fire.

Only, I knew how those fairy tales ended.

When the people ended.

"All I'm standing on is a bed of false promises." I begged my stomach to steady. It churned, full of favorite foods and lies. "You like Singapore, sure. That's not an answer. Not all of it."

Nash leaned against the counter, hands shoved into his dress slacks pockets. "It's the one you're getting."

"Why won't you tell me?" I edged forward until we stood toe-to-toe. I needed him to look at me—really look at me—and understand I was dead serious. "I'm not going to judge you, Nash. We push each other's buttons. I say you're cruel. You say my name like it's a curse and a sin. But have I ever, for a single second, made you feel like I thought of you as anything less than you are?"

"No." The truth sat between us like an unwelcome visitor, lingering too long as we wondered how it had even gotten there. He rubbed at the back of his neck before returning the palm to his pocket. "The building next door."

"What about it?"

"I stayed there once. Delilah and I ate at the restaurant on the roof. Outdoors. No ceiling. Shitty fucking food, but I felt high enough in the sky to touch Dad, far enough from Eastridge to breathe, and close enough to the ground to convince myself it was reality. It's the only time I ever wanted to do this. Run Prescott Hotels, instead of burning it to the ground. I'm buying the building next to it and constructing a skyscraper that's taller, better, closer to the moon."

I tipped my head back and eyed the ceiling, wishing we stood outside. "How was the sky?"

"What do you mean?"

Muttering a magic word, I sloped my head back to him. "Were there stars?"

"It's the city..."

"What does that mean? Yes or no?"

"No, there weren't stars."

"A starless night," I whispered, enchanted, unaware that I'd edged myself against him.

It happened so fast.

Our lips crashed together, our teeth clanging.

It wasn't a nice kiss, because he didn't deserve a nice kiss. No matter how much the world thought of him, no matter the savior Eastridge and the press considered him to be, no matter how much everyone at Prescott Hotels or the soup kitchen raved about him, he didn't deserve nice.

Not from me.

Never from me.

He kissed me like the villain he was. Rough and unrelenting. I pulled at his body, skin, neck. Anything I could get my hands on. Sliding my tongue into his mouth, we warred with each stroke.

His hands met my waist and lifted me easily. I wrapped my legs around his back, groaning when he placed me onto the countertop and ground against me. Whatever skin I could reach, I stole, touching it like it was mine. Pretending it was mine.

And by the end, we were panting, and his shirt had a tear down the side, and mine laid somewhere across the room without him ever actually pulling it off.

"Lagom," I whispered, resting my forehead to his, chasing my breaths.

He tasted like something permanent. Something that would be etched on my lips long after we parted.

And it felt wrong.

The kiss felt wrong.

Not because he was my boss.

Not because he was cruel.

Not because everyone would hate us for it.

Not because his brother was my best friend.

Not because I used to think I was in love with Reed.

But because nothing—*and I mean fucking nothing*—should have felt this good.

And anything that did?

Had to be wrong.

Nash breathed against my lips, still parted as he exchanged breaths with me. "What's lagom?"

My hands fell to his chest, thrilled by his heart's tempo. It matched mine. "Not too little. Not too much. Just right."

I didn't believe in perfect, but I believed in lagom.

It meant right, but not necessarily perfect.

And in a world filled with devious lies, it was a truth I latched onto.

Nash dipped his fingers beneath the hem of my jeans, brushing his thumb against the crease of my thigh and sex. "Why not say perfect?"

I shook my head, appalled by the idea. "Perfection is unattainable. It's stained by the suffering required to chase it. Perfect is something you think with your head. Lagom is something you feel with your heart."

His fingers ran a path along my underwear, knuckles brushing so much skin.

"Why are you looking at me like that?" I asked and moved back, but his grip tightened on my waist, shifting me closer for a moment before he released me.

"I thought of a word." He mouthed it like I do, looking a little ridiculous and endearing for once. "Is that what it's like?"

"Like a cure?"

Nash's eyes took in the space between us. "No."

He didn't elaborate, and I didn't want him to. Not if he'd ruin magic words for me. He wielded the power, and I was too protective of words to risk it.

"What's the word?" I asked.

Desperation didn't suit me, but I needed to know.

Nash brushed a thumb across my cheek and slammed

his lips against mine. He kissed me like I was nuclear and he needed to destroy me to save himself. His tongue slipped past my lips, stroking mine. I gripped his shirt, and he gripped my hair, running his hands through it in a way that had me begging to pant *cafuné*.

It ended too soon, before I could even appreciate that it'd begun. Disappointment slithered inside me, expanding at our distance.

"It's late," he said, pulling away from me. "Security in the plaza makes their rounds in an hour."

My shirt had been torn down the middle like a vest, so I wore it backward and used Nash's suit jacket to cover my exposed spine. He managed to look dangerous with the mussed hair and ripped shirt, whereas I resembled a kid playing dress-up.

We walked to the hotel in silence, stopping at the entrance. I opened my mouth when I realized he'd never told me the word, but I shoved my curiosity down my throat and replaced it with my own magic words.

Nyctophilia.

Basorexia.

Ibrat.

Nash eyed my lips, watching them form and pocket the words.

"I'm driving you home." He nodded in the direction of the parking garage. That would go horribly when he realized I didn't have a home. "Before you waste our time arguing, it's non-negotiable. It's late, dark, and cold enough that I see your nipples every time we pass a streetlamp. I know you don't have a death wish, so your stubbornness will only come off as stupidity."

Ignoring all but his first sentence, I backed away, inch by inch. "I'm good." My shoulder lifted. "Maybe you don't know me as well as you think you do, Nash," I taunted, a little pissed that he never told me the word.

"Emery."

"Stop saying my name like it's a demand."

"Emery."

My eyes dipped to the penance tattoo I wanted to taste. I allowed myself two seconds to study it, turned, and walked away.

I pivoted when I remembered how persistent he could be. Better to let him scheme where I could see him. He already had his phone pulled out when he glanced up at me, like he'd known I would return.

Dick.

He'd already opened the Uber app. "Where do you live?"

Shit. Shit. Shit. What do I do?

I kept my mouth shut and held my hand out. As soon as his phone touched my fingers, I moved the dot on the app to a random residential neighborhood close by. Giving him my back, I leaned against the hotel, tapped my fingers on the glass, and stared at the sky.

I'm starting to think Nash isn't the villain, Starless Sky. Maybe you are.

Nash held out his palm. "My phone."

Oh.

I glanced down at it, my eyes pausing on the Eastridge United app before I returned it to him. Of course, he had the app. He owned it. But did he have a pen pal? He didn't seem like the type.

Then again, if I used it for phone sex, maybe he did, too.

That, I could see him doing.

Jealousy coiled around my throat. I pulled at the

collar of my tee, forgetting the huge rip as I flashed Nash with some serious skin.

Ignoring him, I tipped my head at the sky.

Shut up, dude. Even the moon is jealous of the stars. And you, Starless Sky, have no stars. I bet that makes you jealous of everyone.

When I lowered my head, Nash still studied me, so I watched him back, daring him to break the silence. Secretly thrilled at the feeling of his eyes on me.

I had no intention of kissing Nash tonight, but if I had to explain it, I'd chalk it up to the look in his eyes when he told me about the starless night in Singapore.

Nash reminded me of a favorite song. One you play so often you think you can't stand anymore. But in the silence, when the world is quiet and your brain is pliant, the chords repeat in your mind, and you remember it's your favorite melody.

I broke first, dipping my eyes until he followed suit, much slower than I had. We stood a foot apart, neither of us talking as we stared at our phones. He was probably playing Candy Crush, but I opened the Eastridge United app to check if Ben was on. I squashed a smile at the sight of the green dot.

Durga: How was your night?

Benkinersophobia: Satisfying. Until it wasn't. Yours?

Durga: Satisfying. Until it wasn't.

Flicking a glance at Nash, I angled my screen away from him. I didn't need the headache of him catching me on his app and accusing me of whatever shitty things he thought I'd done. Cryptic comments my pride didn't allow me to ask about.

Durga: Tell me something ugly.

Benkinersophobia: My heart.

Durga: That's not true.

Durga: If your heart is ugly, what is mine? What am I?

Ben didn't reply for a minute. I slanted a glance at Nash. Brows furrowed, he typed something fast. My head fell again before he could catch me staring.

Benkinersophobia: You are a fantasy, a goddess, a heroine, a dream. Those have happy endings.

Durga: And what are you?

Benkinersophobia: I am Sisyphus, a treacherous sea that will drown you.

A car honked twice. Dragging my attention from the screen, I caught the telltale Uber sticker before approaching. Nash opened the back door for me, which I ignored. I slid into the passenger side.

Gifting me a scowl, Nash tapped the window, indicating I lower it. I didn't, but the driver listened. The frosty air bit my skin as the car's heater seeped outside.

Nash made a show of pulling out his phone, taking a picture of the driver, then photographing his license.

"Derrick Atterberry, of 8143 Adair Lane, I have your face, your driver's license, your name, your address, and your license plate number." Nash's forearms rested on the open window frame, his hands dangerously close to touching me. "Nod your head if you're following me."

Derrick's throat bobbed. He nodded his head like the Usain Bolt bobblehead on his dash.

Nash held up his phone. "I also have the numbers of every important politician along this coast, including the president; an ability to lie my way into and out of any situation; an ethical code that sits somewhere between Jordan Belfort snorting cocaine off his mistress' asscheeks and using toddlers as test subjects for torture à la MK-Ultra; and a strong repertoire for vengeance, including but not limited to one-starring your ass on Uber." He paused. "Did I tell you to stop nodding your head?"

Derrick cleared his throat and swiped the sweat off his forehead. "No."

"Are you not following?"

"No. I mean, yes." His fingers gripped the steering wheel tighter. "I mean, I'm following."

"Then nod your fucking head."

Derrick nodded his head. He didn't stop, even when Nash continued.

"Get her home safe, wait until her fucking front door closes, and I'll spare you the receiving end of a wrath you've never known and are unequipped to survive." He reached into *my* wallet and tossed three hundreds at the driver. "Do whatever she says," he slid three more hundreds into the inner pocket of his suit jacket I wore, brushing against my hard nipple, "and she'll give you the rest."

My heart still hiccupped as we left Nash behind, skipping a beat every few seconds. The side mirrors showed him watching the car until we left his line of sight. I should have assured the poor driver Nash hadn't meant any of that, but A—I think he did and B—I remembered what Nash once said about not kissing.

I brought my fingers to my lips, grazing them. I couldn't get my mind off his lips on mine. Worse—not knowing why he'd done it would drive me crazy.

"Can you mark the ride as finished on the app, then take me back to the hotel?" I asked when the driver arrived at the random house address I'd chosen.

"Uhh..."

Furrowed brows hovered over his eyes. They peeped at the three hundred-dollar bills littered across the center console. He hadn't picked them up. His hands had shaken too much on the drive here. They still plastered to the steering wheel. Positioned ten and two like a Boy Scout, even with the brakes on.

I reached into my jean pockets for the money. My hand brushed against the note Nash had given me at the soup kitchen before I remembered he'd placed the money inside the jacket pocket. I pulled out the note and retrieved the hundreds from the inner pocket.

Waving the bills, I offered the most innocent expression I could muster. "I'll give you these regardless, but he did say to do whatever I tell you. Please?"

On the drive back, I pressed the car light on and read the note, hunching my shoulders to cradle it with my body.

> *If you think about it, the concept of a photograph is fucking mind-blowing. A moment in time. Captured. Preserved. Forever. I shouldn't have torn your Polaroid of Reed.*
>
> **— NASH**

Nash's version of an apology.

I shut the light off, folded the note as carefully as I could, and peered out the window at the sky.

Not bad, Starless Night. Not bad.

chapter THIRTY-EIGHT

nash

I existed in a state of permanent irritation any asshole with a brain could diagnose as blue balls, because I couldn't fuck the two people I wanted to fuck. One was a faceless username, and the other drove me so crazy, I didn't fully understand why I wanted her.

I just knew I did.

Admitting it felt like holding my arm up to a dog and asking it to bite me. (An actual dog, like a Belgian Malinois or a Rottweiler, not a Rosco. Rosco's teeth would probably fall off if he tried to bite me, and then he'd be hairless *and* toothless.)

Unlike the dumb-fucks that enjoyed teeth play, my masochistic tendencies didn't include physical pain.

And it fucking *pained* me to admit I'd kiss Emery again.

Repeatedly.

For days.

Jesus, are those teeth I'm feeling?

Delilah lapped up the sight of construction workers from her desk. They left the kitchen a goddamn pigsty. Loud drills reverberated to my side of the penthouse. Randell carried in a section of the countertop with ease, whereas his son Bud knocked the cabinet door cradled in his arms into everything.

Delilah: You should have hired Chip and Joanna Gaines.

Setting my phone down, I tossed her a water bottle from the mini-fridge built into my desk. "Who and who?"

"Seriously?"

"You're not sparing anyone by texting." My voice never wavered. If anything, I raised it. I cracked open my bottle and chugged half of it in one gulp. "If you think Randell and Bud are fucking up, just say it."

"*Nash*," she hissed. "What is up with you today?"

Two words—*blue* and *balls*.

I leaned back in my executive chair, eyed the scratched wall, and beckoned Bud with two fingers. The lanky kid ambled over here with the grace of a newborn giraffe learning to walk.

"Bud, define nepotism," I ordered, wondering what the design crew was doing downstairs.

I couldn't remember the last time I'd worked up here, but I had to supervise the kitchen, considering I had half a mill stashed in the safe, and the construction crew had drills, hammers, and saws.

"Um..." His calloused fingers gripped my desk, leaving wood residue. Bud's eyes darted to Delilah. "When someone hires a person because of whom they're related to?"

"Continue."

He snuck a glance at Randell, who watched him suffer with a chuckle. "And, um, it's a...favor?"

"Keep going."

"And... the person hired is... um..."

"Fucking hell," Delilah muttered. She scrawled her signature and set down her pen. "Nash, the kid's sweating enough. This is painful to watch." She put Bud out of his misery. "Bud, what Nash is trying to say is, you and your dad both work for us, which poses the question of whether or not nepotism was involved in the hiring process. People will think so if you continue to make mistakes without learning from them. Can you be more careful from here on?"

"Yes, ma'am." Bud nodded at me and Delilah a second before fleeing. Even the back of his head appeared relieved.

"Mother Teresa," I shot at Delilah. Pulling up an account, I wired a few thousand dollars to the company I hired to move the sculpture from my Eastridge home to the lobby. "You chose the wrong job for mercy."

"I chose the wrong job in general." She closed her laptop, rested her chin on her knuckles, and stared at me. "Is there a reason you asked for the sudden rush on the kitchen? You could've given me a heads up. I would have slept in." Her pointer finger twirled in a circle. "I can't work with this noise, and Rosco hates wearing his puppy earplugs."

"Chill. First, the rat will survive. They live in sewers, for fuck's sake." I peered at the foot of Delilah's desk, where Rosco curled into a ball on a Louis Vuitton four-poster miniature pet bed. Orange faux fur-lined earmuffs covered the two Dumbo flappers sprouting from his head. "Second, the crew has been at it for hours. They're almost done. The cleaners will be here in," I eyed my watch, "twenty minutes give or take."

"You didn't answer the question, which in itself is intriguing." Delilah repeated, "Is there a reason for the rush job?"

"They already had the cabinets drilled in, the flooring placed, and the appliances installed." I tapped my fingers over my keyboard, double-checked that the word *bribe* had been replaced with *a show of gratitude and friendship*, and pressed send on a memo to a Singaporean diplomat. "You act as if they're creating a kitchen from scratch. It's just the counter and cabinet doors."

"You still didn't answer the question."

"Is this what we're doing now? Playing Twenty Questions instead of working? If so, I'll start." I closed my laptop and blanketed her with my full attention. "What's that word called when you dismiss an employee from her job for failure to work?"

She hit me with an unimpressed eye roll. "I detect an unusual and entertaining level of defensiveness."

Of course, I was fucking defensive.

She would be, too, if her first kiss in over fifteen years went to a girl who talked more to the sky than she did with actual goddamn humans, and whispered made-up words to herself, and snuck into other people's beds and showers as if she owned the world, and possessed a level of stubbornness that would make hostage negotiators quit, and wore the same outfit every day with a different 'magic' word on a fucking shirt manufactured by the pathetic bastard responsible for Dad's death.

And every time Emery mouthed something to the sky, or muttered a word, or showed up somewhere uninvited, or declined food she clearly needed, or wore one of those stupid fucking shirts, my lips wanted to devour her, followed by her body, and finally her mind.

It drove me goddamned nuts.

Clearly, I didn't disclose any of this. For a lawyer, Delilah had the tact of a socially unaware toddler when it came to me.

I exited my browser and focused on her. "What happened during your trip to Cordovia that makes you flush bright pink every time I mention the country?"

Her cheeks flamed.

Called it.

All I knew about her trip to the tiny European island was, she left single and ended up with Kingston Reinhardt VII, second in line to the throne, as her husband.

Delilah greeted the cleaning crew to save face, giving me her back.

"Thought so," I muttered.

Emery

I MOVED CLOSETS last night.

It shouldn't have made me sad, but it did.

Like leaving a relative you saw once a decade. In theory, you weren't supposed to get attached in so little time, but it happened. Next thing you know, you're crying into a bottle of pinot, promising to see each other soon.

Or, in my case, running around the hotel, putting out fires. Bags lined my eyes. I wore my t-shirt backward, but the energy required to run to the restroom and flip it convinced me backward tees could be the new trend.

I zipped up the hoodie I wore to cover my shirt and set out to find Cayden. Two floors later, I spotted him arguing with the foreman.

"You look like shit."

"I feel like shit." I unsaddled bags of dresser knobs from my arms and shoved them into Cayden's. "You were supposed to help me arrange carpets on the fifth floor."

The foreman yawned before sacrificing Cayden to deal with my wrath. I'd spent last night sneaking my things three floors up to a closet on the 19th floor, because the 16th floor would get its finishing touches in a few days.

With the project further along and expensive furnishings involved, hotel security had beefed up. It made me paranoid. I lunged from door to door, dodging shadows in the hall. No one caught me, but I panted by the time I lugged my t-shirt printer to the corner of the new space and passed out.

"Sorry. I forgot." He scrubbed at his face, blinked

away the lethargy, and sifted through the knobs. "Mr. Prescott requested a rush on his room, so I had to reassign the construction crews and find replacements."

Cayden handed the bag to someone.

I trailed him to the elevators. For a fleeting second, excitement energized me. "We're getting a centerpiece."

"I know." He pressed the button for the lobby.

"Already? How do you know?"

"It's downstairs." He leaned against the wall and kicked one ankle in front of the other. "Near the entrance. Come on."

I followed him out of the alcove of elevators. "What's it of?"

"Not sure. It's covered in thick canvas. We're not supposed to remove it until the grand opening of the hotel. Look."

He jerked his chin straight ahead. I pivoted and took in the monstrosity. The architect had gone with one-hundred-foot ceilings, which spanned the equivalent of about seven stories. Thick canvas covered something that descended from the ceiling and hit the floor.

The sheer size of it struck me, rendered me speechless, and had my eyes darting left and right to make sure I wasn't hallucinating. For the life of me, I had no clue what it could be. I wouldn't put it past Nash to mount a giant middle finger in his hotel lobby and call it a day.

The press would somehow spin it into Nash making a statement against the pervasive evils contributing to world hunger. They loved him that much.

"We're not allowed to unveil it." Cayden tapped the heavy canvas material. It didn't budge. "Mr. Prescott was adamant about it."

"Why?" I wanted to rip it off and feast my eyes.

"How are we supposed to design if we don't know what we're designing around?"

Sometimes, I thought Nash did these things to fuck with me. Like—*yeah, I'll make this deal with you, but even when you get what you want, you're not going to enjoy it.*

"I don't know, but it's massive." Cayden overextended his arms, a poorly done ballet pose. He settled for pointing from one end of the centerpiece to the other. "If anything, we need to focus on simplicity now, since the sheer size of it will take up so much attention, anything else comes off as eclectic. I'll set up a meeting in two days to discuss. The whole not-knowing-what-it-is thing makes it a challenge, but I'm up for it. Plus, I've been told by Mr. Prescott that it'll go with everything."

I shook my head and made my way to the elevators. "I've got this."

"Where are you going?" he called.

"To find Nash fucking Prescott."

chapter
THIRTY-NINE

nash

"What are you doing?" Delilah perched on a barstool, chin on her palm.

Hell if I know.

I hip-checked the fridge door closed, wondering why the hell I was doing this. Why I cared when I didn't even cook for myself.

"Penance."

Delilah never questioned the word, so I offered it like a Walmart rollback deal. Regularly, until its meaning dried to nothing, and still, she never said a thing.

Until today.

"Penance. Really?" She jutted her chin at the concoction on the island. "With that?"

"I'm making a fucking sandwich, Delilah." I didn't bother glancing at her. "What does it look like I'm doing?"

"It looks like you're putting chips into your sandwich and being awfully defensive about it." Her nose scrunched up, two fingers absently tracing a pattern on the island counter. "That's disgusting, by the way. You've lost all street cred in my mind."

I didn't answer.

Just stacked a slice of bread and cut it diagonally.

"Wait." She leapt off the stool and rounded the island to my side. Rosco perked up in his bed and sprinted after her for back up. Fucking rat thought he was the fifth Ninja Turtle. Delilah nodded at the sandwich. "That's not for you."

I slid it into a clear sandwich bag. "Is there a point to your existence, or have you dedicated it to irritating me?"

"It's for Emery, isn't it?"

My eyes snapped to hers, fingers hovering over the multi-pack of chip bags the Insta Cart shopper had delivered.

She continued, "What are you doing?"

Her question held weight beyond the damn sandwich.

"No clue," I muttered and selected the white cheddar popcorn.

I shoved the sandwich, a bag of popcorn, and a can of vanilla cream soda into a brown lunch sack with a napkin on top. Making my way to my desk, I pulled out a pen and hotel stationary.

"What are you writing?"

"Cool it, Veronica Mars." The pen moved fast across

the paper before Delilah could force her way over here. "You're the less shiny knock-off of Nancy Drew. Let's not exhaust your brain, sweetheart."

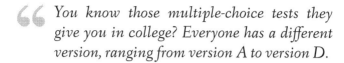 *You know those multiple-choice tests they give you in college? Everyone has a different version, ranging from version A to version D.*

Except the professors don't tell you that when you take it. So, people waste their time cheating off their neighbors... only to completely fail because they copied others when no one's test is the same.

If there's a metaphor for life, it's that.

I bet you were the girl who bubbled in your own answers.

— **NASH**

I read the note twice over, returned to the kitchen, and slid it into the lunch sack.

"Can we not mention anything Veronica Mars related? I can't get over the ending." Curiosity still brimmed in Delilah's eyes. They darted from the bag to me, as if considering whether she could steal it. "King was ready to kick me out of the house when I spent a solid week crying at everything."

"Cool story, bro." I folded the top over the bag and clutched it in my grip. "You should write a book about it."

"For the record, if I did, it'd be a bestseller. With Rosco on the cover. Who's a handsome puppy?" She lifted the rat into her arms and pressed wet kisses all over his naked face, sans ear muffs since the construction crew had taken off a few hours ago. "Who wouldn't buy a book with this beautiful face on it?"

"Literally, everyone on this planet and any extraterrestrial life on every other planet. If you showed up on a cult's doorstep and told them Rosco is the second coming of Jesus, they'd find a different cult to worship."

She ignored me and set Rosco down. He ran to the mini four-poster dog bed, I still couldn't believe I allowed in my penthouse. "Blows my mind that no one has figured out who Emery is. Yeah, she's going by a different last name and none of them are from the area, but she looks just like Virginia Winthrop. It's obvious to me."

"Yeah, if you're blind in one eye and have a field of cataracts in the other."

"They could be twins," Delilah protested.

"Virginia looks like Cruella de Vil's platinum blonde sister. You're bullshitting me, right?"

She slanted her head, staring off into space. "I think it's the face."

"What about it? Emery's nose is more upturned, she has a gray iris, and her eyes are bigger. Not to mention the long black hair compared to Virginia's hacked-off bob."

"Hmm..."

"Hmm, what?"

"It's just..." Delilah grinned. "You seem to notice a lot about Emery Winthrop."

"She's my brother's best friend, and I lived on her parent's property for nearly a decade."

And I've been in her, on her, all over her.

"Why are you two talking about me?"

Our heads swung to the voice. I hadn't heard Emery enter, but of course, she let herself in. She had a damn key, which I should have demanded back after the shower incident. Her hoodie engulfed her, but I noticed no magic word on this tee.

It threw me off balance. I recovered slowly, like I'd suffered a career-ending injury.

Kobe and his torn Achilles.

Beckham and his snapped Achilles.

Durant and his torn Achilles.

Why are all these motherfuckers injuring their goddamn Achilles?

I swore, I felt my heels burning.

"Oh, my God. What is that?" Emery stared at Rosco with her nose scrunched up.

It was almost enough to make me laugh.

Almost.

"He's a Hairless Chinese Crested dog." Delilah rocked him against her chest. "They get cast in a ton of movies and shows."

"For their ugliness." I regarded Emery's blank shirt again. "Let it be known, they often win competitions for world's ugliest dog."

"Hmm... I kind of like him."

Delilah offered Rosco to Emery, who stroked his naked flesh twice and pressed a kiss to his forehead.

I opened the front door and said, "Delilah, your rat looks like he's ten seconds from pissing himself."

She took the hint, sparing me a parting arched brow. Rosco barked when she scooped him up. "Come on, baby. Let's go for a walk."

Emery rounded on me as soon as I slammed the door shut. "What the fuck, Nash?"

"You'll have to be more specific than that. To which fuck are you referring?"

"Remove the canvas from the statue."

The fucking statue. I knew it would bite me in the ass.

I didn't budge. "No."

"No?"

I eyed her lips. "Nope."

Now that I remembered what it was like to kiss, I kicked myself for stopping in the first place.

"That's all you have to say? We made a deal."

"Actually, the deal was that you ate, and I found us a centerpiece." I wandered into the kitchen. "Neither of us said anything about anyone seeing it before the unveiling. You'd make an awful lawyer, by the way."

"So, we're just supposed to design without knowing what it is?" She followed me and propped her hip against the island. "What if it doesn't go with anything?"

"Nice try. It's mostly metal. It goes with everything."

"But—"

"No buts, Emery. It's non-negotiable."

"What if it's ugly?"

"It's not."

Far fucking from it.

"I'm supposed to believe you found a centerpiece and had it delivered in under twenty-four hours?"

"Yes."

"What nice centerpiece can be found, bought, and shipped in twenty-four hours?"

"One I already own."

I'd been housing it on its side in a barn at the far end of my thirty-acre property in Eastridge like a mistress hidden in a secret apartment. Out of sight, out of mind.

"Oh." Her head tilted, nose wrinkling.

"Yes." I studied her shirt, conjuring some scenarios on what happened.

She ran out of ink.

The words washed off in the laundry.
I'd become selectively blind.
She left her shirt at some douche's place after making out with me last night.

Emery blew a lock of hair from her face, eyes lighting up seconds later. "What about the placard?"

"The placard will be engraved and ordered once it's written."

"I can write it if you'll tell me what the centerpiece is."

"Cute, but no." My eyes flicked to her shirt again.

"I put it on backward, okay?" She threw both arms in the air. "You can stop staring now, or I'll have to assume you're a creep."

I stared for one more second because I loved riling her up, then tossed her the lunch bag. Emery caught it on instinct. Her brows pushed together when she realized what it was.

"It's Turkey & Ruffles." I set the knife and cutting board into the sink.

"Wait." She studied the bag as if she had X-ray vision. "You ordered a rush on the kitchen today... and the first thing you made was my lunch?"

I swallowed, twice, and wondered when my throat had gotten so dry. "Technically, it's a snack, considering midday has passed."

"If we're getting technical, it's technically a sweet thing to do."

"Just eat the fucking sandwich, Emery."

A glint returned to her eyes. It screamed mischief. "Let us remove the cover."

"No."

I shouldn't have given up that sculpture in the first place. It belonged on the corner of my farm, never to be seen again. I only did it, because Emery had been right. Ma would be at the grand opening.

Why the fuck would I disappoint her if I didn't have to?

"Fine." Emery slid the lunch onto the island. "I'm full. I think I'll head to the lobby and figure out if neon pink rugs are neutral enough to compliment your canvas-covered monstrosity of a centerpiece."

"There's a note in the lunch sack." I approached her side of the island. "Maybe I should toss it."

Her hand darted out and snatched the bag. I smiled, disguising it as a taunt. She craved my words, just like I craved the ones on her shirt. I didn't know when that had happened, but could you blame me?

The girl looked like a dictionary. Ink-colored hair on pale skin. Rare words printed across her chest. I wanted to devour her, memorize her words, and dog-ear my favorite pages.

Instead, I swiveled, strode to my desk, and sat. "Are we done here?"

"The centerpiece—"

"Will remain covered." I opened my laptop. "If that's all..."

Her eyes found the scorched leather on the perimeter of my desk. She cocked her head to the side and trailed a finger down the spine. My pulse choked me. I considered snatching the ledger and shoving it into my drawer.

I left it out, because like my penance tattoo, it reminded me to never lose sight of revenge. Delilah knew not to touch it, but Emery clearly wasn't Delilah. She had no sense of boundaries. Just her and a world she thought belonged to everyone equally, which apparently meant what's mine was also hers.

She released the leather, looking unperturbed by its

current condition. "That looks kind of like Virginia's notebook, except it's, um, burnt."

"What?"

If she hadn't already had it, she'd have my full attention now.

"The notebook." She motioned to it with a tilt of her chin. "Virginia has one just like it. Well, similar. The same shape and size, but hers had a crown logo on the front and was less... burnt. Like yours, leather wrapped all around it to protect it from fire, water, and dirt."

I remembered what it looked like, considering that was how this ledger had looked before I tossed it into the Winthrop's fireplace, barely retrieving it in time.

Finished leather was resistant to fire at high temperatures, so the encasing had protected most of the interior pages. The exterior looked charred as fuck and unrecognizable, however. Obvious proof that I'd tried to burn evidence, which was pretty damn illegal and why I never turned it in to the F.B.I. or S.E.C.

I'd thought I could handle it myself.

I was wrong.

And Dad died.

Emery continued, oblivious, "She used to carry it into the library before bed, obsessing over it. Then, she lost it one day and went absolutely berserk."

"It was your mom's?" I clarified, because What. The. Fuck.

I'd found it in Gideon's office after hearing him talk about the company's finances. Balthazar even said, *as long as there's no evidence of embezzling...*

My eyes glimpsed out the window, confirming a lack of flying pigs. A window cleaner bobbed his head to music, standing on a metal contraption suspended by wires. His hands held a rag and a squeegee.

He inclined his chin to me as if to say, "'Sup."

Just my mind exploding. Nothing to see here, but you'll have some chunks of brain to wipe off the windows by the end of your shift.

"Your mom had a notebook like this one?" I repeated, knowing it changed everything.

Fucking. Everything.

"Yes." Emery's lips quirked up. "Do you need Q-tips? I bet I can find some." She folded her lower lip into her mouth, taking her time to wet it. "When Virginia lost it, she tore apart the house to look for it. Her eyes rimmed with so much rage and panic, I assumed she wrote about her affairs in there. She and Dad were always done. Their marriage was the shotgun type after she got pregnant with me."

Her eyes returned to the ledger and she continued, "Actually, she was convinced someone on the staff stole it. She wanted to fire everyone, including your parents. Called it a clean sweep. Dad convinced her not to. Told her she could find another notebook. He was always good like that."

My foundation rocked.

Everything I thought I knew morphed.

I stood on a cliff in the middle of a landslide.

The only way to go was down.

chapter FORTY

Emery

Ida Marie and I stared at a painting, our heads tilted, trying to figure out if the subject's V tapered to an oddly shaped penis or a flesh-colored loin cloth.

As soon as the curator had told me the Triumphant Sisyphus was still available for sale, I'd requested for the gallery to be emptied and reserved today.

Proof Nash Prescott had become a household name in North Carolina.

"Are you lonely?"

Ida Marie's question rocked me. She wasn't even

supposed to be here. No one was, but Chantilly had turned it into a field trip once she'd overheard my call with the curator.

"What?" I swapped my view of the penis-shaped loin cloth or loin-cloth-shaped penis for Ida Marie's doe eyes. "Why would you say that?"

"We've been working together for, say, two months now? I haven't heard you talk about anyone. No family. No friends. No boyfriend."

"Gee, thanks."

My attention drifted to Nash. The curator fawned over him, exhibiting an array of paintings and sculptures he clearly gave no fucks about. He wore the same scowl he usually did. The type of face you'd make if you stepped in dog shit.

Chantilly trailed after them, her mouth moving at Formula 1 speed. Two gallery employees hovered at the fringe of the ovular room, gawking over Nash.

I hated that look.

Girls used to do it because bad boys excited them.

Now they did it because his money excited them.

Maybe his attractiveness came into play, but I'd bet it was never for the part of him that mattered most, because no one understood him except himself.

"I didn't mean it like that." Ida Marie grinned. "I just mean, the rest of us jump around from location to location. It's part of the job. We all know how to adapt, meet new people, and live social lives in spite of it. I'm just worried you're having trouble adapting, being new to this."

"I'm okay." I tucked a strand of hair behind my ear and decided the painting depicted a loin cloth-shaped penis. "I promise I'm okay. Thank you."

"Everyone thinks you and Nash are sleeping together," she blurted.

I froze. As if that wasn't a sign of guilt. "What?"

"Um, yeah..." She gazed away, pretending to focus on the painting, but I knew I had her attention.

"Did they"—and by they, I meant Chantilly—"ask you to ask me?"

"Yes, but I won't tell them what you say to me." Her hand touched my forearm before darting away. "Promise."

"It's fine, because we're not sleeping together."

"You've never slept with him?"

"Ida Marie, I can promise you that, in the past several months that you've known me, I have not had sex with Nash Prescott."

See? Not a lie.

Good job, Emery.

"So... are you lonely?"

"Oh, my God." I eyed the ceiling, wishing it were a starless night, so I could vent. "I'm not. I don't need a penis to keep me company."

I wasn't opposed to casual sex. I just didn't need it. Ben kept me company at night, and lately, Nash kept me... *occupied* during the day.

Not sexually.

But mentally.

Emotionally.

He made me lunch every day and left notes like he used to. Sometimes, I'd eat them in his office. He would watch me read the notes. I pretended to toss them with the lunch bag, but I'd slide them into my pocket when he wasn't looking and leave them in my box in the closet.

I told myself the lunches were why I was even at this gallery, about to lead Nash to the Triumphant Sisyphus over the Defeated Sisyphus.

A paid debt.

That's all.

"Are you sure? I can set you up on a date with some friends," Ida Marie offered.

A shadow loomed over us.

I fixed my eyes on the loin-cloth dick.

"We are here to work, not socialize, and his dick looks like one of Rosco's ears."

Nash's voice hit the air, and I felt like I was floating and sinking all at once. Gravity, it turned out, didn't exist. Not with Nash roaming this earth.

"Uhh..." Ida Marie's eyes traversed the room, trying to bullshit two bullshitters. "Chantilly's waving me down. Gotta go."

I turned back to the painting, which did, in fact, resemble Rosco's ear. "Doesn't it bother you that everyone thinks we're sleeping together?"

"No."

He didn't seem surprised.

I waited for him to elaborate.

He lifted a brow. "What?"

"Nothing. Never mind. You're impossible." I zipped up my hoodie until it covered my *wabi-sabi* tee. "Let's get this over with. The sculpture is in the private gallery."

The curator unlocked the private viewing room for us, offering champagne and an exclusive tour.

Nash declined with a polite, "Fuck no."

Her head whipped back, jaw slacking.

"To think she referred to you as the Patron Saint of North Carolina earlier," I said once she left us alone.

I would have felt bad, but A—she looked at Nash like he was a paycheck and B—when she actually did get the commission check from this sale, I was sure she'd be licking her wounds during a beach vacation in Hawaii.

"I fucking hate that nickname."

But he didn't deny its validity. It fit with the Nash Prescott puzzle beside his *penance* tattoo. I was missing the biggest piece. It reminded me of filling out a completely blank Sudoku grid.

Curiosity got the better of me. "Why Sisyphus?"

"Because it's the truth."

"I'm not following."

"Do you know what a Sisyphean task is?" He didn't wait for me to answer. "It's one that can never be completed."

I kept my gaze forward, rounding the bend with him. We passed extravagant paintings, statues, and sculptures. I cared for none of them like I did the Triumphant Sisyphus.

Nash stopped me with a hand on my hip. He continued, "Life is a Sisyphean task. You put out one fire, and another one starts. It's easier to accept it burns."

I couldn't think past his touch, but I tried. "And when there's no place untouched by the fire?"

"You live in a world consumed by fire, but at least it's the truth. You're not lured to sleep with a false blanket of security, telling yourself you exist in a part untouched by the flames."

"That's a horrible way to live."

"Newsflash, Little Tiger, it's life. There's death, and betrayal, and revenge, and guilt everywhere you turn. It's healthier to live it, breathe it, and *participate* in it than to pretend it doesn't exist."

"And when you're burnt everywhere?"

"Don't succumb to the fire. Be the bigger flame." His fingers dipped below my shirt, skimming the sensitive skin.

You are the biggest flame I've ever met, Nash Prescott. You deprive me of oxygen.

We continued down the path. I toyed with his conviction, considered fighting it, and decided against it. The creed suited Nash, the man with the penance tattoo and the unlikely streak for charity. Nothing about him made sense, which was exactly why it made sense.

I liked odd.

Thrived on it.

I accepted Nash for who he was.

Silently, because the second I told him I saw him, he'd morph into someone different, and I'd have to solve the puzzle as the pieces changed.

My very own Sisyphean task.

The path led to the sculpture in the center. My heart rattled its cage when we rounded the last turn. I wondered if I'd remembered it correctly. But the second my eyes reunited with it, I knew I'd made the right choice.

"It's wrong," Nash said five minutes after he saw it.

He'd spent that first five minutes silent.

Just staring at the sculpture.

Not a single word.

I spent those five minutes staring at *him*, only to realize, in this moment, I couldn't read Nash.

"It's perfect," I argued.

"It's not what I wanted."

"It's what you needed."

He raked his fingers through his hair. *Three times.* "It's inaccurate."

"Yeah?" I stroked the base of the mountain. The same reverence you'd give something holy. "What's Sisyphus supposed to be then?"

"Sisyphus is a treacherous sea. One that drowns you."

A response sat at the tip of my tongue, but all I could conjure was silence. Ben had called Sisyphus a treacherous sea. As in, Ben from Eastridge.

Horror dawned on me the same time Nash turned to me and said, "We're not getting it. It's not right. Find another."

"*We* are not getting anything. You are." I released a shaky breath, forcing myself to play it cool. I had no confirmation. Freaking out would be pointless. "This is the sculpture. There's no other."

"Emery."

"Nash."

"It's not happening."

My fingers trembled at my sides. I shoved them into my jeans and stared at Triumphant Sisyphus. The anguish Nash had demanded was chiseled into its face, but the artist laced it with strong undercurrents of triumph.

When I looked at the sculpture, I saw Sisyphus winning.

He carried the boulder above his head like a trophy rather than a punishment.

He reminded me life was a matter of perspective. You can see your losses as failures or lessons. The choice is yours.

My eyes slid to Nash.

Ben.

Whomever he was, he hadn't turned away from the art since we entered.

If I hadn't been blinded by my idea of Nash, I might have considered him as Ben earlier. I inched back, allowing him to study the sculpture. The phone in my palm felt heavy. I chewed on my lip, considering what to text Ben.

Durga: What are you wearing?

I didn't need a response. The read receipt would confirm it. Over ten minutes passed until Nash received a phone call from Delilah. He ended the call, clenched his phone, then held it out in front of him.

My eyes skated between Nash and the Eastridge United App.

The read receipt said, *read*.

A few seconds later, a message popped up.

When Nash slid his phone back into his pocket, the green dot beside his name turned red.

I didn't bother looking at his answer.

It was like the end of a football match.

Fourth down.

Three seconds to go.

One yard from the end zone.

No time outs left, and the whistle blew.

A ref had thrown down the gauntlet.

The end.

Game over.

Final score.

Nash was Ben.

Ben was Nash.

And I was fucked.

Because Ben finally had a face.

A body.

An existence.

He wasn't a fantasy.

He was human.

Real.

Mine for the taking.

Because I lusted for Nash, but I loved Ben.

chapter FORTY-ONE

nash

I reread the messages between me and Durga from two nights ago, feeling oddly guilty about them. And I never felt guilty about Durga.

Benkinersophobia: What are you wearing?

I'd sent her that because she'd sent me the same thing earlier. Then, ghosted me.

Durga: A t-shirt. It's loose and long, hitting the

top of my thighs. I'm wearing nothing under, and if you asked me to, I'd take it off.

Benkinersophobia: Don't take it off.

Durga: Are you on your back?

Benkinersophobia: Yes.

Durga: Flip over.

Benkinersophobia: Tell me when you're done.

Durga: I'm on my hands and knees.

Benkinersophobia: Reach between your thighs and brush your thumb against your clit. Moan my name.

Durga: I don't know your name.

Benkinersophobia: Rules.

She hadn't responded.

Benkinersophobia: Just call me Ben.

Still no response.

Benkinersophobia: You feel the cold air brushing your pussy?

Durga: Yes.

Benkinersophobia: I like the idea of your ass in the air as you cum, waiting for me to enter you, knowing I never will.

Durga: Never say never.

I stopped reading, changed into a tee and sweats, and wandered around the hotel, struck by how goddamned empty it was. Reed would spend this weekend with Basil and Ma, Delilah had flown to New York a few nights ago with her husband, and my plans for the weekend included Durga, who'd been acting weird, and my fist, because the idea of seeking a meaningless fuck did nothing for me.

This was probably karma rearing its head, and it was uglier than Rosco.

I watched a Hornets vs. Lakers replay with a night guard, drank a few beers, cursed appropriately when the Hornets lost even though I gave no shits, and wandered the floors one by one.

When I reached the fifth floor and heard laughter, I counted down the beers I'd drunk with the guard.

Not nearly enough for hallucinations.

Especially considering I recognized the laugh.

I should have turned around and left her alone, but I justified my intrusion with the reminder she'd snuck into my shower and onto *me*.

Emery wore a tee that read *lypophrenia* and headphones in her ears. Her body laid flat on the couch, cocooned by the rattiest quilt I'd ever seen. Checkered with holes and faded to the point where I couldn't tell if the little dots all over were a design or stains.

Her eyes remained closed until she burst out in carefree laughter. They popped open and instantly found mine with unerring precision. I expected surprise on her face, but I got one lifted shoulder and a lazy smile.

A smile.

Weird shit she'd been doing since I caved and bought that Sisyphus statue. Usually when she thought I wasn't paying attention.

She looked pure and innocent and beautiful, like a fallen red maple leaf before someone stepped on it. I wondered how I didn't see it before. Maybe Fika was right. Maybe I'd misheard the argument in the office the night of the cotillion. After all, I'd been wrong about who owned the ledger.

Emery stretched. Her sad excuse for a blanket fell to the floor. The movement lifted the bottom of her shirt, flashing me with skin. "I feel like Sebastian York's voice is the kind of thing that transcends time. Silent films, skinny jeans, and Sebastian York. Things that never get old."

The sudden urge to rip out the asshole's vocal cords gripped me. She never talked to anyone but Reed, and I'd assumed there was no one else.

Fuck, no, you did not just say, no one 'else'.

I rounded the couch.

She caught my look and laughed again. "You'd think I'd just told you I sacrificed a toddler tonight. What's your deal?" She sat up and sloped her chin to scrutinize me. "He's a narrator. I borrowed an audiobook from the library. *Entice* by Ava Harrison." The toe of her Chucks accidentally hit my Brionis. "It's an age-gap romance."

"You borrowed an audiobook. From the library," I parroted, fully aware her Chucks touched my shoes again, *not* by accident this time.

"Jesus, Nash, are you illiterate? Do you know what a

book is? They're these things full of words, and when you read them, you live another life. You should try it sometime. Might help with the crankiness."

The jabs brushed off my shoulders like insignificant flies. "Fuck Sebastian York."

Transparent as saran wrap.

"Really? You kind of sound like him."

"What does he sound like?"

"Like you. I literally just said that."

"Careful." I sat beside her on the couch, taking up most of the space. "It's after hours. I could call security."

"And I could start a Change.org petition. Your wages for interns are embarrassing, and I have a student loan payment due in two days." She set her phone down and nodded to the television. "If I use the company's Netflix account, I get entertainment *and* I can still pay my utilities bill. I was watching *Twilight* before this."

I smelled her bullshit but didn't call her out on it. Mostly because it required admitting I looked into her and knew about the Demi situation.

"Before this—"

She cut me off. "What do you think would happen if Edward Cullen met another mind reader? Who would be reading whose mind?"

I allowed her lame attempts at distraction. "Neither, because mind-reading doesn't exist."

"I don't recall you being this cranky back then."

Ignoring the empty insult, I examined her set up. Phone, charger, blanket, and headphones. "You've been coming here to watch Netflix every night?"

"No." She toyed with the hem of her shirt, teasing me without ever realizing it. "Only recently."

"What did you use before?"

"My ex from freshman year's account. I dated him

for, like, two days. He cheated, but I got four years of Netflix free. I think I came out victorious in that relationship." She leaned against the couch back. "He changed the password a few days ago."

"He didn't know you were using his account?" Something about her right now didn't add up. "Isn't there a watch history?"

"The trick is to create a new user each time you watch and delete that user when you're done watching. Silent revenge is the best revenge."

Her words spiked my impulse.

I wanted to slam my lips onto hers for a second kiss, but I kicked my feet onto the coffee table and sunk deeper into the couch. "You remind me of Delilah."

"A compliment. She's smarter and hotter than you." She retrieved her quilt. "She should be running the company."

"It's like you're asking to get kicked out."

I could have kicked her out, but I wouldn't.

Reed had plans of proposing or whatever, and I had... a company I couldn't give two shits about; a friend I couldn't bring myself to call my best friend, even though she deserved it; Durga, who was acting weird; and... Emery.

"You can't kick me out." Her flippant tone suggested she knew I wouldn't. "It's my birthday next week."

"According to you, the day that doesn't make people special."

"Why is it that you're the one who gets me? When the hell did that happen?"

More pressing question—when had she become so candid about us?

Rather than answer, I ordered delivery from every restaurant still open because she looked like she needed ten cheeseburgers, and I wasn't giving her an excuse not to eat one.

"We could watch a movie while we wait," she offered. "Warning—I'm picky, and given the circumstances, I don't have a Netflix queue, which means it takes me forever to pick."

She grabbed the remote and scrolled through the options. "I'll read the recommended list, but it's mostly Chantilly and Ida Marie watching on the account. *Beauty and the Beast?*"

"If you're into Stockholm Syndrome. *Sleeping Beauty?*"

I imagined hell consisted of Chantilly's Netflix queue on repeat.

"Because kissing solves everything?" Her lips parted when I glanced at them. "Not to mention the DubCon. *Aladdin?*"

"Rub until something comes out. Great lesson to teach children."

"That one's realistic. Lying and stealing always lands you the girl..."

One of the night guards interrupted us with bags of delivery. Peruvian. Tunisian. American. America's bastardized take on Italian. Emery grabbed the Tunisian first, dug through it, and took the first bite out of every item before settling on the *Shakshuka*.

We ate our way through four cuisines, scrolling through Chantilly's Netflix queue and ridiculing every movie until we found one both of us agreed with. *John Wick*, because contrary to Delilah's belief, I didn't hate dogs. Just ones that resembled rats.

I shoved our leftovers into the fridge and sat down again. She glanced at me every minute, fixated on my lips like she wanted to kiss me. At this point, neither of us pretended to watch the movie.

I opened up Candy Crush, because I needed to do something with my hands or I'd cover her body with mine and kiss her until her lips bruised. She pulled out her sketchpad and shaded in a design.

The night continued like that. I moved up ten levels. She watched *John Wick* while sketching fashion designs on her pad. Really, I had no reason to be here other than the penthouse was empty and I enjoyed Emery's company.

There.

I said it.

So fucking what?

When the movie ended, she set aside her designs, pulled her knees to her chest, and asked, "What is up with you and Candy Crush?"

I swiped up, obliterating the level. She waited for me to respond, burning the side of my face with her attention.

I considered my answer, but Dad thought of her as family, which meant she deserved the truth. "Dad used to play it during his treatments. We'd sit side-by-side, trying to beat levels before the other. It distracted him from the needles pumping shit into his arms."

"Like chemo?"

"No." I set the phone down and studied her, content to watch her watch me. "It doesn't eat away at your health like chemo. In fact, it made him better. Healthier. Sturdy when he worked. Kept the heart running great. But the drugs were delivered intravenously and, judging from the noises in the clinic, painfully."

Her front teeth pierced her lower lip. A coat of liquid brimmed her eyes. So fierce, yet so gentle. Typical Emery, longest claws and the biggest heart. "I wish Hank had told me and Reed."

"So you two could suffer, too? Never." I shook my head, remembering how Ma, Dad, and I barely made it work at times. "Ma held it together by a thread most times. She didn't want Reed to suffer that, and Dad didn't want you two to think of him as weak."

"I love Hank and Betty, but it was selfish. We deserved to know each moment with him could have been our last. I could have treated him better."

"You treated him the best, Tiger. He knew that."

I swallowed down the idea of her taking Reed's side on this, of possibly being involved in the embezzlement, though I now had my doubts. She had loyalty to Gideon, but she also had loyalty to us.

"Look," I added, taking in the watery blue and grey eyes, "his illness wasn't contagious, but it spread from him to Ma to me. His heartbeats could be fucking useless. I felt the drag of my heartbeat each time I took a punch for him. Ma felt it each time she worked double shifts. For all my life, I fucking felt it. We stopped it from infecting you and Reed. You think it wasn't my choice to make, and you're right. It was Dad's, because if his heart hadn't killed him, watching two of his favorite people suffer for him would have."

That's the thing about getting sick. You don't suffer alone. You suffer with the people you love, which is too much fucking suffering.

Emery accepted my answer. The silence didn't bother me, mostly because I knew she liked it.

Always had.

"What's with the charities?" she asked ten minutes into the second *John Wick*. "Why do you volunteer at soup kitchens?"

I do it to ease the guilt. I burned that fucking ledger, thought I could use the info to build my company and save my dad, and I ended up too late. Life and regret are my punishments. Giving away every piece of me is my penance.

"Penance," I offered without elaborating.

Her eyes flicked to my tattoo, visible under my tee. The tip of her tongue peeked past her lips. It darted back inside. "What sins are you atoning for, Nash?"

"Stay in your lane, Tiger."

"Let's play a game." She tucked her legs beneath her ass, leaning closer to me.

"Let's not."

"Truth or Dare?"

I shot her a look, knowing which she wanted me to pick and choosing the opposite. "Dare."

"I dare you to pick Truth."

"Jesus, do you ever follow the rules?"

"There are no rules. It's Truth or Dare. Now say, Truth."

"Truth," I said for the sole reason of shutting her up, and not because she still had a tear trail on her cheek.

"How are you really feeling about your dad?" At my silence, she added, "You don't have to answer if you don't want to."

I toyed with a few words. "I don't think there's a word for it."

"Try me."

"I can't," I ground out, "if the words don't exist."

"You want to know why I like words?"

I did, but I didn't tell her that.

She continued, anyway, "I love words, because they're mine. Utterly, completely mine. I can share them with others. I can keep them to myself. I can use them over and over again. No matter what I do, they'll always be mine. No one can take them from me. Want to know what the best part is?"

"I'm sure you'll tell me."

"The existence of a word proves that someone in the history of humanity felt the same way I did and gave it a name. It means we're not alone. If there's a word for what we're feeling, we're never alone."

"Tell me how you feel about my dad."

"Lacuna." She grabbed my hand and squeezed. "Lacuna is a blank space. A missing part."

Bullseye.

I eyed the screen, where Keanu Reeves was running through New York City, bleeding out of every orifice.

When I didn't answer, she asked, "Truth or dare?"

"Neither. You had your turn."

"You didn't answer the question." She inched closer, wanting to know so much about me when no one ever did. "Truth or dare?"

"Just fucking ask the question." I raked my fingers through my hair. "I know you want to."

"Why don't you kiss?"

Everyone has had a piece of me. This is one I don't have to give away.

I could taste her breath. I turned my face, not because I didn't want to be kissed, but because I did. That itself was a foreign feeling. Most people didn't have shit I liked to hear, and the mouth was the biggest perpetrator of disappointment.

Kissing disgusted me.

But kissing Emery?

It didn't.

Batshit, considering I'd stopped long ago. When I started the illegal underground fights, I came home with cuts and bruises I tried to hide under clothes. I'd cover for them by fighting at school, letting everyone assume they came from football tackles and field tussles.

The kiss thing started because my body would get too bruised to be touched. It transformed into a general disdain for people touching me. Why the fuck would I let someone I couldn't stand touch me?

"I kissed you, didn't I?" I shot back, keeping it light.

"Yeah, you did." Her eyes dipped to my lips, holding the heavy gaze. She smiled suddenly and stretched, standing up. "I have to go. The bus leaves soon."

"This again. It's late and dark. I'm taking you home."

"I'm going to Eastridge." She popped a brow. "You'll take me to Eastridge?"

Shit, I promised Ma I'd stay away while Reed visited. But Ma would tell me to make an exception. The Greyhound to Eastridge was long with too many shady stops along with way.

I stole a card from Emery's deck, watching her gather her things. "Yes, but I need something from you."

Your dad's address, please and fucking thank you.

She paused and slanted her head. "Is it illegal?"

"No."

"Is it sexual?"

Fuck, she looked too enticed by the idea.

"No."

"If you accompany me to brunch with my mom, too," she bartered, always set on cinching a victory. "Able will be there, and since Reed is spending the weekend with Basil..."

Get in. Get out, dick.

I would have said no on account of my promise to Ma that I'd stay away from Eastridge, but Able Small Dick

Cartwright was the type of rich prick who thought he could get away with murder.

"Deal."

"Deal," she agreed, betraying her dad with a smile on her face.

She just didn't know it yet.

chapter FORTY-TWO

Emery

Love exists, and it's crueler than lust.

I knew if I loved someone, I wouldn't lie to them. I also knew the idea of telling Nash I was Durga appealed to me as much as contracting a painful strand of crabs.

"What happened to your old Honda?" I asked, sliding into Nash's sleek black convertible. It smelled of new car mixed with him. I shoved my bag in my foot area and waited for an answer.

"Retired."

He didn't elaborate.

I clutched onto my seat when he sped off, thankful he'd left the hardtop on.

Nash Prescott looked like every mom's worst nightmare—and mine for different reasons—in his black jeans and olive-colored Henley, sleeves pulled up mid-forearm. My fingers itched to trace his tattoo.

I dug them into the leather. "I need to make two stops before we get to the country club."

"This isn't a field trip, Tiger."

He rapped the steering wheel with a finger, driving with one hand on it and the other wrapped around my headrest. I couldn't reconcile him with my Ben, but I sometimes saw glimpses of it. Last night, but definitely not today.

Determination inked his body with tight muscles and a set jaw. "You want the stops, I get two more truths."

"Fine," I grit out, knowing I'd regret this, but I couldn't go to Eastridge without visiting Betty.

I also needed to change out of my *sonder* tee and into the dress Virginia hated, in the unlikely event that my belongings hadn't been tossed by the new Winthrop Estate owner. The idea of sitting in a car with Ben had my lips loose, begging to confess.

I busied myself with studying Nash's car, running my fingers along the leather, inhaling its scent. I toyed with the latch to the glove compartment.

"Don't touch that."

Too late.

It flung open.

The latch bounced against my knees. A bag fell onto my lap. I nearly dropped it, but I caught it last minute. The phone I'd broken sat inside. A crack extended across the screen. Tiny flecks of glass peppered the inside of the baggie.

A joke sat at the tip of my tongue, but at the sight of him, I swallowed it. Genuine concern etched his features. I carefully slid the Ziploc bag back into the glove compartment and closed it with a soft *click*.

Silence stretched the next ten miles.

I spent it wondering what had him so on edge. The type of energy he used to radiate when he fought often.

Relief swept through me at Nash's voice. "The phone has the last pictures I took of Dad on it."

And I had broken it.

Guilt stabbed at my stomach, that no longer felt empty, which only added to the guilt.

"Sorry." It felt inadequate. I wanted to give him more words, better words. My vocabulary evaded me. Sand slipping through my fingers.

"I bought the new screen, but I showed up at the repair place, and the guy looked as incompetent as fucking Chantilly."

I traced the leather seat with the tip of my finger. "What's your beef with Chantilly?"

"The corporate masquerade party last year—"

"Ida Marie told me about it."

He slid his eyes to me. "Did she also tell you she grabbed my dick through my pants, pretending to be drunk?"

"Why is she still working for you?"

"Her uncle sits on my board, and unlike his niece, he's both competent and a genuinely good guy." The entire board was. I would not have Prescott Hotels be Winthrop Textiles 2.0. "I buried it. If he found out, he'd probably be mortified and resign, and we're about to close Singapore. Finding a good replacement takes too long.

Chantilly had given me a speech on nepotism, yet she was related to a board member. "I knew her salary couldn't pay for a Birkin."

"Her family's loaded, but also the type to make her work her way through life." He merged onto the left lane without signaling, then the shoulder to bypass traffic. "It was probably a Christmas gift."

The wind rattled the car at this speed. I pushed back in my seat, the car's shakes turning me into a human vibrator. We whipped past another town in silence, breakneck speeds we should have gotten pulled over for.

"I can fix it," I offered, voice low. "I've broken my screen before, and I didn't have the money for a new one, so I learned. I even made a few bucks on the side doing it for some college students. I can fix it. Do you trust me?"

He didn't say anything. We continued to drive until the cars on the road thinned. Each mile tapered my hope.

"You can fix it," he finally said.

"Okay."

I spelled *meraki* on my thigh with my pointer finger, content in his company. Nash drove five miles in silence. We reached a long stretch of highway, empty given the holiday. Another five miles further, he pulled over onto the shoulder.

I peered at the gas level, wondering if being stranded constituted as a valid excuse to miss Virginia's brunch and golf time. "Are we out of gas?"

"Nope." He removed the keys from the ignition and leveled me with his full attention. "I'm asking my three questions in the middle of nowhere, so you can't evade them. If you want to get to Eastridge, you'll answer them. If you don't, we can turn back now."

"But—"

"Question #1—how do you know Brandon Vu?"

What. The. Fuck.

"How do *you* know Brandon Vu?" I countered, completely blindsided.

Did Brandon and Nash know each other? Was the S.E.C. angling to go after my dad through Nash? Loyalty surged within me, lighting up my veins. Uncontrollable embers flickered.

You're supposed to hate your Dad, Em.

"Answer the question." His fingers tightened on the steering wheel. "That's the deal."

"He showed up at the masquerade. I had no clue who he was. Then, he showed up at the tent city and gave me his card." I hesitated, praying Nash wouldn't draw the wrong conclusions. "I remembered him from the day the F.B.I. and S.E.C. raided my house. We stood in front of the cottage. He asked me who lived in there and made me say your names."

"And?"

I swiped hair out of my face to give my hands something to do. "And I did, but I also told him you guys had nothing to do with my dad's business. Now, he keeps showing up... I think he wants to use me to get to Dad. I'm not sure."

"So, he's stalking you?"

"Is he stalking me?" I tipped a shoulder up. "He's an agent. Can it be considered stalking if it's legal?"

"It's fucking stalking." His neck corded, lips pulled back, but he moved on. "Question #2—did you know about the embezzlement?"

My head jerked back like whiplash. "No. Absolutely not." My hand flew to my chest, fingers clutching my shirt. "I don't know if I would have gone to the authorities if I'd known, but I would have told Betty and Hank. They put everything into the company. I didn't know." I chanced a glance at him, taking in his expression. *Oh, Nash.* "Is that why you've been mad at me this whole time? You thought I betrayed your family?"

That meant he thought I was responsible for Hank's death.

A river of pity rushed through me. I flushed it from my system, knowing Nash would hate it if he knew it'd ever been there.

"I'm asking the questions. That's the deal." His restless tapping filled the car. "Question #3—where is Gideon Winthrop?"

I pinched the skin on my thigh, hoping to wake up from this nightmare. Each question was worse than the last and definitely not worth a trip to Eastridge to see Virginia. Trust fund access or not. "Nash…"

"It's an easy question, Emery."

"Not for me."

I hated my dad, but I also loved him. It was the kind of love you gave fiercely. No stipulations. Pure. Wondrous. Permanent. I was pissed at him—so fucking pissed—but he was still my dad, no matter how much or how little I talked to him.

"Chill. I'm not going to hurt him."

My eyes widened. "I didn't even mention anything about hurting him. Were you planning on hurting him?"

I remembered the bruised knuckles he'd come home with. Dad was in his late forties. He wouldn't stand a chance in a fight against Nash.

"Do you trust me?"

"Honestly? Not to keep your hands off Dad, but everything else? Yes."

He muttered a curse and swiped a palm down his face. "The deal is—"

"I know what the deal is." I needed to buy time. "Give me today."

"For?"

"I'll tell you. I promise. Just give me time."

Maybe I could warn Dad first, which required talking to him. I realized, as my heart sped at the idea, how much I missed my dad.

I sank into my seat, grateful when Nash pulled back onto the road.

"Why didn't you go to my dad's funeral?"

"Is this one of your questions?"

"Consider it complimentary for dealing with your ass."

I owed him as much, especially since I wasn't sure if I'd ever give up Dad's location. "Reed asked me not to."

Nash sliced me with his attention, stopping in the middle of the road this time. "He told you not to go?"

"Yes and no."

"I know you buried Hank in his hometown, but Reed grew up in Eastridge. He wanted something done there. We obviously couldn't divide the casket, but he asked me to bury an urn full of Hank's favorite things in the center of the tree maze. While you guys were burying Hank, I buried the urn. It's right in front of the Hera statue."

"What did you bury?"

"His Panthers jersey. The pad of sticky notes he always used to press everywhere." A smile ghosted my lips. "His favorite sunglasses, the ones he kept 'losing' while wearing. The book he'd read to me and Reed when we were younger. The prom king crown you didn't want, but your dad found hilarious and mounted on the wall."

"That's where that went."

"Are you mad I took it?"

He made me wait a few minutes for his answer. "No."

BETTY'S NEW HOUSE straddled the border between the middle class and filthy rich neighborhoods in Eastridge. I assumed Nash had paid for the home, and it suited her. So much so that every time I looked at it in the pictures Reed sent me, little fissures opened inside my heart at the idea of how happy Betty and Hank would have been there.

We pulled up sometime around eight in the morning, which was the equivalent of noon for Betty Prescott. The scent of breakfast lingered in the driveway. Nash cut the engine, popped open the door, and tilted his nose up.

I swung my door before he could, because as much of an ass as he was, his Southern mother had raised him to open doors for women. "How pissed do you think Virginia would be if I pigged out on Betty's breakfast instead of the country club brunch?"

"Like a bear witnessing her cub getting kidnapped, only infinite rage and no maternal instinct."

I grinned. "We should do it."

Nash let us in with his key, my shoulders brushing his arm near the doorway. The smile on my face died at the sight of Basil and Reed sitting at Betty's island. They didn't look happy to see us. Even Betty didn't look happy to see us.

"Fuck," Nash muttered beside me.

I recovered quickly, leaping at Reed for a hug. "Reed!"

He returned it with an awkward one-armed pat. "Why are you here with Nash?"

"I needed a ride to Eastridge."

"Looks like more than a ride, Em."

"Excuse me?"

"Tell me you're not going to do something stupid."

I distanced myself from him, flicking my attention to a wide-eyed Betty behind me. "I have no idea what you're talking about."

This went from zero to a hundred fast, which told me Reed had already been in a mood. I gathered the situation as quickly as I could. Basil looked like herself, but didn't act like herself. No scowl. No eye daggers thrown at me. Disconcerting.

Betty clutched her thin silver bracelet, an anniversary gift from Hank. Also a clue they were discussing something bound to break her heart. The last time Reed looked like this, he'd been cuffed in my living room.

He edged closer to me, which made Nash shift behind me. I held a hand out to my side, stopping them both.

"Tell me what's going on," I demanded, "before hounding me with accusations you cannot take back."

If this was his reaction at the sight of me and Nash, how would he react upon learning we'd had sex?

On. His. Bed.

"Ask yourself this," Reed began, ignoring me, "do you want to be with someone willing to let his brother go to jail?" He jerked a finger at Nash. "Better yet, ask him how he got his millions or billions or what-fucking-ever."

"Reed..." I didn't know what to say to that, except I knew I'd hate the answer.

Nash positioned himself next to me. Reed narrowed his eyes at us. We looked like a unified front.

"You told Emery she couldn't go to Dad's funeral?" Nash's voice pitched low.

Betty gasped and clutched onto the kitchen rag on the counter. "Reed!"

"You made her stay in Eastridge and bury an urn by herself?" Nash stood nose-to-nose with Reed. "And when Ma asked where Emery was, you didn't tell her the truth? And you're pissed at *us* for lying?"

I expected an argument.

I expected some yelling.

I expected Betty to cry.

I did not expect Reed to swing his fist at Nash.

Reed's knuckles connected with Nash's face. It barely budged.

"Close your fist if you intend on doing real damage, little brother." Nash stepped forward into Reed's fist the second time, allowing Reed free reign on his face.

Punch. Uppercut. Another punch.

"Stop!" Betty shouted.

Basil cocked her head and observed the situation, elbow resting on the island counter.

Meanwhile, I slithered between them, knowing it was a bad idea but doing it anyway. Nash's eyes cut to mine at the same time Reed's body fell forward, pushing me onto the hardwood.

Nash split his attention to me, lingering on my wrist

cradled in my palm. He sprung into action, twisting Reed into a headlock. He bumped his knee against Reed's, forcing him to kneel.

"Don't fight it." Voice low, his arm tightened around Reed's neck. "Tap out, and I'll let go. Don't make Ma watch this."

"Emery!" Betty rushed to me, hands flying over my face, but I couldn't look away from Reed and Nash.

I imagined this was what watching an asteroid hit Earth would be like. Fascinating, destructive, and oddly beautiful.

It made sense how Nash had won so many fights. Boardrooms and offices were child's play. *This* was his element.

He wasn't a cruel prince. He wasn't a twisted warrior either. He was both, and it turned him into a man who would rather break than bend.

"Are you okay?" Betty brushed hair out of my eyes.

"I'm fine." I thrust myself off the floor, enchanted by the enigma of Nash Prescott.

"Enough!" Betty grabbed a hot pink fly swatter and swung the thin plastic near her sons as if she wielded a knife. "Stop it! I will not have you stain my floors with your sweat and blood. I will not have you ruin my holiday. And I will not have my sons fighting in my kitchen like poorly trained dogs battling over scraps."

Nash released Reed, who coughed a few dozen times. He beat at his chest, forcing more air out it.

"It's my fault, Reed." Betty set the swatter down and helped Reed to his feet. "Okay? I was the one who wanted to keep Dad's illness from you. I was the one who told Nash to let you take the fall. It was *me*. Be mad at *me*."

"Ma—"

"Let me finish. It was selfish, okay?" She cupped Reed's cheek. "Nash shouldn't have done that to the Cartwright boy, but when he tried to tell the cops it was him, I begged him not to. We needed him."

"You needed the five hundred bucks he sent you and Dad each month," Reed spit out. "I almost went to jail over five hundred dollars."

"No, baby, I needed my family together." Betty's fists seized his collar. "You were a minor. He was an adult. I thought there was no way they'd actually arrest you, so I made a choice. I know now it was a wrong one..."

My lips parted. The wall caught my weight. Leaning against it, I sliced my gaze to Nash.

I remembered that night.

Broken nose, rib, and leg.

Separated collar bone.

Dislocated shoulder.

The scar on Able's forehead I liked to smirk at.

Nash tried to tell the cops it was him, but I always thought he'd been covering for his brother.

"That was you?" I whispered to him.

Nash nodded. Once.

Tension coiled his neck. The fight mode hadn't fled. Two clenched fists hung at his side. Blood trickled down his temple. A gash opened above his eye, which I figured would become swollen and black by tomorrow.

This warrior, with the cuts and bruises and scars across his chest, had fought for me.

"Why?" My murmur went unnoticed by Reed and Betty.

Nash, however, never looked away from me. "He hurt you."

It never got that far, I wanted to argue, but I knew it was the same thing to Nash.

"Why did you let Reed hit you?"

"He needed it."

Can you be any more selfless?

It might have been a flaw at this point.

Nash had a brash tongue, a lack of filter, and the uncanny ability to pinpoint the exact thing to say to throw someone off balance. He pushed people away, never allowed anyone to see beneath his skin, and had no problems hermiting himself for eternity.

He also gave so much of himself, the only thing he kept was his kiss, and I'd taken that from him, too. Sacrifices littered his past and would probably stain his future. And it was a very Nash thing to hurt someone to heal them.

People measure love by how much someone receives, but I measure it by how much someone gives. No one in the history of the universe has ever or will ever have more love than Nash Prescott.

My villain.

My knight.

My prince.

My Ben.

I had to tell him.

"**I'm fine, Ma.** Don't worry about it." Nash tossed the blood-stained rag into the trash, pressed a kiss to Betty's forehead, and drew her in for a hug.

"You sure, baby?"

"Right." Reed leaned against Basil, who slid a palm into his back pocket. "Coddle him some more, Ma. Good going."

They ignored him.

Reed swore, grabbed his phone and keys, and swung an arm around Basil's shoulder. "I'm sorry for ruining our breakfast, Ma. Basil and I have to get going. We'll be back later, but I don't think we'll make it to Pastor Ken's sermon."

Betty turned to him. "It's okay, baby. The walls of a hospital have heard more sincere prayers than Eastridge's church. We can stop by the children's unit later and donate some teddy bears."

"Sounds good, Ma."

Reed locked eyes with Nash before kissing Betty's cheek. I followed him to the door, surprised when Basil tipped a shoulder up at me, as if to say, *boys, what can you do?*

I slid my hands into my pockets after Basil left for the restroom. "Are you mad at me?"

Fury lined Reed's face for a second. He released a sigh and gathered me into a hug. "No, but I hope you know what you're doing."

I don't.

"I have no idea what you're talking about." I offered him a lazy grin and rested my forehead against his shoulder.

I hadn't had an opportunity to mourn the idea of me and Reed, to dig a grave, and label it friendship. In reality,

I should have years ago when I'd slept with Nash. But standing in Reed's arms, I realized why I never had to.

My heart didn't caper inside its cage.

My body didn't experience an earthquake.

I wanted to understand him, but I didn't yearn for it.

I felt loved, but not *in* love.

He was just... Reed Prescott.

My best friend.

That's all.

Only ever my best friend.

chapter
FORTY-THREE

nash

I palmed a stash of joints.
I'd poached them from Reed's bag before he left, just to fuck with him for the punch. Leaning against the hood of my car, I watched Emery run her fingers across the massive double gates to the Winthrop Estate.

She crooked her head to study its height. "How likely are we to get arrested for trespassing?"

The weed wafted to my nostrils. I reeled a joint out of the bag and tossed the rest through my open car window. "Considering it's the Fourth of July and

Eastridge is about as corrupt as a North Korean election, not at all."

I neglected to mention I was the unhappy owner of the sixty-one-acre property. Maintenance fees for groundskeeping and cleaning staff auto-paid from one of my personal bank accounts.

My efforts started and ended there.

Emery tipped her chin at the joint nestled between my thumb and forefinger. "Are you going to light it up?"

Half my damn face throbbed, but I ignored it. "No."

"Why not?"

"Corrupting you sounds more fun than it actually is, Miss Winthrop," I lied. Mostly because the opposite was true, and she tasted of bad decisions and something to fight *for* instead of just something to fight.

Her blue-grays glinted with the challenge. Two fingers drifted down her shirt and thumbed the rim of her jeans, dipping just inside. "Do you like it?"

I swallowed, following the path of her fingertips. "Yes."

She tugged a fraction, flashing me a peek of smooth skin. "How much restraint does it take to not *devour* it?"

"Fucking all of it." Tossing the unlit joint to the leaf-covered ground, I crushed my heel on it. "Are we breaking and entering or what? I'm beginning to think you're too vanilla for this criminal lifestyle, Jailbait."

Emery gifted me with her throaty laugh, so pure and fucking genuine, it traveled straight to my cock. Her teeth grazed her lower lip, chancing a final glance at me before she began climbing the gate.

If I pinned her to it and fucked her hard, she'd probably beg me to fuck her harder. She'd been giving me those eyes since I let Reed go to town on my face. Blue one darkening. Gray one lightening.

They spoke all the words she'd never say.

I need you inside me, they challenged. *Give me everything you've got.*

It took all my self-control not to slide her jeans down her legs and sink inside her.

She was still a walking, talking, breathing rift between me and my brother, and I needed Gideon's location.

A conversation was long overdue.

Not to mention, Ma had pulled me aside at the house and told me Brandon stopped by a few times to talk to her, too. I realized I'd been so wrapped up in discussing Emery that I never asked Dick the PI who the second party to profit from the Winthrop Scandal was.

Now, Brandon was on my ass like a rash, stalking Ma and Emery. I'd burn myself with him, just to see him wither to ashes.

Emery whooped from the top of the gate, straddling it on either side. I edged forward in case she fell.

"How's this for vanilla?"

I tilted my head. "The sun's shining right on your tits. Are those hearts on your bra?"

"I'm not wearing a bra."

Fuck.

She covered her palms with her hoodie, slid down one of the gate's iron pillars, and landed with a Selena Kyle crouch. Her brow lifted as if to say, *beat that*.

I skated into my driver's seat, inched to the gate box, typed the code, and pulled up beside Emery.

She swung the passenger door open. "What the hell? You know the code?"

"It's the same one."

"And you didn't tell me?"

"Worked out just fine." I parked in front of the

mansion's double doors. "I'm in the company of a criminal mastermind."

"Do you think someone's in there?"

"No, but we'll knock in case."

Emery followed me up the steps. She knocked while I retrieved the spare keys beneath a rock. "It doesn't bother you that we're breaking in?"

"Word around town is no one lives here." I swung the door open.

Her lips parted at the sight of the foyer. The ridiculous Dionysus statue welcomed us, pristine given the weekly cleaning service I paid for.

Emery's fingertips trailed along the staircase's railing, coming up without dust. "Isn't this weird to you?"

"What?"

"Somebody bought this place, and it looks like they never touched it." We walked past a few rooms and into the kitchen. "Even Virginia's Swarovski dinner plates are set in the dining room. They're not even dusty."

"What I find weird is you calling your mom Virginia."

Actually, I found it weirder she hadn't called her that from the start. The woman made the evil step-mom from *Hansel and Gretel* seem like a peach.

"What I find weird is that I bothered to call her Mother for twenty-two years, and it took a text from her to get me to stop." She flung open the refrigerator, which the staff kept stocked for themselves, and pulled out a bag of frozen peas. "This isn't even expired."

I said nothing, watching her as she approached me.

She pressed the bag to my eye, gentle at first but firm when I didn't react. "It was always you, wasn't it?" she asked. I had no idea what she was talking about. She sucked in a breath. "Able was a dick, and I had revenge on my mind. If you hadn't hurt him, I would have. Thank you."

She was staring at me hard, looking at me like I might have a heart. I pulled at my collar, remembering after that I wore a Henley, not a button-down. Her breath fanned my cheeks, rushing to my neck. Mint and the strawberries she'd eaten at Ma's.

If she didn't move, I'd kiss her.

Fuck Reed.

Fuck Gideon.

Fuck Virginia.

Funny, how I never wanted to kiss anyone before, and now all I could think of was owning Emery's lips.

"Keep the ice on it." She replaced her hand on the peas with mine, lingering, eyes jumping to my mouth. "I wonder if my room is the same."

It was.

I didn't tell her.

Her eyes dropped to my lips once more. The sharp inhale confirmed she wanted them on hers, too. Three more seconds of staring, and I'd give it to her.

Two.

O—

She stepped back and strode to her bedroom. We passed the library, piano room, her parents' room, and the game room without stopping in any of them. If I didn't know better, I would think she hadn't grown up here. That these walls, this roof, the fucking statuario beneath our feet meant nothing to her.

In fact, she acted like she had no claim to the place. It bothered me. Not in the fairy tale Emery-and-I-met-here kind of way, but something that had less to do with us and more to do with the fact that she thought she had to be strong by pushing the past away.

She didn't.

I'd been there, done that, bought the t-shirt. It fit three-sizes too small, and every time I wore it, it damn near choked me to death.

Probably why I blurted, "I bought it."

She squinted at me and kept walking. "You bought what?"

"The Winthrop Estate."

Her feet stopped, but her back faced me. "Why?"

"I don't know." Always lying.

Because I thought it would lead to clues to take down your family. Turns out, I was wrong. You're probably innocent. Your Dad is probably innocent. Two more victims of this mess. So much of that going around.

Instead, I offered, "You can have it."

She finally turned to face me, conflict written all over her face like a billboard to her thoughts. "I don't want or need your charity."

"At the very least, the things in this room are yours. You can take them or leave them here to retrieve whenever you want."

The bag of peas hung loosely in my hands, brushing the side of my thigh. She focused on my eye, released a breath, and nodded.

In her room, she walked straight to the nightstand and pulled out a music box. The contents rustled when she shook it. Her relieved sigh piqued my curiosity. Setting it down, she disappeared into the closet.

I peered in the box, skimming over the tightly rolled papers. The corner-most one appeared loosest. Grabbing it, I unraveled the strip as if it were a fortune cookie.

> *You ever look to the stars and wonder if there's life out there? If there is, the aliens are*

probably pissed we keep crowning humans as Miss Universe. I bet they're floating in space with their superior technology, thinking—we could help them cure cancer if only those humans would stop considering themselves as the center of the universe. Think that's why we've never met any aliens?

(Hey, Alien Supreme Leader, if you're spying on me or Emery and read my note, take us with you. This place smells like sewage, and I caught Virginia forcing Em to eat with baby spoons to take smaller bites. By the way, I packed you an extra brownie, Tiger. I hope you eat it in front of Virginia and tell her it's laced with weed.)

— **NASH**

I'd written that after a bullshit astrology breadth course lecture, taught by a philosophy adjunct in need of spare cash.

I opened another.

> *Reed said you're obsessed with stars. I told him, if you're obsessed with stars, you'd be obsessed with daylight, considering the sun is a star and we lose its light at night. He said I'm wrong, that you stare at the night sky because it proves light peeks out of the darkness. (What in the actual poetic bullshit is that?)*
>
> *Wanna know what I think?*

It's the darkness you're after, Little Tiger.

Isn't it?

— **NASH**

And another.

> *One day, you'll reread this, and it'll be like spying on your own memory. Hope it's a happy memory. Also, Virginia tossed the cottage, looking for weed. She thinks I'm dealing. I take it you ate the brownie. Worth it.*

— **NASH**

Emery's footsteps approached. I rolled the letters up, deposited them back into the tin box, and leaned against the vanity.

It dawned on me that we shared the same memories.

"Almost ready." She exited the en suite in a dark dress so short, it would have been lewd if she didn't look so fucking pure in it. "I've grown a few inches since I wore it last, but Virginia hates this dress, so it is what it is. You think it's too short?"

No.

Yes.

I didn't answer, watching as she cocked her head and examined herself in the mirror. Satisfaction unfurled across her face at the sight of the dying roses printed on the dress. She reached behind me on the vanity and grabbed a tube of mascara at least four years old.

I snatched it from her. "You don't need it, and I'd

rather avoid explaining to the press why my Fourth of July brunch date has pink eye."

She hummed in the back of her throat. "There's golfing involved, too. Neither of us are dressed for it, which will probably be the only fun part about it."

Her hand found an ancient tube of Chapstick. She rubbed it across her lips, probably infecting them with some disease, but I'd still slam my mouth onto hers.

Her legs kicked at the four giant boxes beside the vanity, dress sneaking up her thigh. "Think I can fit these in the closet?"

"The closet?"

Her hand shot to her mouth. "*Shit.*"

"The closet?" I repeated, trying to figure out why she suddenly looked panicked. "Spill."

"Nash—"

"I'll find out." I opened one of the boxes. Piles of Winthrop Textiles shirts filled it. I didn't know what to think of it other than I needed her shirts, but I hated where they came from. "You know I'm persistent. It's easier for both of us to tell me."

"It's not a big deal."

"Tell me." I emphasized, "No lies."

She caved at the word lie, guilt crossing her face for a fleeting second. "I've been living in a closet at the hotel."

I blew up.

Fucking. Blew. Up.

She pissed me off.

Could she be any more self-sacrificial, infuriating, contradicting, confusing, generous, deviant, remarkable, or fucking goddamn consuming?

My body shook with the vigor of a pipeline drill. I needed to sprint a marathon, swim the entire Pacific, or trek the Amazon. Literally, *anything* to expend this energy, because mostly, I pissed myself off for not seeing any of this sooner.

I'd started this revenge quest with somewhat noble intentions, but I'd chosen the absolute last person I should have tormented.

"I'll move." Emery had the decency to look guilty, just about the wrong damn thing. "I swear, just give me some time to find a place."

"You think that's why I'm mad?!"

I shook my head, then shook it again, wondering if it'd rid me of this nightmare situation.

Nope. Still your fucking reality.

Piece of shit, meet your twin. Me.

Backing away from the vanity, my footsteps pounded against the carpet like artillery fire.

"Are you serious?" I didn't wait for an answer. "You're starving and homeless, but you're giving some chick you don't know over two grand a month for tuition? What the actual fuck, Emery?"

"You know about Demi?" She shook her head, as if it would wipe away the shock.

Nope, sweetheart. Tried that. Didn't work, and here I am, feeling like the biggest asshole in the history of Earth. Napoleon Bonaparte, Christopher Columbus, and Nash motherfucking Prescott.

"What about yourself?" I scrubbed my face. "When are you going to start taking care of yourself?"

"When the guilt fades!"

"What guilt?! Why are you guilty?!"

Fucking hell, this was it.

The moment she told me she'd been involved in the embezzlement.

The moment I learned she was guilty and, worse, wanted her anyway.

She glanced at the hickory clock on her nightstand. "We're going to be late."

"I don't care."

"I have to be on time."

"Still don't care."

"Virginia is holding my trust fund over my head…"

Shit. Cocksucker. Dickface.

I folded my arms across my chest. "We're talking about this later."

"Sure," she said, but I didn't believe her. She didn't comment on the frozen peas I'd left on the nightstand, tossing the bag to me. "I said to keep this on your eye. It's already swelling and turning dark."

"I can handle a black eye, Tiger. I've had plenty."

"Suit yourself." She tipped a shoulder up, glimpsed at the full-length mirror again, and fingered a dead flower on the dress. As if she couldn't help herself, she spun. The dress moved with her, drooping petals suddenly alive.

It was such a fucking Emery Winthrop thing to do, my nails pierced the bag to stop my hands from pinning her to the mirror and tearing that dress off her body.

"I like that you're watching me, mostly because I know you hate that you're doing it," she called over her shoulder.

With her spinning in a dress of dead roses, frozen peas pressed to my eye, I succumbed to the fact that I wanted Emery Winthrop.

This was happening.

I'm going to hell.

chapter FORTY-FOUR

nash

Gossip followed us—*me*—as the caddy drove our group to the next hole.

My eye had darkened and swelled to the point where I'd gotten a few whispers. For the most part, the people of Eastridge fawned over me in a way they usually didn't with new money wealth.

The press painted me as a Saint, and to Eastridgers, good P.R. was a coveted gift bag at an exclusive event. They clamored over it, brown-nosed their way into its proximity, and begged for the scraps.

Virginia clutched onto Balthazar's arm like a hanger

hooked on a rod. The wire, dry-cleaner ones no one wanted. Able Small Dick Cartwright inched to the absolute edge of the cart, his undersized checkered-magenta golf shorts pressed as tight as possible against the railing.

"Of course," he continued, darting wide eyes at me every few seconds as if he thought I would give him another scar to match the one on his forehead, "I told him I could get him off."

"Is that what you do during your day job?" Emery offered Able Small Dick Cartwright a serene smile. "Take people into your office and *get them off?*"

"Yes." His enthusiastic nod begged to double as a punching bag. "I'm very good at my job."

"I'm impressed. I hear the market for prostitution is tough these days."

"I didn't mean—I'm not..." He looked to Virginia for help, but she was busy ordering the caddy to disinfect her golf club. "I'm a *lawyer*."

Emery's eyes said, *sure you are*. She hopped off the cart, retrieved her club, and headed to the tee.

I clamped my hand around Able Small Dick Cartwright's neck, disguising the move as a back pat. "I'm about as interested in hearing your prepubescent voice as I am in watching a 24-hour filibuster on C-Span, Small Dick. Take your pink Polo-wearing, Brooks Brothers-drooling ass to the artificial turf rake and kindly scratch your face off. Keep your eyes and hands to yourself today, and you'll live to get off another client tomorrow."

My long strides outpaced the caddy to the tee. Emery stuck her ass out, two hands gripping the handle with proper form. The tiny dress rose up her long legs. Virginia about ruptured a vein in her forehead every time Emery leaned over.

Small Dick had stayed in the cart.

Good.

I stood between Emery and Balthazar. My body angled to cover his line of sight. Dude was a fucking creep. He stared at her every five seconds like he wasn't already banging her mom.

I didn't know if Emery was swinging wide on purpose or if she sucked at golf, but she spent the last eight holes swinging away. Perfect form, yet she'd missed every shot and took pleasure in shouting, "Fore" as loud as she could.

She'd turn to the caddy, insist on recovering the ball herself, and force us to wait in the sun as she took her sweet time doing so. The cycle continued.

Swing.

Miss.

Swing.

The ball landed in a thick covering of trees on the perimeter of the course.

Emery's cheeks flushed from the sun. Our eyes met and held, hers challenging mine. I didn't know if defying Virginia turned her on or if staring at me did, but I was So. Here. For. It.

"I don't need a new ball. I'll get it," she said to the caddy. "I need the exercise. Right, Virginia?"

I selected the thinnest putter from my new set of clubs and followed Emery past the trees. She bent over at the waist, hands dipping to retrieve her golf ball.

"I said I... Oh." She straightened, tiny white ball cribbed in her palm. "Did they send you after me?"

I trailed the putter up the inside of her calves, sliding past her knee, and between her thighs. "Let's play a game."

"We already are." Her eyes fluttered closed. "Golf."

I ignored her, "Slide your panties off, hand them to me, and position the putter between your pussy lips."

"Why would I do that?"

"Because you're mine, Tiger," I declared, soaking in her lust-heavy gaze. "Your lips are mine. Your tits are mine. Your ass is mine. Your soaking wet pussy is mine."

"You're delusional."

"Am I?" I slid the golf putter from her, brought it to my lips, and ran my tongue along the narrow metal edge. She tasted like ambrosia, sweet and crisp. "You taste fucking wet to me, Tiger, and I know you didn't get wet for yourself."

"If I listen to you, you have to make me come."

"Deal," I said, for the second time in as many days.

Always bartering, this one.

Emery turned around and slid her panties down her thighs, bending slightly as she wiggled her ass to shake them off. I caught glimpses of her bare lips from behind, wanting to run my tongue from one hole to the other.

She pivoted and tossed her panties at me. I caught and pocketed them. Her fingers latched on to the slender, L-shaped end of the putter. She positioned it between her legs. I slid part of the tip inside.

Arousal flushed her cheeks red. She lifted her dress at the edge, showing me the way her pussy lips sandwiched the club.

So naughty.

So sweet.

So mine.

"Drop to your knees and take me into your mouth."

She could never refuse a dare. Whatever embers she had, they kindled it.

"Anyone can walk past the trees and see us."

"Kiss the tip," I negotiated, and I never fucking negotiated. "With your tongue."

She wanted to. Her tongue slipped past her plump lips, begging to lick my cock. I ran a hand through her hair and gripped it near the base of her head. Instead of leading her mouth to my cock, I tilted her head up and slammed my lips onto hers.

Shit.

Motherfucker.

Jesus, Joseph, and Mary.

What the hell was I doing?

The caddy yelled our names in the distance. We broke apart. I swallowed each of Emery's pants.

Her wide eyes met mine. "You promised to make me come."

Without a word, I kneeled, fully aware she was the one who was supposed to kneel and take me in her mouth. I lifted her dress, spread her pussy lips, and licked the entire slit. She cried out, clutching onto my hair.

I slid my tongue inside her, savoring her taste. As the caddy's footsteps came closer, I pushed two fingers inside her and sucked on her clit. She came hard, nearly pulling my hair out of my head with her fingers.

When the caddy called Emery's name again, I yelled out, "She's coming!"

Her body shook with the aftershocks of her orgasm. She clutched my shoulders and steadied her breathing. "My panties—"

I cut her off. "—are mine."

She narrowed her eyes, but didn't argue. In fact, she had that glint in her eyes that told me she loved this.

I walked back with Emery's panties in my pocket, grass stains on my knees, the taste of her on my lips, and an erection the size of a skyscraper.

This was the type of shit that spiraled, and next thing I knew, it'd be plastered all over tabloids that I fucked the twenty-two-year-old daughter of the face of embezzlement.

This was definitely not okay.

But it fucking felt great.

THE GENERAL IQ of the fine people of Eastridge, North Carolina sat somewhere between Americans who can't locate America on a map and people who believe the Earth is flat. At least, it felt like that as I overheard four different conversations about the necessity of muslin washcloths.

Between the mundane chatter, gossip of me ran rampant, occasionally brushing over the pending black eye I sported.

"*He's so damaged. Ugh, and he always looks so tortured. Why does that make him hotter?*"

I don't know, Stepford #1. Perhaps you should seek therapy for that. (For the record, I *am* tortured by this brunch, which isn't even a word.)

"My neighbor told me he gave her the best sex she's ever had at last week's gender reveal party."

My blue balls can attest that I haven't fucked your neighbor, and I'd sooner show up to a swingers' night at a retirement community than a fucking gender reveal party.

"I told my wife he's a thug. Look at his eye. Once a poor kid, always a poor kid."

Cool story, bro. It'd mean more if you hadn't passed me your business card as soon as I entered the restaurant.

Our group sat at a table in the center, which Virginia informed us was the best seat in the house.

"I'm looking into becoming a Sir." Balthazar lifted his chin as if what he said should have impressed us. "You'll all have to call me Sir once it happens."

It could have been a joke, but he seemed like the type to expect it.

"A Sir," Emery repeated, drawing the word out like she couldn't quite wrap her mind around the concept. She sat directly beside me, our bodies so close they stuck together.

"Isn't it wonderful?" Virginia squeezed Sir Balty's hand.

I swear if he leered at Emery one more time, I'd ruin his life, then rearrange his face for sport. Douche was gonna be her step-father, and he stared at her like she was a piece of meat he wanted to dig in to.

"Congratulations, Sir Balthazar," Small Dick said, grabbing a menu off the table. This tool looked like every Disney villain rolled into one idiotic, blue-blooded asshole.

I didn't touch a menu as everyone sifted through the options. Virginia darted her eyes away from me. She'd spent the morning caught somewhere between the sneer she used to give me and the brown-nosed chatter because I was suddenly the most powerful man in the room.

One of the white-suited waiters approached.

"Order anything, Nash." Virginia glanced at him before saying, "It's on our country club tab."

"Perfect," Emery cut in, flipped the menu open, then preceded to order two of everything that didn't suck.

"Two of everything?" The waiter gnashed his lips together. Poor guy wanted to flee.

"Of everything." She offered the closed menu to him. "Treat yourself to a two-hundred percent tip, too."

Virginia's fingers turned white around the stem of her mimosa glass. She pursed her lips until the waiter left. "The temper tantrum isn't cute."

"Perhaps not." A sly smile brightened Emery's face. "You know what *is* cute? A spare tire, so I can't wait to dig into the food."

"*This*. This behavior is exactly why I didn't make you maid of honor."

"You're getting married?" Emery finished off her second cocktail of the afternoon.

"Yes. Soon. I invited you here today to announce it."

"You didn't invite me, Virginia. You demanded it, which happens when your own daughter cannot stand the sight of you."

Virginia ignored her. "We have put it off long enough, waiting for you to find your senses and return to Eastridge. No use in waiting now. I'll be a Van Doren soon, and Cordelia will be my maid of honor. You remember Cordelia, right? Able's sister. Lovely girl." She stared at Small Dick like he was her pride and joy. "Balthazar has agreed to make Able his best man. You'll be my bridesmaid and accompany Able as his date."

"The hell she will," I gritted out. "Were you dropped on your head as a child?"

"Pardon me?"

"It would explain the misshaped head, obsession with injecting chemicals into your face, and overall deranged behavior."

For the record, I had no issue with plastic surgery. Virginia consistently prioritizing it above Emery, on the other hand, rubbed me the wrong way.

"You act as if my daughter hates me, Mr. Prescott."

Emery dug her fingernails in my thigh, the message clear—she didn't need me fighting her battles. She thanked the waiter for topping up her drink and sipped it.

"I don't hate you, Virginia. You shaped me, so to hate you is to hate myself... which, if I think about it, might be what you've wanted all along. I am the younger, shinier version of you, and it's always bothered you. Hasn't it?"

"This is exactly why I chose Cordelia. I would have made you my maid of honor, Emery, but you're entirely too untrustworthy for such a gift."

Another gulp of her drink. "Thanks for sparing me, Virginia."

"I expect you at the rehearsal dinner or you can say goodbye to your trust fund."

"Sounds fun." She pushed her chair away from the table and stood. "Nash and I would love to go." She waved at her soon-to-be step-father and Able. "See you there, Sir Balty and Small Dick."

chapter
FORTY-FIVE

nash

We spent the rest of the evening at the bar, Emery chugging down amaretto sours until I'd asked the waiter to switch them to water.

As soon as we entered the car, Emery shimmied into her oversized sweats, ordering me not to look. She flipped the dress over her head and replaced it with a white t-shirt that read, *Easy, Tiger*.

Settling into the seat, she stroked the trim. "What type of car is this?"

I pulled into the gas station and handed an attendant

my card with orders to fill up the tank. "A Lamborghini Aventador S Roadster."

"Hmm... doesn't seem like something you'd drive."

That's because I'd taken an Uber to the nearest car dealership and picked the first car on the lot after my Honda broke down. It happened to be a luxury car dealership. Eastridge, North Carolina for you.

"You know what I noticed about Virginia?" she asked once we'd driven for an hour, the only car on the road now.

"What?"

"She never looks happy. I want to be happy when I grow up."

"You're not happy right now?"

"Hmm... I think I am. Maybe. Just a different type of happy. I want to be balter type of happy." Another made-up word, no doubt. She didn't give me a chance to ask what it meant. "Are you ever sick of the lies?"

"Whose lies?"

"Lies in general." She massaged her temples, probably to fight off all those cocktails she'd downed. "People hold back, say what they don't mean, and hide everything inside."

I didn't answer her, merely inclined my head and let her make of it what she wanted. My car careened down the concrete. The first splash of rain hit Emery's side of the windshield. She reached up and stroked it, the movement reverent.

When she pulled her fingers back, she'd left marks on the glass. "I hate lies. You know what I realized, Nash?"

"Enlighten me. I'm on the edge of my seat."

"You don't hate me." She flung her arms wide as if she'd just made the most profound statement in the world. "You hide behind this rough exterior, because I've found my way beneath your skin, and it scares you. You don't like how I make you feel, because I actually make you feel."

I swallowed, contemplating an answer to whatever the fuck that was. "You're plastered."

"Not really."

The devious smile forced my fingers to adjust on the steering wheel. She pulled out her phone, gave me her back, and began typing.

I cut a glance at her. "What are you doing?"

She slid the phone back into her pocket and shifted. Her leg jostled the box of my notes she'd taken from the Winthrop Estate. "Just Googled something."

Stretching her arms above her head, she rested her hands on her neck. We drove for a few more miles before her hand slithered behind my headrest.

"What are you doing?" I repeated. Second time in ten minutes. I was a parrot at this point.

The rain splashed across the windshield harder now. I turned on the wipers, placing the speed to its highest setting.

Her hand retreated at the same time she said, "Pull over."

"What?"

"Pull over."

She leaned over me in a flash, moving quickly for how much she had drunk. A second later, the roof of the convertible flung off, flying behind us with the speed I drove at. I flicked my eyes down to my lap. Her hand still clasped the lever that released the roof.

Emery looked half a second from snorting with laughter.

Glee brimmed her cheeks while I cataloged the past hour.

She'd asked me my car's make and model, Google'd something, reached behind both our headrests where two of the roof levers were, and leaned over my lap to pull the final one.

Fucking hell.

Water splattered both our cheeks. Rain came down harder as if it knew what she'd done and wanted to taunt me.

"Jesus, Emery. You need a blanket, psych eval, and a drunk tank. Stat."

"I'm not drunk," she insisted. She shot up from her seat, stretched her arms Titanic-style, and screamed to the empty road, "I want to balter!"

I tried to recall how many cocktails she'd had.

At least six.

Probably more.

I slowed the car. This chick was out of her goddamned mind, begging to fall out of the moving vehicle.

She slanted her eyes to me, her body swaying to no music. "Is it the heavy rain? Would you balter if it were mizzling?"

"Balter isn't a word." I pulled onto the side of the road, remembering that she'd written it on her Polaroid of the night sky. "Mizzling is most definitely not a word."

"Yes, it is. It's a portmanteau. It's mist and drizzling together, like smog is smoke and fog and motel is motor and hotel." Her brow arched, and she looked at me as if *I* were the crazy one. "Are you sure we graduated from the same high school? Could've sworn Eastridge Prep had higher standards."

I ignored her words, watching her swing her arms with the rhythm of a one-footed kangaroo. "The fuck are you doing?"

"I'm baltering. I don't have a dad who loves me. I have a high-society mom that dangles my future over my head every chance she gets. I have an angry boss, staring at me like he wants to fuck me." She nearly toppled over the passenger seat. "I'd rather not deal with any of that at the moment, so I'm going to balter."

"What the fuck is balter?"

Her white shirt clung to her skin. Two nipples pointed out. The *Easy, Tiger* taunted me. My own words, used against me. Her hips rolled, chasing something I refused to address with so much alcohol in her body.

"To dance." She peered up at the sky. "Artlessly, with no grace, no skill, but always with enjoyment. Dad used to say, *all you have to do is ask. I will always be here to balter with you.* What a lie. Is everyone I know a liar?"

"You literally just lied to me when you said you're not drunk," I pointed out, mostly because I had a long list of lies under my belt, too.

"You have to stop assuming I'm drunk. The integral of one over x is the natural log of x, plus the constant C. The twenty-fourth U.S. president is Grover Cleveland. And that Area 51 party is the dumbest shit I've ever heard." She sat down—*finally*—and leaned closer to me. "I'm telling you, Nash. I'm not drunk. I'm chasing happiness. I want to balter."

"It's raining."

In fact, water soaked the entire interior of my fucking car, and even if I did drive back, I had no chance of finding my roof in working condition.

"Wow, you have a career as a weatherman if this hotelier gig doesn't work out for you. It might not," she taunted, "considering we're building a lobby around a sculpture we've never seen..." Her fingertips traced my cheek, jumping from one subject to another like leapfrog, because that was clearly sober behavior. "I wish you were happy, Nash Prescott."

My jaw ticked, teeth grinding against each other. "How do you know I'm not happy?"

"You have too much going on in here"—she tapped her temple—"to allow yourself to let loose and be happy." Her sigh suggested she pitied me. "I'm doing something. Don't look." She gave me approximately half a second to turn away before she stripped out of the oversized sweats and said, "I can't dance in these."

"*Fucking hell*," I muttered.

Dad used to shout, "Heavens to Betsy!" when he found something to be insane. I'd never found a more applicable situation than this one.

Emery stole her panties from my pocket, slid them on before I could process what I'd gotten myself into, and darted out of the car. Twirling in circles, she managed to look petite despite her height.

She was small and fierce, and if she was to be believed, a collector of tears, sweat, and blood. Her Chucks—the only pair I ever saw her wear—trampled over the mud. Was this what mental breakdowns looked like?

Because this wasn't normal behavior.

It wasn't even normal drunk behavior.

But it was a little pathetic and more endearing than I'd like to admit, almost enough to make me get off my ass and "balter" with her.

I didn't.

I stared, waiting for her to sober up.

She spun in circles. Water dripping down her white shirt. Without a bra, all I saw were hard nipples. I could have sucked one of those nipples into my mouth, right over the G in Tiger. But she was drunk, and I was more of a tear-you-to-shreds type of asshole than a take-advantage-of-you one.

She laughed, the only source of heat in this damn rain. Even under this starless night, she reminded me of the sun. So fucking warm all the time. Inside *and* outside. And I legit had no clue where this girl came from.

How she bulldozed her way into my life time and time again. How did it make sense for her to show up everywhere? Fill up every crevice of the universe?

"Look!" She jerked her hand above her. "It's a beautiful night. No stars. Aren't you at least gonna look at it?"

"No."

I watched her instead, taking in her arms swinging back as she whirled in circles. Reaching into the center console, I stuck a confiscated joint in the corner of my mouth, wishing I could light it and replace one addicting substance with another.

Fuck this rain.

My eyes dropped to her nipples.

On the other hand, I didn't hate the rain.

I toyed with the joint and observed Emery. As far as mental breakdowns went, this one was cute. Her smile never left, which was a miracle, considering she possessed absolutely no grace when it came to dancing.

Her limbs were too long for it. They got in her way as she twirled and swayed, two-mile-high legs peeking out beneath her shirt. Fucking perfect as she was, she didn't even look like a fantasy, because no mind on this earth could conjure her up.

Emery caught me staring. "Thinking about me?"

"In case you haven't realized, I'm always thinking about you, and I like it as much as I'd like waking up to Rosco licking my face, but here we are."

"Do you think it's lust?" Keen eyes studied me, waiting for an answer to the question we always skirted.

"Tell you what... Ask me when you're sober, and I'll answer."

Zero chance she'd remember any of this tomorrow.

Emery didn't reply. She continued to dance, gracing me with a smile that suggested she knew something I didn't. Cocky, yet somehow sweet. A drug too addictive to be on the market.

I sat in my drenched, six-hundred-and-forty-eight-thousand-dollar car, picking apart the ruined joint. Her lips muttered so many of her words, I couldn't keep up, and even if I could, I was sure most of them didn't exist in any dictionary alive except the walking dictionary baltering in the pouring rain.

"*Fuck!*" Emery dove suddenly for the passenger seat, toppling over the door until her legs stuck up in the air and her head landed somewhere on the floor of the car.

I set the joint down. "If this is part of baltering, I'm out."

"Shut up. I'm saving it."

"Saving what?"

"Pop your trunk and help me up."

"Tell me what you're saving."

"Please, Nash... Just do it?"

"You're a shit show," I muttered, but I popped my trunk, opened my door, trampled through the mud, wrapped an arm around her middle, and hauled her against my body until nothing but soaking wet clothes separated us.

She cradled the box she'd taken from her room to her chest. It was a tin box, waterproof by nature, which she would have realized if she wasn't hammered out of her mind.

Curiosity plagued my thoughts. I was tempted to ask her why she'd kept the notes, but I carried her to the trunk and set her down.

I wanted to crack open her mind like a book and read it, but I was fucked if it became my favorite book to read.

I obsessed.

When I loved a book, I didn't read it once. I read it over and over again—until the pages fell off, until I could anticipate the words before I read them, until they sunk into me and melted inside my bones in a way that never happened with books I'd only read once.

I couldn't dip into her mind.

She reeked of my downfall.

Emery used one of my gym shirts to wipe the rainwater off the lid before shoving the entire box in the corner with a bunch of my shirts covering it for good measure. When she lowered my hood, she sat on it.

"What's your barrier?" She swiped at the wet hair plastered to her cheeks. "What's stopping you from giving in? I'm not talking about just sex. I know if I told you I'm thinking of you bare and inside me"—*fuck*—"you'd give it to me. But what if I like who you are and want more than that?"

"You don't know who I am."

"I do," she argued. "More than you think I do, and it's driving me crazy." Her ankle hooked around my leg. "Is it the age difference? Reed? The fact that I'm a Winthrop? Because I think it's stupid when two people like each other but aren't together."

I grabbed her calf and stepped into her body. She hooked both legs around me.

"What if I don't like you?"

"I'd say you're a liar. Is it the taboo element that's stopping you? What if I told you, as long as I don't touch you, this isn't wrong," she whispered, getting closer. "You aren't ten years older than me." *Lie.* "You aren't my best friend's brother." *Lie.* "You don't hate me." *Finally, a truth.* "Is that what you want to hear?"

Actually, what I wanted was absolute confirmation she had nothing to do with my dad's death.

Legit the only thing I wanted.

Fuck revenge.

Fuck my brother.

Fuck the company.

Fuck the fucking age gap.

I just needed to know, with absolute certainty, she did not have anything to do with my parent's losing their savings, with Dad losing his spot in the medical trial, with Hank Prescott dying.

For that to happen, I needed Gideon's location.

I cupped her cheek, leaning in to inhale the petrichor on her skin. "Tell me where your dad is living, Little Tiger, and I will give you everything you want and more."

"Enough with the subject changes." One of the smartest people I knew, and she still didn't get it. She leaned against my palm and closed her eyes. "For god's sake, take a leap, Nash. You will always be older than me. I will always be younger than you. Maybe we'll always 'hate' each other, too. But will we always feel like this?"

"Like what?"

"Like our fingertips can shoot lightning, but the only target they can hit is each other."

"Talk to me when you're sober."

"I'm not wasted. I'm happy. And I'm finally realizing that two souls don't just find each other by accident." She leaned forward and bit my lip, harder than any sane woman would. "You taste like sin, Nash. So delicious. So wrong. So right."

It wasn't a kiss, but it could be. If I gave in, gripped her neck, and closed the distance, it could be. Was the last time a fluke, or did she really taste and feel as delicious as she looked and acted?

I stepped back from her. "Sober up, Tiger. It's damn near freezing, and we'll get sick if we stay long. You have twenty minutes before I'm taking us to the nearest hotel."

She didn't budge. "Is it about Hank?" Finally, she got it right, and I wanted her to think it was about our ages again. "You know he'd want you happy, right? Life is fucked up. It's a roller coaster ride without an exit, and you're smushed into the same tiny cart with eight billion other people. You can either push everyone off, throw up until you're miserable, or enjoy the ride. Let's enjoy the fucking ride, Nash."

I swallowed, rounded the car, and sat on the driver's seat. "Eighteen minutes. You should probably start baltering."

Her disappointment filled the space between us.

She exhaled. It was loud and long and made me uncomfortable in a place that had laid dormant for a while now. When I thought she'd return to the car, she skipped across the mud and twisted to a pattern only she knew.

"Thirty seconds," I called out after her twenty minutes had been up ten minutes ago.

She ambled over and rested her forearms on the door. "Thanks for letting me balter."

I nodded, wrung out her wet sweats, and handed them to her. "You'll get sick."

They made flapping noises when she slid them on. "This is why I like you."

"Why?" I humored her.

"I don't want someone who holds an umbrella over

my head when it rains. I want someone who doesn't even own an umbrella. Someone who watches me balter in the rain when they don't know the word exists. Someone who stares at me instead of the stars in the sky."

"Sounds like a fantasy."

Fuck, I need Gideon's location, especially if she's gonna keep talking like we're already together.

"Think what you want."

After she shut the door, I blasted the heater. I tore through the road, hoping we'd find someplace to stop soon. The heat gave us seconds of relief before it escaped into the air. I shut it off to save gas and ripped off my shirt instead.

"Put this on."

Her hungry eyes ate up my scars. One of her fingers reached out and traced one. "I liked you today." She slipped the Henley over her head and dipped her nose down to inhale it. "You are phosphenes, Nash. You are the stars and colors I see when I rub my eyes. You feel real in the moment, but you fade away. Don't fade away this time."

What does that even mean?

"And you speak like you're a walking, talking dictionary twenty-four seven, and especially when you're drunk."

"I'm not drunk."

I rolled my eyes and pulled over when I realized I'd missed an exit with a motel. Emery unbuckled her seatbelt.

"Put on your seatbelt. We're not stopping. I'm making sure there are no cars here before I drive the opposite direction on a one-way road."

She ignored me, wearing a content smile on her face.

I considered that maybe I hadn't been watching her break tonight. I'd been watching her heal herself.

"I know your secret," she whispered, climbing onto my lap. "You're my Ben."

And then she kissed me. Hard. On the mouth. And I realized I wanted to own all her kisses. But she'd been drinking, and I was reeling. Spiraling into disbelief.

Ben.

As in, Benkinersophobia.

As in, Emery Winthrop was my Durga.

What were the odds?

Fucking tell me Fate didn't exist.

chapter FORTY-SIX

Every

A battering ram hit my head.
Either I had the worst hangover or I'd gotten a cold. It felt like both.

I watched Chantilly snatch all the yogurt from the fridge. Hannah staked her claim on the sodas. Cayden scarfed down the cold cuts. Ida Marie ate string cheese without peeling it like a psychopath.

I'd grown past refusing Nash's food, but part of me wondered if he'd stop making me lunches if I caved and grabbed snacks with witnesses in the room.

I hid a sniffle in my tissue, tempted to curl into my bed in the penthouse's spare room. An actual mattress and silky sheets with a thread count higher than my bank balance.

This morning, I'd walked into my closet and found it cleared. The panic came first. Fury came second. The return of my vision came last.

A note on the floor read:

> *I'd give you a key, but we both know you already have one.*
>
> **— NASH**

It wasn't Nash's handwriting, which made sense since he'd been with me the entire time. It looked like Delilah's.

I was still staring at the fridge when Nash entered.

"I thought we were over this. Take what you want." He reached into the fridge, somehow grabbed me exactly what I would have chosen, and tossed it on the empty couch cushion. "I'll still make the damn lunches, Tiger. Eat. Whatever. You. Want. *Fuck.*"

I reached for the juice pouch and pepperoni pizza Lunchables. My hip bumped the Jana Sport. A cascade of tissues fell to the floor

Nash spotted them, taking in the sheer quantity. "Are you sick?" A litany of curses sailed out of him. "I told you you'd get sick in the rain."

"I told you so? Really?" I tore open the Lunchables and ate a pepperoni, smiling at him despite the congestion. "Are we five? You can do better than that."

Nash collected my Jana Sport. "Come on."

I tore into another pepperoni slice. "I already opened

this." The tray rattled in my frozen palms. "Can't waste food."

He nicked the meal and slammed it beside Chantilly's yogurt. "Eat this."

She jolted from the desk. "But—"

"Eat it." His back ended her response. A thick brow arched at me. "Problem solved. We're going."

"I'm hungry," I protested, but I followed him into the elevator.

He pressed the G button for the garage. "I'll pick up McDonald's on the way."

I exited the elevator first. "I hate McDonald's."

"Virginia hates McDonald's. You love it." Nash unlocked his car, swung the door open for me, and waited for me to settle into the seat's leather. "You're obsessed with peeling the breading off their McNuggets and shoving them into a McDouble with fries, which by the way is fucking disgusting."

"My McMasterpiece. Yum." A sneeze swallowed my moan. The tissue filled my palm. Being sick sucked. "Don't knock it 'till you try it."

I ate my McMasterpiece on the way to the doctor's office. The final bite spoke of regret. I considered vomiting, but Nash's car still smelled of petrichor and mud. Plus, he no longer had a roof. Maybe I'd done enough damage to the car.

"This is pointless. It's just a cold. It'll go away on its own. One week max, but probably less." Without a heater in my Alabama studio, I'd gotten so many colds, I was a pro at this point.

"We're still going to the hospital."

"You're ridiculous."

I hid my smile, because I read between the Nash-colored lines. He cared. It was cute. Warm, even. Like watching Ben and Nash merge into one being. The affection of Ben, mixed with the brash exterior of Nash.

"Can you finish this?" I held out a little cardboard box. The naked McNuggets filled it, white without the breading.

He wore a scowl, but he ate them all, since neither of us believed in wasting food. A question filled my mouth the entire drive.

Do you think it's lust?

He'd told me to ask when I was sober, but every time it crawled toward my lips, I dug my nails into the leather.

This poor car. So abused by me.

At the hospital, Nash parked in a slot reserved for staff and guided me to a private entrance. We weaved through plain halls, stained by the stale scent of chemicals and death.

The intake room buzzed. Two teens clutched onto burned arms from a Fourth of July pyrotechnic display. An elderly woman rocked in her seat, rubbing at her arms. Patients filled every chair in the waiting room, and more stood to the side in various states of disheveled and broken.

"We'll be here all day." I groaned, brows dipping together when I noticed Nash walking to a door.

He arched a brow as if to say, *Well? You coming or what?*

A nurse approached him. "Sir, you can't go in there."

"My last name is on this building." He flashed her a wolf's smile. "I'll go where I want."

"Oh, Mr. Prescott." The heels of her sensible sneakers squeaked with her retreat. "I'm so sorry. I didn't catch your face. I'll page a G.P." She fled, not once turning back.

I groaned and followed Nash through a hallway he

seemed to know well. "Don't tell me you've turned into that douche."

"That douche?"

"The one who pulls the money card every chance he gets."

"Not usually."

I stumbled after a sneeze and allowed Nash to steady me. "You donated this building and named it after yourself?"

"I named it after Dad." He held a door open for me. "It's the Hank Prescott Medical Center."

"Oh." I racked my brain for a polite way to say, *horrible idea*, but came up short. "He would have liked that."

Nash snorted. "No, he wouldn't have."

"Yeah, he would have hated it." I hopped onto the exam table. "He would have called it useless fanfare. Why'd you do it?"

"For starters, I wanted him immortalized by someone who isn't you, me, Ma, or Reed."

"If someone else remembers him, it makes his existence real."

"Yeah."

No wonder Nash's chest was so broad. It housed such a big heart.

I wanted to apologize again for his loss, but it seemed inadequate. I wanted to ask him if he was okay, but that seemed inadequate, too. I settled for studying him.

Nash tugged at the otoscope covers. Three coasted to the floor. He kicked them near the door. "The doctor that forced Dad off the trial is on the board of this hospital. It's why I chose to rename it. I want that motherfucker to see it every time he attends a meeting."

More words fringed his mouth. They laid dormant

there, unspoken. I would have pressed, but an older doctor stepped into the room.

"Nash."

"Dax."

Dax adjusted the stethoscope around his neck. "Heard you caused a scene out there." He crushed the otoscope covers beneath his sneakers and cursed.

A smile ghosted Nash's lips. "Driving my car through the building until I reached this exam room would be a scene. Civilized conversation, however, is not."

"When have you ever been civilized?" Dax tossed the plastic and exchanged his Paw Patrol gloves for blue latex ones. "Who's this?"

I waved. "Emery, and considering I'm in the room, too, you can ask me your questions directly."

"Right. Sorry." He snapped the gloves and approached. "I'm a pediatrician. I'm used to asking the parents, but it's a full house today."

The lack of a clipboard had me on edge. Didn't all professionals use clipboards?

Nash toyed with the I.U.D. pamphlets, selecting one for the brand I'd gotten from my campus' medical center.

Dax's eyes followed mine to Nash. "Would you like Mr. Prescott to leave? Your confidentiality is a right."

"I'm fine. Let's get this over with."

Doctors creeped me out, mostly because Virginia had raised me on concierge doctors and in-house medical care.

"Not a fan of doctors?"

"Sorry, I'll tone down the bite."

Nash's lips pressed together as if he didn't believe me and found it amusing.

Dax pulled out a thermometer. "I take it you're sick? What are your symptoms?"

"It's just a cold."

When I didn't elaborate, Nash took over, listing the runny nose, coughing, sneezing, and bajillion other things he'd noticed in a single car ride. An otoscope examined my ears and nose. A thermometer determined my temperature. The metal of the stethoscope chilled my back.

And at the end of it all, Dax told me what I already knew. "The cold should go away in three to ten days without medication."

"That's it?" Nash leaned against the wall, face resembling a concerned coach's. "No pills? Remember, it's your head that I'll be after if something happens."

"It's a cold, Nash. It'll go away on its own." Dax handed me a lollipop from his Paw Patrol fanny pack. It earned him a smile. "If you have a headache, take an over-the-counter NSAID like Advil or Tylenol."

I unwrapped the lollipop. "Got it, Doc. Thanks."

Dax left me alone with Nash. His bespoke suit paired poorly with my skinny jeans and tee, but I liked the dynamic. It was us.

I sucked on the candy, waiting for him to speak.

He toyed with one of the tongue depressors in a jar. "Why are you smiling?"

"I love Ben. You are Ben."

The stick stalled in his fingers. "You remember last night?"

"All of it..." I shifted. The paper beneath my thighs crunched. "I might have been drunk, but I remember it all."

Ask the question, Em.

Nash snapped a depressor in half and toyed with the fringe, probably collecting splinters. "Why Durga?"

"Her sacred animal is the tiger. She's known as the Inaccessible."

"Your Insta handle."

The full-blown smile probably looked goofy and obnoxious, but I refused to tamp it. "You stalked me on Insta?"

"Of course not."

My lips remained tipped up. I'd let this lie slide.

"Last night, I asked you a question. You told me to ask again when I'm sober." My free hand toyed with the exam table's paper. "Do you think this is just lust?"

"Ask me again later."

"But—"

"If I say yes, you'll feel like shit on top of being sick. If I say no, you'll want me on you, all over you, *in* you. Do you really want to be sick when that happens?"

When.

Not if.

"I'm a master at healing," I warned him, ruining it with a sneeze.

If he were the eye-rolling type, he would have. I think I'd seen him do it once in my fifteen—almost sixteen—years of knowing him.

"I don't doubt it."

I considered my next words. Ben was obsessed with penance. So was Nash... and he wanted my dad's address.

"What will you do to my dad?"

The question sucked the energy out of the room and replaced it with uncertainty. I knew Nash needed closure, but it hurt that it had to come from my dad.

Nash tossed the sticks into the trash and tilted my chin up with a single fingertip. "I just need to talk to him."

"You promise?"

"Yes."

I shuttered my eyes, rested my forehead on Nash's chest, and whispered, "He's in Blithe Beach."

Turns out, betrayal doesn't sting as much when you do it for someone you love.

chapter FORTY-SEVEN

nash

I bit into the turkey and Ruffles sandwich, tossing a chunk of the bread onto Dad's grave. A bird waddled over and pecked at it.

Finally, life in this miserable place.

Blithe Beach, North Carolina.

A small town of humble, hardworking people. The town I'd grown up in before moving to Eastridge. Shitty houses. Shitty streets. Shitty beach, that's more waste run-off than beach.

But the people didn't suck.

They worked hard, raised good families, and did nice things for each other. Gideon could do worse.

Footsteps approached from behind. The shadow loomed over me, but I faced the tombstone. He sat beside me and leaned against some stranger's grave marker. When he caught me staring, he shrugged.

"You think the dead care about sharing? If anything, they like the company." He combed his fingers through his hair. "I take it Emery didn't send me that email, asking me to meet her here?"

Nope. All me.

"Gideon."

"Hey, kid."

Kid. Wonder if you'd still call me that if you found out what I've done with your daughter.

He picked at his Timberlands, a far cry from the billionaire who never left the house in anything that cost less than a house mortgage. "I take it you're talking to Emery if she gave you access to her email?"

"I'm more than talking to Emery."

My Durga.

I never really gave much thought to Fate, but every time I considered how hard the world must have worked to get our paths to intersect so many different ways, I became a believer.

A war brewed within Gideon's eyes as if he'd considered punching me before the yearning won. He missed his daughter. So obvious, a glass window would be less transparent.

"How is she?"

I rested a forearm on my bent knee. "She's trouble."

"Always was. When she was eight… and you were an *adult*," he slid in, "I used to think she'd burn the world down with a smile on her face and good intentions."

"Still could." I tossed the sandwich to the crow. Another landed.

You eavesdropping, Dad?

I wiped my palms on my sweats. Dad would give me shit if he caught me here in any of the overpriced suits that filled my closet, so I'd stopped by Nike for a pair of joggers. He'd still kill me for these. They cost more than he used to make in a day.

Gideon toyed with a beer can I'd placed in front of Dad's tombstone. "Has she seen Virginia?"

"I'm not here for idle chitchat." I swiped the Budweiser from his palm and chugged it.

He yanked another can from the 6-pack and cracked it open. "Tell me about my daughter, and I'll talk to you."

"Talk to me, or I'll tell the world where you're at."

"You've changed."

"You changed me."

"I did nothing, and I suspect you know that, or I'd be cradling a black eye right now."

True. True as fuck. I'd spent the past four years searching for Gideon, and now that I'd found him, I skirted around the damn questions.

Maybe I didn't want to know the answer, because everything about this felt off. Blithe Beach? The population couldn't fill Eastridge Prep's football stands. Most maps left the place out, and despite the beach, it hardly constituted as a beach town.

Tourists didn't go to places like this.

Billionaires didn't hide out in places like this either.

They flew to non-extradition countries and lived the rest of their lives in luxury. At the very least, anywhere but Blithe fucking Beach.

I emptied the can and crushed it. "Why Blithe Beach?"

"Hank mentioned Blithe a few times." Gideon drank small sips of his beer. "He told me to escape here when the company collapsed. I figured it'd be a good place to settle down."

"Dad told you to come here?" I frowned at the 'loving friend' engraved on the marble.

Always took you as a bleeding heart, Dad.

"Yeah."

"You talked to him?"

"Yeah."

"Do you possess a vocabulary beyond 'yeah,' or have the polluted waters here induced developmental regression in your brain?"

"Fuck, kid." Gideon shook his head. "You're too young to be this jaded."

"I was less jaded when I had a dad."

He ignored my jab. "I heard the trial's board booted Hank. I talked to someone on the research team and found out why they nixed him."

"Because Doctor Douche lost his money with Winthrop Textiles and took it out on Dad," I finished for him.

"No." Gideon exhaled. "That's what I thought, too, but no."

I could punch him. Rewriting history to make himself feel better sat on some low-as-shit rung of hell.

"I'm done with this bullshit." I moved to leave, but he stopped me.

"Hank lied."

"Watch your mouth." I fixated on Dad's marker, wishing ghosts existed so he could haunt the fuck out of Gideon.

"He told you and Betty the lie because it was better than the truth."

"Which was?"

"That he'd die any day. The trial hadn't helped." Gideon finished off the beer and replaced it with another. "It was all a placebo effect."

"He took the medicine." I jacked the can from him. "I saw him. I drove him there myself and waited in the treatment clinic."

"Yeah, and it looked like it was working because he thought it was working. It wasn't. They removed him from the trial after they realized the results weren't there. It had nothing to do with the money. In fact, I offered to pay for more treatments elsewhere. Hank said they wouldn't help, but he did ask for a favor."

I refused to accept this.

If Dad's death had nothing to do with money, I wasn't guilty. I didn't play a hand in killing him. That meant, all this fixation on revenge over the past four years amounted to... *nothing*.

I downed that beer, too. "What'd he want from you?"

"He asked me to take care of his family, but I knew you wouldn't let me."

"No shit." I crushed the can and added it to the stack. Looked better than the dead flowers soiling the other graves.

"I was your seed investor."

My hand hovered above a new can. "My seed investor was a Saudi oil—"

"—prince named Zayn Al-Asnam." His sly smirk begged to be punched. "I know. He's a character from *1001 Arabian Nights*. I had a cover story made, a shell company founded, the works."

The windfall from insider trading on Winthrop Textiles stocks started Prescott Hotels, but Al-Asnam's—*Gideon's*—investment turned it into an empire.

Shit.

No part of my life went untouched by dirty money and devious lies.

I flicked lint off my joggers. "That means you know I had my own money going into this."

"I know where it's from, too."

"Why didn't you say anything?"

Or turn me in?

"I admired Hank Prescott. I enjoyed his company, friendship, and sometimes, advice." Gideon leaned forward and wiped a smudge off the gravestone.

I noticed that it appeared in far better condition than the rest of the ones in the cemetery. How often did he come here?

Gideon continued, "I regretted the way Virginia treated your family, but she needed to control the household. It gave her something to do outside of pestering Emery and scheming. I also know you stole the ledger the night of the cotillion."

"Why didn't you say anything?"

"I saw you burn it. If not for your dad, I still wouldn't have turned you in because of what you did for my daughter. We all knew you hospitalized Able. He only pointed at Reed, since he knew hurting your brother would cut you deepest."

To this day, my relationship with Reed had never recovered. Small Dick was smarter than I gave him credit for.

"How do you know I burned the ledger?" I thought of the charred remnants I'd locked in my safe before driving down here. Still viable evidence. Against the thief. Against *me*. "You were holed in the office with Eric Cartwright and Virginia. You couldn't have seen."

"I saw the replay. I had hidden cameras installed in the mansion when I became suspicious of Virginia."

The second profiting party Brandon Vu had mentioned.

"She was the one who embezzled," I said, a statement. Not a question.

I pieced it together, mostly because I knew Dad would never befriend someone who'd hurt so many people.

"I figured it out too late." Gideon's lament seemed genuine. "I stole the ledger from her and would've turned it over to the S.E.C., but you took it after I confirmed Balthazar and Cartwright's involvements. Why'd you burn it?"

"Emery. She stood up for Reed and got you to negotiate his release." I shook my head and raked a hand through my hair. Regret felt like a bullet to the skull. All this could have been prevented if I'd left the ledger where I'd found it. "She's loyal as hell."

Gideon hummed in agreement. "Why'd you take the ledger back from the fire?"

"I overheard you arguing in the office."

"If Emery finds out, I will cut you off, Virginia, and I will sue you for everything you own, Cartwright," Gideon had warned, his voice steady and threat real.

"Please," Virginia scoffed, *"she already knows. Why do you think I sent her to that shrink to set her straight?"*

"I thought Emery knew about the embezzlement and kept it from my family," I continued, "despite knowing we'd invested everything into your company."

"That wasn't what Virginia meant when she said Emery already knew."

"What'd she mean?"

"Virginia needed money to leave me. I would've given her a divorce settlement to keep her out of our lives, but she'd signed a prenup. It made her uncertain. So, she embezzled from the company. First a little, but she got greedy."

He toyed with his words, selecting them like you would a pet. With careful consideration. "I had plans to turn her in, but she had something over me. If I kept my mouth shut on her involvement in the scandal, said nothing about Eric or Balthazar, and left Eastridge, she'd keep *her* mouth shut."

"They deserve to pay."

"I can't go after them. Not without Emery suffering."

And then he explained the argument I'd overheard in the office.

He spilled his secret, telling me the one thing that could convince me to keep this from Emery.

I didn't agree with lying to her, but I agreed she needed to find out from him.

She was a plot twist. A surprise. The curveball thrown at me near the end of the book. If I wanted to reach the happy fucking ending, I needed to embrace the twist and fight my way to the finish line.

I couldn't keep secrets from her.

If I didn't tell her, I would lose her.

But if I told her, I would hurt her.

So, when the man I'd spent four years seeking revenge from asked me to keep his secret, I agreed.

Even if it meant losing Emery.

chapter FORTY-EIGHT

Emery

"What if the only word people knew was thank you?" I asked from the floor of Nash's penthouse.

I laid on the living room carpet, rolling around in four king-size comforters. Excessive, yes, but so plush. I imagined riding a unicorn through a wave of rainbows and cotton candy clouds compared to this.

Being sick is amazing.

My excuse for missing work the past four days ended

yesterday, but I'd convinced my hot boss to call in sick for me. (Nash. Not Chantilly.)

The *philophobia* shirt rose up my stomach. I didn't bother to lower it. Nash sat on the couch, wearing nothing but dark gray Nike joggers, scars on display for me to feast on.

Tipping my chin at the extra comforter, I summoned it with my eyes. In reality, Nash tossed it on me, adding to the pile of bliss.

He watched me turn myself into a human burrito, lips finally—*fucking finally*—turned up since his visit with Dad. "That's two words."

"Humor me."

"Thank you would become meaningless."

"Or everything would improve. Think of it this way—would you rather say you're sorry for being late or you're thankful someone waited for you? I'd rather be thankful than sorry." I mimicked an explosion with my mouth. "Boom! Game changer. Perspective forever altered."

He muttered something under his breath and gazed at me with hooded eyes. The joint cradled between two fingers came from Reed's stash. He never lit it, but I often caught him toying with them.

"What's with the weed, Seth Rogen?"

He discarded it in the plastic baggie and set another blanket on me. "Fucking hell. Twenty Questions again?"

I rested my chin on my knuckles. "Do you consider yourself sentimental, Nash?"

"Why?"

A hum vibrated the back of my throat. "It's just that you're walking around with weed from the night I baltered for you, and you sent my *Easy, Tiger* shirt to the dry cleaner's instead of donating it like I asked you to."

Even though I wanted to keep the shirt, I always

donated them. I needed all the good karma I could get. That included spreading magic words and helping people who need it. If I caved and kept the tee, I'd do it again and again.

Nash made the choice for me.

"Emery?" He ran his fingers through his hair. *Once*, which I noticed he only did for me.

"Yes?"

"You ask too many questions."

"Fine." I lowered my head into the cloud of blankets. "Another comforter, my servant."

His deliberately blank face drew a smile from me. He dropped another comforter on me.

I groaned into the clean laundry scent. "Remind me to never give up amazing blankets again." *Bye, bye, shitty quilt and your sleepless nights and endless holes.* "Where did you get these?"

"Delilah had our supplier ship them over early."

"Remind me to kiss her."

He lowered himself beside me. "Or you can learn the way capitalism fucking works and reward the person who paid for them."

I rolled onto him. The tips of our noses kissed, the faintest of touches.

Grinding myself against him, I whispered against his lips, "I hate capitalism. People exploit people, and there's a reward for it."

"Really?" Two hands dipped below my shirt and curved around my waist. "Seems like you're good at it." His fingertips brushed the undersides of my breasts. "Seems like you fucking love it."

"Why did I avoid roommates my entire undergrad?" I traced my favorite scar, admiring the grooves. "This is amazing."

"Roommates?" The pad of his thumb circled a nipple. "You're not my fucking roommate, Tiger."

"Yeah? What am I? Wait." My nails dug into him as if it'd make him less likely to avoid the question. "Better question—do you think this is just lust?"

His jaw clenched, and I recognized the moment he withdrew from the conversation. From us. "You're supposed to wait until you're not sick to ask."

"We made out yesterday, and the day before, and the day before."

"Which probably means I'm sick, and now we have to wait until I'm not sick."

I groaned and plopped onto my back. "What happened with my dad?" My eyes pleaded for another smile or, at the very least, a breadcrumb of what had transpired in Blithe Beach.

He avoided the question, a pro at this point. "They're filling the pool tonight."

I accepted the subject change with the reluctance of a starved toddler being fed something she hated. "No, thanks."

"You have something against pools suddenly?"

"I'd rather christen it while it rains."

"Of course, you would."

I propped my head with my fist. "The end of the rain season is nearing."

"I draw the pillow-talk line at discussing the fucking weather."

"We haven't fucked," I drawled out the word, letting him know what I thought of our abstinence. "So technically, this isn't pillow talk."

He'd flipped the switch from scorching hot to lukewarm. It made no sense to me, and given the timing, intuition forced me to consider something had gone down between Dad and Nash. Whatever it was, I had to trust Nash wouldn't keep something big from me.

We were beyond that.

"Let's swim when it rains," I suggested. "I want to be the first in the pool."

Hopefully, on my birthday in two days.

Nash nodded his agreement and stood. He approached his desk, grabbed a box from the drawer, and handed it to me. "It's the stuff for the phone screen."

"Oh."

I unraveled the package, doing my damnedest not to shake at his attention. So much pressure. The familiar steps came to me in an instant. I twisted the pentalobe screws, taped the display, and used the suction to remove the current screen.

Nash never moved his eyes from me during the process. When I finished, I handed him the phone, muttering magic words for good luck. He plugged it into the lightning cable. It took a few minutes, but thank Starless Skies, it turned on.

His fingers toyed with a few buttons. He opened the Photos app first. Pulling up a family album, his thumb raced down the screen until it came to a section of a picnic. He handed the phone to me.

I scrolled through. A lump bubbled in my throat with each passing picture. "Reed told me about the picnic. Your mom's packed food rotted during the hot car ride."

"We ended up splurging on fast food we couldn't afford." Nash laid back on the comforters and watched me savor his memories. "Reed and I agreed to pretend we were okay. Ma and Dad pretended they were okay. A lot of fucking pretending going on."

"I can't tell. Everyone looks happy."

"We were. Eventually. Fuck, I'm glad we had that

day," Nash said, but his eyes carried ghosts. The kind that looked real enough to touch. The kind that couldn't be silenced by anything.

I returned his phone, telling him about the time Hank caught me talking to one of our neighbor's cows. It struck me that this might have been the only time he'd truly talked about his dad since his death.

We stayed up all night, recalling our favorite memories of Hank.

By the time we fell asleep, I'd planted flowers in Nash's graveyard of haunted memories.

Wilted ones, because those were me.

And he watered them with stormwater, because that was him.

nash

"**It's my birthday.** Ask me what I want." Emery wiggled into her jeans, buttoning them.

Don't ask me what Gideon said again.

Every time I skirted the subject or shrugged her off, I felt like a dickhead—or the liar her parents turned out to be.

I downed half my Gatorade and returned the bottle to the fridge. "You want me to ask you what you want for the day you, yourself, claim is meaningless?"

"I called birthdays a lie, said people aren't special, and told you days of birth shouldn't be celebrated, but I never said they're meaningless."

She tossed the lunch bag into the recycling bin and hid the note I'd written her in the Jana Sport when she thought I wasn't looking.

I always look, Tiger.

"Semantics."

"Sure." She tipped a shoulder up, giving me the stare you'd give a D-student when he claimed he earned an A. *Sure, you did, Little Timothy. I believe you.* "Maybe you should get your Insta Cart shopper to pick up some B12 vitamins with your next order. Your brain could use the boost."

"A convenient memory, considering you're staring at me like you want something."

"I often stare at you like I want something." She lifted a brow, making it clear what that something was.

Not like I asked for these fucking blue balls.

I wanted her, craved every goddamn inch. But sex with Emery would only make things worse when—not if, but fucking *when*—she learned the lie I kept from her. Worse, if I saw her vulnerability and had sex with her anyway, I'd be just as bad as her shitty parents.

So, I turned down her advances.

Every. Goddamn. Time.

She waited for my answer. After it didn't come, she

collected a towel from the closet, stuffed it into the Jana Sport, and left.

Dramatic, this one.

Following her, I reached the elevator and stepped in beside her.

Neither of us spoke.

I wore a suit for a teleconference this morning with the landowners in Singapore. Meanwhile, Emery dressed in skinny jeans and an *alexithymia* shirt, which I'd Google'd as soon as I saw it.

Noun.

The inability to identify and express your feelings.

She was the loudest when she was quiet.

Emery selected the lobby button. "Do you miss your dad during your birthdays?"

I read between the lines, taking in the downcast eyes. Torment created grooves between her brows. I could have spilled the lie and eased her pain, but I didn't.

She was glass, chipped all over, and I shattered her instead of mending the fractured pieces.

"Are your birthdays hard without your dad there?" she pressed.

I should have answered her, but I didn't. Of course, I wanted Dad here for my birthdays. I wanted him here every damn day. If only to yell at me for making poor decisions or turning into one of the corporate dickheads we used to make fun of, that'd be okay, too.

My answer didn't matter. Sure, she wanted to know, but what she'd really asked was whether it was normal for her to miss her dad today.

"You can see Gideon." I blocked the doors when they slid open. "You know where he is."

Gideon had deluded himself into believing she'd cave and visit.

She wouldn't.

It takes strength to want something and deny yourself the craving. And Emery Winthrop possessed a strength so great it broke her and pieced her together. Again and again. A diamond, toughening under pressure.

Something drastic would have to happen to bring her to his doorstep. I held that power—that lie.

Sisyphus, I reminded myself.

A liar and a cheat.

I'd come full-fucking-circle, and I wanted off the damn carousel. It reeked of piss and bad decisions.

"I can't." Her palms met my chest and shoved.

I didn't fight it, listening to her footsteps echo.

The hotel resembled a scene from *The Walking Dead*. Moments before the zombies come, when everything is still empty. A rarity, given the quick pace of our construction.

The design crew had escaped for the weekend. Rain gushed down in heavy onslaughts, so none of the construction crew remained.

And of course, *of fucking course*, Emery swung the beach-front exit open with little concern for the tempest and walked straight into the storm. Wind whipped her hair. Her shirt drenched in an instant.

She peered up at the sky, undeterred by the liquid splattering her face. In this moment, I couldn't see a single difference between her and the storm.

I tried and failed to get a read on her. She muttered a few words, my very own siren. About a minute later, two clouds parted, revealing the starless sky. Almost enough to make me believe in her magic. Not magic words, but *her* magic.

"I knew you'd show up for my birthday," she whispered, talking to the sky as if it was her oldest friend. "This storm's not bad, but you can do better."

What did it say about me that watching her talk to the sky got my dick hard?

What did it say that, despite the frigid temperature, it stayed as hard as the forecasted hail?

Emery peeled off her jeans and dove into the pool. When she resurfaced, she swam to its brink. Beneath her shirt, two hard nipples greeted me. My jaw ticked.

Off-limits. Off-limits. Off-fucking-limits.

If she expected me to cave, she wasn't getting it. But I could imagine it, and I did. In my bed, in my shower, in my office. A fucking teenager, jerking off because he couldn't get the girl. Except I had her, close enough to touch her, and I chose to preserve the lie over her. *For* her.

Fuck you, Gideon. Putting me in this position is Grade-A revenge. Now, I know where your daughter gets her fixation for silent revenge from.

Emery quirked a brow. "Are you coming in, or what?"

Loosening my tie, I discarded it with my suit jacket on the deck. I yanked my shirt off, popping every button. Her lips separated at the sight of my scars. It occurred to me that she hadn't seen me fully naked in almost five years, so I removed my boxer briefs, too.

I locked my jaw, Adam's apple bobbing with the movement of her eyes. She took her time sweeping the length of me. My dick saluted her for every second of it.

Rainwater blurred my vision. I dove into the warmed water and emerged in front of Emery. Her ankle trailed my legs. It traced something indecipherable and stopped at my abs. She used them to push off into a backstroke.

The pool extended into the ocean with a negative edge. If I looked hard enough, I could see where the pool ended and the ocean began. In the rain, all I saw was Emery, arms spread, kicking lazy circles with the backdrop of crashing ocean waves.

So fucking wild, I had no idea how Virginia ever intended on taming her.

She startled when I swam beside her. My fingertips teased the edge of her tee. Her arm wrapped around my neck and clung to me.

"Tiger?"

"Yes?"

"What do you want for your birthday?"

"*You.*"

No hesitation.

Just pure need.

I was definitely going to hell, because looking at her in the rain, determination painted on her face, I couldn't say no.

She skated her lips along my neck, not kissing me. Just feeling me. Breathing me. Consuming me. I dragged her shirt up her body, devouring her nipples.

My fingers gripped her hair.

I brought my lips to the curve of her ear and licked the skin. "What are you asking from me?"

What's eating you, Emery Winthrop?

"Break me." She stared at me like she wasn't completely whole and didn't entirely care. "Then put me back together, mismatched, scarred, and chaotic as this storm."

My mouth slammed on those soft lips, body stapling her to the rim of the pool. Behind her, the waves drowned her moans. I tore her panties off. They fell to the porcelain tiles.

Her body quivered, bare and pressed against mine.

"Beautiful," I said, knowing she wouldn't understand the compliment.

"I know." She threw her head back and stared at the moon. "I love starless skies."

"I'm not talking about the fucking sky. I'm talking about you."

If she heard me, she didn't show it. Simply granted me access to her neck, attention above us. My teeth grazed her skin, tongue lapping at the goosebumps.

"Give me a word, Emery."

"Redamancy."

"What does it mean?"

"The act of loving the one who loves you. A love returned in full." She drew her bottom lip between her front teeth and turned away.

I know what you are, and it's not the storm or the clouds.

I lifted her, locked her legs around my waist, and positioned myself at her core. "I'm going to fuck the last asshole out of your system. And I'll ruin every other asshole for you. Nothing will compare."

Her nails dented my shoulders, and she laughed. Goddamn laughed. "You. *You* are the last asshole inside me."

Fuck.

"Good."

I sunk into her, fucking mind-blown over how different she felt.

Her pussy hugged my cock, quaking around me with each thrust.

I fucked her like it was the last time I'd ever do it.

And it probably was.

The second she discovered the lie, she'd never forgive me. If this was the last time, I'd make it feel like forever. I didn't want the before or even the after. I wanted the during, the part of us I chased each second.

I thrust again, faster this time.

She begged me for more, her fingers leaving grooves in my skin. The heat of the pool warmed us, but the storm above cascaded in unforgivable tides. It was messy, and savage, and too fucking good.

Thrust.

"Nash." The rain drowned her cries, but I heard how much she needed me, felt it as her walls shook around me. "Oh god, oh god, oh god."

Something built in my throat when she licked my scar and ran her fingertips along the others.

I thrust harder, creating our own waves to battle the ocean's.

She moaned into my ear, but the storm above us and between us swallowed the symphony. I should have slowed down, savored this, created a memory of it, but my body had different ideas. It hunted an elusive feeling I couldn't name.

Thrust.

I barely made out her words, "Do I feel as perfect as you feel?"

I realized how monumental it was for the girl who never used the word *perfect* to use it to describe me.

"Better." *Thrust.* "Lagom." She clenched at the word. Curses flew out of my mouth. I grazed her jaw. "Just fucking right."

My fingers dug into her ass. I reached between us and rubbed her clit, loving the way I heard her scream above the storm. My hands gripped her waist, and I slammed her down on me.

Again.

And again.

And again.

And a-fucking-gain.

I was ready to explode inside her, but I whispered words against her temple, doubting she heard them above the storm and her ecstasy, "Moira."

Thrust.

She scraped her fingers down my arms, so hard I bled. "Again."

"Nepenthe."

I buried my cock inside her, erratic thrusts that should have been too hard, but she kept fucking begging me for more.

"Again."

My arms burned from her marks, yet it was art. A scourge of red mixed with rain, something that looked awful, but made me feel like a goddamned king. I wanted her to scratch away my scars and replace them with whatever the hell this was.

Instead, I grunted, "Duende."

Thrust.

"Again."

"Lacuna."

Emery shattered around me, unable to hold herself upright. I barreled into her, creating a tsunami in the pool. The waves lapped at my back and fought my hold of her. Her sigh was so opposite to the situation, it was almost comical.

The serene face she wore deserved my mercy, but I didn't give it. I reached between us and pinched her clit, compelling another orgasm just to feel how tight she was around me. Just to prolong this.

She believed in words, and magic, and storms. In fighting back, going down hard, never giving up. In blind loyalty, jumping first, dealing with consequences later.

She was awful. She infuriated me. She drove me fucking crazy.

And, I realized, *I love her.*

"Ask me the question, Tiger."

Her eyes fluttered open, not staring at me but *into* me. "Is this just lust?"

"It's everything."

chapter FORTY-NINE

Every

F*lash!*
I blinked away the sting of the light. Every time he took a picture, the photographer smiled with sadistic glee. Able Small Dick Cartwright wrapped his arm around me. Cordelia perched on the throne-style chair at my hip. Two bridesmaids and three groomsmen bracketed us.

A prom photo out of a horror movie.

The poster you stare at and take bets on who will die first.

Probably me, and it'd be of my own volition. Another second of this, and I'd snap.

"One more picture, y'all!" the photographer promised for the ninth time and proceeded to snap five more. "Emery, hun? Smile! It's an engagement dinner party! Love is in the air. Be happy!"

Stabbing you with the stiletto heel of my mandatory Louboutins would make me very happy.

My fake smile compared to the Joker's, but I found it hard to even put in the effort. Last night came to me in floods each time I tried.

"Give me a word, Emery."

"Redamancy."

I'd wanted to riot, because it looked like he thought he was fucking me out of his system instead of into it. I'd fixated on the memory all morning, and no, I would not fucking smile unless it involved descending vampire teeth and sucking the blood out of every asshole in here.

"C'mon, Emery!" *Click. Click.* "Give me that beautiful smile!"

"No."

Cordelia turned to me, her face nearly identical to Small Dick's, it made me want to barf, too. She soothed a palm to her collarbone. "Excuse me?!"

Her cheeks matched the color of my roses. The only indicator of her irritation. Seriously, her forehead didn't budge. Not one bit.

I shoved the bouquet into her chest. "Here. These match your face. You're welcome."

Gathering the lavender monstrosity Virginia had squeezed her bridesmaids into, I left the alcove of the Eastridge Country Club and entered the ballroom. My eyes sought and failed to find Nash.

Virginia spent the entire opening ceremony seeking a

way to separate us, including sending me off to take pictures I scowled in. Meanwhile, Sir Balty creeped me out with his beady eyes and weird fixation with me. First golf, then brunch, and now the engagement dinner.

Enough already.

Pulling out my phone, I called Nash and remembered his had powered down earlier. I messaged him through the Eastridge United app, knowing he wouldn't see it until he got home and charged his phone.

Durga: Tell me your favorite thing in the world.

I'd have to find him the old-fashioned way—gossip by socialites.

Pocketing the phone, I latched onto the arm of a random rail-thin brunette. "Have you seen Nash Prescott?"

She shook her arm away and sipped her Cosmo, a version of me my mother would have preferred. "He left down that hall with Virginia a minute ago."

"Thanks." I flashed her a fake smile and complimented her dress, because I knew she expected it—and would spiral if I didn't.

Shoot me now. I hate these things.

Balthazar cued a waiter to him. I used it as a distraction and slipped past them. Déjà vu shotgunned into me once I hit the hallway leading to the office. My last time here, I'd barreled into Nash, exactly where he stood now.

He glanced at his watch, brought a whiskey glass to his lips, and entered Virginia's office without shutting the door behind him. My heels rapped against the floor. I slipped them off and crept down the corridor. I didn't want to be dramatic, but I'd sensed something off the whole night.

Nash seemed irritated with Eastridge, beyond his normal threshold. The silent car ride negated our honeymoon phase. It set me on edge, encouraging me to spy, even if I knew, morally, I shouldn't.

Pressing my back to the wall, I inched as close to the door as possible without being seen. Virginia muttered something indecipherable, luring me dangerously near the open frame. I honed in on the scraps I could glean.

"Whatever you're doing with my daughter, I want you gone."

If she expected him to cower like the spineless Eastridgers she'd grown accustomed to, she'd be sorely disappointed. Nash fought. For instinct. For sport. For survival. Anything else equated to giving up.

I anticipated Nash's brash response with a smile on my face. Without seeing her, I knew Virginia's impatience fed her fury. She was a furnace doused in Butane.

Ice cubes clinked together.

He took his time sipping. "Careful with the threats, Virginia. You may look good in white, but you sure as shit look awful in orange."

She sucked in a breath, stilettos dragging on the floor a bit. "You know about it..." *Know about what?* "How—"

That tone. I recognized it. It came before a tantrum.

That neck-and-neck election for the chairwoman of the Junior Society? A Jimmy Choo thrown at the crystal chandeliers.

Gaining two-and-a-half pounds during our Italy holiday? Fat-shaming her debutantes.

After the deliveryman mistook her for my grandmother? A fire poker to the wall.

I leaned forward a tad. Just to see.

Neither of them noticed me.

Nash sat at the desk, back pressed against the leather

executive chair, legs propped on the mahogany. "Doesn't matter. What matters is, I know everything."

Virginia's face paled, body shivering despite the warmth. She fingered her pearls, close to dropping her drink with the other hand. "You won't say a thing. I see how you look at Emery."

"How I look at Emery is none of your concern, considering if you continue to test my patience, the only thing you'll be able to look at is the other side of prison bars." His fingertips met, forming a steeple. He could have been talking about the weather with that tone. "In the interest of time, let's cut to the chase. You'll leave Eastridge. No one will see you again."

Why? Why would she do that? What did he have on her? And my biggest question: *why didn't he tell me anything?*

A lie of omission still counted as a lie.

Betrayal sliced a path up my throat with the finesse of a machete hacking through a jungle. None of this made any sense. I wanted to interrupt with questions, but I feared nothing would be as candid as this moment here.

Without me.

nash

LIES.

Four letters caused so much damage.

Virginia clenched her champagne glass until her knuckles turned white. "You have nothing but wild accusations. A thug with empty threats. So, why would I listen to anything you have to say?"

Ah.

The thug card. My favorite. Mostly, because I'd identified Virginia as a hypocrite from day one. I just never realized how accurate I'd been in my assessment.

"Because you're scared." My eyes scratched a path down her body. I sneered at her balled fist. Unnerved by the help's son. I fucking thrived on karmic justice. "Look at you. You're shaking at the very thought of being someone's prison bitch."

"No one will believe you." Her head shook, but so did her whole body. "You are nothing but the son of my help—"

"Whom will people believe?" My hand made a sweeping gesture at her. "A washed-up has-been, no one in the history of Eastridge has ever liked, or me"—I pointed to myself, flashing her a charming-as-fuck smile that could win every woman over—"the self-made billionaire, who frequently gives back to the community and is referred to as the Patron Saint of Eastridge?"

I almost wished Emery could see the downfall of her mother. This hadn't been my intention tonight. Gideon wanted me to keep quiet. As in, no feathers ruffled. A waiting game he'd endured for four years, suffering without his daughter.

Not your secret to tell, Nash.

True.

Didn't mean I had to sustain a healthy relationship with Virginia. It wouldn't do anyone any favors, and she needed out of Emery's life like I needed to seal the Singapore deal, quit this soul-sucking job, and confess everything to Emery.

At least, that's what I told myself to justify skirting the boundaries of the promise I'd made Gideon.

Virginia resembled a toddler post-tantrum, the moment she realized she wouldn't get her way.

I pulled my handkerchief from my pocket, wiped it across the bottom of my shoe, and tossed it at her face. "You okay there, Virginia? You look like someone who just learned she got knocked up by her high school health teacher. Sounds like the plot to a D-grade flick I've seen before. Spoiler alert: both the student and the teacher are fucked."

Virginia clutched the cotton. "I—You—" She tossed it to the ground and stomped on it, determination so fierce, I actually appreciated it for reminding me of Emery. "You can't do this to me. Literally speaking, you cannot. Gideon wasn't able to and neither are you."

"Here's what's going to happen." I leaned up in my seat, knowing I appeared more formidable than any predator in the animal kingdom. "You'll take your gaudy ass away from Emery, remove yourself as the settlor of her trust fund, round up your clown car of corrupt friends, and leave this town."

"I will do no such thing!" The point of her toe scuffed the hardwood flooring. "You can't talk to me like this!"

"I can talk to you however I'd like. Unless you do exactly as I say, you'll experience worse in prison." In fact, I looked forward to it. I toyed with a pen, nonchalant with my ruthlessness. "Wave goodbye to your chilled fennel soups that taste like armpits, your shitty orange spray tans, and your uneven haircuts, Virginia. Your life in Eastridge is over. Your life as you know it is over."

"I'll tell Emery."

That gave me pause.

The only thing she could have possibly said to give me hesitation.

"You won't." I considered the ledger, more than willing to turn it—and myself—in if it came to that. "I have something Gideon doesn't. Proof."

A smile curved up Virginia's lips. She could've been pretty. Beautiful, even. Too bad she conducted herself with the moral compass of the wicked stepmothers in every Brothers Grimm fairy tale. "You're bluffing, otherwise it wouldn't have taken four years for this conversation to transpire."

The switch flipped. Her shoulders pulled back. So dumb for thinking I would ever relent. If she thought this was over, she'd never met persistence like mine before. Especially when it came to protecting people I cared about.

Virginia turned. I would have parted with the final threat, but when we both shifted our attention to the doorframe, we encountered my blue-gray storm.

Emery.

Emery

VIRGINIA CARRIED herself with an authority she'd never been granted. I would have admired her for it, except she'd raised me to be as cutthroat as herself. That, and I reeled from the revelations, struggling to take them all in.

I needed that moment where everything clicked. It didn't come, and trying to make sense of their fight reminded me of trying to catch rain with my fingertips. Pointless.

Bottom line—I'd been lied to.

It stabbed me in a place I thought had scabbed over. The last big lie in my life spiraled out of control. I barely recovered from the Winthrop Scandal. How many more lies did I have to endure?

"Oh, Emery, honey." That smile looked demented on Virginia's face. "Let's get this dinner started. Why don't you go hug your father?"

My eyes burned with the effort it took not to glance at

Nash. I scrunched my nose. "God, Virginia, don't call him that."

"Why not?" So smug, her face reminded me of Basil's after she'd left our A.P. Spanish exam, having cheated.

"Virginia," Nash warned.

His tone brought chills to my body, so much venom, it should have killed her on the spot. I stared at him, eyes slanted, trying to figure everything out.

And here was the crux of it all. I loved listening to Nash fight for me, but I was capable of fighting for myself. Especially when he kept secrets everyone but me seemed to know. Who lied to someone they cared about? If he could lie so easily to me, what else had he lied about?

"Why wouldn't I call him your father?" She downed her champagne, leaving a blood-colored lipstick stain around the glass's rim. "He is, after all, your biological father."

She'd shocked me into silence, but it wasn't her words or their cold delivery that pained me. It was the lack of surprise in Nash's eyes.

He'd known, and he'd kept it from me.

The satisfied sneer Virginia flashed me before she left wouldn't haunt me tonight.

Nash's lies, on the other hand, crippled me.

They wouldn't haunt me tonight either. They'd haunt me forever.

"Explain," I demanded, barely able to form the word through my hurt and fury.

"Balthazar Van Doren is your dad."

I sidestepped him when he approached. "Yeah, I got that." Dragging my toe across an imaginary line, I said, "This is my half of the room. That's yours. Don't cross it, and I won't knee you in the balls. Now, continue. The truth, please."

His jaw ticked. Actually, his everything ticked. "Sir Balty was your mom's secret high school sweetheart. Her health teacher. She got pregnant and freaked out, because the affair started before she turned sixteen—the age of consent in North Carolina.

"Your dad visited her town over vacation, and she targeted him for his money. They slept together, she told him she was pregnant, and they had a shotgun wedding." The words rushed out, like he thought I'd leave any second.

If I looked flighty, it was because I was. "How do you know all this?"

"Gideon told me."

In the hall, two drunk socialites ambled past, stumbling over their heels and giggling with each other. As if my world hadn't tilted on its axis. I'd never felt more aware of my insignificance.

The world moves on, Emery, and you will, too.

I shook my head, unable to fit these puzzle pieces together, even as he spoon-fed them to me. "Why would da—*Gideon* let Balthazar into our lives?"

So many questions, but I trembled too hard to ask them all. I needed to take a step back, have this conversation tomorrow when the alcohol and adrenaline fled my system, but I feared he'd be less candid.

No, it needed to happen now.

"He didn't find out about Balthazar until you turned six. Balty showed up, looking for some cash. He threatened to claim his parental rights over you. Gideon struck a deal, allowing him to be a partner in Winthrop Textiles in exchange for his silence."

"Why would Dad—" I swallowed, digging my nails

into my palms. My pulse gripped my throat, erratic and unrelenting. "Why would *Gideon* tell you this?"

"Because he's not guilty."

Another lie, maybe?

I tugged at the corset of this ridiculous dress, struggling to breathe. "But the F.B.I. and S.E.C. announced an investigation against him. The whole town calls him a cheat."

"I—" He cursed and yanked his collar hard, causing a button to pop off. Neither of us were made for these clothes, though he wore his easier than I wore mine. "None of this is my secret to tell. At least, not before you talk to your dad."

My lower lip wobbled. "Except he's not my dad."

I wanted to scream, and yell, and claw at Nash. I wanted the same for him. An uncontrollable reaction.

This didn't feel like us. A civilized argument, no magic in the air, no flames we couldn't douse, no fucking fight.

Our age gap never felt more prominent than it did now.

Twenty-three and fatherless.

Thirty-two and fatherless.

We carried it so differently. Him, with barriers erected higher than any skyscraper mankind could build. Me, with tiny thorns that pricked but didn't possess the strength to draw blood. Unbreakable stone versus a fractured heart. I knew which would win, and it wasn't the heart.

"He is," Nash insisted. "In every way that matters, Gideon Winthrop is your father. Even when you never returned his postcards and ignored him after he tried to visit you, he didn't give up hope that you'd return to him."

I remembered the visit. Three years ago, I spotted

him waiting for me outside the diner I worked at. I called the cops and told them some creep stalked me there.

Disbelief clung to me, it's hold nearly choking my neck. "I told you yesterday that I miss my dad."

"I know, and I—"

"You saw me near tears, and instead of telling me the truth, you fucked me."

"That's not why I—"

"I don't care why you screwed me, Nash. I care that you did, knowing how I felt about my dad in that moment."

"*Shit*." He palmed his face. "That wasn't fucking. Don't tell me you didn't feel anything last night. What happened to redamancy?"

I did feel it, but I didn't answer. Maybe tomorrow, but not tonight. Everything hurt too much. Felt too raw. Because I promised myself after the Winthrop Scandal, I'd never let another liar into my life.

No matter how good he tasted. No matter how good he made my body feel. No matter how good he made my heart feel.

My foot inched past the doorframe.

"Emery." He matched my steps.

"I thought I built walls after the scandal. I thought something like this would never happen again. I feel so stupid for not seeing the difference between a truth and a lie."

"Don't blame yourself."

"I don't. Not entirely. My heart was hungry, so you fed it lies. Everyone in this world lies, and I should have realized that."

"Maybe everyone lies, okay? Is that what you want to hear?"

"If it's the truth, yes. And you know what happens

after the first lie? Every truth becomes questionable. How am I supposed to believe anything you say now?"

He didn't answer.

I answered for him, "A liar once told me, *life is a Sisyphean task. You put out one fire, and another one starts. It's easier to accept it burns. We live in a world consumed by fire, but at least it's the truth. You're not lured to sleep with a false blanket of security, telling yourself you exist in a part untouched by the flames. There's death, and betrayal, and revenge, and guilt everywhere you turn. It's healthier to live it, breathe it, and participate in it than to pretend it doesn't exist.*"

I edged closer to him, cupping his face and hating myself for it. "Do you remember what you said when I asked what happens after you're burnt everywhere?"

He dropped his eyes, and it was so unlike Nash, it startled me for a moment.

Even the language of your body is a lie.

My palm whipped away from his skin, and I gave him the biggest truth he'd ever told me, "Don't succumb to the fire. Be the bigger flame."

part four: FINIFUGAL

finifugal

\fi-ni-ˈfU-gal\

(adjective) hating endings; of someone who tries to avoid or prolong the final moments of a story, relationship, or some other journey

Finifugal originates from the Latin word fuga, *for flight. It shows us that endings are fleeting. We may hate them. We may fear them. We may avoid them. But we don't need to.*

Like sunsets, endings can be beautiful. The next morning, the sun always rises again, because there is no such thing as an ending, just a new beginning.

chapter FIFTY

Emery

"Why is it that two people never realize how much they love each other until one of them says goodbye?"

Silence.

No one answered me. Not even crickets. Made sense, considering I laid on my shitty quilt in the unfamiliar twenty-fourth-floor closet, picturing the ceiling as the starless night. Outside, so many stars twinkled, it nauseated me.

"I had a nightmare last night. In it, I never met Nash.

I died in a parasailing accident, and a blue man in a pink suit took me to a white room and showed me Nash Prescott—defending me against Able, feeding me all my life, sending me notes, being the Ben to my Durga, giving me his new first kiss, all the filthy things juxtaposed beside the clean, the baltering, the late nights as 'roommates', making love in the rain, the way he loves the same people I love and sees me better than anyone else."

Ceiling: *Stop talking to me, woman.*

"I watched it all, thinking it was the most epic love story I'd ever seen. Then, Blue Man shut it off, and I nearly killed him for it. He gave me two options for the afterlife. Door One saves me the heartbreak, but I live a life without ever meeting Nash. Door Two takes me back to day one, where I meet Nash Prescott, eventually fall in love, and experience a pain like I've never experienced. Do you want to know which I chose?"

Ceiling: *I'm fluent in silence. Please, learn the language, too.*

"I chose Door Two. Blue Man patted my shoulder and told me I made the right choice. Apparently, Door One is the bad place and Door Two is the good place. Am I being ridiculous, Ceiling?"

Ceiling: *Considering you're talking to an inanimate object and imagining its replies, we've sailed past ridiculous and entered involuntary psychiatric hold territory.*

"It's just... everyone in my life lies to me, and I

promised I'd never put myself in this situation again. Not if I can help it. Dad—I mean Gideon—lied to me most of my life."

Ceiling: *You mean the man who raised you as his own?*

I ignored the buzzkill above me. "Virginia lied to me all my life. Same for Balthazar, but who the hell cares about him?"

Ceiling: *Wow. The mom you hate and a guy you considered to be nothing more than a creep until last night lied to you. You seem so torn up about it. Here's a tissue.*

"Fuck you, Ceiling. Such a damn buzzkill." I made snow angels in the blanket, imagining the comforters in Nash's penthouse. The quilt ripped when my fingers caught in a hole. "Hank lied to me about his illness. So did Betty and Nash."

Ceiling: *It's almost as if they care enough about you to save you from the pain of watching him die.*

"It would be painful, yes, but what's worse is not being given the option to love him like every moment could be his last. There's so much I would have done differently."

Ceiling: *If this moment was Nash's or your last moment, would you be here, annoying the hell out of me?*

"Did you say something? I couldn't hear you. Ran out of Q-Tips this morning." I patted the hole in the quilt as if my touch would heal it. "Do you know what hiraeth is?"

Ceiling: *No, but I'm sure you'll tell me. I'd rather you didn't.*

"Hiraeth is a homesickness for a home to which you cannot return, a home which maybe never was. It is the nostalgia, the yearning, the grief for the lost places of your past. I've always thought of it as the saddest entry in the dictionary."

Ceiling: *This conversation deserves a name. Then, it'd be the most pathetic entry in the dictionary.*

"And on the long list of lies, I can't even wrap my head around the whole thing about the Winthrop Scandal. I mean, if you think about it, the only person in my life who hasn't blatantly lied to me is Reed."

Ceiling: *The kid you once thought you were in love with? Hypocritical, since you never told him... and Nash never told you something. I'm sensing a theme. Why do humans leave so much to be desired?*

I ignored the last half of Ceiling's insults. "Stupid that I once considered Reed a recipient of my love. He didn't compare to Nash. With Nash... It's a vicious love, the kind that beats me down and robs me of all my possessions until I feel bloodied, worn, and bruised, stolen of everything that makes me... me."

Ceiling: *Sounds healthy. Who needs carrots when you have Nash Prescott?*

"I wonder if this is how any of my father's victims felt. Except... If Nash is to be believed, they're not my father's victims."

Ceiling: *You should probably talk to Gideon... and not me.*

"You're right. Tomorrow." I wrapped myself in the quilt like a burrito. One of those sad and skinny ones from Chipotle, that happens when the customer doesn't know how to order. "Hey, Ceiling? Avoiding Nash sucks."

Ceiling: *Awwwwww, did the bad boy break your heart?*

"Don't be silly. He didn't break my heart. He cracked it open."

Knock!

Knock!

I swung the closet door open, bedhead for days. My heartbeats tripped over themselves, racing at the sight of Nash. He wore a navy three-piece suit, tailored to hug every delicious inch of him.

My hair stuck up in several places. The *clinomania* shirt I wore boasted drool stains on the shoulder. I'd stayed up all night, talking to Ceiling, and the night before that—the night of Virginia's dinner—I hadn't slept at all.

Delirium had set in twelve or so hours ago.

I didn't know how to act around Nash, so I went with pretending his lies hadn't gutted me. "How did you know I'm here?"

After we'd returned from the dinner, I'd begged Delilah to grab my boxes and high-tailed to a random floor.

He went along with my ruse, "Full disclosure?"

No. Lie to me again.

"Obviously."

Nash eyed my shirt, my hair, the quilt behind me,

everything. "I checked every room from the ground up. You had to pick the twenty-fourth floor?"

"Had I known, I would have picked the fifty-third."

I examined him, head to toe, telling myself I did it to confirm the truth and not because I already missed him less than forty hours into our fight. Beneath the Kiton suit, his chest rose and fell a little faster. A thin sheen of sweat misted his forehead. His cheeks flushed the softest shade of pink from the exertion.

Jesus.

He really had inspected every floor. Even he looked like he couldn't believe it. Furrowed brows and jaw a bit slack. His fingers combed through his hair. *Once.*

I clutched onto the door frame, trying and failing to delete the question from my brain. "Why do you do that?"

"Do what?"

"Run your hands through your hair. Three times if you hate where you are. Two times if you think someone or something is idiotic. One time if..." I tipped a shoulder up, playing it off as if it meant nothing. "... you're around me."

I sucked at this fight thing.

Ceiling: *Perhaps you shouldn't do it. It'll sure as shit make my life easier.*

Me: *For the record, I am not crazy. As we speak, he is literally holding a secret back from me. A lie of omission is still a lie! Why doesn't anyone get that?*

"Full disclosure?" Nash asked.

"Yes." I wanted to laugh, because he genuinely meant it each time he said it. "Jeez."

"I don't know." He drove me insane.

"That's it?"

"I never realized I did it."

"If you had to guess?"

He stared at both sides of his palms as if noticing them for the first time. "If I had to guess, it's because I need something to do with my hands. Whenever you're around, they always want to touch you."

Me: That was cute. I'm still allowed to hear him and fall for his charm, right?

Ceiling: BRB. Googling how to hide a body.

I toyed with a strand of lint on my jeans. "I'm not ready to have this conversation." *Yet.* "There are so many unanswered questions... and I haven't seen my dad."

I'd missed the bus to Dad's yesterday, and *'Hey, Dad, I figured out I'm not a product of your sperm'* didn't seem like an appropriate text or email exchange. Especially since I had to frame it in my mind as a joke just to think about it.

"I know."

My brows pulled together. "How do you know?"

"Full disclosure?" Again, he looked so serious, like he wanted to make sure I understood he meant everything that passed his lips.

"Oh, my God." I rolled my eyes. "Yes."

"You don't have a car, and I paid some kid a thousand bucks to keep an eye out at the nearest bus stop."

Ceiling: *I've changed my mind. You psychos are both made for each other.*

My jaw slackened a bit before I recovered. "You realize that's borderline psychotic, right?"

His neck corded, muscles so tight, they seemed fake. "You realize Billings and Dickens are on the bus route to Blithe Beach. Murder capital of North Carolina ring any bells?"

"I can take care of myself."

The slow shake of his head bothered me. "I didn't stop here to fight with you. I know you're mad at me. I'm not asking for forgiveness, but you're sleeping in a closet when you can sleep on a bed. I can kick Delilah out of the presidential suite."

I blinked a few times, wondering if I'd heard that right. "You're not kicking Delilah onto the streets."

"She and her husband are worth more than the GDP of some industrialized countries. She'll hardly be on the streets."

"Nash, no."

"My room."

My hands dropped to my sides. "I'm not sharing the penthouse with you."

"Stay in the guest room inside." He adjusted his cuff. "I'm pulling the boss card. This is my hotel. I cannot, in good conscience, have someone sleeping on the floor in a closet without a bathroom or bed or running water."

"You have a conscience?" I bit back the smile, missing the banter I thrived on.

He lied to you, I reminded myself. *Everyone lies to you. Even now, by not telling you, he is lying to you.*

"You're a pain in the ass." He let loose his smile, and I forced myself to breathe.

I hacked out a cough. When it settled, I relented. Kind of. "I'll stay in a finished room inside the hotel, not attached to yours. To be clear, it's because I want to. Because I've never made myself my priority, and that's changing now."

Nash trailed the bus to Blithe Beach.

It should have pissed me off, but when I left the bus for a water fountain break in Dickens and returned to an abandoned parking spot, I might have been thankful. Even in the daylight, I'd panicked.

Murder capital and all.

"I just need a ride to Blithe," I told him, tossing my Jana Sport under the seat. "I'll take another bus back. You don't have to stay."

"Okay. I won't."

I faced the road, ignoring my hair whipping around in the wind. Pain kept me company, an unwelcome companion. I didn't like how easy his response had come, but I also saw the hypocrisy in wanting him gone yet needing him to care.

"*Shit*." He clenched the steering wheel and turned to me. "Lie of omission. Reed is with Basil near Blithe. At

Synd Beach. I planned on heading there, then rounding back to Blithe to pick you up."

"You can stop this all by telling me everything."

"It's not my secret to tell. I shouldn't have said anything. Virginia sure as hell shouldn't have said anything." He ran a hand through his hair. *Three times.* "I promised Gideon I wouldn't."

"What about me? Am I selfish for wondering where I fit into this? Why does everyone get a say in when I learn things that affect me—except me?" When I looked at him and saw an answer I didn't like, I added, "Don't answer that. Tell me this. Do you regret anything? Not with your dad and stuff, but anything to do with us?"

"I don't regret a second, because they led me to you."

"When you lied to me, Nash, you became like every other person in my life. Virginia, Balthazar, and Gideon, who apparently isn't even my dad. I hope I'm looking into things. I hope it's bad timing—"

"Timing? There is no such thing as time. Time is something people made up to give value to each breath we take, to remind us that they're limited, that we should leap first and ask questions never."

How can you believe that when you lost your dad? All Betty wants is more time with Hank.

When he said things like that, things that made me stare up at the sky and consider my place in the universe, I wanted to close the distance and remind myself it was with him.

He pulled up at Gideon's tiny cottage, not unlike the Prescotts', and turned to me. "Will you stop fighting it? Us. Come back to me?"

"No." I retrieved my Jana Sport and snatched it against my chest. "I am literally here because you know some big secrets about me and refuse to share them."

"Can I ask again tomorrow?" Nash Prescott—of the underground fights, the constellation of scars, and the billion-dollar hotelier business—looked like a damn puppy in this moment. And he'd *asked* for permission instead of telling me.

I caved. "Yeah."

I was so fucked.

chapter FIFTY-ONE

nash

The only way to Synd Beach was by boat, which made it the perfect place for shady shit to go down. Small island. No actual police force. The highest property rates in the state.

Rich college students took their summer breaks there, throwing parties, dealing drugs, and fuck if I knew what else. Reed hanging there unsettled me. Ma would flip the second she found out. If she ever did.

I told myself I had to be here, waiting for a fucking boat to Synd, rather than in Blithe Beach with Emery.

Reed had avoided this talk since Dad died, and it never exactly made the top of my to-do list.

Now that I learned Dad's side of the story via Gideon, I at least had something true to tell him. *Truth.* Ha. I was trustworthy in the same way Richard Nixon was—not at all. I fucked over my parents. I fucked over my brother. And I literally fucked Emery.

The parking lot attendant gave me a retrieval ticket. I shoved it into my pocket and walked down the dock. I'd left my suit jacket and vest in the car, leaving me in a button-down and slacks.

It looked ridiculous as fuck, but I kept a baseball cap on my head. I didn't need the press taking pictures of me headed to an island commonly referred to as Synd City. The boat ride splashed water all over the cockpit, ruining my Giannis and soaking my socks.

I spent it staring at the message Emery had sent me before everything went to shit.

Durga: Tell me your favorite thing in the world.

My fingers hovered over the keyboard. I typed out my answer and deleted it. I couldn't send it until Gideon confessed and explained it all. If I thought it was better that she heard it from me, I would have spilled the second I identified Sir Balty as her sperm donor.

Until then, I'd be here for her.

I found Reed smoking a joint at the beach. As in, my salutatorian brother with the D1 football scholarship. I sat beside him, tore it from his fingers, brought it to my lips, and inhaled.

"Nice hat," he greeted, shaking shit out of his hair.

The baseball cap had a bug-eyed gray squirrel above

the bill, the North Carolina state animal. I'd bought it at a tourist stand.

I held up the joint. "The fuck are you doing with this, kid?"

"Not like it's laced with LSD, *Dad*." He paused, digging his heels into the sand. "The stash you stole from me, on the other hand..."

I noticed that shit smelled funny.

"You running with this crowd now?" I signaled to the group of over-privileged posers playing guitar next to a ten-foot-tall bonfire in broad fucking daylight.

"You said you wanted to meet." He spread his arms wide, unapologetic and high out of his mind. "This is where I hang."

"Does Emery know?"

"Know what?"

I gestured at him. "You've turned into this tool."

Fuck, not how I expected this conversation to go.

"Emery doesn't judge." He muttered a curse, swiped the joint from me, and inhaled. "Nah, she doesn't know."

"What's going on with you?"

"Don't worry, I know what I'm doing."

The least assuring words ever, since they implied he was currently doing or had done something shady.

I followed Reed's line of sight directly to Basil. *Jesus.* "Seriously? All this for Basil Berkshire? Why?"

"If I told you, you wouldn't believe me."

"Try me."

I sat back, listening as he spilled. By the end of his story, I sure as shit didn't believe him. Katrina Berkshire's tale of spending two months at band camp over the summer and returning with a new nose and double Ds was more likely.

Reed laughed, digging the tip of the joint in the sand. "You don't believe me."

"I do, but I don't believe the situation." Cursing, I snagged a water bottle from the bright blue cooler beside him.

"It's vodka."

"Fucking hell, Reed. Who are you?"

"Same person." He shrugged. "Everyone considered me to be the golden boy, and I liked it that way. Easier to sneak around as I pleased."

I nodded at Basil. "For her."

"Yeah." A smile softened his face, and it reminded me of us before Eastridge sunk its claws into my family. "You finally here to tell me the truth?"

It defied every instinct of mine, but I did.

We talked about Dad's diagnosis, the fights I got into to raise cash, beating up Small Dick, the ledger, and how I'd unknowingly built my company on Gideon's money.

By the time the sun set and his douche friends moved on from weed to harder drugs, Reed told me he didn't agree with what happened the night of the cotillion, but he forgave me.

Reed swapped his soda for the vodka, pouring in Coke to chase it. "I knew about you and Emery on my bed."

The fuck?

My water bottle hovered before my lips. "Why didn't you say anything?"

"Figured having sex with you mortified her enough." He stole my cap and used it as a trashcan for the junk food he'd eaten. "I saw her running from the cottage, half-naked. Then, she moaned your name one night. I'm talking full-blown *moaned*. I'd passed out on her floor after sneaking back from the Berkshires. Didn't want Ma to find me."

"Thanks for the play-by-play, Jerry Springer." I pretended to check my watch, feeling some sort of cosmic. Like someone had rigged my life against me, and I somehow still had a shot at winning.

Reed tossed the cap, wrappers and all, into the bonfire like a frisbee. He pitched the vodka into it, forcing the flame higher. Tossing the bottle at my feet, he hovered over me. "Consider this your obligatory warning. Brother or not, I'll happily burn your ass if you hurt my best friend."

Too fucking late.

Emery

SWEAT SLICKED my palms.

I sat on the steps of his new house, debating whether to enter. I'd seen it in an email attachment, yet it surprised me. Smaller than the Prescotts' cottage, it countered every definition I possessed of Dad.

Of Gideon.

What else has changed?

I doubted he still dressed in the suits. A sensible Toyota parked in the driveway. The foliage seemed maintained but not immaculately groomed. This wasn't a three-piece bespoke suit kind of place.

Truthfully, I feared looking at my dad and seeing a stranger.

Because if I didn't have blood to bond us, what else was there?

"You coming in or what, sweetheart?"

Querencia.

It came to me with the force of a battle cry. Overwhelming and fierce. The urge to shout it gripped my vocal cords, but I suffered in silence. I mouthed the word, taking in Gideon, who stood near the bend of the house.

He wore a plain white t-shirt, faded blue jeans, a Hornets baseball cap, and a pair of Timberlands. My querencia disguised as a regular guy. He tore off his gardening gloves and tossed them into the nearest topiary.

A smile crinkled the corner of his eyes. "What's the magic word this time?"

He still understood me.

I wanted to fall against him and finally, *finally* shed the tears I'd kept at bay for four years. Relief wobbled my feet forward like a rickety rocking chair. Dad caught me before I fell off the steps.

I clung to his arms, breathed him in, and released my grip on him with the exhale. "Querencia."

"You'll have to explain to an old man what it means." He tapped his temple. "Mind's not what it used to be."

Being near him seemed surreal, like returning home after a long vacation to see all your furniture gone. I still recognized him, but the memories came to me slowly as I pieced together what went where.

"In bullfighting, it's the part of the ring where the bull feels strongest and safest. The place he gravitates to and makes his home. It develops as the fight progresses and becomes the place he is most dangerous, where he is impossible to kill."

He flashed me a brilliant smile, one that had always convinced me of how proud he was that I existed. "I've missed you, Em."

"You're happy," I replied, not a statement or a question. More like an accusation or demand, except I didn't understand what I'd asked of him.

I saw it in the deeper laugh lines. The carefree demeanor. How he'd stopped graying. If being in Eastridge had sucked the life out of him, living in Blithe Beach had granted him more.

It was callous, but I wanted none of this fanfare. I wanted to cut straight to the problem and fix it. "Virginia told me Balthazar Van Doren is my father."

"He's not your father." Gideon's jaw ticked. He pulled back a step. "He's a sperm donor at best."

"Why did you keep this from me?"

"I planned on telling you when you turned eighteen, but the scandal happened."

"Nash told me Balthazar blackmailed you into giving him a share of the company."

"He and Virginia embezzled from it. She needed a cushion in case I divorced her. I found out, so they cut Eric Cartwright into their scam." He swiped his jaw, eyes fixated in the distance. "They had him draw up parental rights papers and threatened me with them. You were a minor. If I told anyone about the embezzlement, I would have lost you."

"And now? I'm twenty-three."

"I've been emailing you every week, trying to talk to you, waiting for you to come see me, so we can do this in person." He clasped onto my hands, drawing me nearer. "I'm not blaming you. It's not your fault. But I need you to realize I tried. Even when you saw me outside your diner and called the cops on me, I kept showing up. I love you. Far as I'm concerned, you're my daughter."

I swallowed, squinting into the distance to avoid looking at him. Did this make me the architect of my misery? I didn't feel like the girl who chased storms. I felt like the girl who ran from them.

"Will you tell me about the rest? I want to know what happened to you after the scandal. I want to know why Virginia isn't in jail. Was there no proof? Was it your word against hers? I want to know how Nash is involved. I want to know how *I* am involved."

"I'll tell you." He flipped the bill of his hat and covered the top step of his porch. "Every Saturday, we can meet up, and I'll explain it piece by piece. I promise."

I sat beside him. "You can't explain it now?"

"I could, but how else am I gonna get you to meet me?" He nudged my arm with his shoulder.

Biting back a smile, I considered the reception he'd get anywhere but Blithe. "I'll come here."

"You sure? I can drive to Haling Cove."

"Yeah, I'm sure. Can we meet at Hank's grave next time?"

"Of course." He appraised me, taking in my black hair and the t-shirt. "I want to know everything about you."

I shrugged and tapped my foot on the step. "There's

not much to know. I can write everything on a sheet of paper and have most of the white space left over."

Except Demi.

My penance.

Why did it feel less meaningful suddenly? Why did it feel different?

My eyes widened. I ducked my head down, processing. Perhaps I hadn't been trying to alleviate my guilt. I was trying to alleviate Dad's culpability. If he could make things right, maybe I could see him again. Maybe I could have a dad.

"What's eating at you?" Dad tapped my shoulder. "There's something else."

"It's a lot to take in." I considered lying, but went with the ugly, painful truth. "And mostly... In the past four years, I knew we weren't talking, but I never felt like I didn't belong here. And now... I'm not sure."

He folded me into his arms and squeezed me into a bear hug, one he used to give me as a kid. Even when he'd known I didn't share the same blood.

"You think I send weekly unanswered postcards to just anyone? You're my daughter, Emery Winthrop. Always have been. Always will be. We don't need blood to bond us when we've got love."

chapter FIFTY-TWO

nash

I found Emery on the beach.
 The one with waters more polluted than the Styx, probably mutating her into one of the X-Men by the second.

She stood waist-deep in the ocean, fully dressed, staring at the dark sky. Waves crashed against her back, but she remained an immovable force. I'd never seen anything so fierce. She reminded me of the Charmaine Olivia painting displayed in the Prescott Hotel in Paris. A sea of chaos and colors consumed the canvas, but all I saw was the subject.

You may not need me, but fuck, I need you.

I was an asshole with an ethical code that occasionally dipped as low as a genocidal dictator's. Someone had to reel me in.

An entire day had passed. Enough time for Gideon to explain everything in excruciating detail. Now I'd get my girl back. Simple.

Pulling out my phone, I responded to Emery through text.

Durga: Tell me your favorite thing in the world.

Nash: You and whatever brought me to you.

She slid her phone from her pocket. Her tongue peeked past her lips, fingers flying.

Emery: That's two things. You never follow the rules.

"Fuck the rules."

She glanced up at me and waded through the water, hungry eyes eating a path down my body. The waves pushed her back and forth with their current. Each step she took seemed like a battle with gravity.

We met somewhere in the middle, where the waves hit her knees but didn't do much damage.

"What threads tie us together?" No hello. Straight into the philosophical musings. So fucking Emery, my dick hardened. She splashed the water with her foot. "Isn't it crazy how we mind our own business, not knowing our next step can be the one that determines our forever?"

I inched closer to her, settling into familiar territory, recognizing her like this. She always searched for meaning, for an explanation, for something to tell her *why* when the answer would likely do nothing for her.

But I'd give her the best response I could and hope she came back to me.

"Do you know what Moira is?"

"Moira?" Her head slanted. She tossed me a look that suggested she hated the fact that I knew a word she didn't. If she could, she'd probably reach out and steal it, just like she'd stolen a piece of me.

"Moira is Fate. It's the threads that bind us together."

"You, me, Gideon, Virginia, Hank, Balthazar. We're tied together." Her hands wrung her shirt, bunching it at the front. "I know this, but Dad hasn't explained everything to me. You won't. So, I'm standing here, aware these threads exist and blind to what they look like. Help me, Nash. Dad is holding the info over my head until I return for each visit. I don't blame him. I ditched him for four years."

Fuck you, Gideon Winthrop. Fuck the position you've put me in.

I didn't have an answer for her, other than I wanted her. "Come back to me?"

"Never." Her lips quirk up, the moonlight performing a devious dance in her eyes. She kicked the water and watched the waves splash my suit slacks. "Not until you tell me."

I wouldn't. She knew this.

Every time she spoke of her dad, she made a face. Confused. Lost. Warring with whether to forgive him. She needed to hear this from Gideon, or she'd never recover the relationship they'd shared.

I toggled with the words, wondering how to say this

without sounding completely whipped, then realizing I didn't give two shits. "You are at war with yourself, and I've never wanted to pick up a suit of armor and fight for anyone more than I do now, but I know I can't. This is your battle. This is your war. You'll come back to me, Emery, or words like fate and destiny wouldn't exist."

"Fate? Destiny?" She shook her head. "You're throwing some serious words around."

I stepped closer, pushing a small wave onto her. "What are the odds I was in that bed the night you snuck into Reed's room? That you are Durga? That I am Ben? That you ended up in the elevator with me? That it got stuck? That you worked for me? That I ran into you at the soup kitchen? I can go on, but what are the odds?"

"High!" She threw both hands up and began ticking her fingers. "You are Reed's brother, and Betty took over your room. Of course, you'd sleep there. There aren't that many people in Eastridge, and even less using the Eastridge United app. Makes sense that you'd be Ben."

She ignored my you've-gotta-be-kidding-me stare and continued, "I got a job from Reed, and he's your brother. It was late, several people were trying to get into the elevator. There are power outages all the time during storms. And that's the only soup kitchen in miles. Maybe there's fate. Maybe there's not, but are you really using us as proof it exists?"

"You—the girl who believes in magic words and starless skies—do not believe in fate?"

She lifted a shoulder. "I don't know what I believe in, but it could all be a coincidence. Not fate."

"It exists." I closed the distance and wrapped a palm around the nape of her neck. "Fate is a hurricane. You think you know where it's going. You think you're safe. And just when you think you've weathered the storm, its path moves directly into yours. You, Emery Winthrop, are my hurricane. My fate. My Durga. My Tiger."

I kissed her, running my fingers through her hair and tilting her head up to meet mine. Her fists clung to my shirt. A button flew off, but fuck if I cared.

She wrapped her legs around my waist. I brought my hands to her ass and pressed her against me. The waves pushed us deeper into the ocean. My cock fought to escape my pants, hard as fuck for her.

Emery pulled back and leaned her forehead against mine. She panted, still rubbing herself against me. *Fuck.* "We shouldn't have done that."

I knew she wouldn't without knowing the full story, but I asked anyway, "Come back to me?"

"Not yet."

Yet.

I'll fucking take that.

Emery

KNOCK!
Knock!

"Coming!" I muttered, "Please, tell me you have not developed a habit of waking me up this early every morning."

I padded barefoot to the door, passing a spare room, the living room, and the kitchen before reaching it. These upper-level suites were the real deal. Ida Marie once mentioned they went for a cool five-figures a night.

When finished, Nash's penthouse would span two floors, the first story sharing real estate with two presidential suites. Delilah's and, now, mine.

I swung the door open, expecting Nash. A cherubic face greeted me. I recognized him from a meet and greet with the staff. They came in last week to get a lay of the land before employee training began.

"Hi." I kept a palm on my door. "Can I help you?"

He hopped from one foot to the other. "Mr. Prescott told me to sit outside and wait until you wake up."

"I'm sorry." I blinked, taking in his uniform. "What? He wants you to babysit me?"

"No. Oops." Cherub Face reached down and collected a giant blue cooler. The type hospitals used to transport organs. He shoved it into my arms. "Here. I was supposed to get this to you when you wake up, but I really have to pee."

"Thanks, I think?" I opened the cooler, heartbeat a fucking goner at the sight of my packed lunch. My fingertips ghosted my lips, remembering my kiss with Nash two nights ago.

Cherub Face's feet tapped against the hall's carpet. "Can I use your restroom?"

Uhhh... Hard pass.

Letting a stranger inside equaled the premise of every slasher flick.

Ceiling: *Oddly sensible of you. Gold star.*

"No." I pulled out the lunch bag and set the cooler on my entryway table. "But you can use Mr. Prescott's."

"Are you sure?"

Lunch bag clutched in one fist, I pulled Nash's keycard from my back pocket, led the guy down the hall, and let him inside. "Guest bathroom's right there."

As soon as he left, I tore open the bag. A note sat at the top.

 Hey.

I'm not greeting you, Emery. You would think that. Control that ego, Tiger.

I'm saying hi to the voice in your head. The one you're using to read this.

'Sup, sweetheart.

Tell Emery her ass looked fuck-hot in her jeans yesterday, her idea about alternating curtain colors was a stroke of Einstein-level genius, and it drives me fucking insane every time she whispers magic words.

Really, I think that's you whispering them, isn't it, Emery's Inner Voice?

If you could tell Emery to come back to me, that'd be great.

— **NASH**

I tamped a smile and rifled through a kitchen drawer for one of the hotel notepads. I wrote my answer on it.

> *Not happening.*
>
> **— EMERY**

P.S. *All you have to do is tell me.*

And so the cooler saga began.

I'd wake up to one in the morning and drop it off in front of his door at night, along with my reply. On Saturdays, Nash drove me to see Dad, whose idea of telling me everything consisted of literally telling me every single detail as slowly as he could.

I wanted him to speed to the juicy bits, gloss over the yucky aspects of my conception, and get to the part where Nash somehow discovered everything before I had. At the same time, I knew Dad cherished my visits, so I let him take them at his pace.

Even if patience had never been my strong suit.

And every morning, when I woke up to a note in the cooler, I'd smile.

> *Fate is the Universe kicking Coincidence's ass. We are an example of Fate proving to the world it exists. Come back to me?*
>
> **— NASH**

I'd toyed with the paper, knowing Nash would ask this every day until I said yes, knowing I'd want to cave every time. Dad or Nash could put me out of my misery, but neither did, so I'd written back:

Never.

— **EMERY**

P.S. Unless you tell me. In which case, I'm curious: If Fate and Destiny went to war, which do you think would win?

We worked together every day, with the exception of a few trips Nash took with Delilah. He'd leave by chopper on the roof, but he never failed to make me lunch and a note. The following morning, he replied:

 Whichever brought you to me.

(Cheesy enough? Covering my bases here, since deep and philosophical didn't work. I could also go with—the universe wants us together. Who are we to defy the universe? Pure gold. You could put that on a shirt.)

Come back to me?

— **NASH**

I ran to my room and printed the shirt.

Who are we to defy the universe?

It felt like wearing Nash.

Chantilly left with Cayden, Ida Marie, and Hannah to do an interview with an architectural magazine about the hotel's upcoming soft opening. Nash spent the morning with Delilah, schmoozing a local politician at an MLB game.

He entered the office around noon, sporting dark denim, a white Henley, and a baseball cap. When he caught me eating the sandwich he'd made, in the shirt he'd come up with, he leaned against the door frame, crossed his arms, and watched.

Self-satisfied and so damn cocky.

I popped the last bite into my mouth, incisors crunching on the Ruffles. "Are you going to tell me?"

"Will you trust that I have my reasons?"

"Yes, you want Gideon to tell me."

"The fact that you're calling him Gideon and not Dad is exactly my point."

Actually, I always called him Dad to his face and mostly called him Dad in my head. In fact, I only used Gideon with Nash because I feared the unknown. So far, I understood the motivations behind everything Dad had recounted.

He stayed in a loveless marriage with Virginia, so he could keep me.

He made Balthazar partner, so he could keep me.

He didn't turn them in, so he could keep me.

Understandable.

But what if the day came when he confessed he or Nash did something so bad, I could never forgive them? Or worse—I forgave them, because I wanted them both in my life that much.

I wrote my note in front of him and slapped it to his chest.

 Nope.

— **EMERY**

P.S. The only cheeses I like are white cheddar and string cheese eaten correctly (re: peeled).

A few days later, Nash arrived late to take me to Dad's, which meant I'd walked to the bus stop, boarded, and watched him trail the bus until the next stop. I hopped down and ambled toward him.

"I got held up at the mechanic's." Nash raked his fingers through his hair. *Once.* "You could have waited. I doubt Gideon would care if you showed up late."

He leaned against his car, arms crossed. He had replaced the roof. Through the windows, I noticed the leather chairs appeared reupholstered. All evidence of our night baltering... gone.

Pain lashed at my stomach. Ridiculous, but also proof I cared.

"Actually, I waited *and* texted you." I opened my Jana Sport. "When I didn't get a response, I left. Couldn't risk it."

I retrieved my sketchbook, barely glancing at the "Come back to me?" on his note from this morning. My pen moved fast across the paper. I yanked the note out, crumbled it into a ball, and handed it to him.

 No.

— EMERY

P.S. Out of all the lies, my favorite was you and me.

He unfolded it and read it with a raised brow. The amusement did nothing for my irritation. "I just realized something."

I sighed, shoved the sketchbook into the Jana Sport, and dumped it into the car. "What?"

Nash closed the door for me and entered on his side. "Temper tantrums can be cute."

Nash Prescott—the master of the backhanded compliment.

"For the record," he continued, "my phone powered down. The mechanic forgot to return the charger to the car after he finished reupholstering."

The following morning, my letter from Nash read:

> *You couldn't look away from me yesterday. I know we're waiting for Gideon and you fear what you'll learn. I promise you, there's nothing to be afraid of.*
>
> *Ask yourself: what do you have to lose when being scared? What do you have to lose when being fearless?*
>
> **Come back to me?**
>
> — **NASH**

> *P.S. Tell Gideon to hurry the fuck up. I'm impatient by nature and prone to getting my way. You could've finished a hundred fucking Ava Harrison audiobooks by now.*

I did, in fact, relay the message to Dad the following week, who only laughed and told me Nash could wait. The answer would have pissed me off, but he said it with such ease and comfort, I'd never felt more certain that we'd be okay.

We spent the day talking about all the events that had to happen to lead Virginia to him.

"Things happen for a reason, Emery." Dad pressed a kiss to my forehead. "You've got to trust that."

That night, I struggled with a response for the first time.

> No.
>
> — **EMERY**

P.S. What if it was fate that led me to you? When I ask myself questions like this, this path we're on feels beyond us.

At this point, Dad and I had gotten into a groove. We'd fought our insecurities and found a relationship reminiscent of the one we used to share. This *1001 Arabian Nights*-style blackmail could end without either of us feeling like we no longer had a reason to meet.

I could have told Dad to give me a quick rundown, so Nash and I could finally be together again. I didn't.

Oddly, I did it for Nash.

He wore a distant look every time he dropped me off, and I knew he left for the cemetery to visit his dad while he waited. I also knew he felt so strongly about maintaining my relationship with Dad because he no longer had a chance with Hank.

So, I drew the meetings out, even when it gutted me and I sometimes caught Nash staring at me as if he was trying to figure out if I felt the same way.

Over a month later, the moment I feared came.

The Nash talk.

I wanted to hear this from Nash. How he'd found the

ledger and burned it for me. The company he'd built off of the Winthrop Scandal and Dad's secret investment. About the way he'd mistakenly blamed himself for Hank's death. How he'd helped so many people to pay penance.

I'd already suspected most of it, so it didn't come as a surprise. But at the end of it all, I realized something.

I'd seen it on his desk. The burnt leather, pages preserved inside.

Nash still had the ledger.

The one thing that could prove my dad's innocence.

And he'd kept it to himself.

chapter FIFTY-THREE

nash

"Those motherfuckers. Fuck them. Fuck everyone. Fuck the whole fucking world." Delilah shuffled past me, sheer rage plastered all over her face. "We need to go."

We left the reception area of the D.C. skyscraper and speed-walked our way to the rental car. After dropping Emery off in Blithe this morning, I'd arranged for Gideon to drive her back to the hotel.

Still, Emery and I had made plans for tonight. I'd helicopter to North Carolina in time for take-out and poking holes in every movie on Chantilly's Netflix queue.

"Care to explain what's going on or are you having another temper tantrum?" I slid into the driver's seat. "Unlike Emery's, yours are not cute."

"You're amused. Good. Hold on to that, because you won't be in a sec. We're headed to the airport." She pulled out her phone, dialed a number, and signaled for me to be quiet with a finger. Her middle one. Charming. "Yeah. Did you read my text? I need the soonest flight. Commercial or private, so long as it's the first one out."

I took off to the airport, sensing her urgency. *Fuck.* I needed a charger to text Emery and let her know I'd left.

"Spill," I said as soon as Delilah flipped her phone shut. "Also, do you have Emery's number? Or Reed's?"

"No, I don't have your girlfriend's number. And no, I don't have my boss' prepubescent brother's number either." She shoved her phone into her Birkin. "That should be the least of your concerns. They changed the meeting from the building we were just at."

I turned into the airport. "Not a big deal. Which terminal?"

"International. Air Singapore."

"One—we're flying commercial?" I abandoned the rental at the curb, not caring. Singapore was too important.

Always prepared, Delilah slammed down our passports at the VIP ticket counter. "Why does it matter if we're flying commercial? I never took you for a diva, but it all makes sense now."

I ignored her jab and plucked our tickets from the haggard employee. "I need to charge my phone or buy a new charger."

We rushed to the TSA Pre-check line, shouldering

our way past people, just shy of an actual tackle. Half the time, I thought Delilah wanted Singapore as much as I did. Either for me, or because she'd worked so hard on it for too long to lose now.

"Fuck, I do, too." She strode through the metal detector. "But we have no time. We literally need to sprint to make this flight."

I placed my phone in a bin on the conveyor. "Two—how the fuck did we get the location wrong?"

The TSA agent scowled at my harsh language. I ignored her and led Delilah into the terminal.

She shoved our passports into her bag and handed our tickets to the airline attendant. "We'll make it if we land on time and chopper directly onto the adjacent building. I've cleared it with their security." Her heels click-clacked down the passenger boarding bridge. "The landowner changed the auction site and time, and a glitch somehow wiped our emails from their CC list."

"A glitch," I deadpanned.

She didn't say it, but we both knew Asher Black's reputation. Mafia ties and a less than legal history.

Her shoulders tipped up as we took seats across from each other in fucking economy class. "Black Enterprises wants this property."

My knees bumped the seat in front of me. *Fucking hell.* Commercial flights weren't made for anyone taller than a toddler or wider than a stick of gum. The C.I.A. must've designed this shit as a torture experiment. Cram two-hundred people into a forty-five-ton hunk of metal, force them to pay for it, and see who cracks first.

"There's no property left in Singapore like this. One-of-a-fucking-kind." I ignored the appalled expression on the mother beside me. She covered her son's ears and inched away from me—even as her eyes swiped up and down my body, checking me out. "It's zoned for the highest buildings."

Exactly why I fucking needed it.

I reclined the seat as far as it would go, pretending I didn't hear it knock against the person's knee behind me. I'd fly to Singapore, win the land auction, and find a phone charger on my way back to the airport.

Emery would understand.

She knew what Singapore meant to me.

ASHER BLACK looked like he'd be a cocky motherfucker, and he was.

The smug son of a bitch had practically tattooed *ENTERTAINED* across his forehead. He brought his wife Lucy to the negotiations, reaching a level of ball-less sap I was tempted to address.

"Nash Prescott in the flesh." He leaned back in his seat and stretched, his tone flippant. "You look smaller in person."

Lucy dug an elbow into his ribs. "Asher, stop." She smiled at me, so opposite to her husband, I wondered why she'd chosen the dick. "You look perfectly proportionate."

Fucking hell, she looked like she legit meant that as a compliment.

"Mr. Prescott. Mrs. Lowell." Elliot, the auctioneer for today, glanced between us. He seemed uncomfortable around Asher, which I didn't blame him for. "Cheng explained the mix-up. We're so sorry. Please, allow me to extend an apology on behalf of myself and my colleagues."

"Don't worry about it, Elliot." Delilah perched on the seat I pulled out for her. "It's not a big deal. Truly."

The five of us looked ridiculous in a conference room meant for thirty. Twenty-five empty chairs stretched the length of the room.

Elliot sat at the head of the table, the backdrop of Singapore visible through the glass behind him. "I'll cut to the chase here. Mr. Black, our board has reservations about your... reputation. You'd have to make a substantially larger bid than Mr. Prescott for them to approve the sale."

Delilah pulled out a pad of sticky notes, scribbled the damn dictionary, and slid it to me.

> *Good news. I expected this. I'm betting Asher did, too, which is why they had our emails hacked. If you bid in the upper threshold of your budget off the bat, we can make it clear that he'd have to pay substantially over market value to win.*

Thank fuck.
Something needed to go right today.
I scrawled back:

> *Good.*

Asher leaned forward in his seat. "If you intended on bringing me here to screw me over, you could have saved me and my wife a trip and done it over the phone."

Elliot adjusted his collar, looking like he'd rather jump in a pool with sharks than be in a room with Asher. "I'm sorry, sir. It's our policy not to disclose details before an auction. You request—"

"I don't care what I requested. Common courtesy..."

I tuned them out and read the note Delilah passed back.

> *This is perfect news. Haling Cove is nearly done anyway. With the soft launch next week, you can assure everything is on the right track for the grand opening, which gives you the opportunity to leave for Singapore the day after.*
>
> *They'll need you here for at least two months to 1) navigate your re-zoning request and 2) finalize the purchase.*

What the fuck? She'd never mentioned two months in Singapore. My pen strokes left fucking indents in the pad and possibly the table.

> *Two months? Can't it be done remotely?*

If I'd known, I wouldn't have bothered flying here. I figured by the grand opening of the hotel, Gideon would have gotten his shit together and spilled to Emery. Maybe I could fly back and explain my part of the mess to her myself.

Even as I thought it, I knew I wouldn't. Given the Sir Balty situation, she needed to cement her relationship with her dad. If I had a chance to talk to my dad, I'd do it. Every fucking day, not just once a week.

Asher continued to demolish Elliot, but I gave no fucks. I snatched the Post-Its from Delilah, not bothering with subtlety.

1. Walking naked in your own home.

2. Chewing gum.

3. Smoking.

4. Noise after 10 P.M.

5. Leaving the toilet un-flushed.

6. Using someone else's WiFi.

7. Hugging someone the same gender as you.

8. Singing in public.

9. Feeding pigeons.

10. Alcohol and parties between 10:30 P.M. and 7 A.M.

Lucy tilted her head from across the table, studying me. I angled my pen to block her view of the pad.

> *Are you on drugs or is this your pathetic bucket list?*

The ledger sat in my safe. Delilah knew it existed, but she didn't know what the contents held. Really, I should have confessed to Emery by now. It possessed enough evidence to free Gideon of all accusations.

No more hiding out in Blithe for him. He'd be able to visit his daughter without fear of a mob. She could drop the Rhodes last name and become a Winthrop again.

But—*fucking but*—it meant a possible jail sentence for me. I wanted one damn month of me and Emery on some stranded island, talking, laughing, fucking on every inch of the beach before I spent twenty years in jail.

(I Google'd it. That was the maximum sentence for insider trading, not to mention the whole burning evidence thing.)

Delilah slid the pad to me.

> *No, just listing illegal things to do in Singapore. Now, imagine the strict property laws. But go ahead. Try closing remotely and fuck up this deal WE've been working on for years. (And by we, I mean ME, while you obsessed on the sidelines.)*

She had a point.

I obsessed over this project.

Sitting on the roof of the building next door, I'd never felt closer to Dad. The skyscraper boasted nearly eighty floors. I bribed so many politicians in the past several years, just to rezone mine for one-hundred-and-thirty floors.

Higher than the fucking Empire State, the Shanghai Tower, and the Makkah Clock Tower.

Dad.

Emery.

Having to make this choice should have compared to voluntarily sticking my neck under a tractor. It didn't.

The consequences hurt, yes, but choosing Emery came easy.

"Eat a Snickers, Asher. You're too you when you're hungry." I tossed Delilah's pad in the trash and stood. "Prescott Hotels formally withdraws from this auction."

Everyone in this room—aside from Lucy, and seriously what the fuck—shared dumbstruck expressions.

Delilah recovered first. "Excuse me while I confer with my client." In the hallway, she paced twice and rounded on me. "What the hell, Nash?!"

"Careful, D." I made a show of studying her forehead. "Those wrinkles are showing. I count one, two—"

"This is not funny." Delilah Jr., that vein on her temple, looked ten seconds from bursting. "Do you know how long I've worked to make this happen for you?"

"I've compensated you for your time." I swallowed and turned away.

Even with the burn of her disappointment, the decision felt easy. I picked Emery. Simple as that.

"It's not the money or the time. It's the fact that I worked my ass off, knowing how much this project meant to you... And now you're pulling out? Why?"

I didn't answer.

Her head whipped back. She rocked on her heel and gave me a shit-eating grin. "It's Emery, isn't it?"

I said nothing, waiting this out.

She continued, still with that fucking smile. "I always

knew you were capable of falling in love." With that, she turned and walked to the room.

"Delilah?"

She paused, fingers on the door handle. "Yeah?"

"Thank you."

Her brows shot up, like she couldn't believe I'd uttered a thank you. You'd think I was a fucking monster or something.

"Let's get you your girl."

I SPENT THE flight back to the U.S. lamenting the fact that I had to choose between buying a new charger and taking the first flight out of Singapore.

With only one seat available, Delilah stayed behind. I tried to feel bad about it, but A—I wanted to return home to Emery and B—Delilah seemed excited to maul the Singaporean street food. So, really, she should thank me.

Free trip to Singapore on the company.

By the time I landed, I had zero patience for customs. I cut past people when they stopped paying attention— and did it again even when they *did* pay attention.

At the kiosk, I handed the customs officer my passport, ignoring the irritated whispers of the people I'd skipped over.

The officer swiped the passport and tilted his head at the screen. He swiped it again.

"Is there a problem?" I glanced at my watch.

It had taken nineteen hours to fly from D.C. to Singapore, then twenty-five hours to fly from Singapore to North Carolina with a quick layover that required me to sprint from one end of the airport to the other like I was Eric fucking Liddell.

With the meeting, all in, Emery hadn't heard from me in over two days.

I blinked away the jet lag, in time to catch the officer waving a coworker over. "If this is about cutting in line, can we hold off the time-out until tomorrow? *Fuck.*"

"Sir, come with me." Officer Two snagged my passport from Officer One and led me to a back room, while I wondered what the hell was going on.

A metal bench pushed against the wall in the corner. The rectangular table filled the space, two chairs on each side. It looked like the mall cop version of an interrogation room.

I arched a brow and turned to the officer. "Do I need to call my attorney?"

Goddamnit, Delilah.

She was probably scarfing down *bah kut teh* on an overcrowded street this very second. Also, even if I had a call to use, my phone had powered down, and I hadn't memorized any numbers.

"Sir, I need you to lower your voice and calm down."

"I am fucking calm."

"A law enforcement agency has placed a flag on your

passport." The officer gestured to a seat. "Please, wait here while we alert the appropriate authorities."

Appropriate authorities.

"Goddamn rent-a-cops." I made a show of yawning and laying on the table instead of sitting on a chair.

The first hour pissed me off.

The second hour made me stir crazy.

And on the third hour, the puzzle pieces fell into place. The door swung open, and the 'appropriate authority' walked in.

Brandon Vu.

chapter FIFTY-FOUR

Emery

Since I didn't get a note this morning, or yesterday morning, or the morning before that, or the morning before that... I've decided to be proactive and leave you one.

Before you ask, no, I will not come back to you.

— EMERY

P.S. You're a bad stitch job that can't be undone. No matter how hard I try to untangle us, we become messier than when we began.

B<small>ILE CHASED</small> my breath.
I chugged half a bottle of water, hoping it'd make me less queasy.

Nope.

Still a quarter second from spewing my empty stomach all over the floor.

I'd felt this way since realizing Nash had kept a ledger that could exonerate my Dad for almost eight years. I'd gone through every scenario, trying to justify it, but Ceiling always cut through the bullshit.

I tried again.

"Maybe he thought Dad participated in the scandal?"

Ceiling: *You are worse than a broken record. At least record players can be turned off. Let me say it slower this time—he took you to see your Dad.*

Repeatedly. Why would he do that if he thought your dad was guilty?

"Maybe he lost the ledger since then?"

Ceiling: *Really? This again? Hun, people lose things like their virginity or their car keys. People don't lose evidence in famous fraud cases unless it's on purpose. Because you're particularly dimwitted, let me spell that out for you—I'm talking about destroying evidence.*

"Maybe he's keeping it to ask me what to do with it?"

Ceiling: *And in the almost eight years since he had it, has he ever once asked you what you want to do about it? On second thought, don't answer that. You have conversations with inanimate objects. I wouldn't put it past you to hallucinate conversations with Nash, too.*

"If he's innocent, I shouldn't have left that letter on his door. He didn't show up to our date, so I couldn't even confront him about the ledger like I'd planned. Then, he sent me straight to voicemail the fifty billion times I called him. And he hasn't brought me my lunch or notes in days."

My emotions exceeded a single word, so I hadn't bothered printing a new t-shirt since he left. I wore a plain t-shirt, feeling so unlike myself, it was almost embarrassing.

Office gossip placed Nash with Delilah in Singapore for a meeting.

I'd believed it… until I spotted Delilah yesterday,

walking down the hallway, coffee cup in hand. When I asked her about Nash, she seemed surprised I hadn't seen him, mentioning he'd flown in before her and she hadn't seen him since either.

I checked the flight logs for all the local airports, then all the ones in the state. Every direct and connecting flight from Singapore in the past five days had arrived.

Ceiling: *Obviously, he's avoiding you. He deserved that note.*

My feet dragged across the carpet with each step. I had carpet burns on them from pacing. Still, I sprinted to the door at the knock and swung it open.

Nash.

Relief swept through me like a current. The violent kind that pummeled your body, pulled you under, and dragged you places you didn't want to go.

He waved a sheet of paper, looking more exhausted than I'd ever seen him. Frankly, a little smelly, too. His eyes dipped to my shirt, noticed nothing on it, and returned to my face.

A frown turned his lips down. "Before you speak, I wrote you a letter. This was before I got your letter, by the way, but I still mean every word of mine. I want to see your face when you read it."

I traced him with my eyes, cataloging the wrinkled button-down, abandoned suit jacket, and slacks that had lost their pleating.

My lower lip folded into my mouth. Even disheveled, I wanted him.

Sighing, I yanked the letter from his fingers and scanned the first line.

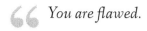 *You are flawed.*

A hate letter?

I jerked my gaze up. "Are you serious?"

"Did you want me to send it to an editor first?" He seemed a little unhinged, the whites of his eyes peppered with red from lack of sleep. "Come on, just read it." His hand raked through his hair. Once. "Please."

It was his hands through his hair that undid me, but the please cemented it. I dropped my gaze back down to the letter and read.

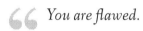 *You are flawed.*

You talk to yourself.

You talk to the sky.

You know words that mean nothing to most people.

You don't care about words that matter to everyone else.

You are harder on yourself than others.

You love the dark more than you love the light.

Your heart is too big, so you do stupid shit like give up food and shelter for a complete stranger to get a college degree.

You love small moments more than big ones.

You believe in magical words, yet you don't believe in fate.

You are so fixated on the stars—whether or not they're there—but to be fucking honest, the sky could be full of them or completely empty, and I'd still be looking at you.

You are flawed, but you're also perfect. (Of course, you don't believe in the word perfect either.)

And if I could give you anything, I wouldn't save you (from yourself or me). You're more than capable of doing all the saving.

I'd give you the ability to look at yourself through my eyes. You'd see that you are not the storm. You are <u>lightning</u> in the storm. You are what pierces <u>through</u> the clouds and shines brightest.

You'd see exactly why I love you.

"Nash," I started, unsure what to say.

I struggled to find words, swallowing each emotion as they took turns throttling me. His fingers reached for the letter when all I wanted to do was grab it, frame it, and make it mine.

I released it, because the idea of it ripping in my hands devastated me.

My eyes refused to leave him. He looked like a

favorite memory, one you replayed until everything reminded you of it and became déjà vu.

Nash broke the silence with an infuriating, self-satisfied smile. "Yep."

"Excuse me?"

"Just wanted to see your face as you read this. You still love me."

"Still?" I shook my head. "I never said I love you."

"You did. Not with your words, but with your actions. You put so much weight in words, but sometimes, the things you do say more than the things you say. See you tomorrow, Little Tiger. Shit's about to go down."

I stood there, slack jawed, clutching my door. He pressed a kiss to my temple and left. His whistles echoed down the hallway.

Ceiling: *See? I told you he's not avoiding you. You shouldn't have written him that note. You can be such an asshole sometimes.*

nash

DELILAH WALKED into the penthouse, midway

through my conversation with Chantilly. I spared her a glance and returned to the psycho sitting across from me.

She tucked a red strand of hair behind her ears. "We've been working closely the past two weeks."

"Yes," I dragged out. "You, me, and four other people."

She spread her legs, an invitation. Did she really think I didn't remember her trying to accost me?

Her fingertips ran across her collarbone and circled the cross necklace around her neck. "I see you staring at me."

"Only when I'm appalled at how quickly you're able to run through millions of dollars in budget money." I leaned back in my seat and drew up some documents, fucking exhausted with today. "Also, I won't ask you again to close your legs. I have to sit in this office for another three hours, and your pussy smells like a fish market."

What she didn't understand was, I had no use for someone who nodded every time I did. I have a shadow for that, and I sure as hell liked it more than I liked her.

Delilah cleared her throat and set Rosco down. He sprinted to his four-poster bed.

Chantilly tilted her chin up, cheeks flamed red when she noticed the company for the first time. "I have to check on something, um, on another floor."

"You do that." I motioned her to shoo.

She darted around Delilah and slammed the door on her way out. Rosco jumped, yelped, and pawed at Delilah's leg to be held.

Bending, she scooped him up. "You look like shit."

Yeah, and you know why, asshole.

I'd told her through email last night, sparing her any incriminating details but enough that she got the gist.

"Shut up." I lied, "I'm sick, you cold-hearted monster. Chantilly cornered me this morning to talk about budgets. She had a cold, Delilah. She coughed in my mouth, Delilah. I ate her cold, Delilah. I ate it. Do you know what that is like? I could demonstrate."

"I feel like you're saying my name a lot."

"I feel like you're not listening."

We skirted around the elephant of the day, because I'd been fucking held in federal custody for the maximum forty-eight hours allowed by North Carolina law. If I had a working phone, I would have called Delilah to get me the fuck out of there.

I hadn't.

So, I sat through Brandon's incessant questions without speaking a word.

"Did you know about the Winthrop Scandal before the F.B.I. and S.E.C. announced our formal investigation?"

"What is your involvement with Virginia Winthrop, Balthazar Van Doren, and Eric Cartwright?"

"We spotted you at Balthazar and Virginia's engagement dinner. Her daughter was your date. Would you say you are close with her? Did she know about the Winthrop Scandal before it began?"

"We don't have to be after you, Nash. Strike a deal with us. What do you say?"

If it were just me, I could deal with the pressure from the S.E.C. Fika had done a good job of covering my tracks, and insider trading cases could be difficult to prove. But the fucker went after Ma and Emery.

Instinct urged me to fight with my fists, but that had never worked out well in the past. Good thing I had something better than a fist. A Harvard-educated lawyer on payroll.

I spit it out, "Delilah, I need a favor."

"How desperate are you for it?"

Sighing, I closed my laptop and clasped my fingers together. "What do you want?"

"Hmm..." She tapped a fingertip to her lip. "Tell me how desperate you are first."

I stared at her until she fidgeted under my attention. Even then, she didn't relent.

"Desperate," I seethed, knowing she'd toy with me as revenge.

I deserved it for making her do all the work on Singapore for nothing. Didn't mean I had to enjoy it.

A smile consumed her face. She looked like the less green offspring of the Grinch. "I want you to kiss Rosco on the lips and tell him you're sorry for being an insufferable asshole." She held him out to me. "Also, tell him you think he's cute."

I didn't budge. "I'm not doing that."

"You can do the favor yourself." She made a show of shrugging and shooting me a sympathetic grimace. "I hear self-care is all the rage these days."

"You're an ass, and not a nice one." I transferred Rosco to my grip, brought the rat up to my face, stared it in its beady fucking eyes, and said, "You look like someone shaved a teletubby baby and glued a used wig to its head"—Delilah coughed—"and I guess you're cute. Sorry, dude."

I leaned forward, wondering if I'd entered a different dimension disguised as hell. The things I did for Emery Winthrop. *Goddamn.* As if he had a sixth sense, Rosco leaned forward, too.

And then He. Bit. Me.

On the nose.

For a tiny thing, he had razor-sharp teeth. Blood trickled down my nostrils. I released the rat, letting him fall to my lap and hop off. He ran to his bed, circled the doggy blanket, and curled into a ball.

When I stared at him, he barked. Twice.

I gave him the finger and focused on Delilah. "Now that it's established your rabies-ridden dog and I dislike each other, can we move the fuck on?"

She yanked a few tissues from her desk and tossed them to me, not hiding her amusement in the slightest. "I know I'm supposed to look serious right now, but I'm not worried at all. Frankly, the worst part is that you kept this from me all these years. I could have helped you out earlier."

I read between the lines and saw her question, but I ignored it. Instead, I broke everything down for her, from stealing the ledger to burning it to building this company off money obtained through insider trading.

Delilah sighed, sat at her desk, and booted her laptop. "I have good news and bad news. Which do you want first?"

"The bad news."

"Of course, you do," she muttered, clicking a few times with her mouse. "The maximum sentence for insider trading is twenty years."

"I know. I have Google."

She ignored me. "The good news is, the average sentence actually given is just over one year, usually in a cushy country-club facility if you're rich enough. The time served is often half of that on good behavior. So, about six months we're dealing with."

"I can do six months."

"You probably won't have to." She shut her laptop and peered at me. "I think you can get the six months waived if you agree to testify and pay the maximum fine, which is five-million dollars."

Worth every cent if it got Brandon off Emery and Ma's backs.

"Done."

She pulled out her phone and penned a text as she spoke, "I have a friend who specializes in fraud cases. She can attend the meeting with you as your lawyer. I can be there if you want."

"I do," I cut in.

Her soft smile made me roll my eyes. "For moral support?"

"For catering. People are less inclined to lash out when fed."

"Sure," she dragged out. The smile never left her face. "Let's go with that excuse. We can outline terms of agreements before the meeting, including confidentiality, so the company doesn't get bad press."

"How are you so sure I'll get off?"

"You're really looking at six months max. That's your negotiating point, so the S.E.C. has little to lose and a lot to gain. Besides the logistics, Brandon is motivated and ambitious. He's looking to go places bigger than the S.E.C. He won't do that arresting North Carolina's golden boy, but he will do that with the testimony of an anonymous whistleblower."

"I'll make that fucker's career," I muttered.

I'd pay a five-million-dollar fine.

Brandon Vu would get the career bust of a lifetime.

I should have cared more, but I didn't.

He was just another step to getting Emery back.

chapter FIFTY-FIVE

Emery

I laced my Chucks beneath a gown, feeling like a knock-off Cinderella. The same floor-length dress I wore at the masquerade, because I refused to make another for a soft opening, which was really just an excuse to throw a party.

Ida Marie popped her head into the office. "We need an extra set of hands down there. Mr. Prescott never attends the soft openings, and no one can find Delilah, so we're short some mouths to talk to the press."

Talking to the press appealed to me as much as

ingesting a banana stolen from a porn set. I considered forgoing the event entirely. Nash wouldn't care.

Nash.

Every time I tried to push him out of my mind, he popped back in. If I was a storm, he was hail, and he came down harder, faster, and did more damage.

Ceiling: *Funny. That's how I feel about you.*

"I'll be there in a sec," I promised, adjusting the slit of my dress.

She rifled through Cayden's drawer and handed me a safety pin. "Hannah downed two cocktails. She's tipsy and getting loose-lipped. You can take her spot in front of the centerpiece. Have you seen it yet?"

"No." I latched the ripped seam together with the pin, hiding it beneath the fabric. "Why is Hannah pissed?"

"You didn't hear? Chantilly has been ranting all morning. Prescott Hotels pulled out of the Singapore deal."

"What?!" I squeezed the pin too hard. It pricked my thumb and drew a bead of blood, but I ignored it.

"Delilah sent Chantilly a memo, informing her that Nash would leave for Singapore for two months. Then, all of a sudden, they both returned from Singapore, and Delilah told Chantilly they're no longer building a hotel there."

I swallowed, reading between the lines. Two months gone? Did Nash give up Singapore for me? The timeline made sense if you excluded the part where I'd seen Delilah a day before Nash. He arrived with that note, left me reeling, and mentioned shit was about to go down.

Straightening, I marched to the elevator, hoping to

catch Nash in the lobby. I'd checked the penthouse earlier, but he'd already left. I didn't want this conversation to happen through the phone either.

Ida Marie followed me. "You should see the centerpiece. Not even that. You should read the placard. It's insane. The press has been all over it. Technically, we probably don't need to talk to them. They're hungry to learn more about the centerpiece, which none of us know anything about."

I tuned her out the second my feet hit the lobby, careening to a halt. Shock bloomed from my toes to my head.

The centerpiece.

A waterfall stretched the seven-story height. Shards of metal cascaded down from the ceiling. When I peered closer, I noticed the pieces had been welded from car parts, including his old Honda and the used junker I'd sold Virginia's Birkin to buy. She had Hank drive it to the junkyard. Nash must have kept it.

Rising from the water, the shape of a tiger emerged. Almost like a bird with raised arms, painted the same color of the starless sky. It stood on a bed of geode crystals. The rock shells had been cracked open. Thousands of crystals spilled out in blue and gray waves of all sizes.

The sight wrecked me.

"Excuse me, ma'am." A reporter shoved her way up to me, regarding my name tag. "Do you work here? Do you know who the Little Tiger is? Who is she to Mr. Prescott?"

I struggled to avert my eyes from the statue. "I'm sorry?"

"From the placard."

That caught my attention. It stood at the base of the

centerpiece, mounted to the floor. A monument of its own. I could barely see it through the crowd.

Giving the reporter my back, I asked Ida Marie, "When was the placard placed?"

"Umm..." She cocked her head and tapped her lip. "The day we went to pick up the couches for the lobby."

Before our fight. Before Virginia's wedding. Before that night in the pool. Before everything.

I didn't fully understand why it mattered, but it did. Maybe because I knew it wasn't an apology. Whatever he'd etched onto the placard would be a revelation before the apology was ever needed.

Shoving my way through the masses, I stood in front of the placard, words engraved into thick stone.

"Moira"
by artist Anders Bentley

Dear Little Tiger,

You wear black and white, but you are a rainbow.

It's the first thing I noticed about you after I *really* noticed you. The realizations spiraled from there. I noticed all your fucking minutiae (I bet that word gets you wet), without ever realizing it.

Your damn pride cripples you, but it also proves you're the most determined person I've ever met. You are somehow both fire and the water that extin-

guishes it. You fixate on words, but your actions are what gut me.

I want to do all the things I've never done with you—and all the things I've already done again, because fuck, I know they'd be better with you.

When everyone else saw the angry kid with the busted lip and the bruised knuckles, you simply watched me. When my employees saw crass behavior, you saw my humor and returned it. When I didn't see myself, you still did.

I hope you're looking at the centerpiece. I hope you're staring at the geodes, the cascading waterfall, and the tiger. I hope you're overwhelmed by it. I hope it fucking shatters a piece of you when you stare at it. I *don't* hope you want to fuck the shit out of it, but for the sake of this analogy, let's say I do.
Because that's what it's like for me when I stare at you.

In case it's not blatantly obvious by now, I fucking love you.

— NASH/BEN/YOURS

Nash's version of a love note.

Littered with profanities, yet still charming.

And on display for photographers, press, and guests to fawn over.

All of North Carolina, who idolized him, would see this.

Ceiling: *He didn't break your heart. He cracked it open. Remember?*

"Like a geode," I whispered, shaken by the realization. "Geodes need to shatter for their beauty to be seen."

Around me, the room shifted. Nash appeared near the alcove of elevators, flanked by Brandon Vu, Delilah, and a few more people. Shock slowed my breathing before panic took over and turned my heartbeats into a pop song.

Blood coated Nash's fist and smeared beneath Brandon's nose. They'd been in a fight, and now he was being led outside, accompanied by his lawyer and what was probably more agents.

Oh, Nash.

What have you done?

nash

I WAS A SNITCH.

A rat.

Officially, no better than Rosco.

But sending Virginia, Eric Cartwright, and Sir Balty to prison fucking fueled me. Biting back a smug smile, I signed the contract where Francine, Chantilly's lawyer friend, told me to. No jail time. Not even the full five-million-dollar fine.

Truthfully, I'd rather be up here, making deals with the S.E.C., than down there.

Soft openings.

I hated them. I'd avoided every one for the past four years. They dowsed me with memories I refused to remember. Each body-slamming into me harder than the next.

"Nash? Your dad had a heart attack. He fell off the building at the construction site. They called the ambulance. You don't look so well. I can drive you there."

"Are you the family? Mr. Prescott died before he arrived. I'm so sorry for your loss. We have a grieving room to your left and a chapel down the hall. Please, feel free to use either. If one of you can identify the body..."

"I'm going to remove this sheet, and it will be a shocking sight. All you have to do is nod your head yes or no. Is this Hank Prescott?"

The day Dad died, I'd attended a soft opening for Felton Hotels near Eastridge. I shadowed their C.E.O., knowing I'd buy the hotel and eventually merge it into the Prescott Hotels empire.

The day had begun with a round of drinks and celebrations and ended with me staring at my father's dead body, because no way in hell would I put Reed or Ma through that.

I hadn't been to a soft opening since.

"We have to drive you out to the office to write a statement and answer some questions." Brandon slid his seat back and nodded to one of his two coworkers. "It will probably take the rest of the day. I know you have a party going on. Is there a rear entrance?"

"Not yet accessible. Doesn't matter." My head jerked to the other two agents. "Tell Thing One and Thing Two to take off the windbreakers." I stood after Brandon, the picture of serenity. "Hey, Brandon?"

He turned back to me.

I swung. Once. But it was enough. Blood spilled from his nose, dripped to his white button-down, and splattered onto the fresh carpet. Delilah didn't react. To her credit, neither did Francine. One agent moved for me, but Brandon held up a hand.

"It's fine," he spit out and clutched his upper cartilage. "I deserved it."

Damn straight.

It was one thing to bother me. An entirely different one to harass Emery.

I also realized he'd only said that because an assault charge would fuck up my credibility as a key witness and, thereby, ruin his career-making case.

Brandon rubbed at the blood with his hand, smearing it. I didn't offer to show him to the restroom or bother to apologize. Frankly, I'd do it again, but jail time didn't appeal to me. Plus, I needed to see my girl.

I handed the documents to Brandon, who shot me a glare before shoving them into his briefcase. We left for the elevators together. He led me through the lobby with blood on his face. To an outsider, it looked like a weird group of people walking.

Not even a perp walk.

I wore no cuffs. They wore nothing to identify themselves as agents. The confidentiality clause Francine had placed came into effect as soon as I'd signed the document. Delilah and Francine flanked me with Brandon and his merry band of agents before and behind me.

The colossal centerpiece had drawn a crowd. Within it, I spotted Emery. She stared at me with panicked eyes. Frozen. My fists clenched and unclenched. Dried blood cracked all over them.

I ran my fingers through my hair. *Once.*

We held eye contact until Brandon flung the door open. A row of black SUVs lined the front of the hotel. We headed to the one in the middle. He clutched the handle at the same time Emery sprinted out.

"Wait!"

Panic engulfed her face. She chased after us, giving me less than a second to react before she jumped on me and kissed me hard. The slit on her dress tore. I covered it with my palm, trying not to laugh at how Emery this situation was.

(Of course, she was a verb, adjective, and noun.)

Still clinging to me, Emery faced Brandon. "Please, just give us five minutes."

Why the fuck was she asking him?

He offered her a shrug and stepped to the side with his agents, Delilah, and Francine. I ignored the crowd and focused on Emery. She loved words so much, but it looked like she had none for me.

"I read your placard," she finally whispered, threading her fingers together behind my neck. "You say I fixate on words, and you're right. Yet, I'm here, wondering why I can't put my feelings into words, thinking that love is too inadequate a description, and I realized it doesn't matter. It doesn't matter because I'm not alone. I don't need words to keep me company. Falling in love with you is like diving blindly into a book, not knowing it's destined to be my favorite. Whatever's more than love, I feel it for you. I am only ever going to be in love with you."

I popped a brow up, tightening my grip on her. "You more than love me."

"Yes. I don't care if you have," she glanced at Brandon and lowered her voice, "*you-know-what* that can exonerate Dad, and you didn't tell me. Maybe it's fucked up, but I don't care about anything but us. I'm sorry I never said this sooner. I love you. I'll wait for you. However long it takes."

"However long what takes?" The puzzle pieces clicked together. I set her down, so she wouldn't fall with my laughter. Only she could make me crack up on the same day I signed a plea bargain. "I'm not going to jail, Little Tiger. I'm a witness. I made a deal."

Brandon piped in. "Confidentially."

"Brandon, seek help for your obsession with hearing your own voice." I angled us away, shielding her with my body. "I made a deal with the S.E.C. I'll serve as a witness against Balthazar, Eric, and Virginia. Your dad will be absolved. I'm not going to jail. I promise."

The girl with all the words—speechless again. My ego could get used to this.

I tugged at her dress, using it to reel her to me. "Come back to me?"

"Always."

epilogue

nash

TWO YEARS LATER

I don't believe her when she tells me she *may* be happy.

My devious fucking liar.

Her black hair flies everywhere, resembling a wild horse's mane. Outside, the ground has frozen over with snow, thick layers that have hardened into crystal cement.

Fire saves us from the frost. The flames flicker, shadows dancing on the wool walls. My Tiger looks like royalty, her hair glowing each time the flames climb.

Red lips tempt me. Her gray eye—the color of moonstone—shines so bright, it's almost colorless. The other is as frosty as Lake Baikal, a bottomless courier of wisdom, flecks of white battling the blue.

Neither will win.

There never is a victor with Emery.

Only a battle.

Constant.

Fervent.

Beautiful.

A love that deserves chasing to fuel it.

"There's no may," I enunciate. "You *are* happy to see me." I try to flatten a few strands of her hair, but it's useless, and taming Emery would be like taming a tiger. If I try, I'd be changing everything that makes her who she is.

And I love who she is.

I love her wild and reckless and fierce.

I love her *mine*.

"I thought you were done telling me what to do." She turns to face me, nipping at my neck.

"Outside of the bedroom," I correct.

"Outside of the bedroom," she agrees, lips parted, two mismatched eyes darting to the entrance to confirm we're alone.

I'm not supposed to be here, standing in front of my fiancée, making fun of her flushed skin and the orgasm I just gave her. Gideon will kill me (he can try), unless Delilah gets to me first (she would succeed).

"I'm not telling you what to do, baby. I'm stating a fact. You're fucking happy to see me." I flick one of her nipples through her dress and smirk. "Admit it, Little Tiger."

She shakes her head, and I accept the challenge.

I grip her chin. Firm. Exactly how my fiancée likes it. She holds eye contact, so defiant, I want to flip her over and sink into her again. My lips dip to press kisses on her collarbone.

No matter how many times I kiss her, claim her, mark her as mine, it will never be enough. The way I crave her is insatiable. It's proof of immortality.

I reach behind her and undo the zipper to her dress before circling around and tracing her spine with my tongue.

She spins and swats at my face. Her fingers scratch my eyes, eliciting a curse. "I just zipped that up."

"And I need your pussy to warm my cock up." I grab her fingers and place them on my erection over my suit slacks. "It's so cold, I can feel my balls shriveling up."

"They are not shriveling up." She squeezes me once as if she can't help herself, then nods to the center of the yurt—a fucking yurt, that's how whipped she's got me. "The heater is on, Nash."

"Two logs of wood and a packet of matches from Prescott Hotels does not constitute a heater."

She's about to argue. She always does. I lick my lips in anticipation, loving this foreplay we share. Every word, every glance, every touch—an appetizer until the second I'm inside her.

Reed interrupts, entering the yurt without knocking. "I would have knocked, but there's no door."

Emery squeals at the sight of my brother, clutching onto his shoulders. "Is your mom here? I'm so glad you didn't get lost."

Her dress is short, a horrible idea for a wedding in Norway in the middle of September. I told her this, but what the fuck do I know? It's forty-something degrees out, the beginning of the cold season. Chilly but manageable, especially when her nipples have been permanently hard since we set foot in Norway.

"Yeah," Reed drawls out, nodding to me. "Everyone's waiting on y'all to come out."

Reed is here as Emery's maid of honor. He's not my biggest fan, but I'm no longer his worst enemy. We're getting to a point where we're content in each other's company. Ma says we're one step away from being brothers again. Emery acts like it's a foregone conclusion, and maybe it is. After all, I've started to accept a lot of things are inevitable.

Emery squeezes Reed's hand. "Give us five minutes."

When he leaves, she returns to me and rubs at the lipstick stain she left on my suit. Dad's suit. Emery tailored it for the occasion. I almost regret not stripping out of it before entering her, but fuck it. Dad would want me happy, and I am.

Balthazar is in jail. Not some billionaire retreat with security guards for show. An actual jail, with prison bitches, yard fights once a week, and world-worn men who hate rich pricks like Sir Balty.

Cartwright is locked up in the same joint, his assets frozen and his son so broke, he has no money to send his dad for the prison dispensary. Dude can't even afford instant ramen packs. He exchanges *favors* to eat.

With Balthazar's assets frozen, Virginia moved to a trailer in a small town in inland North Carolina. She still lives there, hawking anything she can from her previous life as a Winthrop. It's not much, since I bought the Winthrop Estate and gave it back to Gideon.

"We're getting married," I whisper, ego brimming at the way Emery can't help but smile every time I say it.

"Thank God." She nudges my shoulder and bites

down on her lower lip. "I was getting sick of you sliding 'my fiancée' into every sentence."

"You were not, and you'll pay for lying." I swat her ass once before leaving, turning back in time to see her wink at me.

"I'd expect nothing less."

Reed and Gideon are at the entrance of the yurt, waiting for Emery. I nod at them both and take everything in.

Tromsø, Norway is the kind of place you visit for the first time and never want to leave. Emery fell in love when we flew here last year to balter under the stars and Northern Lights, so I popped the question with the ring I'd been keeping in my pocket.

Above me, the emerald, blue, yellow, and pink streaks fight for dominance in the sky. It's the same mating dance each time.

Our first time in Tromsø, we star-gazed every night. (I stared at Emery. She stared at the sky.) She always rooted for the lilac, but the emerald won every time.

I asked her why it matters.

She squeezed my hand and said, "The lilac reminds me of your dad. When I painted the cottage mailbox black, Virginia yelled at me for not behaving like a lady. Your dad patted my head and told me, *It's okay. I'll like the pink for you.*" She stared up at the sky as if her attention would spark more life into the lilac. "I guess I want the underdog to win this time."

It looks like it's no different tonight, the emerald swaying, nudging all the other colors out of its path. In front of me, a sea of floating candles leads to our makeshift altar of crimson rose petals scattered across the snow.

I wait for her amidst the roses. It takes longer than I

anticipated, or maybe I'm just impatient to marry the fuck out of her already. Delilah stands beside me, laughing at my mom, who's already crying.

Reed is the first to leave the yurt. Delilah swallows her snort. He strolls down the aisle with a black bouquet of roses cradled between two palms until he's directly across from her.

"Shit, it's cold. Does anyone else feel their balls shriveling up?" Reed mutters, even though—aside from me—the only other human male within hearing distance is Tiger Bro (short for Broduski). He's the vegan, tie-dye shirt-wearing spiritual guide Emery hired to marry us.

We ignore Reed.

Dermot Kennedy's version of "Lover" plays from white speakers hidden in the snow. Wind whips thousands of rose petals into the air. They fly around Emery as she walks past rows of floating candles, an arm clutched to Gideon.

The Northern Lights turn her skin different colors, lighting up the lace gown she wears, the same black color as starless nights. A crown of black crystals, gray moonstones, and dark gray diamonds sits on her untamed hair, attached to a massive black veil.

She looks like a goddess come to life.

Durga walking this very earth.

A tiger roaming her territory.

When Gideon places her hand in mine, I press a kiss to her knuckles and part the veil, taking in her face.

"You changed," I accuse.

"I knew you'd sneak in and see my dress." She lifts a brow, daring me to argue.

I can't. She's right. I lasted an hour before I dipped into the yurt to, well, dip my dick inside her yurt.

Tiger Bro begins the ceremony.

I say my vows as a rare gold overtakes the emerald in the sky. When it's her turn to say her vows, she stands on her tiptoes and whispers in my ear.

One word.

A secret for us to share.

Ya'aburnee.

I have no fucking idea what it means.

She doesn't elaborate, just smiles a secret smile that makes me love her more. A second later, she slams into me, knocking me against Tiger Bro as she presses her lips against mine. I swipe a hand out, blindly pushing Tiger Bro away. Wrapping my arms around her waist, I drag my tongue against her lips.

Emery grazes her teeth along my bottom lip. I want to lay her down on this snow, strip her bare, and lick a path from her toes to her lips.

She pulls back before we maul each other in front of an audience. Our foreheads rest against one another.

"What do you want to do, Mrs. Prescott?" I ask.

Low, just for her to hear.

"Balter," she whispers against my lips and presses another quick kiss to them.

She dances under the stars with our family, her head thrown back, absolutely no rhythm to the movement in her body. When she begs me to dance with her and promises to make it worth my while, I do.

With her in my arms and our family surrounding us, I notice something.

Above me, the lilac has taken over the sky.

Pink and purple streaks have consumed the other lights.

The underdog has won.

Emery

NINE YEARS LATER

"**I fucking swear,** I can't stand this shit." Nash scrubs his face with his palm. He leans his head against the back of the couch, staring at our ceiling like the television's existence is an insult to him.

My eyes dart between the two twin eight-year-old demons sandwiched between us. "Language!" A half-hearted scold.

"We hear 'shit' all the time, Mom." Hallie glances at me, wide eyes the same color as Nash's. "Last week, Mrs. Kimberly was teaching us about the Egyptians trading in the Red Sea. She kept talking about their shits."

"She meant *ships*." Lawson pinches Hallie's arms. He has my eyes. One blue. One gray. "Mrs. Kimberly can't pronounce anything for *shit* through her retainers."

I cannot believe Lawson and Hallie shared my womb at the same time without killing each other. They share the same black hair and literally nothing else. Not even the same gender. Lawson is pale and ruthless, whereas Hallie is tan and sweet.

Nash's fingers inch toward the remote.

I dig a fist into the white cheddar popcorn and toss a handful at his face. "Don't you dare." The kids squeal between us as it rains popcorn. I hip-check Lawson and ask, "What do you think about the movie?"

Lawson glances at the screen and shrugs. "Cinderella's hot, I guess."

"Lawson, she's eleven years older than you!"

"So? Dad's ten years older than you."

I shut up, because the kid's got a point. "Hallie?"

She puckers her lips and squints her eyes at the screen as if that'll help her form an opinion. "She's really clumsy, but I'd want to be her. I like her dress and her shoes."

"Unbelievable," Nash mutters, but the kids hear him. They throw more popcorn at his face.

The front door opens and slams shut.

The kids jump off the couch and shout, "Uncle Reed!"

"Where are your kids?" Nash asks him when he enters the living room with his wife.

It's still weird seeing Basil's face without the permanent scowl etched onto it, but here we are. To top it off, Reed's wife helps me run my company, a non-profit fashion line that takes recycled materials and turns them into one-of-a-kind pieces. The proceeds go to soup kitchens across North Carolina. Nash calls me a bleeding heart, but I know he likes it.

Reed presses a kiss to my temple. "Ma stole them for a few hours."

A second later, the kids whisk Reed and his wife

away. Nash shuts the T.V. off the first chance he gets. His fingers meet his temple and rub. I roll my eyes at his dramatics and flick his arm.

He latches onto the arm and yanks me to him.

"Ya'aburnee."

The word brushes against my temple. I mouth it back, a smile tipping my lips upward at the secret vow we share.

Ya'aburnee is Arabic for you bury me.

It is the hope that you will die before your one true love because you cannot bear to live without them.

There's magic when we say it, but it doesn't come from the word.

It comes from us.

The End.

acknowledgments

Chloe, I keep flashing back to the little moments, wondering why they're the ones I remember the most. I miss your minutiae, every small quirk that made you... you. This book's for you—and every book after.

Rose and Bauer, my absolute obsessions. I love you. Thank you for making my life better. I smile more, laugh more, and live more because of you two.

L, thank you for loving me with your actions and not your words, because we both know I'm into jerks. LOL.

Heather, thank you for putting up with my craziness! You're always there for me. I appreciate every conversation, phone call, and message. You are so invested in my career. I have no idea what I did to deserve you, but I'd do it a thousand times over again. I'm so blessed to have you in my life.

Ava, you nut case. I'm pretty sure you are responsible for 115 of the 116 hours I spoke on the phone during the month of October when I was supposed to be writing this book. I don't know whether to thank you for them or curse you for those hours. (We were productive, right?) Obviously, I love you. I'd love you more if you upgraded your WiFi, but I don't think the world can handle that type of love.

Heidi, I love that you make ugly things beautiful like helping caterpillars turn into butterflies and my first drafts into actual books. I love the beauty you see in unexpected places—the photographs you capture, the way you treat me and our friendship. I love how you don't handle me with kid gloves and treat me like I'm made of tough stuff—and as I'm starting to realize, I am. I love how you came into my life so kind and unassuming, a sweet reader whose words I didn't know would have the large footprints they do today. I love how you get me, how you love dogs, how you understand my words—and when you don't, you work to understand them (and me). I love your selflessness and the time you give as if it is not the rarest, most precious gift you could give me (aside from your friendship). And mostly, I just love you. Thank you.

Professor Harloe, thank you for being my cheerleader and offering a helping hand always. You're so supportive of me and deal with all of my craziness without a complaint (even when I am level ten dramatic, spouting crazy conspiracy theories).

Leigh, thank you for all the momager duties, making me get my ass in gear, and loving/beta-ing this book even when I was so frustrated at having to scrap the first 60K. I couldn't have done this without you!

Jose, I have no words. I struggled to find a cover for Nash, but you sent me this one as if you just knew I needed it. Seriously, I didn't even tell you I was cover searching, which is why I think it's 100% fate.

Ryan, thank you for being Nash! I'm in love with this cover.

Desireé and Sebastian, thank you for bringing Emery and Nash to life! Des, you put up with my crazy and go above and beyond. I am so grateful to have you in my life.

Juli, you are always so supportive of me! When I need a pick-me-up, I go to the Romano IG page you made and am just in awe that someone out there is sweet and talented enough to do that for me.

Brittany, thank you for beta-ing this book and loving Nash for me. I can't begin to describe how much I value your friendship and appreciate you.

Elan, your Battleship game is weak. Bask in my awesomeness. Also, thank you for being my friend.

Gem and Janice, thank you for your diligent work on my manuscripts. They'd be a mess without you both.

Ashlee, you are such a talent!

Thank you to my amazing admins: Gemma, Ava, Krista, Heather, Amanda, Brittany, and Leigh.

Thank you to my wonderful author friends: Giana Darling, Lylah James, SM Soto, Heather Oregeron, Claudia Burgoa, Nicole French, Logan Chance, and Amara Kent.

Thank you to the amazing group of people who helped get this book into as many hands as possible:

- Jenn Watson, for dealing with my crazy, especially my rambling phone calls
- Sarah Ferguson, Shan Brown, and everyone at Social Butterfly PR—total rockstars
- Cecelia Mecca and Bridgette Duplantis, two gems

- Harrison, you're probably realizing that giving my neurotic self your number was a big mistake. THANK YOU!
- Daniel, Daniela, and Luiz—I appreciate all you do for me!

Bloggers! I am in complete awe at all the love this book has received. You guys help me spread the word, and I cannot be more grateful!

Lastly, my readers! To the new ones, welcome! I can't wait to continue this journey with you. To the ones who've been with me for longer, thank you for your continued support and patience. I know you all wanted a mafia book this release, but you guys have greeted Nash's book with open arms, supporting me more than I can ever imagine. I'm so lucky and blessed to have you all.

SO MUCH LOVE,

Parker S. Huntington

about PARKER

Parker S. Huntington is from Orange County, California, USA. She has a Bachelor's of Arts in Creative Writing from the University of California, Riverside and a Master's in Liberal Arts in Creative Writing and Literature from Harvard University.

She was the proud mom of Chloe and has two puppies, Bauer and Rose. She also lives with her boyfriend of seven years—a real life alpha male, book-boyfriend-worthy hunk of a man.

REACH ME AT:

Fan Group: facebook.com/groups/Parkerettes
Website: www.parkershuntington.com

- facebook.com/parkershuntington
- twitter.com/authorPS
- instagram.com/ParkerSHuntington
- amazon.com/author/parkershuntington
- bookbub.com/profile/parker-s-huntington
- goodreads.com/goodreadscomparkershuntington